THE
EYES
OF
TEXAS

Also in
The Lone Star Legacy

LONE STAR LEGACY

BOOK 3

THE EYES OF TEXAS

A Novel

GILBERT MORRIS

INTEGRITY®
PUBLISHERS
Nashville

THE EYES OF TEXAS

Published by Integrity Publishers, a division of Integrity Media, Inc., 5250 Virginia Way, Suite 110, Brentwood, TN 37027.

HELPING PEOPLE WORLDWIDE EXPERIENCE *the* MANIFEST PRESENCE *of* GOD.

Published in association with the literary agency of Alive Communications, Inc., 7680 Goddard Street, Suite 200, Colorado Springs, Colorado 80920.

Cover Design: Brand Navigation, LLC—DeAnna Pierce, Terra Peterson, Bill Chiaravalle; www.brandnavigation.com
Cover Images: Corbis, Punchstock, GettyOne
Interior Design/Page Composition: PerfecType, Nashville, TN

ISBN 0-7394-5253-3

Printed in USA

DEDICATION

To Jill Van Der Lee
The Scripture tells us that there is rejoicing in heaven whenever a single soul is saved. So I join the angels in rejoicing that you, my dear Jill, have been made a part of the family of God!

PART ONE:

END OF THE REPUBLIC

CHAPTER ONE

Y ou'd better keep your distance, Lucifer! I'm in a *bad* mood this morning."

Jerusalem Taliferro broke stride and stood in the middle of the yard, staring at the red-and-black rooster that circled her. She had named the ornery fowl "Lucifer" because he was the most evil rooster she had ever seen in her life. Now she watched his beady eyes as he turned sideways and lifted his feet, clucking low in his throat in what seemed to her a threatening tone.

"Mind me!" she warned. "I've had enough of your depraved ways."

As the rooster circled slowly, lifting his feet and putting them down onto the hard ground, Jerusalem turned and surveyed the land that surrounded the Yellow Rose Ranch. She had grown up in the hills of Arkansas, and the endless spaces of Texas had frightened her at first, but now she had grown to love it. The open spaces made her feel alive and free in her spirit.

Turning, she looked to the west, where the Humpback Blue Hills stretched for miles along the horizon. They looked like lumps of wet bread, and the winter sky of Texas now obscured their jagged outlines. Far to the east the Spanish Peaks touched the sky. Her eyes narrowed as she looked at them, for she knew they were the favorite lurking places of the Comanche raiding parties. Turning slightly to the south, she squinted her eyes as if she could see all the way to the Gulf and then to Mexico across the Rio Grande. To her, Mexico seemed an evil place where blood-thirsty Mexicans lurked, full of resentment and hatred toward all Texans. They were convinced that their country had been stolen from them, and so they rode across the border at night to steal cattle.

A shiver passed over Jerusalem Ann, and when she turned to look to the north, she thought of the terrible land that lay there. The Mexicans called it *the Llano Estacado*—the Staked Plains. It was the home of the Comanches, who were feared for being the most deadly and merciless of all the tribes on the plains. They came not in huge numbers, but in small bands of no more than ten painted warriors. They could travel a hundred miles a day on their tough mustangs. When they found a lonely homestead isolated by distance from other Texans, they came and killed the men, some of the women, and carried off the children.

The sound of lowing cattle floated to Jerusalem Ann. When she turned to see the longhorns far off out in the distance, a sense of ownership and pride filled her. She and her children had left the hills of Arkansas, a place she had learned to despise. For years she had grubbed in the thin mountain soil, struggling for a bare subsistence while her husband, Jake, had wandered away. He'd come home for a spell, then he would grow restless and leave her again with another baby in her womb. Her memories of Jake Hardin had dimmed for her now. He had died at the Alamo. When the word of his death had come, Jerusalem Ann had said barely, "Jake died better than he lived."

The longhorns that she watched were more like wild animals than the docile cows she had been accustomed to in Arkansas. They were wild-eyed with enormous, sweeping horns that could do terrible damage. It took a fine rider to make them do what the cattlemen wanted them to do. She watched as Zane, her brother, rode at a full gallop, chasing after a cow and her calf. It gave her a sense of satisfaction to see Zane herd the two back toward the herd. The size of the herd gave her a good feeling, for since she and her new husband, Clay Taliferro, had decided to become ranchers instead of cotton farmers, life had been different.

Different but very hard. Looking around at the large house, the two barns, and the corrals, memories of how difficult it had been at first filled her mind. From the start they had worked long hours. At the same time they had been forced to keep close guard against the Comanches from the north and east and the Mexican raiders from the south. Besides these constant dangers, they also had to be on the outlook for white cattle thieves who would strip a ranch if it were left unguarded.

"Ow!" Jerusalem Ann uttered a piercing cry and looked down. Lucifer had strutted over and pecked her on the calf. Jerusalem Ann Hardin Taliferro was not a hot-tempered woman, but from time to time, a sudden surge of fiery wrath would appear—usually when one of her children was threatened. This time, however, her anger was directed toward this stupid rooster that had pecked her one time too many! Stooping down, she grabbed him by the neck and whirled him in a circle, giving a tremendous wrench at the apex of the third cervical vertebra. The body separated from the head and went wheeling through the air, striking the ground a few feet away. Jerusalem Ann watched, waiting for what she knew would happen. The headless body gained its feet and began running around in circles. It never ceased to amaze her how a headless chicken could show more activity than any other chicken in the barnyard! She watched as the headless chicken began to stagger and finally flopped over onto the cold ground.

Glancing down at the head, Jerusalem said, "Well, Lucifer, you pecked me one time too many." She threw the head away from her and went over and picked up the body by the feet. She held it out as the last of the blood drained out, then spoke to the headless carcass. "Reverend Morgan would say it was predestined for you to die this morning, but I don't believe that. If you'd kept your bill to yourself, you could still be running around loose and free. But you had to do it, didn't you?"

She turned and walked toward the house, holding the chicken clear from her body. As she turned the corner, she stopped suddenly when she saw her husband, Clay, and the children in the corral. She stood there and watched, a warm feeling flooding her, for she was very much in love with her husband. Clay Taliferro had been a mountainman with her first husband, Jake. Then one day Clay had appeared out of nowhere with a message from Jake. If it had not been for Clay, she knew that she and her kids would have all perished. He had loved her while she was still married to Jake, but he had never spoken of his feelings for her. After Jake died at the Alamo, it had been Jerusalem Ann who had had to make the advances.

Now she watched closely, extremely proud of her second family. They had faced many hardships since leaving Arkansas years ago, but now life seemed brighter for her. Her older children—Clinton, Moriah, and Brodie—were all grown now. Mary Aiden was a young woman of sixteen. She had borne Clay's twins, Sam and Rachel Belle, now eight, and another son, David, who was barely three. Her eyes went quickly to her grandson, Ethan, who was now six. Her eyes lingered on him the longest, for his father was a Comanche war chief named Bear Killer. During a raid, Bear Killer had stolen Moriah and kept her captive among his tribe. During those long years living among the Comanche, Moriah had borne him a son. After months of trying to find where Bear Killer spent the winter, Quaid Shafter and Brodie finally came upon an Indian who tipped them off. They had risked their lives to rescue her and Ethan. Now, watching the boy with his clear-cut features, like both his mother and his father, a pang pierced Jerusalem Ann's heart. She knew what sufferings could come to anyone with Indian blood in Texas. Prejudice ran deep for half-breeds out here on the plains.

She stood there watching while Clay held a yearling calf for Sam to mount.

"Ride him, cowboy!" Clay yelled and jumped back as the yearling began arching his back and bucking. After a few hops, Sam tumbled off the cow. He hit the ground, rolled, and came up, his green eyes flashing and his red hair catching the sun, throwing out reddish gold tints.

"Let me ride him again, Dad!"

"No, you had your turn," Clay said.

Jerusalem was proud of her husband as she watched him with Sam. Clay was not a tall man, no more than five ten, and weighed a hundred and fifty pounds. But he was strong and wiry and had the quickest reaction time of any man Jerusalem Ann had ever seen. He moved so fast at times that he was just a blur. He was forty-four now, Jerusalem Ann's own age, but there was a youthful look about him, for he carried his years well.

"All right, Davie, it's your turn."

As Clay grabbed the calf with one hand and reached for Davie with the other, Jerusalem Ann suddenly cried out, "Clay Taliferro, you stop that this minute!"

Clay turned around, and surprise washed across his face. "What's the matter, Jerusalem?"

"You're not letting that baby ride that wild calf! He could break his neck."

"Well, shucks! How's he going to learn to be a tough cowboy if he don't learn to ride?" Clay said. He stood there holding Davie, who was begging to be put on the calf.

Jerusalem came over and said, "You children go inside right now."

"Aw, Mama, we're havin' fun!" Rachel Belle had the same bright red hair and green eyes as her brother. They both had an adventurous nature with hints of a wild streak. When they got into one of their scrapes or showed this adverse side of their character, Clay would shake his head and say, "That's your mama's side comin' out. Them Satterfields were always a wild bunch. I'm afraid you'll come to no good."

Jerusalem opened the gate and lifted her voice. "All right. Now! Inside and wash. You're all filthy as a bunch of pigs wallowing in the mud."

Protesting, the children all left to go and clean up. Ethan grabbed Davie's hand and led him away with the others.

"Every time we start havin' fun, you always come out and put a stop to it. Why is that, wife?"

"You're too rough with Davie."

"Too rough! Why, when I was three years old, I was practically breaking broncos." Clay came over and suddenly grabbed Jerusalem Ann and kissed her. He hugged her tight and began to nibble at her neck, which drove her crazy.

"Stop that, you fool!"

"Why, a man ain't a fool because he wants to give a good-lookin' woman some affection."

Jerusalem Ann tried to shove him away, but he held her tightly. At that moment Jerusalem wished she could tell Clay all that she felt in her heart for him. How does a woman tell a man that he's become such a part of her that he's like the air she needed to breathe? How does she tell him how it feels when he returns from a long trip, and something inside just turns over when she sees him grinning crookedly at her as he comes through the door? How does she tell him what it's like when fearful thoughts fill her mind in the night to have a man there to reach out and just touch and know that he would die to keep her safe? All these thoughts overwhelmed her as Clay held her in his embrace. It was Clay, strangely enough, who said the sweet and intimate things. Jerusalem had been puzzled by his romantic tenderness. She did not know a single other man, with the possible exception of Rice Morgan, who had married her sister, Julie, who could say things like that without being embarrassed. Most men seemed unable to express their deep feelings, if indeed they had them.

"You've been a good wife," Clay whispered in her ear. "I'm gonna think up a real good reward for you tonight. See me later."

Jerusalem laughed. "You and your rewards! I know what you're doing."

"Why, I ain't doin' nothin'."

"Yes, you are. You know you were wrong to put Davie on that calf, and you're trying to sweet-talk me so I won't chew you out."

Clay looked pained. "It hurts me down to the core when you say things like that. It purely does. I'm hurt."

"It would take a broad ax to hurt you, Clay Taliferro! Now, you go get cleaned up too. You're just as dirty as the kids."

"What happened to Lucifer? It looks like he met up with an accident."

"He pecked me once too often."

Clay reached over and pinched her. "Well, a feller would have to be careful and not step across no lines with you."

"Stop pinching me!"

As the two approached the house, Clay said, "Gonna be big doings tomorrow. Texas is becomin' a State. Better mark that down on the calendar. February 18, 1846. You know, it makes me kind of sad."

"But you wanted Texas to come into the United States bad."

Clay shrugged his shoulders. "I know, but we're givin' up our freedom. I kind of like bein' an independent country. All we had to do was listen to Sam Houston. Now we got to listen to a whole bunch of senators and Washington politicians."

"You haven't changed your mind about going to the celebration, have you?"

"Nope. Zane says he and the hands will take care of the cows and watch over the place. What about Clinton? Is he going?"

"He's taking Aldora—if he had the sense to ask her."

They had reached the back porch now, and Jerusalem said to the young Mexican girl who had come out, "Maria, clean this rooster. We're going to eat him for supper tonight."

"He is not enough for everyone, señora."

"Well, go out and kill another one, then."

"Which one?" Maria asked.

"The most stupid one."

Maria suddenly giggled. "All chickens are stupid."

"Then grab the first one you see."

The two stopped, and Clay watched as Jerusalem washed her hands. He lounged against the outer wall of the house, his eyes moving, from time to time, out toward the herd of cattle. He had a watchful air, as all Texas men did, and finally he remarked, "I've been expecting Clinton and Aldora to get hitched someday."

"Well, you may wait a long time for that," Jerusalem said.

"Why's that? Clinton's twenty-five. He needs to get married, settle down, and give us a passel of grandchildren to put on the calves and get bucked off."

Ignoring his remark, Jerusalem plucked a towel off a nail and began to dry her hands. "It's been three years," she said, "since Clinton discovered Aldora was a woman. As a matter of fact, Clinton knows less about women than any man in Texas—except for you."

"Well, there you go hurtin' my feelins again. Shucks, I know *all* about women."

Jerusalem came over and could not help smiling. She put her arms around his neck and kissed him but shook her head, saying, "I know you think so, but Clinton has been quite foolish. Aldora would make him a good wife, but he hasn't done anything about it."

"Come on inside. I want some coffee." The two went in, and Clay sat down, his spurs making a soft jingling. He watched as Jerusalem poured coffee from a black pot that stayed on the stove constantly. He tasted the coffee and said, "What about Moriah? I guess she'll be going to the doings."

"No. She won't."

Clay lowered the cup, surprise washing across his face. "Why not?"

"She won't subject Ethan to what he'd hear."

Clay understood instantly what she meant. There had been several instances already when Texan men had made slighting remarks about Moriah's half-Comanche son. Zane had whipped one of them badly, and since then the remarks had not been made in the presence of any of the family. "She ought to go. If anybody makes any remarks about Ethan, I'll shoot 'em."

Jerusalem shook her head and rolled her eyes. "You can't shoot every big-mouth fool in Texas, Clay. You couldn't afford the ammunition."

The two of them sat there at the large table for a while and talked about all that was happening on the ranch and with the family. Jerusalem Ann's first husband, Jake, had been gone for most of her first marriage, and for years she had had no adult to talk to. From the first day Clay had appeared at her home in Arkansas, she discovered he liked to talk as much as she did. As she sat there sipping her coffee, a warm feeling filled her as she studied Clay's tanned face. *I've got a good man,* she thought, *but he doesn't understand what it's going to be like for Ethan and Moriah.*

Moriah Hardin stopped abruptly and took in the sight of the man and the boy who stood in the bright sunlight. Quaid Shafter was one of the most striking-looking men she had ever seen. His hat was shoved back off his head and suspended by a leather thong, exposing his pure silver-colored hair. At first glance, people thought he was an old man, but, in fact, he was only thirty–two years old and at the height of his strength. He had deep-set, light blue eyes that seemed to glow, set off by his tanned face. His face was V-shaped, and he had a wide mouth and a rather youthful expression.

Moriah's eyes went to Ethan, and a feeling of pride mixed with fear filled her heart. Ethan was tall for his age and a handsome boy by anyone's measurements. His hair was not pure black, as most Comanche children. Instead, it was a dark brown with a surprising hint of reddish gold in it. Moriah knew that his hair color came from her, as well as some of his other features. He had her chin and her mouth. The deep-set, penetrating brown eyes were a gift from his Comanche father, Bear Killer.

The two were shooting a bow, and Quaid was kneeling down to put himself on the same level as the boy. She heard him say, "All right, Ethan, let's see what you can do." She watched as Ethan, his face intent, drew the bow and loosed the arrow. It hit on the outside edge of the target.

"Why, that's plum good, son!" Quaid exclaimed. "You're gonna be a real marksman someday."

Ethan had extraordinary hearing as well as phenomenal eyesight. He turned quickly and saw his mother. "Hello, Mama. We're shooting arrows."

"I see you are."

"Mama, Quaid says we're going on a trip to Houston."

"No. We're not going."

At his mother's words, Ethan frowned. "But all the others are going."

"No. We can't go this time." She waited for Ethan to argue, as most boys would, but he simply turned and gave the bow to Quaid and walked away downcast.

Quaid came to his feet and stood there, a tall, strong figure. "Why aren't you going, Moriah? The boy's been looking forward to it. He doesn't get much entertainment. Going to the festivities would be good for him."

"You know why," she said curtly.

Quaid stared at her. "You can't keep Ethan in a box somewhere. He's got to grow up and face the world."

Moriah knew that Quaid was right, but still the fear ran deep in her of what people would say. "People will be cruel," she said finally.

"He's got people that love him."

"I know that, Quaid, but maybe when he gets older."

"It won't be any easier then."

The two stood there awkwardly. Quaid Shafter had always felt responsible for Moriah's being captured by the Comanches. He had driven her to town that day, but instead of driving back with her, he had gotten drunk and tried to force a kiss on her. Disgusted at his behavior, she attempted to make her way home alone, but she had been caught by the Comanches and carried away. She had told Quaid more than once that even if he had been there, it would have made no difference. They would simply have killed him, and she would still have been carried off as their captive.

Quaid did not argue with her. For some time now, he'd had eyes for this woman. As he studied her, he wondered how to say what was on his mind. He took in the dark red hair, the brown eyes, the strong figure, and finally he said, "How about if I take him hunting?"

"That would be good, Quaid. Thank you," Moriah said, then she turned and walked away without another word.

Quaid watched her go and shook his head. He knew that Ethan had been hurt, for the boy had already spoken to him with excitement of going to Houston. He circled the house and saw Ethan over at the corral, watching one of the hands break a half wild mustang. He walked up and said, "Hey, Ethan!" When the boy turned, he said, "How about you and me going to hunt antelope tomorrow?"

A light sprang into Ethan's eyes at once. "Really! Just me and you?"

"Right. Just me and you. We wouldn't want no lesser hunters along to slow us down." Quaid always made it a point to stoop down whenever possible when he was around the boy. He squatted now, avoiding the huge spurs that he always wore. "You'll have to bring the meat down. I got that light shotgun of mine. That ought to do."

"Aren't you going to shoot them?" Ethan asked.

"Well, I got something in my eye."

"Mama might not let me go."

"Sure she will. She's already said you could."

"Quaid, why doesn't she let me go to Houston?"

Quaid never knew exactly how to explain to Ethan the difficulty that could come with Texans because of his Indian blood. "Well, she's afraid you might get your feelings hurt."

"Who would do that?"

Quaid reached back, pulled his hat on his head, and settled it firmly. He shrugged and reached down and picked up Ethan and set him on the top fence. He did not answer for a while, then he said, "You know, some white men don't like Indians."

Ethan thought that over and said, "Well, Indians don't like some white people."

"That's right, they don't."

Quaid kept his eyes on the boy's face. There was a maturity in Ethan

Hardin. Quaid was never exactly sure what went on in his mind. He had that much Indian in him that he was hard to read.

"Why don't white men like Indians?"

"Well, there have been some pretty bad fights between them. But listen, son, you've got to look for the good white men. The ones that don't care what color a man's skin is."

"Like you?"

"Yeah, like me. Anyway"—he reached over and put his hand on the boy's shoulder—"you and I are partners. We always will be. Okay?"

"Okay," Ethan said, smiling.

"Right. We'll leave at dawn. We'll have to have a keen eye, Ethan. Come on. Let's go pick out our horses and something to cook those antelope in case you shoot one."

CHAPTER
TWO

C linton Hardin drew the sharp razor down across his cheek, cutting a swath through the thick foam of shaving cream. He wiped the straight razor carefully on the towel before him, then methodically finished his shave. Laying the razor down, he splashed the water from the basin on his face, dried his face with the towel, then lifted his head and peered into the small mirror fastened to the wall. He turned his head critically both ways, then picked up a comb and ran it through his crisp, brown hair. He was no more than five ten, but he was strongly built and there was a virile handsomeness about him. His mouth was wide, his ears lay close to his head, and his eyes were deep-set and widely spaced.

He picked up a long-neck bottle, stared at it, and then pulled the cork out and filled his cupped palm with the lotion. Putting the bottle down, he splashed the lotion all over his face, spilling some onto his shirt. He inhaled deeply. "That smells plum good!" he said with satisfaction. "I'll be the best-smellin' fellow at the whole celebration." He turned, left his room, and encountered his sister Mary Aidan coming down the hall. She had bright red hair and gray-green eyes, and the dress she wore had enough green in it to set them off.

"What's that I smell?" she asked. At the age of sixteen, Mary Aidan had a most direct way about her. She was a beautiful girl with a figure that turned every man's eye. Already she had suitors practically lined up at the Yellow Rose Ranch trying to catch her eye.

"That's me." Clinton nodded with satisfaction. "Ain't it elegant?"

Mary Aidan's eyes sparkled. "Well, it's *strong*. I'll say that for you."

"I got it off of a Frenchman the last time I was in New Orleans. Been savin' it for a special occasion. Here, smell."

Mary Aidan laughed as Clinton bent forward. She put her hand on his chest and said, "I could smell you fifty feet away."

"You smell pretty good too. Where'd you get that perfume?"

"Zane bought it for me."

"Who you going to the doings with, Mary Aidan?"

"Barton Singleton."

"Why, he's a big, ornery thing, and that dress you're wearing is plum immodest."

"What are you talking about, 'immodest'? Mary Aidan said sharply.

"It's too tight. The Lord don't approve of tight dresses."

Mary Aidan's temper flared like a flash of lightning. "Clinton," she demanded, "where did you get the idea that you're called on to make everybody so blasted holy?"

"Why, it's a fellow's Christian duty to see that his sister acts right in public."

Mary Aidan had a special affection for Clinton, but he was unbearable at times with his priggish ways. He had been converted at the age of fourteen, baptized in the Ouachita River back in Arkansas, and since then had considered himself the spiritual head of the family. He corrected even his mother at times, and as Zane had once said, "Clinton's so holy he wouldn't eat an egg laid on Sunday."

The two argued about the dress for a while, and finally Mary Aidan shook her head. "How would you like it if I started telling you all the things you do wrong?"

Clinton stopped midsentence and stared at her with surprise. "Me? Why, I don't do nothin' wrong!"

"Clinton—Clinton . . ." Mary Aidan shook her head in despair. "If you ever get a wife, she'll have a horrible time with you."

"What are you talking about? Of course I'll get a wife. The Bible says that's what a man ought to do. It says to leave his mama and daddy and cleave to his wife, and that's what I aim to do."

"Well, it won't be Aldora."

Clinton's eyes flew open, and he stared at Mary Aidan. "What are you talking about? Why would you say a thing like that?"

"Because it's true."

"It ain't true, either. I'm practically almost ready to start courtin' her real serious."

"Clinton, it took you a whole month to find out that Aldora wasn't a boy!"

This was nothing but the truth. Aldora Stuart had dressed like a boy in shapeless clothing and worn a hat pulled down over her head. For some time Clinton had paid so little attention to her he thought she was a boy. His illusion was helped by the fact that everyone called her Al, short for her real full name. He eventually discovered that Aldora was a girl. During that time he had delivered several lectures to his young friend, thinking she was a boy, on how tricky and subtle females were. In time Aldora had blossomed into a beautiful young woman, and all the young men in the area had not been slow to come seeking her.

"Well, she wore them old, baggy clothes," he protested, "and kept her hat pulled down over her face! How was I supposed to know he . . . she was a girl?"

"Mama took one look at her and knew she was a girl the first time she saw her. And even after you found out, you didn't act like a man in love."

"Well, what does that mean?"

"You only take her to church, Clinton. When was the last time you gave her flowers?"

"Flowers?"

"Yes, flowers. Those colored things that grow out in the woods and on the prairie."

"Why, I didn't know she needed any."

"Clinton, you're impossible! Did you ever write her a love letter?"

Clinton was obviously getting annoyed at his sister as he ran his hand over his hair. "Well, I wrote her a note that time she went to New Orleans."

"What did you say?"

"I told her to be careful about the men in that place. They ain't moral. And I told her to wear loose-fittin' dresses, not like that one you're wearin' right now."

"You are impossible, Clinton Hardin!" Mary Aidan exclaimed. She reached out, slapped him on the chest, and walked away.

Clinton stood staring at her and finally shrugged. "Mary Aiden's plum foolish sometimes."

As Clinton drove the buggy up to Aldora Stuart's house, he saw that another buggy was already there. He got down, hitched the team to the rail, and then walked up the steps. Aldora's father, Caleb Stuart, opened the door for him before he knocked.

"Come in, Clinton."

"Howdy, Caleb."

Caleb Stuart sniffed the air. "What's that I smell?"

"That's me," Clinton said proudly. "Don't it take the rag off the bush?"

"I reckon so." Caleb grinned. "Come on in the parlor."

Clinton followed Stuart into the room. He saw Aldora first and then the man who had risen from the chair from across the room. Clinton took one look at Aldora and exclaimed, "Why, Al, you are as pretty as a red heifer in a flower bed!"

Aldora stared at him, then laughed. "You always know how to turn a pretty compliment, Clinton."

"Charles, this here is Clinton Hardin," Caleb said. "Clinton, meet Charles Maynard."

As Clinton reached out and shook the man's hand, he examined the man carefully. Maynard was a tall man at nearly six feet, and was wearing a fine brown suit. His white shirt was crisply pressed and almost glowed. He obviously was not a working man—at least not a farmer or a cowhand.

"Clinton's family runs the Yellow Rose Ranch, Charlie," Aldora said. "I told you about him."

"Yes. I hear the ranch is going well."

"Pretty well," Clinton nodded. "What do you do?"

Before Maynard could answer, Aldora said, "Charles has bought out the Cockrell and Jones Hardware in San Antone."

"That's right. I met Miss Aldora last month when she came in to buy some things."

Clinton was troubled by the man's confidence and his obvious interest in Aldora. "You sell hardware, then."

"I have two other stores. Keeps me pretty busy."

Clinton turned and said, "It'd drive me crazy bein' cooped up in a store all day."

"I expect it would be hard on men that like the out-of-doors. I guess I like my creature comforts too much."

"He's building a fine home in San Antone," Aldora said, her eyes sparkling. "It wasn't finished, but I saw it when I was there."

"You'll have to come back and see all that I've done to it since then. I had carpet sent in all the way from St. Louis."

"Carpets on the floor! Wouldn't that be lovely?" Aldora said.

Clinton studied Aldora's dress and said, "That's a nice dress, Aldora. It looks new."

"It is new. I bought it just for the celebration. Look," she said. "Charles brought these for me. Aren't they beautiful?"

Clinton looked at the flowers in the vase that Aldora was gesturing toward. "I never seen flowers like those."

"They're chrysanthemums. I'm going to plant them out in the yard. We'll have them every year." There was a moment's silence, and then Aldora said, "Well, this is a surprise."

"What's a surprise?" Clinton asked, puzzled.

"Why, I didn't expect to see you."

Clinton stared at her. "I don't know why you're surprised. I told you I'd take you to the celebration."

Aldora stared at him. "I'm going with Charles, Clinton."

Clinton shot a glance at Maynard, who was watching this scene carefully. "Why are you going with him?"

"Because he asked me."

"Well, shucks! You should have known I was gonna ask you."

"I'm not a mind reader, Clinton."

Clinton turned to face Maynard and said with a marked determination. "Well, Maynard, you see how it is. Al's my girl, and I'm takin' her to the celebration."

A sudden flush touched Charles Maynard's cheeks. "That's up to her, Hardin."

"I'm telling you how it is. Now, I think it'd be better if you'd leave."

"I'll leave when Aldora asks me to."

Clinton Hardin had a straight-forward type of mind and one way of solving problems. He attacked them head on. He suddenly reached forward, grabbed Maynard by the arm, and said loudly, "Evidently they don't teach manners in San Antone. I'm telling you that Al is my girl, and she's going with me! Now, you just get in that buggy of yours and get out of here!"

"Clinton—" Aldora cried out, but Clinton paid no mind.

Maynard jerked his arm away from Clinton's grasp and said, "Don't put your hands on me, Hardin!"

Clinton reacted instantly. He reached out to grab Maynard again, but Maynard struck with a lightning-fast move. His fist caught Clinton in the chest and drove him backward. It was a hard blow, and Aldora cried out, "Don't fight! Please don't fight!"

A sudden anger rose up in Clinton, and he seemed to lose control of himself. It was a sin that he often had to repent of, but now his temper overpowered him. He threw a high hard punch at Maynard, but Maynard simply picked it off with his left hand and came around with his right hand, striking Clinton right in the mouth. The powerful blow drove him backward into a table, which fell with a crash, breaking the flower vase with the chrysanthemums.

Clinton did not even hear Caleb saying, "Now, boys, we can't have this!" But he did hear Aldora crying out, "Clinton, you stop that right now!"

Lunging to his feet, Clinton came wind-milling at Maynard. Clinton was a strong young man but awkward, and apparently Maynard had had some experience in fighting. He was a fast man, and he caught Clinton again just over the eye with a left. Then a blow that seemed to come from nowhere caught Clinton squarely in the jaw. He went down at once and felt the blood trickling from his lip, and fiery stars seemed to glow across his mind.

He sat up groggily and tried to focus on Maynard. After a moment, he got up and demanded, "Well, Maynard, have you had enough, or do I have to do it again?"

Maynard shook his head and turned to say, "Aldora, this is no fun for me. I don't want to spoil a friendship for you."

"Charlie, I'm just one of the boys to Clinton. Let's go."

Clinton got to his feet, still unsteady. The blows had come fast and hard, harder than he had imagined for a city man.

"I wouldn't have thought a hardware salesman could fight like that," he muttered, shaking his head, which was throbbing.

"He was tougher than he looked," Caleb said.

"Well, I took it easy on him." Clinton saw Caleb staring at him strangely and cleared his throat. "Let me clean up this mess."

"No. I'll do it." Caleb was studying the young man, whom he liked very much. Clinton had been a great help on the place, always ready to pitch in when there was something that needed to be done. Caleb Stuart was not in good health and appreciated all the help. He had hoped that Al and Clinton would marry, but for three years now the courtship hadn't seemed to go anywhere. "I think you'd better start courtin' my girl more seriously, Clinton."

Clinton stared at him. He pulled his handkerchief out and wiped the blood from his face "She'll be sorry, Caleb, that she went with Charlie to the celebration. You watch, she'll be crawling back. Don't you worry. I'll forgive her—when she's repented enough. Well, I guess I better be gettin' on to the celebration."

Caleb watched as Clinton left. Going out on the porch, he saw Clinton climb into the buggy, wave, and then drive the team off. He shook his head and muttered, "That boy sure is headed for a big heartache!"

CHAPTER
THREE

Sitting loosely on the wagon seat, Zane Satterfield held the lines loosely in his hand and listened to O. M. Posey, who sat beside him. Listening to Posey was a full-time job, for the small rider talked incessantly about everything. Glancing over, Zane saw that Posey was holding his left arm carefully to keep it from moving and remarked, "That's tough getting your arm broke like that, Posey. That's the way it goes sometimes."

The wheels of the wagon jolted into a pothole, throwing Posey to one side. He gripped his arm hard and turned and stared with contempt at Satterfield. "It was all that bird's fault."

Zane grinned, for he was accustomed to Posey's odd remarks, which seemed almost meaningless at times. "What does a bird have to do with your getting a broken arm?"

"Why, I told you, Zane. You just don't listen."

"Well, tell me again so I get it clear this time."

Posey reached into the pocket of his coat, pulled out a plug of tobacco, and bit off a large chunk. He moved the cud around in his mouth, carefully getting it in a position that pleased him before he answered. "I told you. A bird got in the bunkhouse last Tuesday."

Zane's eyes were on the road ahead, which led into Jordan City. It was a crooked, winding road, circling outcrops of rocks thrust up from the earth. During the summer the road was buried in the long grasses, which made it almost impossible to traverse. The flat Texas country did not please Zane. He preferred the mountains with their forests and rushing streams. He spoke to the horses, slapped their backs with the lines, and then said, "I forget what you said a bird had to do with getting your arm busted."

"Why, everybody knows a bird in the house brings bad luck!"

"It's just a bird, Posey. It was that horse's fault."

"T'wasn't either! That horse didn't have nothin' to do with it. It was that bird." Posey spit over the side of the wagon and then grimaced and grabbed his arm. "I'm just glad it ain't worse. Why, back home my second cousin Phoebe Trimble let a bird get in the house, and no more than three months later her brother Dave died."

"What'd he die of?"

"I forget. Some kind of sickness, but it was that durned bird's fault."

Zane suddenly laughed aloud. He was a lean six-footer, a hundred and eighty-five pounds of muscle. His eyes were gray, and crisp brown hair with a slight curl escaped from the hat he had shoved back on his head. "Don't be foolish," he said. "You're too superstitious."

"Me? I ain't superstitious a'tall. I just know the facts."

As the wagon jolted over the prairie, Zane only half listened to Posey, who for the next mile insisted he wasn't superstitious in the least. He was, of course, terrifically so. Everything that happened seemed to bode ill for Posey. Satterfield had no such strange superstitions, and finally he was glad to see Jordan City break the lines of the prairie. "Well, there's town," he said, gesturing at it. "I hope we can find Doc Woods."

"Why wouldn't we find him?"

"He might be gone to tend somebody."

"That'd be just my luck, wouldn't it? He probably won't be there, and this arm will fester, and he'll have to cut it off when he does wander back into town. Or else it'll heal crooked, and I won't be able to work no more."

"You don't work much anyhow." Zane grinned. This was not true, for Posey was a hard-working rider, perhaps the most industrious of all of the hands that worked for the Yellow Rose Ranch. The ranch was owned by Zane's sister Jerusalem and her husband, Clay. It had come as no surprise to Zane that Jerusalem had decided to make the Yellow Rose one of the biggest ranches in Texas. Clay did not have that sort of ambition being a happy-go-lucky sort of man, but he wanted to make Jerusalem happy, so he had hitched his wagon to her star. And in time, he grew to love the ranch as much as she did, working long, hard hours to make it succeed.

Zane guided the wagon into Jordan City, which was composed mostly of one main street with narrow alleys between the buildings. It was a typical Texas town. Most of the buildings were made of adobe, but a few had been built with lumber that had been hauled in.

Pulling up in front to the rail, Zane tied the horses, then walked around and said, "You want me to carry you in?"

Posey gave Zane a disgusted look. "That's foolishness! I can walk. It's my arm that's busted, not my leg!"

Zane and Posey walked inside the door and found a Mexican woman listlessly moving a broom around, stirring up the dust more than anything else. She looked at them with tired dark eyes and said, "The doctor ain't here."

"Where is he?" Zane said.

"At the saloon getting drunk."

Zane grinned. "It sounds like Doc Woods, all right. Posey, you stay here. I'll go fetch him."

"Bring me somethin' back to drink from that there saloon. It will ease the pain I'm feeling."

Zane grinned but did not answer. He left the doctor's office and walked down the main street until he reached the Golden Lady Saloon. For a moment he stopped and looked at the sign on the outside that bore the faint imprint of what was once a very large nude lady. She was almost faded now, and Zane shook his head. "You need a new coat of paint, lady." He turned and entered the saloon and at once saw Doctor Phineas Woods sitting at a poker table across from Frisco Farr, the owner of the Golden Lady and a well-known gambling virtuoso. Woods was a big man in his mid-sixties, with salt-and-pepper hair and beard. His weaknesses were cards and liquor, and at the moment, both had a good grip on him.

Zane walked over to the table and said, "You need to find some new sins, Doc. Why don't you take up chasin' scarlet women?" Zane grinned at Woods' profane response to that remark.

"Hello, Doc. Hello, Frisco."

Doctor Woods was holding his hand and studying the cards over the top of his glasses. "What do you want, Zane?"

"I brought a patient for you. He's down at the office."

"I'm busy. Is he dying?"

"No. I don't reckon so. Just a busted arm."

"It won't hurt him to wait, then."

Frisco Farr leaned back in his chair and laughed aloud. He was a man of no more than medium height and dressed in a neat black suit. A black string tie contrasted with the snowy white shirt, and his curly brown hair was neatly cut. "Sit down, Zane. As soon as I take all of Doc's money, I'll start on yours."

"I got a little better sense than to play with a professional gambler, Frisco."

"I guess that means I don't have any sense!" Doctor Woods snapped. "Go over there and sit down. When I trim this sharpie here, I'll go fix that arm. Who is it?"

"Posey."

"Won't hurt him to wait a spell."

Knowing Doctor Woods could not be rushed, Zane headed toward the bar, where he saw Sheriff Joel Bench sitting at a table. He had a bottle of soda pop in front of him and was carefully pouring a little into a shot whiskey glass. "Hello, Sheriff," Zane said. "Mind if I join you for a spell?"

"Sit down, Zane. Albert, bring Zane one of these soda pops."

Zane grinned. "I don't know about them soda pops. I heard they ain't good for ya."

Sheriff Joel Bench was a small man with icy blue eyes. He had silver hair, and his face was lined. No one knew much about Bench's past, but everyone knew he was one tough sheriff. He lived alone except for his cat Omar, and his voice was soft in peace or in trouble. "What are you doing in town, Zane?"

"Posey broke his arm. I brought him in to get it patched up."

"Too bad. How'd it happen?"

Zane explained Posey's theory that it was a bird in the bunkhouse that had caused his misfortune. As he spoke, his eyes went to a woman wearing a shiny maroon dress. She had dark, lustrous eyes and hair as black as coal. Her eyes met his, and she came over and said, "Hello, Zane."

"Hello, Bev. Sit down and have a soda pop."

Bev laughed. "You're living pretty recklessly, you two, drinking soda pop. No telling what'll come next."

Bev Despain was an attractive woman, but working in the saloon had brought a certain hardness to her. She had a beautiful olive complexion, and her lips, when they were relaxed, were soft and curved. She was smiling now at Zane, and it was not a professional courtesy. She had always liked the big man and said, "Why don't you ever come and see me anymore, Zane?"

"Too much competition. I'm through running around after good-looking women."

Bev took the soda pop that Albert set in front of her and tilted the bottle back. "What are you going to chase around after, if not good-looking women?"

"I'm gonna find me a homely woman and settle down and have ten kids."

Bench was interested in these two. He had always felt he saw something between them, and now he asked, "Why do you want a homely woman when you can have a pretty one like Bev here?"

Zane leaned back in his chair, lifted the glass of pop, and studied it as if it had some deep meaning. He sipped it slowly, then humor danced in his eyes as he said, "Well, if a fellow marries a good-looking woman, somebody's likely to run off with her."

Bev grinned. "But fellows run off with homely women too."

"Oh sure," Zane shrugged, "but who cares?"

Bench laughed. "You're a caution, Zane! I've got to go keep law and order. The soda pop's paid for."

"You're the last of the big spenders, Joel," Bev said. She reached out and traced a figure on the scarred top of the table, but her eyes remained fixed on Zane. "What have you been up to?" she asked.

"Cows. I heard a fellow once that said bein' a cowboy was romantic. He didn't know what he was talkin' about. I can't think of anything less romantic than following around after a bunch of smelly cows that don't want to go where you want 'em to."

Bev stuck her finger in the pop and then put it in her mouth. "I don't know why anybody drinks this stuff," she said. After a moment, she looked up and said, "Why haven't you ever married, Zane?"

"I thought about it once."

Bev Despain looked up suddenly. The remark surprised her. She had always wondered why a handsome fellow like Zane Satterfield had never married. "Why haven't you done it, then?"

Zane leaned forward and clasped his hands together and studied them for a moment. "It seems like I missed out on everything important."

"Like what?"

"Why, a family. Kids. That's about all that counts in this life."

"Well, you're not too old to start, Zane."

"I'm forty-six." He unclasped his hands and placed them flat on the table and looked across into Bev's eyes. "Nothin' much to show for my life. Just some empty years that don't seem to mean anything." The words seemed to strike against Bev Despain in a way that Zane could not really understand for a moment.

She blinked and then murmured, "Me, too, Zane."

At that instant they both heard Doctor Woods curse loudly. They turned and watched as he stood up from the poker table and stalked toward them. When he reached their table, his face was flushed with anger. "Might as well go set that fellow's arm."

"All right, Doc, I'm ready."

Doctor Woods glanced over at Frisco Farr, who was raking in a sizeable pot. "I don't know why I play poker. I can't ever win."

"You need a wife to keep you occupied," Bev said.

"I had a wife, a good one too."

"Find another one, Doc. A man like you needs a good woman." Bev smiled.

Zane found the remark interesting. He turned to face Bev and said, "Let me go back with Doc to be sure he don't cut that arm off Posey because he lost that pot." He smiled then, and his whole face seemed to light up. "I'll come back, and we'll try to cheer each other up."

"All right, Zane. I'll be here waiting."

★ ★ ★

"Houston sure don't look like much, does it? For the capital of a whole country, it sure seems like Texas could have something a little fancier."

Jerusalem, sitting beside Clay in the front seat of the wagon, laughed. "What do you want—New York out here in the middle of nowhere?"

"Well, I reckon not New York. St. Louis, maybe."

The two were tired, for the trip to Houston was long and tiring. The children were asleep in the backseat, and as they entered town, suddenly Jerusalem said, "Look. There's Julie and Rice."

Clay looked over and grinned. "Sure is, and they got that new young'un of theirs with them."

Clay pulled the wagon over and hollered, "Hey, Preacher!"

Rice Morgan looked up at once when he heard his name. He was a trim, well-built man of thirty-five with black hair and blue-gray eyes. "Clay!" he called out, and taking his wife's arm, he waited until the two dismounted.

"You brought the whole bunch," Julie Morgan said.

Jerusalem went up to her and took the baby from her arms. "Hello, sister," she said. "Let me hold this girl of yours."

"A big, fat wad of a girl she is." Morgan grinned, the strain of old Wales in his voice. "It's proud I am to have two good-looking women in my house."

Julie laughed. "That's not what you say when you have to get up in the night and carry her when she has the colic."

Julie Morgan was a little old to be having a baby at the age of thirty-nine; however, she looked ten years younger. Her hair was a bright red and her eyes a brilliant green. Her life had been hard for many years, and everyone in the county had been shocked when Julie, a saloon girl, had married Rice Morgan, the pastor of the Baptist church in Jordan City.

"She's so pretty," Jerusalem said, touching the baby's rosy cheek. "She looks just like Rice."

"Bad luck for her, then. I wanted her to look like Julie. Maybe the next one will look like her."

The two sisters stood there admiring the baby as Jerusalem's brood came piling out of the wagon. "You children come with me," Jerusalem said. "I've got some shopping to do. Come along, Julie. You can help me keep these wild Indians in line."

"Ethan and Moriah didn't come with you?" Rice asked quickly as the women prepared to leave."

Jerusalem hesitated. "No, they didn't."

"She should have brought the boy. It would have been exciting for him."

Jerusalem didn't answer, for she knew Rice would have told her the same thing Quaid had. Handing the baby back to Julie, she said, "Clay, you stay out of saloons today, you hear."

"Well, I'll be with a preacher. If we go in one, it's no harm to anybody."

The two men moved down the street, which was more crowded than Clay or Rice had ever seen before. Both of them had made many good friends during the years since the Alamo had fallen to Santa Anna and Texas, shortly afterward, had become an independent republic. They stopped often to speak to old friends, and then Rice said, "Look, there's Houston. Let's go listen to him."

The two moved through the crowd, shouldering their way where they could get a good view of the president of the Texas Republic and soon-to-be senator of the brand-new state of Texas.

Sam Houston towered over most of the other men. He stood six feet four in his stocking feet and was thickly built. His face looked like a map, seamed, and at the moment he looked almost happy. He had had a checkered career, but everyone agreed that it was Sam Houston's forcefulness that had kept Texas together against marauding Mexicans and raiding Comanches.

Clay admired the man and listened as someone said, "Why do you reckon the United States let us in, Sam? They fought giving us statehood for ten long years."

Houston's eyes suddenly gleamed, and he looked out over the crowd. "It wasn't so much that they wanted Texas, men. They wanted everything between Texas and the Pacific Ocean. The way to get it was through Texas. Watch what I tell you. They'll snap up New Mexico next and then go all the way to California."

"But that belongs to Spain."

"It does now," Sam Houston said, grinning, "but you mind what I'm telling you. I'm not a prophet nor the son of a prophet, but one day this

United States will reach all the way from the Atlantic Ocean to the Pacific Ocean."

"We'll have to whip Mexico first," someone shouted from the crowd.

A secretive look swept across Sam Houston's face. He smiled enigmatically and shrugged his massive shoulders. "I reckon that can be arranged," he said loudly enough so that every man heard him.

"That's what's going to happen. We'll have a war with Mexico," Rice said, "and then, one way or another, we'll take everything between here and the Pacific, including California."

"Sure is a funny way to get a country together, ain't it, Rice?" Clay remarked. Then they both leaned forward to catch Houston's remarks.

A large wooden platform no more than six feet high had been built in front of what would serve as the capitol building. A band composed mostly of Mexicans was playing with all their might, and Mary Aidan was in her glory. Barton Singleton had brought her to the festivities, but he had been forced to stand aside and watch while Mary was claimed by many men as their partner to dance.

Finally, Barton went forward and said, "I believe this is my partner."

Mary Aidan's eyes were sparkling. She said, "Oh, Barton, I'm sorry. It's just that—"

"I reckon this here's my dance, sonny. You can scratch for it," said a large man.

Barton was actually surprised. He turned to see a huge man, even bigger than himself, wearing two guns standing before him. The guns he saw were the new Colt forty-fours that fired off six shots without reloading. There was wildness in the man's face, but Barton was determined to stand his ground. "You'll have to find another partner," he said forcefully.

"I'm claimin' this one, boy. Now, leave us alone!"

Mary Aidan was staring at the scene. She watched Barton to see what he would do, because she knew he had an explosive temper and no fear of fighting.

"What did you say?"

"Get out of here, sonny boy!" The big man put his hand on Barton's chest and shoved him backward. Barton was shoved with such force he nearly lost his footing. His face flushed with rage, he readied himself for a violent showdown.

"What's the trouble, sis?"

Mary Aidan turned quickly to see her brother, Brodie Hardin, had arrived. "Hello, Brodie."

"Hello, Barton," Brodie said. He was a tall man, six feet two and lean, with the same auburn hair and greenish eyes that all of the Hardins had. "You gonna save me a dance?"

The big man had paused to look at Brodie and grunted, "Get out of here, boy."

Mary Aidan knew that Brodie was a fighting man, like Barton, who preferred to resolve arguments with his fists.

"Brodie, don't...don't fight him."

"Why not?" Brodie remarked. He turned and faced the big man and said, "You can leave now."

When the big man reached out to shove him away, Brodie's hand moved so fast that Mary Aidan could hardly see it. Brodie simply reached out, plucked one of the huge pistols from the man's holster, lifted it, and brought it down over his head. The hollow sound was like someone striking a watermelon. The big man's knees collapsed, and his eyes rolled upward so that she could see only the white. He sprawled forward, his face striking the floor with another thud.

"Hey, you get on with your dancin', sis. Barton, it's yours, I guess." He reached down and got the man by one leg and dragged him off of the stage that had been built for the festivities.

The music continued, and laughter filled the air.

"It's a good thing for that guy Brodie came along. I would've killed him," Barton snorted as he grabbed Mary Aiden's hand and pulled her from the platform.

As Brodie dumped the inert figure of the bully on the street, a voice said, "That was right neat, young fella. What's your name?"

Brodie turned to see a rather unimpressive man who was watching him carefully. He wore a single revolver on his right hip, and he had watchful eyes, though he was mild-looking. "Brodie Hardin."

"I'm James Macklin. People call me Captain Mac."

"Captain of what?"

"That's what I want to talk to you about. You got a minute?"

"Why not," Brodie said.

Macklin walked away, and Brodie followed him, towering over the smaller man. When they had moved away from the dancing area, Macklin turned and said, "I'm captain in the Ranging Company. I need some more men to join our forces. I think you'd fit right in."

"Ranging Company?"

"That's right. Texas is going to need some help against the Comanches and the Mexicans."

"Why, the army will take care of that!" Brodie said with surprise. "We're a state now. They'll have to send blue coats in to defend us."

"If you think soldiers can catch a bunch of Comanches on the warpath, you've got a better opinion of the army than I have. You've been in Texas awhile, haven't you?" Captain Mac said.

"For quite a spell."

"Then you know the Comanches. They can hit a ranch and be a hundred miles away in twenty-four hours. You think a bunch of marchin' soldiers can catch 'em? No, sir, it's going to take Rangers to do that."

"Well, I'm flattered, Captain, but I'm helpin' my family. We're building a great ranch—the Yellow Rose."

Macklin nodded. "Yes. I know that. But you're going to find it hard to build a ranch where you're located. The Comanches will come down on you from the north, and the thievin' Mexicans will come up from the south. But I don't ever beg for men. If you ever change your mind, Mr. Hardin, come and see me."

"Sure, Captain. I'll do that."

"I'd say it's time for you to marry me."

Mary Aidan looked up with surprise. Barton had directed her away from the dancing area to a relatively quiet spot and had proposed so abruptly that it caught her off-guard. Well, not exactly off-guard, for she had seen it coming. At only sixteen, Mary Aidan had an innate knowledge of men, it seemed. Her beauty had drawn them to her ever since she was only fourteen, but now she was a fully developed woman.

"Why, Barton, I'm surprised!"

"No you're not," Barton said. "You knew I was going to propose."

Mary Aidan flushed. "Am I that transparent?"

"I guess you are. You know men pretty well or think you do." He waited and then said, "Well? You are gonna marry me, ain't ya?"

"Barton, I like you so much, but—"

Barton suddenly grinned bitterly. He was not a very practical young man, but he shook his head, dumbfounded at her audacity. "What do you mean you *like* me? You know you're the girl for me, Mary Aiden. So why are you stringin' me along?"

"I'm not, Barton. It's just that—"

"So why won't you say yes?" he demanded.

"Why, I don't love you, that's why."

"But I carry guns, and I like to go around shooting people and bashing heads. That's what you want, Mary Aidan, a man of action like your brother Brodie, right? Well, I'm that kind of a man!"

"That's not true."

"What? You don't think I'm that kind of man?"

"No—that I want a man who's a fighter and a gunman."

"Stop and think about the men you admire, Mary. I've known you for a while. You've got some silly romantic notions about the perfect man. Well, I'm the perfect man, and no man would make a better husband than me—certainly not some tame man."

Mary Aidan was half angry. "I think that's unfair, Barton!"

"You think you're pretty smart, but you don't know yourself. Come on. We'll have a good time, I'll take you home, and you can think about what I said. The next time I ask you, you will say yes."

"Mama, Barton proposed to me tonight."

"What did you say?" Jerusalem Ann asked calmly. Mary Aidan had found her mother to tell her of Barton's proposal.

"Why, I told him no."

"That's good. He's not the man for you."

Mary Aidan blinked with surprise. "I thought you liked him."

"He's not the meanest rooster in the yard, but he's pretty close. I know you want a man like Brodie or your dad, but Barton is too rough of a sort."

Mary Aidan was stung by her mother's words. "That's just what Barton said."

Jerusalem put her arm around her daughter and said quietly, "The man you'll marry won't have an easy time, Mary Aidan."

"Why would you say that, Mama?"

"You expect too much of a man. You've got this picture in your mind, and if a man doesn't fit it, you don't think he's worthy. It would be good if you could get that thought out of your mind, but I don't expect you can."

The two were interrupted, for suddenly they heard a blare of trumpets. "It's the ceremony," she said, "hauling the flag down. I'm going to find Clay."

Jerusalem made her way through the crowd and found Clay not twenty feet away from the flagpole. When he saw her, he grinned, reached out, and took her hand. He stood there holding it, and Jerusalem felt a sudden warm glow. It was the sort of thing her first husband, Jake, would not have done. *Most men would never hold their wife's hand in public*, she thought. It made her happy that Clay showed affection openly and unashamed.

"Well, there it goes," Clay murmured. The flag of the Lone Star Republic slowly came down the pole, fluttering in the late afternoon breeze.

"Somehow it seems kind of sad to me," Clay whispered.

"Why's that?" Jerusalem asked.

"I don't know. The Republic of Texas suited me just fine." He sighed and then shook his head. "Well, she was fine while she lasted, but we'll see what comes now."

CHAPTER
FOUR

F ine dust arose like incense into the air, but to the men struggling to brand the longhorns, it did not smell quite as sweet. Two crews of three each were working. Zane was roping the wide-eyed long-horns and dragging them up close to the fire while Clinton and Brodie did their best to wrestle them to the ground. The other crew was headed by Quaid Shafter, with Ike McClellan and Johnny Bench doing the branding. The sun had nearly set in the west, and the men moved much slower now. They had been working for hours and were worn out. From time to time one of the men working on the ground would complain that they had the hardest part of the job, Clinton being the worst offender.

"Zane, let me do the roping for a while." Clinton's face was coated with dust, and when he licked his lips, he left a track outlining his mouth. "I'm tired of eatin' this dust."

Zane Satterfield was recoiling his rope and grinned while Brodie slapped the red-hot branding iron on the longhorn. "Why, Clinton, I fig-ure I'm doing you a favor by lettin' you take the hard part of this job."

"Well, I don't want no favors. You got the easy part."

"Now, you know the Bible says man's born to trouble as the sparks fly upward, so I'm just seein' to it that you get your share. I wouldn't want to rob you of suffering. You told me a hundred times that's what makes a man better."

Brodie was as coated with dust as Clinton but was much tougher. "There you go, brother," he said. "You ought to thank your uncle for letting you have all this suffering. He could have hogged it all for himself."

Zane shook his head, ignoring Clinton's wild reasoning and turned his mustang and laid his rope over the sweeping horns of a brindle steer. His pony immediately stopped and began backing up, dragging the struggling animal with him. When Zane got close to the fire, Brodie dodged under the steer, grabbed a front leg, and then he and Clinton wrestled the animal to the ground. "You slap the brand on him, Clinton. I'll hold her."

Clinton walked stiffly to the fire, picked up a brand, and stared at it. "This ain't no proper brand," he said. "Who ever heard of a ranch named the Yellow Rose? Why, it sounds like some kind of perfume made by a Frenchman."

"Just slap the brand on. I can't hold this critter much longer," Brodie panted.

But Clinton was staring at the smoking branding iron, which was red hot. "I wonder how bad it hurts. It must be awful to get one of these things slapped on your hide. There must be an easier way."

"What do you want to do, hang a sign on them, Clinton?" Brodie shouted. "Brand this critter before I brand you!"

Clinton, lost in philosophical thought, hesitated too long. The steer managed to get away from Brodie. With one sweep of the mighty horns, the steer caught Clinton right across the seat of his pants. Clinton was tossed through the air but managed to hang on to the iron as he rolled in the dust.

The steer, wild-eyed and huffing, started for Brodie, who dove into the dirt. Zane quickly guided his pony to drive the steer away.

"Well, ain't that a pretty come off!" Brodie said, getting to his feet and dusting off his knees. "You ain't worth dried spit, Clinton!"

"Don't say that," Zane said, his eyes dancing. "You know Clinton's theology. He says whatever is to be will be. I think he calls himself some kind of a Calvinist. Is that right?" Clinton merely glared at him, and Zane gathered up his rope and continued his mild teasing. "Well, I guess it was to be since before the world began that this cow was gonna slap you right across the butt. Just be glad you got that behind you, nephew."

The three men working fifty feet away at another fire were all laughing. Quaid Shafter was roping for Ike McClellan and Johnny Bench. McClellan had taken the scene in and then turned to say to Bench, "I wished I had paid more attention to my ma and pa and done what they wanted me to do."

Bench, a six-foot muscular man, turned to face Ike, who was short and shaped much like a barrel. "What'd they want you to do?"

"Wanted me to be respectable. What they had lined out was for me to be an undertaker."

Johnny Bench shook his head. "I'd rather wrestle cows than fool around with dead folks."

"Why, there ain't nothin' to it. My grandpa was a fine undertaker. I used to watch him all the time. As a matter of fact, he let me help him. Why, I've given many a corpse a shave."

"You shaved dead men? Why, you won't even shave yourself, Ike!" Quaid called out.

He had coiled his rope and was ready to put it on another steer, but Zane suddenly called out, "I guess that's enough for today, boys!"

"Well, I was ready to quit a long time ago," Ike said. "We're gonna be late for supper."

Zane sat on his horse and watched as the dusty cowboys walked wearily to their mounts. He noticed that they were all tired and said to Quaid, "We worked them pretty hard today, Quaid."

"It won't kill 'em. I've eaten my share of dust."

"So have I. That scared me, though, when that mossy horn got Clinton. He could have hurt him bad."

"Clinton's too holy to get hurt," Quaid said, grinning. "It'll be sinners like me and you that gets whacked a good one when we're not watching."

Zane laughed and rolled a cigarette expertly and stuck it in between his lips. He struck a match on his thumbnail and lit it as his eyes took in all the cattle scattered in the corral. "I wish we had a market for these steers."

"We're gonna have to make a drive pretty soon."

"You're right about that. If we don't, the bean eaters will come across the Rio Grande and steal 'em."

Quaid laughed, his teeth flashing against his tanned skin. "We could steal 'em back."

"I reckon we could. Some of these steers have been stolen back and forth across the border so often that they're gettin' old and worn out."

Quaid turned and looked far to the south, as if he could see all the way to Mexico. "I don't think those Mexicans are ever gonna give up."

"No. From what I hear we're gonna have a war before you know it."

"If it comes to that, I think I'll join up. I feel almost like Clinton does. I'm tired of eatin' dust. I'd like to have a little more excitement than wrestling steers."

Quaid laughed shortly. "If the Comanches come down from the north, you'll get all the excitement you want. They've been mighty good lately, but I don't trust 'em. They remind me of a mule I had once. He'd be good for a whole year just to get a chance to kick me a good one."

Zane turned his horse and started back for the ranch. As the others followed, he thought about how hard the life had been on the Yellow Rose. Building a big ranch was Jerusalem's idea, but Zane was afraid she didn't realize how hard it was going to be. Even the three months since Texas had achieved statehood, they had been raided once by Mexican cattle thieves, who took nearly a hundred head of cattle back across the Rio Grande. They had taken them from the southernmost part of the ranch. By the time they realized the steers were missing, it was too late to trail them.

As for the Comanches, they were like dry lightning. The sun could be shining and the flowers growing, and the world could seem right, when suddenly out of nowhere a half-dozen Comanche warriors would appear and literally annihilate a small ranch or homestead. They picked their targets well, and after torturing and killing and raping, they would disappear, headed back for the Llano Estacado.

As they approached the ranch house, the shadows were growing long, but Zane's thoughts were longer still. *It seems like I ought to be making more of myself. A whole life is going by, and what have I got to show for it? Nothing! Just the horse I'm riding and the clothes I'm standing in and my gun.* These thoughts troubled him as they never had before. It came to

him that a man lived his life thoughtlessly and woke up one day, then realized that he was an old man and that his days were numbered. Although
he was only forty-six, life was hard in Texas, and men died young.
Something stirred in Zane Satterfield. Even as he swung off the horse and
got ready to wash up with the others for the evening meal, he knew that
he was going to do something different. Suddenly, a thin vein of humor
crossed his mind. *A man bends over to pick up something, and when he
straightens up, the whole world has changed. Well, I reckon it's about time I
did some changing.*

With this thought in mind, he unsaddled his horse, grained him, and
then turned him out into the pasture. The other riders were doing the
same, and as the hands started for the bunkhouse, Zane, who loved to nee-
dle Clinton, said, "Hey, Clint, them fellers need to say grace over their
food. You'd better go take care of it, or they'll be eatin' an unsanctified
supper."

Clinton had turned his horse out and came over beating the dust out
of his shirt with his hat. "Uncle Zane, you ought not to be makin' fun of
sayin' grace."

Zane suddenly felt a streak of compunction. "I know it, Clinton. I'm
sorry. I don't mean to pick on you all the time. As a matter of fact, I don't
know of a better young man in this whole country than you."

The unexpected compliment caught Clinton off-guard. He stopped
dead still, for it was the best compliment that his uncle had ever paid to
him. "Well, you sure kept quiet enough about it," he said stridently.

"I know it. I'll try to do better."

"Uncle Zane, don't you believe in God at all?"

"Yes, I do."

Clinton had tried to talk to his uncle Zane many times, but as the two
walked toward the house, he realized that there was an opening here.
"Well, why don't you get baptized and come right up and admit you need
the Lord?"

Zane stopped and turned toward Clinton, for he had touched on a
spot that was tender. "I don't know, Clinton. It just never came my way."

Brodie had approached and had been listening to the conversation.
"Stop preachin' at Zane all the time, Clinton."

"I won't either."

"It don't do no good all this preachin' you do!"

Clinton shot his brother a superior look. "You don't know that! The gospel is like seed. The Bible says so. Some of it falls on good ground and some on stony ground."

"Well, save your preachin' until after supper."

Zane ordinarily would have joined in with Brodie, but instead he dropped his hand on his nephew's shoulder. "It's all right, Clinton. You just keep on preachin'. I don't mind it. I know you're right about the Lord, and I'm wrong. Maybe someday I'll get it right."

For once Clinton was speechless. For years he had tried to talk to his uncle about the Lord. Suddenly and for no apparent reason, his words were finding good soil. "Here," he said, "I got somethin' I want to give you." He reached into his shirt pocket and pulled out a piece of paper. "You read this part I got marked."

Curious, Zane unfolded the paper. "Why, this is a page out of the Bible!" he said.

"Yeah, it is."

"You tore a page out of your Bible?"

"Oh, I do that all the time. I find a good part, and I tear it out and then give it to someone."

"Well, that's right thoughty of you. What part did you want me to know?"

"I got it all underlined, and out at the edge I put a little star. Of course I didn't know it was for you, but I figure it might help some."

Zane had spent a great deal of his life being amused at Clinton, but somehow the sincere action of the young man touched him. He tightened his grip on Clinton's shoulder and said, "I'll keep it. You believe it, Clinton, and thanks a lot."

The three men washed up on the back porch, and as they entered the house, the smell of good home cooking filled the air. Jerusalem and Moriah were loading the big rectangular table with food. Clay was already seated at the long table. He looked up and said, "You boys come in. After a hard day's work, we all need something to nourish us."

Zane, who was as old as Clay and felt more free to speak his mind, sat down and stared at him. "I don't remember seein' you out there wrestlin' with those ornery steers today."

"Why, no. Somebody has to do the thinkin' around here," Clay said, and his eyes danced as he spoke. "Why, if it wasn't for me to think, there wouldn't be no thinkin' done around this place. And then we'd all be in a fix."

"Well, I'd like to see you think a brand on all them steers," Brodie grunted as he sat down.

"Why, I wouldn't want to deprive you young fellas the privilege. You know the Bible says that when a man gets married, he has to take some time off and make his wife happy." Clay reached out and grabbed Jerusalem, who was passing by with a huge bowl of mashed potatoes. "And this here woman takes lots of tender care. Isn't that right, wife?"

"Turn loose of me!" Jerusalem admonished. "You haven't done a thing but play with the children all day."

"Well, that's what the Bible says."

"Where does it say that?" Jerusalem demanded and moved away from his grasp.

"Well, it says it somewhere because I read it," Clay said. "Come on. All this thinkin' has made me mighty hungry. Everybody get set so I can bless this here food."

There was a rush for the table, which was crowded now with Clay, Jerusalem, Zane, Moriah, Mary Aidan, and Clinton, as well as the children, Sam and Belle, Dave, and Nathan. All of them squeezed in as best they could.

"Now, everybody bow their heads because I'm fixin' to bless this food," Clay said. He had not been a Christian long, but he loved to bless the food and give thanks for all the blessings his family had.

"Keep it short, will you, Pa?" Brodie pleaded.

"Now, Brodie, we don't want to short-change ourselves on our prayers. You young'uns all bow your heads and shut your eyes." Clay waited until the children obeyed, and then he looked around to see that every head was bowed before closing his own. "Now, Lord, we wouldn't want You to think that we're not grateful for this food. I know there are people eatin' awful food like frog legs and oysters and snails, but we're grateful for the good Texas food that You've allowed us. So, Lord, I thank You right now for these beef steaks. They might be a little bit tough because my dear wife hasn't found out how to tenderize them always yet, but we thank You for them, tough as they are. Thank You for this gravy, Lord, which I know is good because it's one of the best things that Moriah makes. We just pray that there'll be enough so that the gluttons won't eat it all up before the rest of us get some of it. The potatoes, Lord, they came straight out of the earth, but we know that You made 'em grow. And there's nothin' I like better than steamy hot potatoes with butter on top of 'em. So we thank You for the butter and even for the pepper and the salt that's gonna make 'em taste so good. . . ."

On and on Clay went, naming every item of food, and finally after blessing the buttermilk and the coffee, he ended by saying, "And I'm sure there's some kind of dessert that's gonna be comin', and whatever it is, I just know I'll be able to keep it down. So, Lord, we're—"

"Amen!" Jerusalem Ann said loudly. "That's enough, Clay! The food's gettin' cold."

"Why, wife, I'm surprised at you. Here you got me all trained to be a good Christian, and now you're raisin' a fuss because I'm thankful for the food the Lord has blessed us with."

Everyone at the table, even the younger ones, grinned, for they all knew how Clay loved to tease Jerusalem Ann. He sat there trying to look hurt, but he could not disguise the humor that flickered in his eyes.

"You done hurt my feelin's now, wife. You surely have."

"I couldn't hurt your feelings with a pick ax!"

Bob came over at that moment and nudged Clinton's leg. He was always good for a hand-out. The big dog was an absolute beggar, and although Jerusalem had forbidden anybody to feed him, he generally managed to scrounge something from someone at the table. Clinton turned around and said, "Get away, Bob! You're not supposed to eat with people."

The big dog gave Clinton a hurt look, then dropped his head and shuffled mournfully across the floor. He went to the corner, plopped down, and stared at the wall, the picture of hurt pride.

"You see there? You done hurt his feelings," Clay said. "He's sensitive—like me."

The food began to disappear at an alarming rate, and the room was filled with plenty of talk and laughter. Finally, Mary Aidan asked, "Clay, what's going on in the state now that we're a part of the United States?"

"You need to call me *Father* or maybe *Father dear*, Mary Aidan. It ain't right for you to call your father by his first name. It don't show respect."

Mary Aidan giggled. "All right, *Father dear,* what's going on?"

"I can't see no difference at all. Nobody's gotten rich. The Mexicans are still stealin' us blind, and the Comanches raided a ranch not forty miles away from here last week."

Everyone's eyes went to Clay, and Zane said, "Anybody we know?"

Clay swallowed a huge mouthful of potatoes and shook his head. "I met the man once at a stock sale, but I really didn't know him. One thing's for sure. We're gonna have to keep our eyes open. We don't want to be taken off-guard by the hostiles."

"Is that why you hired those two Indians to keep watch?" Moriah asked.

"Well, more or less," Clay admitted.

"Well, you might as well get rid of them."

"Why's that, Moriah?"

"They're tame Indians. Any real Comanche brave would kill them before they could blink an eye."

A brief silence fell around the table, and every eye was on Moriah. She had spent years as a captive with the Comanches and knew their ways better than anyone else. She never spoke of her captivity, and everyone at the table avoided looking at Ethan, the son she had borne to Bear Killer, the war chief of that tribe.

"Well," Clay said, "I reckon that's the best we can do for now. By the way, how many steers did you boys put the iron on today?"

"Not as many as you would have liked," Brodie said, smiling at Clay.

The talk continued for some time until Zane, who usually lingered and talked while drinking coffee, got up and walked over and plucked his hat from a peg on the wall.

"Where you going, Zane?" Clinton called out.

"Reckon I'll drift into town for a spell. See you all later."

As soon as he was out the door, Clinton said loudly, "He's going to see that saloon woman, Bev Despain. That's where he's goin'." He got up to his feet and said, "I'm gonna go stop him."

"Clinton, you set yourself back down!" Jerusalem's voice hit Clinton like a blow, and he stopped dead still. Turning to her, he said, "But, Ma, somebody's got to—"

"You set down and eat your pie."

Clinton opened his mouth to argue, which was the thing he did best in the world, but one look at his mother's face convinced him of the foolishness of that. He sat down with a hurt look and ate two huge slices of pie without saying another word.

After the meal was over, he pulled his mother aside. "Why wouldn't you let me go after Zane?"

"I want you to leave Zane alone. What he does is none of your business."

"Why, it is so my business! He's my uncle, ain't he? I'm concerned for him, Ma."

"Yes. He's your uncle, and he's been an unhappy man all his life. He's never had anything good happen."

"But that Bev Despain is a saloon woman and she'll do him no good."

"Your aunt Julie was a saloon woman, too, but she's a good woman now. If you want to do something fittin' to help your uncle, stop naggin' him and pray for him and for Bev Despain also. She's as unhappy as Zane."

"How do you know that, Ma?"

"All women in her place are unhappy. Now, you mind what I tell you."

As Zane entered the Golden Lady, his eyes swept the room. The smoke hung like incense on the air, only it was strong and rank. Walking up to the bar, he leaned over and spoke over the tinny piano music that filled the place. "I don't see Bev around."

"She didn't come in today. She sent word she wasn't feeling well."

Albert watched as Zane Satterfield took this in, then turned without a word and left the saloon. He picked up a glass and began polishing it, when suddenly Frisco Farr walked over.

Frisco's eyes went to the door, and he was quiet for a moment. "What's the matter with Zane?" Farr asked. "He didn't have much to say today."

"He's looking for Bev," Albert said. "You don't reckon he's serious about her, do you, Frisco?"

"Maybe he is. Who can tell with that feller?"

"Can't see that. Why, he's part owner of that big ranch, and she ain't nothin' but a saloon girl. I just can't see it."

Frisco fingered the large stone on his ring finger and said, "You don't have to see it, Albert."

The knock on the door startled Bev Despain. She was lying on the bed fully dressed, staring up at the ceiling. A frown crossed her face, for she had stayed away from work because she didn't want to see anyone. "Go away whoever it is!" she called out.

"It's me, Zane."

Instantly, Bev sat up. "Zane?"

"Yes. Let me in, Bev."

Coming off the bed, Bev walked over and opened the door. She looked up at Zane and said, "I don't want to see anybody today."

"Are you sick?"

She did not answer but turned around and walked over to the window and looked out. She was not wearing one of the colorful, low-cut dresses she normally wore. Today she had on a simple light blue dress. Her hair was down, and she looked vulnerable.

Zane stood looking at her for a moment and then came over and said, "What's wrong, Bev?"

"Nothing." She turned and sighed. "Sit down, but I'll tell you, I'm not good company today."

Zane put his hat down carefully on the small table and sat down. The room was neat and clean and had a pleasant smell to it. Like Bev herself, it was neat and well kept.

"What's going on with you?" Bev asked.

"Just cows," Zane said. He was troubled by the look on Bev's face. She was a woman that appeared out of place to him in the saloon, but he was sure men had told her that before. For a while, he talked about the ranch, and finally he said, "You look sad."

Bev always tried to keep a cheerful spirit, but years of a hard life had caught up with her. Lately, she had become more and more aware of how shallow and meaningless her existence was, and now suddenly, to her horror, tears sprang to her eyes. "I don't know what's the matter with me, Zane. I'm not much of a crying woman."

"No, you're not." He sat silently for a while, and then he said, "I wish I could do something to make you feel better."

"You can't. Nobody can."

For some time the two sat there in silence, and then Bev began talking. It was as if a dam had burst, and she found herself telling Zane how she had wound up working in a saloon. It was an old, old story. A man had deceived her with his declarations of love. She had run off with him, convinced that he would marry her. In the end, he had used her and then dropped her when he had grown tired of her. She had been so hurt and disgusted and angry by it that she had taken the path of least resistance to make a way in life.

Zane listened, for he had never heard her talk like this before. Finally, he said gently, "I hate to see you down like this, Bev."

"It goes with the kind of life I lead."

Zane reached over and took her hand. Startled, Bev turned to stare at him. She expected to see the sort of thing in his eyes that most men had, but instead she saw real compassion. He had always had something in him that she was not accustomed to. Most men she met only wanted one thing. But Zane Satterfield seemed different from most of the rough, wild men that came into the saloon with their lust practically written across their foreheads. Yet years of being used still caused her to wonder about his intentions. His hands were hard and strong, and she did not try to pull it away.

"Both of us are in pretty poor shape," Zane said quietly.

"You're not like me."

"Sure I am. I've always thought you and I were a lot alike."

Zane's words struck at Bev Despain, and she waited for him to move, to become what other men had been in her life. But when he spoke, she was so startled she could not answer.

"Maybe we could help each other."

"Help each other? How could we do that?"

"Well, if we had each other, we wouldn't be alone anymore."

"You mean—you want us to live together?" Bev asked, surprised.

"No," Zane said, and his eyes were fixed on hers, holding her attention. "I want you to marry me, Bev."

For a moment Bev thought she had misunderstood him. "Why, that can never be."

"Why not?"

"Men don't marry saloon girls."

"The preacher, Rice Morgan, did. My sister Julie worked in this very saloon. You know that. But Rice married her, and I've been thinkin' about that. They've got a good life together now. Julie's changed. She is so different now you'd never know the kind of life she led before. I never thought people could change, but Julie found God and look at her. Maybe we could change too—both of us."

The silence seemed to fill the room as Zane stopped speaking. Bev was staring at him almost wildly, and then her eyes filled up, and tears ran down her cheeks.

"I didn't mean for you to take it like this, Bev." He reached over, put his arms around her, pulled her to him, and kissed her cheek. When he released her, he said, "You think about it, Bev. Take a few days." He got up, turned, picked up his hat, and started for the door. When he reached the door, he turned and said, "Neither of us have been angels. Lots of things we've done we wish we hadn't. But I believe we can start over."

"Why, Zane, your family would never accept me!"

Zane straightened up and said firmly, "You're wrong about that. You think about it, Bev. I'll come back in a day or two for your answer."

Bev watched, unable to move or speak as the door closed. Then she began to tremble, and she buried her face in her hands and began to weep uncontrollably.

CHAPTER
FIVE

~~~~~~~~~~~~~~~~~~~~~~~~~~~~~~~

The moon was round as a silver dollar and tinted a rich shade of orange as it floated across the dark velvet sky. As Bev Despain sat halfway down the steps that led to the alleyway, she gazed up at the heavens and was gripped by a sense of sadness. Despite the brilliant display of the stars that burned and sparkled across the entire heavens, she found no joy in nature's display. The sound of the tinkling piano from the saloon on the floor beneath floated up to her, and the harsh laughter of the men and the women underscored her somber mood. It only reminded her of the life she had been living.

May was a month that Bev usually liked, but lately, nothing seemed to please her. Life had become nothing but a dull routine that left her feeling more and more ashamed each day. A sound drifted up from the alley. She looked down and saw a cat carrying the limp body of a large rat in its mouth. The cat was yellow with a wide, flat head and seemed intent on his business. She watched as he disappeared in a hole that led to the dry goods store next to the saloon.

A group of cowboys rode up, the hooves of their horses sending up clouds of fine dust. They piled off their horses and eagerly walked down the wooden boardwalk to the Golden Lady. Bev knew they would stay until they were drunk, and some of them probably would have to be carried out. Some of them would get into fights and wake up the next morning penniless and in jail, their hard-earned wages spent on the liquor and the women in the saloon. Leaning over, Bev put her forearms across her knees, then placed her forehead against them. She tried to shut out the sound of the raucous pleasure-seekers from the saloon. It had become part of her life, and it was hard for her to remember when things were any different. She was not a crying woman, but she wanted to cry as she sat there, her face pressed against her arms.

"Bev?"

Quickly, Beverly lifted her head and looked down to where the alley intersected the main street. She saw Zane Satterfield standing there clearly outlined by the yellow light of the moon. "Can I come up?" As he stood there waiting, a slight smile spread over his face.

"Come on up, Zane," she said wearily. She did not move but sat there. As he came up the steps, his high-heeled boots punctuated his progress as he climbed the stairs. He sat down beside her, and she could smell his odors—leather, sweat, tobacco smoke—and she said, "Just come to town?"

"Had to come and bring a horse to get shoed. What are you doing sitting out here all alone?"

"I like it when it's quiet. I get enough of that noise from the saloon."

Zane turned and studied her carefully. Zane was suddenly aware of the lovely turnings of her body within the light blue dress she was wearing. She was tall and shapely in a way that had often attracted him. He stared at her face, as if trying to read the thoughts that reflected in her sad eyes. The bony structure of her face made strong and pleasant contours, her lips made a slight curve at the corners, and she made a little gesture with her shoulders.

"I'm not very good company tonight, Zane."

"Well, I'm not either, so I guess we can sit here and bore each other for a spell."

The remark brought a slight smile to her face, and a thought came to her. She said, "You'd better go down in the saloon. There's no fun up here on this balcony."

"I guess I'll stay here." Zane shifted slightly so that he could see her head-on. He saw an expression on her face that stirred his curiosity, and he found himself trying to find a name for it. It was a heaviness that comes when someone has seen too much of the hard side of life. The smile was gone now, and the shadow of a hidden sadness took its place. "Pretty night."

"I guess so."

"Always liked the nights like this, a yellow moon and all those stars." She didn't answer for a long time, and he let the silence run on. From far off came the sound of a coyote yodeling, and the two sat there listening to the strange sound.

"You know, Zane, I can't keep time anymore."

"What do you mean by that?"

"I mean every day is just alike. The days pass by. It's like the ticking of a clock that doesn't have any face and not even any numbers." She turned to him then, and the grief in her eyes was easy to read. "It's hard for me to remember what it was like before I got into this life."

Zane had always found this woman different from the rest of the girls in the Golden Lady Saloon. She kept aloof and was not full of meaning-less laughter that filled most of them. Now he wanted to reach out and hold her, but he did not. He pulled his hat off, turned it around in his hands, and said, "I guess maybe that's the way it is with most of us."

"I wouldn't think it of you."

"I don't know why not. Sometimes I think my life is like a river that meanders and wanders but never gets anywhere. All rivers wind up in the sea, I reckon. Mine doesn't seem to be going anywhere."

The two sat there for a long time, and a sense of futility settled over Zane. He said, "I've been waiting for you to say whether you'd marry me or not." Bev turned, and he saw tears in her eyes.

"I can't do it, Zane."

"I reckon I'm not much of a man that a woman would care for."

"It's not that." She reached out and put her hand on his arm. "It just wouldn't work. I've lost something I can't ever get back."

Zane knew she was trying to tell him something about the life she had lived. "We all feel like that," he said.

"No. It's different for a man."

"Why, Bev, there's such a thing as starting over." He put his arm around her and felt her tremble. She seemed vulnerable, and there was a softness in her that she did not let other people see.

"I can't do it, Zane. I've ruined my own life. I can't ruin yours. You need to find a decent woman." She suddenly got up and climbed quickly up the steps to the door that led to her room above the saloon. Zane sat on the steps and watched her go but did not even call out after her.

As soon as she stepped inside the room, Bev went to the bed. Her eyes were so blinded with tears she almost stumbled over a chair. She fell across the bed and pressed her face against the pillow, muffling the sobs that rose from deep within her.

As soon as Zane knocked on the door, he heard his sister's voice yelling, "Well, come on in! The door's open."

Zane opened the door and stepping inside found Julie standing at the table preparing a meal. "What are you makin', sis?"

"I'm makin' my husband's favorite dish. Deviled fish eggs."

Zane grinned. "It sounds awful. Does Rice really like 'em?"

"He eats 'em like they were peanuts. It's a good thing. They're easy enough to make."

Zane walked over and stood beside Julie. He could smell the fragrance of violets, faint but unmistakable. It had always been her favorite scent. He watched as she worked and said, "It looks just like hard-boiled eggs to me."

"Well, that's what it is, but looky here." Her hands moved as she continued slicing the hard-boiled eggs and removed the yolks. "What you do is you put in a little vinegar, a little sugar, a dash of black pepper and some butter. But here's the secret," she said. She picked up a small jar and a deep spoon. Spooning out the contents into the mix, she said, "This is what makes 'em good."

"What is that? It looks awful!"

"It's fish eggs."

"Fish eggs? You're eatin' fish eggs?"

"That's what this is. Deviled fish eggs." She stirred the mixture and then picked up a spoon and filled half of an egg with the mixture. "Here. Try one," she said.

"Well, I like fish, but I don't know about the eggs."

"Why, people over in Europe pay a big price for that. They call it caviar."

Cautiously, Zane took a bite of the egg, getting mostly the white.

"Go on. Taste it," Julie urged.

Zane bit off half the egg, chewed it, and then his eyes opened with surprise. "Why, this is *good*!"

"You ought to see that husband of mine eat 'em. You'd think he had his hand in the candy jar."

"Where'd you get the fish eggs?"

"Mose Crosby brings 'em to me. He goes fishing every day, and when he catches a fish with eggs in it, he saves it for me. Sit down, Zane, I'll get you a cup of fresh coffee. I just made some."

"Why, that'd be right nice of you, sis." Zane sat down and watched as Julie walked across the room. It was a rough little house, nothing fancy, and she was wearing a plain brown dress. He thought of how different it was now from when she had worked in the Golden Lady Saloon along with Bev. Julie Satterfield had led a wild life, and it had caught the town of Jordan City off-guard when Rice Morgan, the preacher born in Wales, had courted her and married her. Zane watched his sister, and as she sat down, he noted her eyes were sparkling. As she talked about her life with Rice, she would stop and sip from the coffee, then wave her hands about expressively, laughing at her own efforts to become a housewife.

"I didn't know how to boil water, but I'm learnin'."

"Married life agrees with you, I see."

Suddenly, Julie grew serious. She was thirty-nine now. Her hair was as red as ever, and her green eyes sparkled. She had a strong spirit, and she had thrown herself into becoming the wife of a preacher with the same exuberance with which she had sought pleasure most of her life.

"God's been good to me, Zane," she said. She studied him and was silent for a moment. She knew this brother of hers very well, and finally she said, "What's wrong?"

Zane stirred, shaking his shoulders together, and said, "I thought I had a plan, but it's not worked out the way I'd thought." When he saw that she was waiting for an explanation, he said, "I asked Bev to marry me, but she won't do it."

"Why not? It'd be good for both of you."

"I think she's got the fool idea that she's not good enough for me."

Suddenly, something changed in Julie's eyes. She loved this brother of hers and wanted him to find peace in his life. "I'll go and have a little talk with her."

Zane looked at her with doubt. "I don't reckon it'll do any good."

"You ought to know I don't quit easy. You sit there and fill up on these deviled fish eggs. Wait'll I get back. If God can change me, then He surely can help Bev."

"Hello, Bev."

Bev had opened the door to her room, and her eyes were still red from weeping. "I'm not much in the mood for visiting right now, Julie."

"I didn't come to waste time, but I've got to talk to you."

"Well, come on in, then."

Julie entered the room, and as soon as she did, she said, "I just talked to Zane. He says you won't marry him."

"That's right. I won't. It wouldn't be right," she said, looking down.

"I know why," Julie said. "I had the same problem when Rice asked me to marry him."

"Then you know what it's like. This life leaves scars on a person."

"It would be a good thing for you, Bev. Here, come on, let's sit down and talk." There was one chair in the room, and Julie sat down, drawing it up close to the bed, where Bev sat down across from her. Bev seemed to have difficulty speaking.

"It wouldn't work after the kind of life I've led. Zane would never forget."

"Bev, I had the same problem, like I said, but everybody is pretty well faking it. Everyone has a past they wish they could get rid of."

Bev's eyes opened with surprise. "What do you mean?"

"You may work in a saloon, but the banker's daughter and every other woman has something they're not proud of. Men learn how to fake it before they're into long pants, and women learn even quicker. All of us have something in our past we're ashamed of. Not just saloon girls—everyone. Rice says that everyone has done something that needs God's love and forgiveness to wash away."

Bev stared at her and said, "I wish I could believe that, Julie, but you know what a woman's life is like working in a saloon." She straightened up and crossed her arms across her chest and was quiet for a moment. A softness filled her eyes, and she whispered, "I remember how innocent I was when I was a girl. You know what I did one time? I took a penny and put it on the sidewalk, and then I took a piece of chalk and drew a line around the corner. At the end of the line, I wrote in big letters MONEY THIS WAY."

The corners of Julie's lips turned upward. "That was a strange thing for a girl to do. How old were you?"

"Oh, I don't know. Maybe seven or eight. I just wanted to do something good for somebody."

"There's goodness in you, Bev. All of us have a little good, I guess, but most of us bury it. I know I did. But this is your chance to change." She got up from the chair and quickly sat down beside Bev. She put her arm around the woman's shoulders and said, "Jesus is what you need. He can make you a new woman. He did it for me."

"I can't be a woman of God. I can't forget all the—"

"You know, when a person comes to Jesus, and He comes into their heart, He takes all the sin away. The Bible says He throws it into the ocean and puts it as far as the east is from the west. There's a story in the Bible about that. I don't know where it is offhand. I'm just now really learning the Bible. Rice told me that His blood makes me as white as snow."

"I don't think so. I don't know much about the Bible."

"Well, these men came to Jesus and brought this woman and threw her down at His feet, and they said, 'This woman was taken in adultery.'"

"Where was the man? Why didn't they bring him?" Bev asked.

"That's just it. They didn't say anything about him. They just wanted to see this woman punished for what she had done. Back then, it meant being stoned to death."

"What did Jesus say?" Bev asked.

"He didn't say anything for a while. He just stooped down, the Bible says, and began to write in the dust."

"What'd He write?" Bev said, her curiosity growing sharper.

"The Bible doesn't say. Rice said he always thought He was writing the sins of those men who brought this woman, but He told them if they weren't sinners, they could throw the first stone, and the men began to fade away. And then Jesus turned to the woman and said, 'Where are your accusers?' The woman said, 'They're gone.'"

A silence filled the room, and Bev seemed to be holding her breath. "What did He say to her, Julie?"

"He said, 'Neither do I condemn thee. Go and sin no more.' Don't you see, He was telling the woman that she could start all over again. That's what I've come to talk to you about."

Bev Despain was not a woman who knew a great deal about church. She had not been inside one since she was a child, and her life had been hard. But she sat there listening, twisting her hands together as Julie spoke of Jesus and His sacrifice on the cross. She bowed her head and did not move, and finally she whispered, "Well, what do I have to do?"

"The Bible says you have to turn from your sin and call on the name of Jesus, and then you'll be saved. You'll be different on the inside. I was. Will you do that?"

"I don't know how." .

"I'll help you. Let's kneel down here. I'll pray out loud, and you just pray in your own heart."

Bev Despain knew she was at a crossroads in her life, and this moment might never come again. She had the feeling it was the last chance, and with a sob she fell on her knees, leaning against the bed, and buried her face in her hands. She felt Julie's arm around her, and she heard her praying fervently, and then she herself began to cry out, "Oh, God, I'm just a sinner. Save me for Jesus' sake!"

Time passed, but Bev was not conscious of how long she was there kneeling. She had been weeping and trembling for some time, but now a great peace and sense of feeling clean inside came over her. She turned with tears streaming down her face and said, "Is that it, Julie? Am I a Christian now?"

"Yes! You've got a husband now too." She smiled as she saw Bev's eyes open wide. "The church is the bride of Christ, so you've got a heavenly Husband, and you're going to have an earthly husband too."

"I don't know if I can do it, but I'll try."

"Tomorrow is Sunday. I want you to find a nice dress, as plain as you can find, and come to church."

Fear tried to fill Beverly Despain, but the new peace that had descended upon her gave her a new strength. "All right, Julie, if you say so." The two women got to their feet, and Julie threw her arms around the taller woman and kissed her on the cheek.

"The devil will try to get you to believe that there's nothing to all this, but Jesus wants you to follow Him. First thing you do is go down and tell Frisco you're quitting."

"What'll I do?"

"You're coming and staying with us tonight. Bring your things—everything. You're cutting all your ties with your old life. Will you do that, Bev?"

Beverly Despain took a deep breath and straightened up. Her face was stained with tears, but there was a holy light in her eyes now, a light of hope and joy. "Yes. I'll do it."

The church was crowded, as usual, for Rice Morgan was a fine preacher. He also had a good voice to lead the hymn singing. The church was new and still smelled of the turpentine and the sap of the unpainted wood of which it was built. The benches were rough and splintery, but no one seemed to mind.

Zane had come early and taken a seat up front. Even though he knew most of the people there, he felt out of place, for he was not a church-going man. Suddenly he sensed a rustle in the congregation, and heads turned toward the door at the back. He turned quickly and saw his sister Julie come in, and at her side was Bev Despain. Furtive whispers ran across the congregation, but Zane paid them no heed. He saw that she was wearing a plain blue dress, modest and nothing at all like her usual attire at the saloon. She was wearing no makeup, something he had never seen her without. His eyes followed the two as they walked up the aisle. They stopped at the end of the bench where Zane sat, and he heard Julie say plainly, "Sit by Zane. I'm going to sing in the choir."

"All right, Julie."

Zane stood up as Bev moved past the three people on the end. When he sat down beside her, he reached out and touched her arm. When she turned to face him, he noticed a difference in her. He whispered, "Good to see you, Bev."

Bev did not answer, and he saw that she was tense. They had no chance to speak, for Rice had suddenly appeared up on the rostrum.

"And now it's some good singing we'll have. Let's sing loud the praises of our God."

There were few singers better than Rice Morgan, and he led the congregation in a hearty round of old songs. Zane remembered some of them from the dimness of his youth. He saw that Bev was not singing at all. She was sitting with her head bowed. He could not imagine what was going on in her mind. All that Julie had told him was that the two had prayed together and that Bev would be at church. He stood there feeling nervous, not knowing what was going to happen next. He was well aware that the congregation's eyes were all fixed on Bev from time to time, and he felt a sense of urgency he could not define.

After the singing was over, Rice Morgan took his Bible and said, "This morning, if I had a title to this sermon, I would say it's 'How to Follow Jesus.'" He looked out over the congregation and began to quote Scripture, going through his Bible and talking about the life of Jesus. He stressed that He was a man of the people, the friend of sinners. "That got Him in trouble," Rice said, his clear voice filling the building. "The Jewish leaders in the synagogues didn't like it when Jesus went to the house of Levi the tax collector. They didn't like it when He talked to a Samaritan woman at the well about her soul. They accused Him of being a wine bibbler, but Jesus didn't care what others said about Him. He loved people. He loves sinners. If you are a sinner today, then glory to God. Jesus is your friend."

Finally, the sermon was over, and Rice closed his Bible and put it down. He turned and let the silence run on. "It's easy to become a Christian," he said quietly, "but it's difficult sometimes to keeping walking the path of righteousness. The Lord is telling me that there may be one of you this morning who needs to choose to follow Jesus. He loves you. He died for you. He shed His blood on the cross that you might turn away from your sins and have an abundant, eternal life. Now, the question is, will you have Him to be your Lord? If you will, you get up and come to the front. We'll pray together, and God will save you."

A song began, and Zane suddenly started, for without hesitation Bev started moving toward the aisle. He could not see her face until she reached the end of the row. Her face was pale, but she had a certainty about her. She walked to the front of the church and stood in front of Rice, and the two of them spoke. Every eye was fixed on them, and suddenly Zane knew this was *his* time as well. Zane Satterfield had been in many dangerous situations and never felt shaken, but now his knees felt weak. He knew that God was speaking to his own heart. He began to step out and move toward the front. As he did, he saw faces turn toward him with surprise. His sister Jerusalem Ann and Clay and Clinton and Brodie were all staring at him. He saw the joy in their faces at the decision he was making.

When he got to the front, he waited until the preacher looked up, and he said, "I guess it's my time, but I don't know how to do it."

Rice's face was filled with joy. "Will you kneel with me here and ask the good Lord to come into your heart?"

"Yes," Zane said hoarsely, and he knelt. And as he did, he heard people begin to cry out, "Hallelujah! Praise the Lord! Glory to God!" Somehow he wasn't surprised to hear the loudest cry come from his nephew Clinton.

No one ever forgot that service at church. From that time on, many of them dated things by saying, "That was a few weeks after Zane and Bev got saved," or "That happened a month before Beverly Despain came to the Lord."

Zane knew he would remember this service vividly for the rest of his life. His calling on God and the exact moment God entered his life were marked forever in his heart. He felt overwhelmed at how all the people were crowding around him and welcoming him to the family of God. His family and the rest of the church all seemed to want to touch him and Bev. It was a glorious time for all of them.

Finally, Rice's voice rose upon all the people. "All right. We're going to have a baptism at three o'clock today. Everyone be at the river."

Suddenly, Zane spoke up above all the talking. "Bring your marryin' book, Preacher."

Every eye turned to Zane, but he ignored them. He turned to Bev and said, "Will you have me, Beverly?"

Beverly Despain put out her hand, and when Zane took it, she nodded and said, "Yes, Zane Satterfield, I will. We'll have each other for the rest of our lives."

Everyone heard this exchange of words, and a piercing cry filled the building. Clinton Hardin's face was about to burst with joy. He was dancing and hollering and finally came and threw his arms around Bev and then his uncle Zane. Clay turned to Jerusalem and said, "I think Clinton's lost his mind."

"No. He's happy just like I am. Isn't it wonderful?"

"Yes it is," Clay said. "I've never seen anything like it."

"Neither have I."

The day was beautiful as practically everyone in Jordan City had come down to the Brazos River. Eleven people stood in a group to be baptized as the crowd on the bank sang hymns. One by one Rice Morgan put them under the water and brought them up again. Each time he did, Clinton shouted, "Hallelujah!"

Finally, Rice came to the bank. He dried his hands off and took his book from Julie, who was smiling and crying at the same time. He turned to Zane Satterfield and Beverly Despain. His voice carried loud as he said, "We are here today to unite this man and this woman in matrimony."

Beverly stood there listening to the solemn words, and when she heard Rice say, "I now pronounce you man and wife," she turned and let Zane kiss her. She surrendered herself to his embrace, and then she heard Rice say, "All right. You've got an earthly husband. Now, let's baptize you both into the bride of Christ." Moving back into the river, and accompanied by the two, he baptized first Beverly and then Zane. As they stood there for a moment holding hands looking into each other's eyes, they heard Reverend Rice Morgan say with victory in his voice, "I wish every marriage could start like this."

★   ★   ★

Far away at a Comanche camp the chief of the band stood looking down at the dead body of his son. He reached out, and his hand shook as he closed the boy's eyes. He turned and walked out of the tent, and as soon as he did, he was met by Black Eagle, his brother.

"How is the boy, Bear Killer?"

But there was no need for Bear Killer to speak, for the death song was being sung by Bear Killer's wife. Black Eagle said, "He has gone to be with the spirits, then?"

"Yes."

"I am sorry, brother." He was silent for a moment, and then he studied the face of Bear Killer and said, "You do have another son."

Bear Killer looked up, and his eyes were filled with grief for the loss of his son. But something else flickered in his obsidian eyes. He had never forgotten Moriah, the white captive that everyone called the Quiet One, whom he had taken for his own wife. She had borne him a strong son. His mind quickly went back to those days. Now, with the death song for his son in his ears, he said, "Yes, I still have a son."

"You have never forgotten."

"A man does not forget his son." Bear Killer thought of the two men that had come and taken the white woman Moriah and his son away from The People. He did not know their real names—Brodie Hardin and Quaid Shafter. They were called among the Indian tribes the Tall One and the Silver Hair.

"What will you do, brother?"

Anger and rage mingled with grief in Bear Killer's eyes. When he spoke, his voice was low but clear. It grated like stone as he said, "I will have the scalp of the Silver Hair and the Tall One—and I will have my son back again!"

CHAPTER SIX

August had come to Texas, bringing its heat-burdened days and breathless nights. Zane and Bev had settled down into a small cabin not far from the main structures of the ranch. It was only a two-room cabin thrown up originally as a bunkhouse, but the two had found a peace and contentment that they had not dreamed possible.

Bev had thrown herself into learning how to be a good wife. She had spent hours learning to cook from Jerusalem and Moriah, and the simple life agreed with her and flowed over her spirit like a soothing balm. She was amazed at how the memories of her past had faded away. It had been Rice Morgan who had told her, "God takes away some bad memories for us, sister." She had believed that, and each day had been a new adventure for her as the wife of Zane Satterfield.

The sunlight touched her face, and she opened her eyes slightly, noting that it was later than usual. She stretched, arching her back, and reached up and touched the top of the walnut bedstead. It was pure luxury. The sheets were smooth and still had a pleasant smell, for she had washed them just the day before.

Opening her eyes widely, she drew her head back and then came fully awake, for Zane had his head propped up on his hand and was regarding her steadfastly.

"What are you looking at, Zane?"

Zane's lips curled upward in a smile. "You know, wife, I sure wasted a lot of years waking up. The first thing I saw was a bunch of dirty, hairy-legged men." He reached out and gently stroked her cheek with his hand. "I'll have to admit you're an improvement over all of them."

"Well, I should hope so!" Bev covered his hand with hers and held it to her cheek. "You know, I had a funny thought lately, Zane. I don't know how to explain it, but somehow it seemed like my whole life has been pointed toward what we've found here in this place." Her face grew solemn and still as she struggled for words, and then she said, "It's like . . . it's like I've been a bell all my life waiting to be struck." She smiled and put her forefinger on his lips. "And now I have."

Zane regarded her, admiring the strong contours of her body and the strength in her face. "I know what you mean. You know what Rice preached about last Sunday?"

"About Jacob struggling with the angel? I'd never heard that before. It was wonderful."

"He's a fine preacher. Well, I felt like old Jacob. I felt like I'd been struggling all my life with God."

"But Jacob got crippled in that struggle. He limped ever after that meeting with God."

"Yeah, but he was never the same after that. And God gave him a new name," Zane said. "I'm just grateful God never gave up on me."

The two lay there talking about the sermon, and finally she said, "We've wasted so much time."

He saw the regret in her face and said, "Remember what Rice told us when we got baptized. He told us the Lord will restore the years that the locusts have eaten. So let's not waste any more."

"All right. I'll get up and cook us some breakfast."

Zane reached out and pulled her close. "You can cook breakfast when we're old and wore out."

In the strength of Zane's arms and in the love she saw in his eyes, Bev Despain's dormant dreams came to life.

★ ★ ★

"I declare, Brodie, you need to watch Bob and learn a few lessons from him."

Brodie, who had been pacing around the kitchen getting in Jerusalem's way as she worked, looked over at the huge cinnamon-colored dog. "How could I learn anything from that old hound? He don't do nothin' but sleep most of the time! Look at him!" Brodie walked over and picked up Bob's front legs. He dropped them and Bob didn't stir. "It's like he dies every time he goes to sleep. What could I possibly learn from him?"

"Because you're restless, that's why," Jerusalem said.

Brodie shot his mother a quick glance. She knew him better than anyone, but he denied her charge. "I'm no more restless than anybody else."

"Yes, you are. You take Clinton. As long as he gets to go to church and shout a little bit and go a-courtin', that's all he wants. But you're different."

Brodie came over and forced himself to sit down. He watched his mother peel potatoes and said, "I'd help you with those, but I always used up too much of the potatoes. How do you peel 'em so thin?"

Ignoring his question, Jerusalem continued to work as she studied the face of this fine son of hers. He was always the more serious one, the one who was more responsible than her other children. She listened then for the sound of the children, who were playing outside making mud pies. Sam's and Rachel Belle's voices were clear but also interwoven with David's and Ethan's. It gave her a sense of satisfaction and strength to know that even though she was old for children, she and Clay had been blessed with their own. But she turned her attention to Brodie. He was twenty-nine and should have married by now, but he never had. She stopped peeling the potatoes and suddenly asked him, "Do you still think a lot about Serena?"

Serena Lebonne had been Brodie's first love. She had been a beautiful woman with black hair and strange violet eyes. She and her mother had gone back to Mexico to live with Mateo Lebonne, who had become something of a legendary figure after serving in Santa Anna's army and winning the battle at the Alamo. Those who lived in north Texas, however, considered him nothing more than a ruthless bandit. To the Mexicans, he was sort of a Robin Hood. The trouble was he robbed the Texans of their cattle and gave them to the poor Mexicans.

"Why, Ma. Why would I be thinkin' about her?"

"You were in love with her, that's why."

"That was a long time ago."

"I don't think it changes all that much."

Brodie grinned and reached over and grabbed his mother's hand and held it tightly. "Why, Ma, I think you been readin' them love stories again."

"Don't be foolish! I don't read such silly nonsense as that, but I think love, if it's real, doesn't leave so easy. Once a heart has been touched by love, it's hard to forget."

"She's in Mexico, and her brother's a bandit."

"He was your good friend once. He saved your life at Goliad."

"Sure he did, but I saved his at the Battle of San Jacinto, so now we're even."

Brodie changed the direction of the conversation quickly. They talked some about Zane and Bev, and then he got up and left the room. Jerusalem put the knife down and sat there at the table and thought about Brodie. It concerned her to see him so downcast. "Lord," she prayed, "please help my boy. Only You can touch his heart and help him move on." She did not move for a long time, and then she heard steps and looked up to see Zane come in.

"What do I smell?" he said, grinning.

"Gingerbread. I don't suppose you want any."

"Oh, come on, sis. You know I can refuse anything except temptation and gingerbread."

Getting up from her seat, Jerusalem Ann stepped over Bob's inert body and went to the pantry. As she cut a large slice of gingerbread, Zane studied the dog. "Is he dead?"

"No, of course not. He's just asleep."

"Well, he sleeps like the dead."

"He's a good enough watch dog when he's awake. This gingerbread isn't very good."

Zane took a large bite and chewed it thoughtfully. "There's no such thing as bad gingerbread," he said. "The worst gingerbread I ever had was real good." His eyes went back to Bob, and he said, "You remember that big tom cat that we had named Jerry?"

"Sure. I remember Jerry."

"He'd come when you called him, just like a dog."

"That was a long time ago, Zane." She sat down and studied him. He was a big man, and his hair was sprinkled with gray now, for he was in his mid-forties. He sat loosely in his chair and began speaking of their child-hood together. "You remember the time Ma cut off the tip of her finger with a hatchet?"

"I won't ever forget it. It scared me to death. I thought she was going to bleed to death."

Zane shook his head. "She acted like nothin' had happened. She reached out, got that bit of her finger and stuck it back on, then bandaged it up."

"It grew back," Jerusalem said.

"It did, but she never had any feeling in it after that."

"I remember seeing her hand in the coffin the day she died. That lit-tle white ring around the tip of her forefinger was still there."

"I think about those days a lot," Zane said. "Things were simple then."

"Well, they're not now."

Zane looked up quickly, brushing gingerbread crumbs from his lips. "You worried about something?"

"Not worried exactly, but I don't know how we're going to make it in the cattle business. There's just no market."

"There will be," Zane said. "All we've got to do is hang on."

"Working from dawn to dusk can be a dull life, especially for young fellows like Clinton and Brodie."

Zane studied his sister and asked, "You worried about them?"

"I'm worried about Brodie. I wish you'd spend some time with him, Zane." A glint of humor touched her eyes. "If you can tear yourself away from that new wife of yours."

Zane flushed. "Well, it'll be mighty hard," he admitted. "I know I'm actin' like a young fool, but I never knew married life could be so agreeable."

"I'm glad for you, Zane."

Zane shook himself and said, "Tell you what. I'll take Brodie out on a hunt and get his mind off things. Maybe we can bring back some game. What's wrong with him, really?"

"I think he's still in love with Serena Lebonne."

"Why, she's been gone for years! Probably fat and married with a bunch of papooses now."

"She's a Mexican, not an Indian! She wouldn't have papooses, but I wish you'd talk to him."

"I'll do it. You'll probably have to comfort Bev while I'm gone." He got up and mischief twinkled in his eyes. "She's so much in love with me she might plum starve herself to death."

"She can spare you for a couple of days. You go on now."

Brodie studied the antelope steak on the end of a sharpened stick, poked it gingerly with his fingers, and then put it back over the fire. "This tastes better outside, don't it, Zane? Don't know why."

"I think it does. Tell the truth, though, antelope is pretty sorry meat." He bit into the steak he had taken off the stick and said, "This is tough as boot leather."

Brodie watched his uncle, who was trying to chew the tough meat. "How do you like married life, Uncle Zane?"

"Should have done it a long time ago."

"Well, you've made Clinton happy. He's proud as a cat with two tails over your becomin' a Christian."

"He's a good boy."

"Drives us all crazy with his constant preaching. He never gives up. He thinks the world's on fire, and he's got the only bucket of water." But Brodie grinned as he talked about his brother. He watched his steak as it sizzled over the flame, pulled it back, and burned his finger on it. "What's it like to be married, Uncle?"

Zane swallowed the mouthful of tough meat, then reached down and picked up the canteen and washed it down with a swig of water. "You know," he said, "I went on a ship once down to South America."

Brodie laughed. "You sound just like Clay. Half the time you ask him somethin', and he'll come up with an answer that has nothin' to do with the question. What in the world does goin' on a ship to South America have to do with married life?"

"Well, if you'd listen, you'd learn." Zane leaned back against the mesquite and scratched his shoulders. "I went on this ship to South America, and it was awful! I mean, when we headed for home we hit a powerful storm and got blown off-course. The waves were so high everybody thought we were gonna sink to the bottom. It was the worst time of my life, I reckon." He poked at the fire with a stick that had bore his steak, then looked up and grinned briefly. "But then we got back to Galveston just as the storm ended. After fightin' all that wind and those waves and bein' scared to death, we came into that port. Everything was quiet and peaceful and safe." He tossed the stick down and looked over at Brodie. "That's what it's like for me, Brodie. I feel like I made port."

The two sat there in the darkness, the fire making a crimson dot in the blackness of the night. From time to time a coyote would howl, and once a large owl swept silently overhead, looking for prey. Finally, Zane said, "I can see you're restless, Brodie. That's natural for a young fellow like you. But I want to warn you. Don't waste your life like I did."

"Your life's not wasted!"

"Well, it seems like it to me." Zane reached down and picked up a small twig and stuck it in the fire. He waited until it ignited and then held it up before his eyes, studying the yellow flame. "I guess I'm like the bear that went over the mountain to see what he could see." He blew the flame out and then said with regret, "But all he could see was the other side of the mountain. Do your wandering, Brodie, for a while. A young fellow has to do a certain amount of that, but there's nothin' better than having a home and family to come back to at the end of the day. You know that Scripture that the preacher quoted? I don't know where he got it from. It's in the Bible somewhere."

"What Scripture was that?"

" 'As a bird that wanders from her nest, so is a man that wanders from his place.' That's what I wanted to tell you, I guess. Do a little wandering, but find yourself a good woman and marry her and make yourself a home. Have kids. I'm too late for most of that, but you're not."

"You're not too late. You're just right. You got a good woman."

The two sat there soaking up the silence of the plain, listening to the sounds of the night. Zane studied the young man and seemed to have difficulty seeing what future lay ahead for his nephew. Brodie Hardin was unhappy, and he knew what that was like. "Lord," he said, "don't let him waste his life like I've done most of mine."

"That's the stupidest thing I ever heard of, Posey!"

Bill Manning, a short well-built man who did most of the horse-breaking for the Yellow Rose Ranch, was standing beside O. M. Posey. He and Posey spent a great deal of time arguing about Bible doctrine. Posey was dogmatic, and he had started in earlier talking about his favorite subject—predestination.

"It's right there in the Bible, Bill. All you have to do is read it. It's plain as day."

"I know something's in the Bible about being elected by God as His own, but that don't mean we ain't got to do our part."

Posey at once began spouting off verse after verse of Scripture. One arm was in a sling, but he waved the other in the air violently as he spoke. He had a phenomenal memory and could not only quote the Scripture but give the chapter and verse, something Manning could never do.

The two had been out in the corral working with the half-broken broncs. Posey looked over and saw Moriah and Ethan gathering eggs. "That son of Miss Moriah is growin' like a weed, ain't he?"

Even as he spoke the last word, Posey heard a whistling sound and then a solid thunk. Curious, he turned around and stopped dead still. Bill Manning was standing there looking down at his chest. An arrow had pierced his body just below the shoulder blade, and its head now dripped with bright, crimson blood.

"Bill!" Posey yelled. He stepped forward and saw Manning reach out and touch the arrowhead and then lift his head. Disbelief filled his eyes, but he was already falling, for the arrow had pierced his heart.

Posey heard a shrill scream, and he whirled to see three Indians break from cover behind the barn, where they had been concealed. Posey always carried his pistol. He pulled it out and leveled it and fired. He missed with the first shot but continued to fire and yelled at the top of his lungs. An arrow sizzled by his head, and he saw one Indian go down, and the others faded away. Posey ran for the house, yelling loudly.

Clay had just sat down with the family to eat breakfast. Most of the crew was gone, but the sound of the shots and Posey yelling brought Clay out of his chair in a flash. It fell over backward, and he grabbed his gun out of the gun belt that was hanging on a peg and raced out of the door, shouting, "Keep the kids inside, you women!"

As soon as he stepped outside the door, a flash of movement caught his eye, and he whirled to see four Comanches running straight for him. Clay had always been an expert shot with a pistol. He lifted his gun and pulled the trigger and saw the leading brave stop dead in his tracks by the heavy slug. It drove him over backward, blood spurting from his chest. At the same time a red hot pain struck Clay's knee, and his leg was driven out from under him. As he fell to the ground, he got off two more shots. One of the braves was struck and turned, but he was not seriously wounded. Clay kept firing, but when the hammer clicked on empty, he saw a large Indian wearing war paint bearing down upon him. He tried to roll over, but there was no time. Clay knew he could not dodge the tomahawk the brave raised above his head.

Suddenly, a black round hole appeared in the brave's forehead, and at the same time Clay heard the boom of a rifle. He turned and saw Jerusalem chambering a new shell. Staggering to his feet, he yelled as he hobbled into the house, "Get inside the house! Keep the children down!"

His leg was almost useless, but Clay heard Posey still yelling and firing from outside. When he got to the window, he looked out and fired at an Indian but missed. At that same time, he saw that Moriah and Ethan had been trapped outside. They tried to run, but a brave caught them before they could reach the house. "Load this pistol," Clay shouted. "Give me the rifle, Jerusalem."

Jerusalem had grabbed another rifle off the wall. She gave it to Clay, took the pistol, and began loading it with cartridges. "That devil's got Moriah!" Clay cried bitterly. "I can't shoot or I might hit her."

"It's Bear Killer!" Jerusalem cried. "I always knew he'd come for Ethan."

It had been a fear they had all lived with since Brodie and Quaid had rescued Moriah and Ethan from the Comanches' winter camp years ago.

But now that it was happening, Clay was furious because he was wounded and couldn't run out and help them. He could not get a clear shot, but right then he saw dust from horses approaching. "Look, it's Zane and Brodie!" he yelled.

As he watched in horror, he saw Bear Killer lift his hatchet to strike at Moriah, who was fighting fiercely to keep Ethan away from the Comanche war chief. The hatchet did not come down, however, for Zane had got off a quick shot. It had merely grazed Bear Killer in the neck, leaving a red, bloody mark but doing no mortal damage. Bear Killer shoved Moriah backward and reached down for the rifle lying in the dirt.

Zane yelled, "I'll take care of this one! Go help Clay and Jerusalem!"

Zane drove straight at Bear Killer, who had managed to get off a shot. Zane felt a bullet strike him, but he ignored the pain and urged his mount on. The buckskin struck Bear Killer, knocking him down, and Zane came off his horse. He pulled the trigger on his pistol, but it was out of ammunition. He had no time to reload, for Bear Killer had drawn a large knife and leaped at him. Zane could see the hatred in his obsidian eyes. The Indian was quicker than Zane could have believed. He felt the knife puncture his chest, but he managed to reach out and grab the Indian by the wrist. The two struggled, but Zane felt his strength leaving him. Blood was gushing from his side, and the knife had drawn blood also.

Bear Killer wrenched the knife back and drew his arm back to strike a fatal blow, but suddenly a yell startled him and a bullet raked his side. He looked up to see the Tall One, the one he had sworn to kill, riding straight for him, his gun blazing. Quickly, Bear Killer swung himself onto Zane's buckskin and kicked his heels into the horse's side. He yelled, and the surviving members of his band echoed the yell. As quickly as they had come, Bear Killer and his braves disappeared in a hazy cloud of dust.

Brodie fired twice after them, then his hammer clicked on empty. He came off his horse and knelt beside Zane, who had slumped to the ground. "Zane, are you all right?"

"I reckon he got me, Brodie."

Moriah was there holding Ethan with one arm but kneeling down. She saw the blood flowing from Zane's wound and said, "We've got to get him in the house."

"Posey, help me!" Brodie yelled. The bandy-legged rider came running over, the heat of battle flushing his face. "Did they get Zane?" he asked.

"Yes. We've got to get him in the house. He's hurt bad!"

Beverly had heard the gunshots and seen the Indians riding away. She had run to the house and seen two dead Indians and Bill Manning lying with an arrow all the way through his chest. Her heart almost failed her then, and she ran inside.

Jerusalem caught her and said urgently, "Quick, Bev, come in here! It's Zane!"

When she got inside the house, she saw Zane lying on the couch. He was bleeding from some terrible wounds, and his face was taut and drained of color.

"I can't stop the bleeding," Jerusalem said in a tight voice.

The two women tried to stop the bleeding, but it was obviously too late. Zane's eyes were closed, but he opened them. When he saw Bev he called her name.

She reached out and took his hand and said, "Zane!"

Zane had been around death long enough to recognize that it had come for him. He managed to say, "You gave me love, Bev."

Beverly, knowing she was losing her man, leaned forward and said, "I'm bearing your child, Zane. I'll never let him forget you."

Zane smiled, but his breathing was coming in short gasps now as he said, "We found the Lord, didn't we?"

Those were his last words. He coughed, and bloody froth spattered Bev's face. She held him and felt his life slipping away, and then she turned and saw Clay holding his bloody knee and Jerusalem looking at her. The children were all in a group, and Bev whispered, "He's gone. Zane's gone."

The funeral for Zane brought out nearly everyone in Jordan City. All the ranchers and their families for miles around knew Zane. His marriage to Bev, the former saloon girl, and their conversion to the Lord had been the talk of the country.

Jerusalem Ann had sat beside Bev during the brief sermon and then walked by her side out to the graveyard, where Rice Morgan finished the service.

"You'll have to stay with us now. When the baby comes, we'll help out," she whispered.

"All right." Bev had said very little, for the joy of life seemed to have drained out of her.

The family stepped away from the grave and walked slowly back to the house. The neighbors had brought food in, but nobody seemed to be hungry. The children were all strangely quiet. Many of the church members were trying to comfort Bev, when suddenly Brodie spoke up and said, "I'm going to join the Rangers. Those Indians are going to pay for what they did," he said bitterly.

Fear gripped Jerusalem's heart, for she knew what dangerous, hard lives the Rangers led. She started to speak, but Brodie interrupted her.

"I know you don't want me to, but I'm going to kill Bear Killer. He's touched our family." No one spoke for a time, and then Brodie added, "I've already talked to Captain Macklin. I'll be leaving tomorrow."

"That's a hard life, son," Clay said. His leg was bound up and would always be stiff from the wound. The bullet had done considerable damage to the kneecap, and he knew he would not be the man he had been before.

Jerusalem went to this tall son of hers and looked up at him. "Do you have to do this thing, Brodie?"

"Somebody's gonna have to do it, and I think it will be me."

Jerusalem knew from the look on his face that Brodie had made up his mind and would not be changed. Her greatest fear was that he would become hardened as some men who became law officers or man hunters. She could not speak, for fear filled her.

"Don't worry, Ma. Me and Captain Mac, we'll get him." He looked over at Moriah and said, "Don't you worry, Moriah. He won't get you or Ethan. I promise."

"I'm afraid for you, Brodie," Moriah whispered. "You don't know what Bear Killer is like."

And then Brodie Hardin, his arm around his mother, nodded, his face stony. "Then I reckon I'll find out," he said.

PART TWO:

CLINTON'S DRIVE

CHAPTER
SEVEN

B rodie Hardin stretched himself wearily, groaned, and looked down at his horse. "Red," he said through dry, parched lips, "you wouldn't think the Colorado River would be such a hard thing to find, would you?"

The big stallion was weary, but he lifted his head and neighed slightly and then made a slobbering sound.

"I know. I'm as thirsty as you are, but it ain't my fault if nobody in the whole blamed country can give directions." Brodie had been given two sets of directions, and both were wrong. Now as the sun was reaching its zenith, he was beginning to wonder if he would ever find the Ranger troop. He had left home on a fresh horse, fed up to the neck bone by Moriah and Jerusalem, but that had been four days ago. Now he leaned forward and peered off into the distance. All he could see was scrub sage, outcroppings of reddish brown rocks, and barren landscape. "Come on, Red," he sighed. "If we don't find the blasted camp by night, I'll carry you."

For the next two hours, Brodie sat loosely in the saddle. Red was tired, but he was a big, strong animal and was good for many miles yet.

Far off to the left, high in the sky, movement caught Brodie's eye. He saw dots high above and knew they were buzzards. "I hope they ain't feedin' on the Rangers," he spoke aloud. He had gotten in the habit of talking to himself, since there was no one else to talk to. Now, as Red ambled along, picking his own path through the cactus that rose up, Brodie thought about his decision to leave home and join the Ranger troop. It had been on his mind for a long time, and the murder of his uncle Zane by Bear Killer and his band of Comanches had pushed him over the edge. Actually, he was a mild-mannered young man, but he had been very fond of Zane, and it had infuriated him that the Comanche had come onto the Yellow Rose Ranch and killed Zane and Bill Manning. "He had no business comin', Red. He was comin' for Ethan and Moriah, but he won't pull that stunt again. When I catch him, I'll turn him wrong side out."

An hour later he saw something breaking the horizon. As he moved forward, he saw a line of trees. "Got to be the Colorado," he said, "so the troop can't be too far from here."

Following the last directions he had received from an old prospector, Brodie hit the river and turned north, but not before he had lain flat on his face and drank out of the muddy brown water. He let Red have a drink, not all the horse wanted nor all he wanted. He still had a ways to go, and to drink too much dirty water could make both horse and rider sick.

September had come to Texas, but the air was still hot. Summer had not loosened its hold on the land yet. As he looked off in the distance, Brodie knew that the winter could come quickly. Almost overnight it could turn the brown grass white with frost and kill every plant in its path.

"Well, looky there, Red. I do believe we've finally found them." The big horse nodded as if he understood and picked up the pace from a walk to a bone-jarring trot.

"You're shakin' my teeth out, Red! Gallop if you've got to. Rain on all this trottin' business!"

As Brodie moved closer, he saw a cabin set back from the river a quarter of a mile and sheltered by a bunch of towering cottonwoods. He had sharp eyes and could see some men moving about. When he got closer, he pulled Red down to a halt and walked the big horse toward the man he saw outside the cabin. He was well aware it wasn't safe to go galloping in unannounced.

"Hello, the house!" he shouted from a distance.

"Hello, yourself!"

The speaker was an undersized young man in his late teens, Brodie guessed. He was wearing clothes that were patched, had a pair of light blue eyes, tow-colored hair, and a wealth of freckles. "Git down and set. I'm Pokey Reese."

Brodie came out of the saddle, conscious of his weariness, and turned to greet the young man. "I'm Brodie Hardin."

"Right glad to meet up with you." He looked at the horse and shook his head with admiration. "That's a fine piece of horse flesh you got there, Brodie."

"Best I ever had. I'm lookin' for the Ranger camp and Captain Macklin." As he spoke, Brodie was hoping that the camp was somewhere else, and that this ragged, undersized individual was not one of the Rangers. He had a picture in his mind of big, strapping men with steel gray eyes and broad shoulders. Pokey Reese was none of these.

"Why, the captain he's been gone for a spell, but he'll be back soon. Reckon you got business with him?"

"I came to join the troop if he'll take me."

"Oh, he'll take you, all right," Pokey said. "He's takin' about anything these days."

The sentence seemed to grate on Brodie's nerves. "Why is that?" he said. "I thought it'd be hard to get into the Rangers."

"Well, it pays eight dollars a month, and for that you get shot at, maybe scalped, or fried over a fire by the Comanches. None of us ain't gonna get rich at it. I hope you didn't think so."

"No. I guess I knew better than that," Brodie said, wondering if he had made a mistake.

"Come on and unsaddle your horse. It looks like he could use a feed. We got a little grain we can spare."

"That'll be good."

The two men walked toward a ramshackle barn, and Brodie unsaddled the stallion. He pulled the bridle off, and Pokey Reese poured some grain out into a box. The big horse ate eagerly, and Brodie slapped him fondly on the neck. "There's a good horse," he said.

"He looks like he can run," Pokey said as he admired the horse.

"As fast as lightning," Brodie said, smiling.

"Are you hungry?" Pokey asked.

"You bet!"

"Well, Peach is cookin' up somethin'. Let's go see how he's doin'."

As the two men walked toward the back of the cabin, Reese explained, "Peach is about the best cook I've ever seen. Reckon he's the most valuable man in the troop. If anything happened to him, we'd probably wind up shootin' each other over bad cookin'. And that ain't all he can do. He can track most anything." He turned suddenly and said, "He's black. I hope that don't bother you none."

"Not a mite."

"Him and the captain have been friends just about forever. They really growed up together. Peach was his slave, but the captain he done set him free."

Pokey Reese evidently was a fount of information, for he talked constantly. They turned the corner, and there on the back porch was a wood stove with a pipe jutting up through the tin roof. A lanky black man was busy cooking, and he turned to look at them as they approached.

"This here is Brodie Hardin, Peach. He's come to join up with us, and his backbone's knockin' against his stomach. What you got to eat?"

"Howdy, Mr. Brodie."

"Hello, Peach."

"I got some venison cookin'. Won't be long."

Reese leaned over and looked into one of the big skillets over the fire. "That ain't venison over there on this side."

"No, that's for Mr. Snake."

"Mr. Snake!" Brodie said. "You got somebody named Snake?"

"Oh, his real name's John Jones, but everybody calls him Snake." A look of distaste came over his face, and he shuddered. "They call him that because he likes to eat snake. Myself, I'd rather not."

Brodie laughed. "Snake's pretty good eatin'."

"Yes, sir, it is," Peach said. He was black as a man could possibly be, and his eyes were a dark brown. When he smiled, his teeth contrasted with his ebony skin. "This be about ready, Mr. Pokey. You want to go tell the boys to come and eat?"

★ ★ ★

The group of men that tramped into the room that was used as a kitchen, as well as for other sociable activities, were a disappointment to Brodie. They looked like a bunch of tramps. Their clothes were tattered, and even their weapons looked old and worn out.

"This here is Brodie Hardin, men. He's come to join the Rangers—lookin' for fame and fortune."

"Well, he won't get it," a big, hulky man said, staring at Brodie with distaste.

"Aw, Hack, don't be so down-hearted. We're gonna be famous and get our pictures in all the papers," Pokey said. "This here is Hack Wilson," he said, pointing to the big man. "This here is Simon Gore, a genuine, cer-tified Indian fighter and mountainman."

Simon Gore wore buckskins so tight they seemed to be molded to his skin. They were blackened and dirty, and looked as if they had never been changed. Simon's hair was long and tied with a leather thong in the back. He could have been anywhere from fifty to eighty, but though he looked old, his hazel eyes were alive.

"Come to fight the Indians, have you, sonny?"

"I guess so," Brodie said.

"Well, you ever fought 'em before?"

"Not really."

"Well, you'll get your chance, maybe, if you hang around this bunch long enough."

"This here's Snake Jones." Pokey indicated a short, heavy-set man with muddy brown eyes and a round face. "He's a good feller 'cept he loves to eat snakes. But he knows this country better than anybody else. That's the reason the captain keeps him on. And this here is Sally Duo."

"Hello," Duo said. He was a small man with black hair, brown eyes, and an olive complexion. He spoke with an accent and appeared indiffer-ent to the new recruit.

"Sally here plays the fiddle. He carries it with him everywhere he goes. He speaks Italian too."

"Well, that'll be handy," Hack grunted. "No tellin' where we'll run into a bunch of Indians speakin' Italian."

"This here's Ollie Franz."

Ollie was even younger than Pokey. He was a short man, but he was very muscular. "He can't shoot straight, but he's stout."

"Howdy." Franz grinned. "Welcome to the Rangers. Glad to have you."

"This here's Denny Womack. He ain't weaned yet, quite, but we all got hopes for him that he'll be a real Indian killer."

Denny Womack was an awkward-looking young man, tall and lanky. He came forward and put his hand out. "Howdy," he said. "Where you from?"

"Texas by way of Arkansas," Brodie said.

"Whereabouts in Arkansas?"

"Don't tell him," Pokey said. "If you do tell him, he'll want to know who was the mayor of the town and what was the population and what was the annual rainfall in the place. Nosiest fellow you ever saw."

Denny Womack grinned. "I just like to get information, that's all."

Pokey gestured toward the table. "You gentlemen gonna sit and eat or jabber all day?"

They all went to the table, and Peach brought the food in. Brodie sat between Franz and Womack. Across from him, Simon Gore was eating indifferently. After taking a bite of the food, he said, "I'm hopin' we hit the herd pretty soon. Could use some good meat."

"The captain wouldn't let you take time out from huntin' Indians to hunt buffalo!" Snake Jones grunted. He was stuffing his food in his mouth and could hardly talk, his mouth was so full.

"Yeah, he would. The captain likes good buffalo tongue good as I do."

"Buffalo tongue!" Denny Womack said. "You eat the tongue of those critters?"

"It's the best part except maybe for the liver."

Denny Womack shook his head. "Not me. I ain't eatin' no tongue off no buffalo. How're the steaks?"

Simon evidently had said enough for the moment. He had a taciturn manner about him, and his eyes were never still as he forked his food into his mouth.

"How come you joined up with the Rangers, Brodie?" Denny asked.

Brodie felt the eyes of every Ranger on him and decided to keep it brief. "A Comanche named Bear Killer raided our ranch. He killed my uncle. I aim to see he pays for it."

Simon Gore stopped chewing, swallowed, and then stared at Brodie. "Bear Killer, you say? Well, you ain't likely to get a hold of him. He's about the slickest Comanche in these parts. He killed a partner of mine out on the Llano Estacado. I couldn't do nothin' about it. They caught him and cut him to pieces. I was hidin' in the brush. It was just one of me and near on to fifteen of them." He took a bite of meat, chewed it slowly, then said, "I'd like to get a hold of that Indian myself."

"I intend to get him for what he done," Brodie said, and then was sorry. It sounded boastful. The only real Indian fighter in the room, apparently, had said he had no luck with him, and here he had boasted he was going to have his revenge on Bear Killer.

"We don't need another braggart around here," Hack Wilson grunted.

"I wasn't braggin'. I'm just statin' my intention."

Hack Wilson stared at Brodie as if he wanted to argue, but Pokey Reese quickly changed the subject. They finished the meal, but Hack Wilson would not let it drop. He was the kind of man, Brodie sensed, who would have to try his strength out and prove himself on a stranger.

"So you're gonna catch Bear Killer. Why, you'd run like a rabbit if you ever seen him!"

"No, I wouldn't," Brodie snapped.

"You callin' me a liar, boy!" He evidently had been drinking, for his face was flushed, and he stepped forward with the full intention of grabbing Brodie.

As soon as he moved, Ollie Franz stepped in front of him and grabbed Wilson's outstretched wrist and said mildly, "Now, Hack, we don't want no trouble here. Especially with a newcomer who's come to help us fight the Indians."

Brodie was prepared for trouble, and he was shocked to see Hack Wilson, a big burly man, struggling to free his wrist. Even though Ollie was a much smaller man, he had grasped Hack with tremendous strength. There was no sign of stress in Ollie's face as he watched Hack struggle to free himself.

"Turn loose of me!" Hack growled.

"Why, sure, Hack." Ollie released him but stood watchfully. "We don't want any trouble. You hear me?" he said.

Hack Wilson glared at Ollie as if he were weighing the possibility of launching himself at him. But there was a strength in the young man that gave him pause. He cursed, turned, and walked out of the cabin.

"You have to excuse Hack," Simon said. "About the best he can look forward to is gettin' scalped or maybe a genteel hangin'."

Brodie turned to Ollie. "Thanks. I usually like to handle my own problems."

"Oh, Hack ain't mean. He just smells bad. Come on. I want to show you my horse. I got a real dandy. Can beat any horse in the troop."

"He can't beat mine," Brodie said.

The two men left and went out to look at Ollie's mare. She was steel gray with sleek lines. "She looks fast," Brodie said as he admired the powerful horse.

"Like I said, she can beat any horse in the troop. What you ridin'?"

"Come and see the best horse in these here parts," Brodie said. The two went to look at Red, and Ollie's eyes filled with admiration when he saw the size of Brodie's mount.

"Well, if anybody can beat Molly, I reckon it'd be that big hoss. You have him long?"

"For a spell," Brodie said as he stroked the horse's mane.

The two men stood there talking for some time about horses, and Brodie was glad to find that some of the Rangers were young men and just as untried as he was. "Have you been in lots of Indian fights, Ollie?"

"Never been in *one* yet. Neither has Pokey or Denny. We're all green as grass. For that matter, Simon's the only one that really knows Indians. Hack's claimed to have been in some scraps, but I don't know about that. He tends to boast a lot."

"The rest of the crew will be comin' in tomorrow. It'll make about fifteen, but most of 'em are green as I am," Ollie confessed.

"Doesn't sound like a prosperous undertaking."

"Oh, Captain Mac won't let us go wrong. He knows Indians better than anyone. Just wait'll he gets back. He's all kinds of a feller."

"You really like him?"

"Like him? Well . . ." Ollie scratched his chin thoughtfully. "I don't know if I like him, but I trust him to tote the key to the smokehouse!"

For three days Brodie stayed with the troop, enjoying the excellent food that Peach seemed to be able to prepare out of the least of supplies. Except for Hack Wilson and Snake Jones, he felt comfortable with the rest of the men. Every chance he got, he tried to talk to Simon Gore to find out what it was like to fight the Comanche, but Gore was gone most of the time. He seemed uncomfortable in the company of the others and was a loner.

The three young men, Reese, Franz, and Womack, seemed to have a camaraderie of their own. Although Brodie was much older, his same lack of experience in fighting Indians seemed to help draw the four of them close.

"The captain is comin' in!"

Pokey Reese had called out loudly, and Brodie, who had been currying Red, left the corral and came to watch as the single horseman came riding in. He had met Captain James Macklin once at a dance where he had had a set-to with a bully. The captain had come to him later and given him an invitation.

"If you ever want to join the Rangers, I'll be glad to see you," Macklin had told him.

Now, as the rider dismounted from a weary gelding, Ollie moved forward to take the lines of the horse. Macklin's eyes picked out Brodie at once. He smiled slightly and came forward and said, "Well, I didn't really expect to see you, Hardin. Welcome to the Rangers."

Brodie took the hard hand that the captain extended and shook it firmly. He felt as if he were under a magnifying glass as the man's eyes scrutinized him. Captain James Macklin was forty-five, no more than average height, thin but very active. He had light blue eyes, black hair, and a trim black beard. According to all that the men had told him, the captain was absolutely fearless. It was as if he had been born without that emotion. He had started out to be a lawyer but hated it. Then tragedy struck, and he lost his wife and three children to cholera five years earlier. He had joined the Rangers to fight against the Indians who were raiding and killing many of the settlers. The Indians hated him, for he had gained a reputation among The People of the plains for never giving up on a trail.

Macklin nodded and said, "Glad to have you as a part of the troop." He asked no more questions but turned and faced the other Rangers, who had come out of the house. "You came at a good time," he added to Brodie. "We'll be riding out early tomorrow morning."

"Where we goin', Captain?" Sally Duo asked.

"I caught a glimpse of Victorio's bunch."

"Big party?" Simon Gore asked.

"No. Only eight. A small war party."

Denny Womack pulled off his hat and slapped his leg with it. "Why, we'll wipe 'em out! Only eight!"

Simon Gore gave him a disgusted glance. "Not likely!" he snorted.

The troop rode out at dawn, and Captain Mac kept them at a hard pace in their saddles all morning. They paused at lunch for a short break and then when twilight started to fall hours later, they camped beside a small stream for the night. As usual, Peach fixed a good meal almost effortlessly. He had brought enough meat with him to cook up, and he made cold water cornbread, which Brodie had always liked.

"This is great cornbread, Peach. My ma makes it the same way."

"Ain't hard to make cornbread like this. Just put in some meal and water and fry it up in a good hot pan. A little better if it's fried in fat of some kind."

The men all ate heartily. They had ridden hard all day, so they all spread out their bed rolls and within minutes were fast asleep. Brodie, however, sat up staring into the fire, casting his eyes from time to time on Captain Mac, who was reading.

Suddenly, Mac lifted his head, and his blue eyes seemed sharp by the fire light. "You a Christian man, Hardin?"

"Yes, sir. I take it you are too?"

"I'm not sure." Macklin looked at the book and didn't speak for a while. "I lost my wife and three children five years ago. I got mad at God. Haven't forgiven Him yet."

Brodie was uneasy by the idea that anyone would think he had to forgive God. He didn't know what to say to ease the pain he could sense at the man's terrible loss.

"What about your family?"

"Well, I've always had a good family. . . ." Brodie went on, speaking of the Yellow Rose Ranch and his stepfather, Clay Taliferro. But finally he said, "I guess the reason I joined the Rangers was to get revenge on Bear Killer. He killed my uncle Zane a few weeks ago during a raid on our ranch. Another man was killed too. I aim to nail his hide to the fence for it."

"Well, you can plan all you want to, but things always happen to a plan."

"Will we catch Victorio, Captain?" Brodie asked as he watched the flames dance in the fire.

"I doubt it."

Brodie was surprised at his answer. He had expected to find assurance from a man like Macklin. "Why not, Captain?"

"This is their country, Brodie. They know it better than we do. They know where to find the water, where to hide." He looked out in the darkness and shook his head. "They know we're tracking them too. We can't sneak up on them, but they can sneak up on us. Why, they might be out there right now just waiting for the right moment to attack."

Brodie looked out into the thick darkness, and a chill ran through him. The very idea that Comanches might be creeping in to cut their throats brought fear to him that he did not like to admit. "Well, Captain, you might as well know right now that scares me a little bit."

Captain Mac gave him a rare grin. "You'd be a fool if you weren't. Anybody that's not afraid of Comanches is a fool."

For two days the Rangers tracked Victorio's small band of warriors. They rode through some rough country, and the Indians were apparently traveling very fast. Simon Gore, the scout, would go out each day early in the morning, and when he would find their tracks, he'd come back and lead the troop. Once Brodie was close enough to hear him say, "Captain, they're just ahead of us. They ain't tryin' to hide." Gore pulled off his hat and scratched his gray hair. "Can't understand why they're so careless."

"I don't like it either, Simon. Where are they now?" the captain asked.

"Why, they ain't more than five miles ahead of us. We could catch up with 'em easy."

Captain Macklin said instantly, "All right. It's the best chance we'll have. Check your weapons, men."

Brodie had brought two six-guns and one rifle along. He checked all three of the weapons. They were fully loaded.

When Captain Mac saw the two Walker Colts, he said, "Well, you got more bullets than there are Indians ahead of us."

"That's right," Gore said, grinning. "All you have to do is see 'em and knock 'em over."

The men were all tense, for it would be the first encounter with Indians for some of them. Captain Macklin led them out at a fast pace. They rode hard, and after about an hour, Simon yelled, "I see 'em. They're headin' for those rocks over there!"

The troop was galloping headlong, and Brodie caught a glimpse of the Comanches ahead as they headed for cover. His heart began to beat faster as the group of Rangers began to close the gap. When they reached the hills that rose up, he heard Hack Wilson cry out, "They're gonna hide in those rocks!"

Brodie was leaning forward in his saddle, his heart beating with excitement, when suddenly he saw Captain Mac's horse go down. He had stepped in a hole and sent Macklin flying. Brodie fell back from the rest of the Rangers.

"Are you okay, Captain?" he asked as he rode up beside him.

Macklin stooped to pick up his hat that had fallen off. His face was covered with sand, and he brushed it away. "Let me get on behind you, Hardin! We have to hurry!"

"Sure, Captain."

Captain Macklin kicked the horse into a run and began shouting, "Pull back! Pull back!"

"What's the matter, Captain?" Brodie demanded.

"Those Indians have gone into that canyon to lay an ambush, and the men are following right after 'em. They'll get themselves all massacred!"

"You think it's a trap?"

Macklin did not answer. He pulled out his pistol and fired it off, but it had no effect on the Rangers, who, except for Gore, were headed straight into the narrow gap. Gore was yelling something, then he turned his horse and came back.

"I couldn't stop 'em, Mac," Gore said. "They won't listen to reason. They've gone crazy!"

He had no sooner spoken than a fuselage of gun shots began to sound, ricocheting off the canyon walls.

"They'll be cut to pieces!" Macklin shouted. "We'll have to go after 'em."

Red seemed not to know he was carrying two men, for he pulled ahead of Simon's mount with ease with his long strides. As soon as they entered the narrow entrance to the canyon, Brodie was shocked at what he saw. Several of the men's horses had fallen down and were kicking. Others were lying still. At least two men were stretched out and not moving. The rest of the Rangers were milling around shooting wildly at nothing.

"The Comanches are in the rocks!" Simon yelled. "We got to get out of here!"

Captain Macklin yelled in a stentorian voice. "Rangers, follow me!"

The surviving Rangers, those who still had horses, turned at once. Sally Duo's horse went down, but Snake Jones stopped and pulled him on behind him. As they filed out, Brodie looked desperately for the enemy, but he could see only rocks and the puff of rifles.

He had expected the Indians to fight with bows and arrows, but they were as well armed as the Rangers.

When they were out of range of the canyon, Macklin halted the group. "Where are the others?" he said.

Hack Wilson said, "Will Sandford and Links Barnes got knocked off first thing."

"Where's Denny Womack?" Macklin asked. "I don't see him."

"He may have gone down too," Snake Jones said.

"What do we do, Captain?" Brodie asked.

The Rangers were pale and shaken by how it had happened so quickly.

"We can't do anything," Macklin said grimly. "We're in poor shape.

We've got five men without horses. We'll have to ride double. We're not likely to catch a bunch of Comanches like that."

He would have said more, but suddenly a piercing scream rang out, high and unbelievably shrill.

Ollie Franz suddenly cried out, "Look! They got Denny!"

Brodie turned to look and saw four Indians surrounding Denny Womack. They had stripped his clothes off. With one swift motion, one of the Indians ran a knife down across his forehead and yanked his scalp off. The young man's screams made Brodie's blood run cold.

"We got to help him, Captain!" Franz said and started forward.

"Stay where you are, Franz!"

Franz stopped and protested. "But look. They're going to cut him to pieces!"

"Give me your rifle, Pokey." Macklin took the rifle that Pokey gave him and stepped off his horse and took a dead aim. The screams of the young Ranger were the most awful thing that any of the men had ever heard. The shot rang out, and the screams were cut off.

"All right. Let's get home—if they'll let us. We'll be lucky if they don't follow us and pick us off one at a time."

As they rode away, no one spoke. One of the Rangers, whose horse had been killed, was riding behind Brodie. Peach came up to ride beside them and turned and looked at Brodie's face. He saw the pain in the young man's expression and said, "It's the way it is, Mr. Brodie."

CHAPTER
EIGHT

Clay Taliferro carefully made a loop in his rope. He had been determined to break this horse for some time. As he watched the wild-eyed sorrel turn to face him, he began to sing. He had found that sometimes singing helped to calm the nerves of a wild horse. His singing had never calmed anybody else's nerves that he knew of, but it was a song he loved, for it had been one he had used to court more than one woman:

I found a rose in New Orleans,
Sweetest flower I'd ever seen.
Coal black hair and sparkling eyes
And rosy lips for telling lies.

Moving cautiously with a distinct limp, Clay enlarged the loop and sang the chorus:

Deep in the heart!
Oh, deep in the heart!

Naught can be lost
That's deep in the heart!

Suddenly the sorrel broke and threw herself wildly to the right. Clay followed as well as he could, but he was slowed by his gimpy leg. The bullet he had taken from the marauding Comanches had caused some serious difficulty. Doc Woods had said he would probably limp the rest of his life, but Clay had stubbornly refused to believe him.

Once I held her in my arm,
She swore we would never part,
But now I only hold her charm
Way down deep in the heart!
All flowers may fade
Their fragrance depart—
But my New Orleans maid
Will ever be deep in my heart!

It was the last day of December 1846, and the cold weather had numbed Clay's hands. The frigid weather was not the best thing for a lame knee, and Clay rebelled against it. "I can be as good a man as I ever was," he had stubbornly told Jerusalem, who had urged him to take things easy. Now Clay tossed the rope, but it fell short, and the sorrel jerked to one side. The horse seemed to be enjoying the chase—which Clay was not.

Clay Taliferro was not a man who liked profanity. In fact, he had gotten into more than one fight over what he called "rude language." Now, however, the bitterly cold weather, his aching knee, and missing a cast of the lariat he could have made easily before the Comanche raid forced out of him a single word that was even ruder than he intended.

To his surprise, the word came floating back almost like an echo. Startled, Clay turned to see Rachel Belle and Sam, along with Ethan, standing at the edge of the corral watching him. His eyes fixed on Belle, for it had been her voice he had heard uttering the rude word. He limped over and stood staring down at her.

"What did you say?" he asked, hoping he had imagined the offense. But Rachel simply looked up at him with a defiant look and said the word again.

"What do you mean sayin' a word like that?" he demanded.

"Because you said it, Daddy."

Vainly, Clay tried to think of an argument, but nothing came to him. He assumed a stern expression and said, "Well, I'm not going to have you sayin' rude words like that. It ain't fittin' for a child to use rude language."

"That's right, Daddy," Samuel nodded. "You have to wait until you're grown up before you can cuss."

Somehow this did not seem exactly the lesson that Clay wanted to impress upon his children, and he said quickly, "I don't condone cussin' even in grown-ups."

"I know you don't," Sam said. "I saw you beat the soup out of Hayden Fry because he cussed in front of Mama. I thought you was gonna wallop him to death."

"Well, that's how I feel about cussin'. I don't want none of you young'uns usin' it."

"Well, how come you did it?" Belle said. She was an outspoken precocious child and already showed signs of a rebelliousness that reminded Clay of Jerusalem's independent spirit at times.

"Never you mind what I did. It was just a mistake. It just slipped out."

Ethan had been taking all this in and pushed his hat back on his forehead. "All grown-ups cuss, don't they? Except the women, some of them."

"It ain't fittin' for a girl to cuss—or for a boy either. Now, I don't want to argue about this anymore."

He turned to walk away, and Ethan said, "Does your leg still hurt?"

Clay turned to look at the boy. He had become very fond of Ethan and grinned at him crookedly. "Well, it's better than gettin' poked in the eye with a sharp stick. I don't—"

Clay whirled quickly and stared at the house. "That's Miss Beverly cryin'," Ethan said. "Her baby's comin'."

Sam shook his head dolefully. "Poor little fella. He won't have no daddy."

Clay immediately contradicted him. "Sure he will," he said loudly. "I've got the hang of this daddy business. I'll be his daddy." Even as he spoke, however, he heard a sharper cry and bit his lip. "You fellas go down to the creek and bring back some fish to fry up."

"It's too cold to fish!" Belle argued.

"Then go do something else. Now scoot!"

Beverly's face was twisted with pain and was white as chalk as she labored to bring her child into the world. Moriah bent over her and mopped her head with a damp cloth. "You're doing fine, Bev," she said, hoping to encourage the woman.

"I'm afraid, Moriah," she gasped in between contractions.

Jerusalem, who had gone across the room, came back at once. "You're doing fine. That baby's going to come soon, and you're going to be all right." She spoke with more confidence than she felt, for Beverly had been struggling in hard labor now for over twelve hours and there seemed to be no progress. Jerusalem had experienced relatively little trouble bearing her own children. Even Ethan had been born with a minimum of pain. Both women knew something was wrong here, and Jerusalem said, "I'm going to step outside. You stay here, Moriah."

"All right, Mama."

Moving outside the bedroom, Jerusalem turned and walked to the hall. She met Clay, who had just come in from outside, and noted again how badly he limped. Doctor Woods had said he would never be the same, and although Clay denied the doc's assessment vehemently, Jerusalem agreed with the doctor.

"How is she, Jerusalem?"

"Not good at all. I think something's wrong. Maybe the baby's turned the wrong way. I'm afraid for her."

"I'd better go for Doctor Woods."

"No. You stay here. Send Clinton and tell him to hurry."

"I just hope Doc's not drunk or out of town," Clay said as he turned to go find Clinton. He went back outside, moving as rapidly as he could, and headed for the stable. He slipped a well-worn saddle on Baldy, the old horse they used for plowing the garden, and cinched it tightly. He was easy to catch, for he was not the fastest horse in the world. Clay grunted with pain as he threw his leg over and then said, "Come on, Baldy, let's go."

The cold wind cut through Clay as he kicked the old horse into a rough gallop. The jolting hurt his knee, but he ignored the pain and urged the horse on to his full speed. Ten minutes later he saw the cattle that had been rounded up for feeding. At the sound of the approaching horse, Clinton turned toward him.

"What's the matter?" Clinton said as Clay pulled up.

"It's Bev. She's havin' a hard time with the baby. Go in and get Doc Woods and make it quick."

Alarm filled Clinton's face, and he nodded. "Sure, Pa. I'll break a record."

"Don't take a horse. Go back and take the wagon. You may have to bring him out if he's drunk."

"That'll be slower."

"It might save time. Doc's gettin' too old to ride a horse at a fast clip. Now git!"

Clinton nodded and kicked his buckskin into a dead run. Clay turned and kicked at Baldy's flank with his good leg. "Get goin', but you don't have to run so fast." As he rode along, watching Clinton skim over the ground ahead of him, he said, "That Clinton never does anything by halves. He'll probably kill the horses gettin' 'em to town."

Clinton drove the team into town at a furious pace. He brought them to a halt by hauling up on the reins and slamming on the brake. They were not even completely stopped when he jumped off his horse and ran to Doctor Woods's office. The doc had a small office for people to wait in, and as Clinton came rushing through the door, he saw a Mexican woman cleaning the office.

"Where's Doc Woods?" he shouted.

The old woman looked up and said, "Drunk."

"Is he in there?" Clinton pointed toward the inner office.

"No. He's probably down at the saloon. That's where he usually gets drunk."

Clinton wheeled on his heels and ran out of the office. In his hurry, he had not even tied up the horses to the hitching rail. As he headed for the saloon, he paid no attention to the people he passed. One of them said, "What's wrong, Clinton?" But he didn't even stop to answer.

Reaching the Golden Lady Saloon, he burst in, shoving the bat-wing doors open, and paused to sweep the saloon with a glance. He saw Doc Woods over at a table playing poker with two men. He took note that one of them was Lou Burdette, foreman of Skull Ranch, which adjoined the Yellow Rose. Along with him was Dee Nolan, one of his riders. Dee Nolan had administered a severe beating to Clinton at one time. He was a brutal, burly man with a broad face and delighted in proving his strength by beating other men senseless.

Ignoring the two, Clinton walked over and said, "Doc, come on. You're needed out at the ranch."

"What's that?" Doc Woods looked up.

Clinton could tell that he was even drunker than usual. His eyes were blood-shot and unfocused, and his voice was thick with a heavy slur. Doctor Phineas Woods had been a good doctor once. Even at the age of sixty, he was still good when he was sober. He was a big man with a fat stomach and the signs of hard living on his face, but Clinton paid no attention to that. "Come on, Doc," he said, putting his hand on his shoulder. "Miss Beverly's havin' her baby, and it ain't goin' right. She needs your help."

Dee Nolan glared at Clinton. "He ain't goin' nowhere until we finish this game. Now get out of here you whelp before I give you another beatin'!"

Clinton stared at the big man. He remembered the last time he had crossed the big man and knew he was no match for him in a fight. For one thing, he hadn't had the practice that Nolan had, and now was not the time to start a fight he would certainly lose.

"Nolan, there's a woman in bad shape out at the ranch. It's more important than any poker game."

Nolan cursed and said, "We're finishin' this game. Now git!"

For one instant Clinton wished that he had brought a gun along. He might have used it, but he doubted it. Lou Burdette, the foreman of Skull, was a quick man with a gun, and only Clay could match him in a draw.

"I'm sorry to bust up your game," Clinton said carefully. "You can take it up later, but right now Doc's got to go." He leaned down and got Doc by the arm, and the old man lurched to his feet.

Clinton had no time to do more than that, for in a surprisingly swift move for so big a man, Dee Nolan came to his feet, reached out, and grabbed Clinton by the arm. "I told you to get out of here!" he said. He swung a powerful blow that caught Clinton in the chest and drove him backward. He careened into another table, where two men were playing dominos, and fell sprawling as the table overturned. He knew Dee's style of fighting was to kick men once they were down, so he quickly rose to his feet. His quick action saved him from a crushing kick from the tip of Nolan's boot.

The big man was smiling and said, "I'm gonna stomp you, Hardin, just like I did once before."

Clinton knew he had little hope, but suddenly Frisco Farr stepped in front of Clinton and stared at Dee Nolan. The owner of the Golden Lady was dressed immaculately, as he always was. Clinton had often made fun of his fancy clothes by saying, "Well, if you drop dead, Frisco, we won't have to do a thing to you except put a lily in your hand."

Frisco Farr wore a pearl-handled pistol at his left side. He was known to be a dangerous man, and now he stood there, staring at Dee. The menace in his eyes was unmistakable as silence fell across the room. "I expect you'd better back off, Dee."

"What are you buttin' in for, Frisco?"

"Beverly is a friend of mine." Farr remembered her more fondly than as just a hostess at the Golden Lady before she had married Zane Satterfield. She had not been like the other women who worked there, and Frisco had sensed this. His eyes looked almost sleepy as he let his hand linger near the pearl handle of the forty-four in his holster. "Get out of my saloon, Dee. You make too much noise."

"You runnin' me out?" Dee grunted.

"Do you need help going?" Frisco said quietly, and a grin touched his lips. "I can accommodate you."

For a moment everyone in the saloon held their breath, waiting to see if Dee was going to draw on Frisco. The silence seemed to grow thick and palpable, but finally Dee brushed his hand across his face and said in a sullen tone, "You don't have to get so rambunctious about it."

"Second thoughts are usually best, Dee. Now get out of here. You can come back maybe later." He glanced over and said, "Lou, you better teach

this hand of yours a few manners. I may not be so easy on him next time."
He turned then and said, "Doc will never stay on a horse back to the
ranch."

"I got a wagon down the street," Clinton said.

"Go get it. I'll help you put him in it." Frisco turned as Clinton left
and said, "Doc, you need to sober up quick. Beverly's a good woman, and
right now she needs your help to have her baby."

Doc Woods had been taking in the scene and said wearily, "Somebody
ought to shoot me. I'm nothin' but a miserable drunk."

"Maybe they will someday, but not before you take care of Beverly
and her baby."

Frisco guided Doc out the door, and when Clinton drove the wagon
up, he shoved the old man up into the front seat.

"Thanks, Frisco," Clinton said.

Frisco nodded and heard Doc say, "We've got to go to the office and
get my bag." He watched as Clinton turned the wagon around, then
shook his head. When he went back inside the saloon, Lou Burdette came
over and said, "Sorry about Dee. I'll have a word with him."

"That might be wise. I nearly got upset with him."

"Hope it goes all right with the woman. I always liked Bev."

As Clinton pulled the team to a halt in front of the main house, Clay came
out and stared up at Doc. "Doc, you're drunk."

"I know it."

"I'll shoot you if you don't take care of Bev."

"You won't need to. I'll shoot myself."

Clay suddenly grinned tightly. "Well, I'm glad you're here. Come on.
She's having a rough time trying to bring this young'un into the world."

Clinton sat on the wagon seat and watched Clay help the old man up
the stairs. "Too bad about Doc. He's a good man, but I sure would like
to see him become a Christian before his time comes. Maybe I ought to
have a talk with him." He looked up, then slapped the lines on the horses
and said, "Okay, boys, back to the barn for you."

★ ★ ★

At suppertime those gathered around the table were quiet. Usually, it was a noisy bunch with the children, for either Clay was telling one of his tall tales, or the children were arguing about something. Now they all sat quietly, intimidated by the moans that came from the bedroom, where Beverly still struggled to have her baby. Rachel Belle looked up at Jerusalem and said, "Why does it hurt when women have babies, Mama?"

"I can tell you that," Clinton said. He was spearing an enormous bite of steak with his fork and jammed it in his mouth, talking around it. "It's all in the Bible because of that woman Eve and that snake. That's part of the curse that women would have babies with lots of trouble because Eve disobeyed God."

"Well, what about old Adam? What happened to him? It shouldn't have been all put on poor old Eve," Sam said.

"I'm gonna have to start a Bible class around here," Clinton said. "Ma, these children are plum ignorant of the Bible. They need to know what God says in His Word."

Jerusalem could not help but smile. Clinton had considered himself the spiritual head of the family ever since he had been saved while in his early teens. He had become quite unbearable and self-righteous for a time, but she knew he had a good heart and meant well. "I think that'd be a good idea. Maybe you can get Brother Morgan to help."

"Why, shucks, Ma, I don't need any help teachin' the Bible! I know all about it."

Clay laughed. "People have been arguing about what the Scripture means for now onto two thousand years, and suddenly Clinton Hardin comes along, and he knows all about it."

"Well, I do!" Clinton said stubbornly.

Clay leaned forward and said, "Do you? Well, answer me this. Where did Cain get his wife?"

"What'd you say?" Clinton sputtered.

"I said, where did Cain get his wife?" Clay enjoyed confounding Clinton's theology, and he grinned at the young man's confusion. "Well, I mean, after all, who was there for him to marry?"

Clinton swallowed a bite of meat and glared at Clay. "Well, I don't know, Pa, but if she suited Cain, she suits me all right."

Jerusalem giggled. "I guess you'll stop trying to beat my boy with theology." She put her hand on Clinton's neck and squeezed it. "Don't let him get the best of you."

As she spoke, Doctor Woods came into the dining room. His face was tense. "Could I have a cup of coffee, Jerusalem?"

"Doc, you'd better eat something."

"No. No time for that. Not hungry anyway." He took the scalding cup of coffee that Jerusalem handed him in a big mug and stood there sipping it. His face was worn and haggard, and he did not seem to see the people gathered at the table.

"When's the baby going to come, Doctor?" Rachel asked.

"It'll come when it comes. There ain't no schedule for this, honey."

"She won't die, will she?" Sam asked, a worried look on his face.

"No. I don't think so, but she's havin' a hard time."

The doctor stood there silently, and finally, when he had drained the cup, he said, "Thanks, Jerusalem," then turned and walked back to the bedroom. His shoulders were slumped, and he moved slowly toward the door.

"Doctor Woods is gettin' old," Moriah said.

"He's not but sixty," Quaid replied as he pushed the piece of pie around on his plate before eating it. He ordinarily ate with the cowhands, but he had gotten in late and had joined the family. He got up finally when the women started cleaning off the dishes and said quietly to Moriah, "Did you have this kind of problem when you had Ethan?"

"No. It was easy."

"It must have been rough having a baby among the Indians."

Moriah looked up at him and paused for a moment. "Everything was hard with the Comanches."

"You reckon you'll ever forget it?"

"Forget it? Never. And I can't hate them like other white people do. There are some good people among them."

"I reckon you're right." He looked over at Ethan, who was sitting next to the fire with the other children. "Ethan's a fine boy."

"He's going to have a hard life," Moriah said, sighing.

"I wish you'd let me help more."

"Why, Quaid, you do help. You spend more time with Ethan than anyone. You've taught him more than anybody, and he admires you for it."

"I hope I don't let him down—like I let you down."

"Quaid, I've told you to forget that."

Quaid shook his head. "Hard to forget when a man acts like that."

Moriah felt a sudden compassion for Quaid Shafter. She studied his tan V-shaped face and his silver hair, thinking what a fine-looking man he was. He had a masculine air about him that gave him a certain attraction. She put her hand on his arm and said, "Forget it, Quaid. We have to learn to put things behind us."

Light flashed in Quaid's eyes then. "That's good of you to say so, Moriah, and I promise to always do the best I can for you and for Ethan."

"You need to get yourself a wife and a family of your own," Moriah said quietly. Then she turned and walked away, leaving Quaid to stare after her.

At midnight the children were all asleep, but the adults were sitting around the table drinking coffee. The clock struck, sprinkling the night with its twelve silver chimes. "Well, we got a whole new year to use up," Clay said. "It's 1847 now."

Jerusalem was sitting beside him. She reached over and took his hand. "You've done fine, Clay, with the ranch."

"Don't know if I can do so good with a gimped knee."

"A knee's not a man," Jerusalem said quietly. She squeezed his hand and said, "You're the best man I know."

Clay turned to face her. "Why, wife," he said, "if I didn't know you better, I'd expect you was lookin' for some affection!"

"I wouldn't mind it a bit."

At that instant Doctor Woods came out in the room. He looked younger, and his step had a spring to it.

"Well, our new visitor is here," he said, smiling.

"Was it before or after the clock struck?"

"About the same time, I reckon. What difference does it make?"

"Her birthday. It'll either be December the thirty-first or January the first."

"Well, I say call it January the first," Woods said. "Come in and see the newcomer."

They all traipsed into the bedroom and gathered around the bed. Beverly's complexion was pale, and her face was damp with perspiration. Despite her weakness she managed to smile at them all.

"A fine baby girl," Moriah said, bringing over a bundle and putting the child into Beverly's arms.

Clay walked over and put his hand on Bev's face. "I'm glad it's a girl," he said. "They're a lot prettier than boys."

Beverly reached out and put her hand over his. "Isn't she beautiful?"

"Sure is. Most new babies look like six pounds of ground meat, but this one's a real beauty. Look at that black hair. I think she looks like Zane."

"What will you name her?" Jerusalem asked.

"I'd like to name her after Ruth in the Bible. And my mother's name was Anne, so she'll be Ruth Anne."

"Fine Bible name," Clay said.

"That's what I told Zane. You remember when Ruth decided to go with Naomi. That's what I told Zane. That I'd go with him always." She touched the black hair of the infant and whispered, "You'll never see your daddy, sweetheart."

"Why, we got a whole bunch of daddies around here. Me and Clinton and Brodie and Quaid over there. We'll spoil that girl child rotten. You just see if we don't!"

CHAPTER NINE

Jerusalem woke slowly and stirred beneath the sheets as the yellow beams of sunlight filtered down through the window over her bed. She always came out of sleep feeling groggy and envied Clay, who seemed to wake up all at once. Stretching her toes and arching her back, she began to think of the work that had to be done today. But when she opened her eyes, she saw Clay, his head propped up on his palm, with his elbow resting on the mattress. He was watching her silently, like he did so many mornings, and his eyes were wide in the early morning light.

"Why are you always watching me like that?"

"Why, I was just thinkin' how blessed you are, wife."

"What are you talking about?"

Clay reached over and put his free hand on her cheek and stroked it. He had been a rough man most of his life, and Jerusalem had been shocked after they married to find out that he had a gentleness in him she had never suspected. Her first husband, Jake, had been rough in all his ways, and she had been pleased beyond measure to find this tenderness in a man like Clay.

"Why, I was just thinkin' how the good Lord has poured His blessings down on you." He let his hand run down on her neck and onto her bare shoulders. "Why, just think how blessed and fortunate you are to have such a good-lookin' husband."

Jerusalem giggled and twisted in the bed and threw her arms around Clay. She caught him off-guard, and the force of her motion threw him over on his back. She grabbed two handfuls of his hair, pressed herself against him, and said, "You are a good-looking brute!"

"Wait a minute," Clay said. "I don't know if it's good for a man in my condition to be subjected to all this mad passion, woman!"

Another trait she loved about him was that he was full of fun, always teasing her. For a time Jerusalem held on to him. And then finally she whispered, "You're right, Clay. I am lucky. You're the best husband in the world."

"Well, if you say so, I guess it must be true."

Jerusalem laughed and rolled over on her back. "You're not the most humble, modest man I ever met."

"A man's got to recognize his strengths."

The two lay there talking, enjoying each other's company, but finally Clay grew silent, and Jerusalem turned again to look at him. She saw a studied expression on his face that she didn't understand. "What's the matter, Clay?"

"I've been thinking about Bev and Ruth. I miss 'em."

"So do I, but it was a good thing for her to take the baby back east to her family." Bev had surprised them all by her decision to take Ruth and return to her family in Missouri. "I disappointed my folks when I left and came west," Bev had said. "But they need to know that I did two good things when I married Zane and had Ruth Anne. They love children, and Ruth needs her people as she grows up."

Clay nodded. "She done the right thing—and like we told her, she can always come back here anytime. . . . I'm not doin' too well with the ranch. I thought we'd be a lot better off by this time."

Clay fell silent, and Jerusalem could tell that he was troubled about the lack of progress. She knew all the hard work he had put into it, and the disappointment she sensed in him bothered her. "It's hard times in

Texas," she said, reaching over and stroking his hair. "Times will get better. You just wait and see."

"They better is all I can say."

"You know, Clay, Texas is kind of like an adolescent. You know how they are at a certain age. They're not a child because they're not grown. Just blundering around somewhere in the middle. But they grow out of it, and so will we. We just need to keep on trusting God to bless the Yellow Rose."

"You're right, wife, as usual."

"It's been hard, but we'll make it. I know we will."

"This Mexican War that went on last year," Clay said. "It made a big difference in this country."

"You think it'll make a difference to us here in Texas?"

"Bound to."

"I never understood what that war was about," Jerusalem said.

"Well, it's not hard to figure out. The United States wanted the land Mexico owned, so the greedy politicians looked for an excuse for a war, and they found one." Clay lifted his leg and stared at the scar where the Comanche bullet had ruined his knee. He put it down again and said, "We got a territory four times the size of France from Mexico for fifteen million dollars. Mexico gave up all claims to Texas and set the boundary at the Rio Grande. This is a big country we got now. It goes all the way from the Atlantic to the Pacific."

"Some of the Mexicans don't think it settled it. Take the Lebonnes for one. Mateo Lebonne is not going to pay any attention to what politicians call the border. He's gonna come over and steal cattle just like he's been doing since the Alamo."

"I hate what the war did to people. The Lebonnes were good friends, and the war ruined that. I think Brodie is still in love with Serena."

Clay was silent for a time, and then he sat up in bed and stared out the window. "This is a fine place we got here, Jerusalem, but we're gonna have to decide something."

"What's that, Clay?"

"We're going to have to decide if we're going to keep what we've got and be small potatoes or whether we're gonna go for broke. Should we buy more land and grow with this state?"

Jerusalem was stirred by his words. The thought of owning a larger ranch and providing for her family made her think of the hard years scrabbling on an Arkansas farm no bigger than eighty acres. Those memories were deeply ingrained in her. She sat up and looked out the window at the boundless expanse outside, and then she turned to Clay. Her voice was steady as she said, "Let's go for it, Clay. All or nothing. Let's make the Yellow Rose the biggest and the best ranch in all of Texas!" She grew still for a moment, then said, "You know, I dreamed of our place last week. I dreamed that everyone in Texas was watching us to see if we'd stick it out or quit."

"That's quite a dream," Clay said. "Like the eyes of Texas are on us."

"That's it! And if the eyes of Texas are on us, we've got to go on!"

"Could we have some soda pop and some candy, and can I buy me a new doll?"

Quaid and Moriah had brought all the children into town to buy supplies. Belle had piped up, making her request. Moriah started to speak, but Quaid beat her to it.

"Why, I don't see why not. What's the good of bein' rich if we don't spend money on good-lookin' kids like you?"

"Quaid, don't promise them that. You'll spoil them."

"Well, that's my aim, Moriah. I had a little luck in a poker game, and I can spend my winnings any way I want."

"You're gonna spend away your winnings on us?" Sam said with amazement. "If Clinton were here, he would say give it to the church."

"Well, Clinton ain't here. Just an old, hardened sinner like me. So I say let's go in and get soda pop and hard candy and maybe some licorice too."

Moriah laughed and shook her head as they all entered the store. Seeing the kids make a beeline for the candy case, she felt a keen pleasure in the moment. Ethan was climbing up and trying to see in the glass case. Something stirred in her heart as she watched Quaid pick him up and say, "Okay, buddy, pick what you want. Buy enough to make yourself sick."

Not only Ethan, but Sam, Rachel, and even David ordered candy as fast as Cal Lockhart, the clerk, could dish it out. After he stuffed it in four sacks and handed them out, Quaid said, "Now, let's have soda pops all around."

When the kids got their soda pops, Quaid looked down at them. He was, Moriah thought, a strange-looking man. He was six feet tall, lean, and muscular. His V-shaped face was tanned by the Texas sun, and his light blue eyes seemed to pierce whatever they looked upon. His most striking feature was his hair, which was pure silver. He no longer wore it in a pigtail but cut it just off at his collar. He was the kind of man, Moriah thought, that turned heads when he walked into a room.

"You kids go outside now because you're gonna be sick. I don't want you bein' sick all over this store."

"Just a minute," Moriah said. "I'm not going to have sick kids. Here. Let me show you what you can eat." She selected several pieces of candy and said firmly, "Don't you eat any more. We'll save some for the trip home. Now, go outside."

As the children ran out, she turned to Quaid and said, "You shouldn't spoil them like that."

"Won't hurt 'em. Besides, I've got more spoilin' to do."

"What are you talking about?"

"That was a pretty big pot I won. I want to buy you a birthday present."

"My birthday was a month ago."

"Sure it was, and I didn't get you anything. But I'm going to today." Quaid was in a light mood, and he looked at her with a smile dancing in his blue eyes. "Why, a good-lookin' woman like you needs to have fine clothes. I want you to buy an entire new outfit. From the hat down to the shoes."

"I won't let you buy me any clothes!" Moriah protested.

"You'd better, or I'll throw a blue-faced hissy fit right here. You ain't never seen one of them. It's a sight to make strong men pale, send children runnin', and make women faint."

Moriah argued against it, but actually she was pleased at his attention. Finally, she said, "Well, I suppose it won't hurt me to be spoiled a little."

"Of course it won't. Come on now. I'm quite an expert on women's fashions. I'll help you pick an outfit."

When they reached the area of the store where women's ready-to-wear was displayed, there was not a great deal of choice. But there were three dresses that Moriah liked.

"I like this one the best," Quaid said. He picked a light blue dress off the rack and said, "This'll look good with that ugly red hair you got. Go try it on."

"My hair's not ugly and it's not red. It's auburn."

"When the sun hits it, I see nothin' but red. Oh, let's pick you out some underwear first."

Moriah snatched the dress away from him, and her face flushed. "I'll pick my own underwear out, thank you!"

Quaid laughed at her. As she went off to change clothes, he wandered over to the case where the pistols were kept. Lifting one out, he studied it. As he waited, he felt good that he had found a way to please Moriah and Ethan.

"You better not eat any more of that, Belle," Sam said. "You already ate what Ma told us to eat."

"Well, one more won't hurt," Belle said.

Ethan had carefully made his candy last, but he reached into the sack and said, "Here. You can have one of mine, Belle."

Belle took the hard candy and popped it into her mouth. "Now, I didn't eat any more of my candy than Ma said. She didn't say nothin' about eatin' Ethan's," she said, giggling.

The four kids were sitting outside the store enjoying the last of their soda pops when two adolescent boys came by. Carl Emery was one of them, and he stopped to stare at Ethan. He was twelve years old, raw-boned with pale hair and brown eyes. His friend Jake was with him, and he winked and said, "Look here, Jake. Look what we got here."

"What is it?" Jake said. "I don't see nothin' but a bunch of snotty-nosed kids."

"Why, you ain't looked close, Jake. Look at that one there. He's a redskin tryin' to pretend that he's white."

Instantly, all four of the youngsters came to their feet.

"You keep your mouth shut, Carl Emery!" Belle said loudly.

"What'll you do if I don't? You gonna whip me?"

"You better watch out, Carl," Jake said. "That girl looks dangerous to me."

Carl ignored Jake. Turning, Carl reached out and knocked Ethan's hat off. "Look at him. Nothing but a filthy redskin."

Ethan said nothing, but his dark eyes seemed to blaze. He'd turned seven years old recently, but he threw himself against the big boy with abandon. Emery had to take two steps backward, but then suddenly he yelled, "Why, you dirty little redskin!" He swung his fist and caught Ethan right in the mouth. Ethan fell to the ground. Before Emery could turn, Belle flew at Carl like a ball of fury, clawing, spitting, and kicking him with all her might. At the same time, Sam joined her. The big boy was rolled over backward by the onslaught. He shouted and tried to shove the youngsters off, but Ethan had joined them now. It was all he could do to protect himself. Every time he threw one off, another was battering at his face.

Les Emery, Carl's father, had approached and had laughed when his son had knocked the boy's hat off. He hated Indians, and so did his brother Jack, who was with him. "Look at that, Les," Jack said. "They're gettin' the best of Carl." Stepping forward, Les grabbed hold of Sam's arm, jerked him off, and thrust him backward. Sam went sprawling, and Les slapped Belle, his blow catching her on the cheek. He started to reach out for Ethan, but a solid blow caught him on the back of the neck. It drove him down, and for a moment he was totally confused. He rolled over to see Quaid Shafter standing over him, his light blue eyes blazing.

"You're pretty rough on kids, Emery. Why don't you try it with a man?"

Jack Emery, a big, burly man, was standing over to Quaid's right. He stepped forward and swung a tremendous right that caught Quaid on the forehead and knocked him down. "Come on, Les. Let's make a believer out of this redskin lover."

Quaid scrambled to his feet in time to ward off the first rush. He dodged a blow by Les Emery, but his brother Jack was a faster man, and he caught another blow right in the mouth that drove him backward against the wall. The two men came at him and began to pummel him with merciless blows.

Moriah had heard the yells and stepped out of the store. She was wearing the new dress and took in the scene at one glance.

"He called Ethan a dirty redskin, Moriah," Belle screamed, "and then they both started punchin' us around!"

Moriah Hardin looked around, and her eyes fell on a barrel just beside the door of the general store filled to capacity with ax handles. Without a moment's hesitation, she stepped forward and plucked one out. She grabbed it, stepped forward, and swung with all her might. The impact of the hickory club against Jack Emery's head made a dull thumping sound. It did not knock the big man down, but he staggered around, and when he turned, his eyes glazed, she hit him right in the face, driving him to the ground.

Les turned to see what was happening, which gave Quaid an opportunity. He stepped away from the wall and brought his right hand with every bit of his weight around it well below the belt buckle of Les Emery. Emery gasped as all his air was knocked out of him. He fell to the ground at once, groaning in pain.

Quaid's face was puffy where he had taken some blows, but he was laughing. "I never knew a woman could brawl so well, Moriah."

"What's goin' on here?"

Quaid turned to see Sheriff Joel Bench, who had come hurrying across the street. Bench was fifty-three, a tough man with white hair and sky blue eyes. He looked down at the two men and said, "What's this ruckus about?"

"They called Ethan a dirty redskin," Belle said. Her eyes were sparkling, and she said, "They tried to whip us, and then they jumped on Quaid. That's when Moriah hit 'em with an ax handle."

Joel Bench had little use for the Emery family. They were shiftless, lawless men who were in and out of jail constantly for drunkenness. He also knew for a fact that both men were wife beaters.

"Put 'em in jail, Sheriff," Sam demanded, jumping up and down.

"They're stupid, Sam," Sheriff Bench said, shrugging his shoulders. "If I arrested all the stupid people around here, we'd have to build a bigger jail."

Moriah was still holding the ax handle, and she was furious at the two for what they had called Ethan. "Sheriff Bench, if there's any charge, you'll know where to find me."

"Won't be no charge, I guarantee you. I might arrest these two for disturbin' the peace."

Moriah turned and walked to the barrel. She put the ax handle back in and said, "Come on, children, we're going home. This town living is not for us."

Sheriff Bench was looking down at the two men. Jack's face was a bloody mess, and his brother was still clutching himself and moaning. "It does me good, Quaid, to see these sinners get their comeuppance."

"I was of a mind to shoot 'em."

"You can't do that. There's a city ordinance against it. Now, you take the lady and these kids out of here. I'll take care of these two."

Quaid enjoyed the scene that took place when he drove the wagon into the ranch. All of the kids jumped out and went running to tell Jerusalem and Clay about the fight. Quaid smiled to himself as he watched Clay listen with interest. After each of the children told a part of what had happened, Clay smiled and said, "Well, I see you done the necessary thing, Moriah."

Moriah, however, said little, and Quaid followed her when she walked away. "What's wrong?" he said.

"You know what's wrong. Every time Ethan gets around other kids, they taunt him horribly. I'm worried about how it makes him feel."

"Why, he's all right. Those two got what they deserved."

"I can't hit every man in the face with an ax handle who makes a remark about Indians."

Quaid reached out and took Moriah by the arm and turned her around. "As long as you're in Texas, there's going to be that kind of trouble. There's mean people in the world, and you can't stop them from opening their big mouths."

"I know. There's nothing I can do about it." Frustration filled her voice, and her shoulders slumped. "It's just something I'll have to live with."

"Marry me, Moriah, and we'll move to Santa Fe. It's different there. I traded there years ago, and the Mexicans don't look down on the Indians like Texans do. Marry me. We'll have a good life there."

Moriah was shocked at his sudden proposal. She looked up into Quaid's eyes. "I . . . can't do that, Quaid."

"Why not?" he asked, puzzled by her quick refusal.

"This is my home. My family's here. I couldn't up and leave them."

"Women have left home and families before. And you need to think of Ethan. It'll be a whole lot easier for him there."

He suddenly reached forward, put his arms around her, and kissed her. He had never done such a thing before. Moriah was taken off-guard, but as his arms tightened around her, she was glad that she had the power to stir this man. She had never gotten over her experience with the Comanches. Being taken and forced to be a squaw to a Comanche war chief and bearing his child had left deep scars in her heart. From the day she had been rescued, she had thought that no white man would ever care for her. Yet as Quaid held her in his arms, she knew that this man did. She felt an impulsiveness in her to put her arms around him. Moriah Hardin was a proud woman, and the force of her emotion in her was deep and strong, but something held her back. She put her hand on his chest, and at once he released her. Faint color stained her cheeks, and she held him with a glance that he could not understand. For a moment something whirled between them, swaying both of them, and the temptation to give in was strong.

"I can't do it. Texas has become my home, and I want Ethan to grow up around his kin even if it's hard on him."

"Do you care for me at all?" Quaid asked simply, gazing into her eyes.

She averted his look, even though her heart longed for a man to love and care for her. Yet the hardness of her ordeal with Bear Killer kept her from trusting. She shook her head and said, "Find yourself another woman."

"Every man sees his own kind of beauty, Moriah," Quaid said. "And I see a beauty in you that makes me want to be with you the rest of my life. Think about what I've said."

Quaid turned and walked away, and Moriah knew she would be troubled by her decision for weeks. Deep down her heart yearned for a man, and Quaid Shafter was strong. He was already like a father to Ethan. And though her family had accepted her back with open arms and love, the years Bear Killer had taken her as his squaw still filled her with a sense of shame. She turned and walked into the house with her shoulders slumped.

CHAPTER
TEN

As the sun sank out of the sky and began to paint the horizon a soft crimson, Clay tilted his chair back, put his feet up on the rail that surrounded the porch, and let the pleasant view of landscape gently soak into him. It was one of his favorite times of day—when the hard work was done, the heat was passing from the earth, and a sense of proprietorship filled him. He had been a wanderer most of his life. The only home he could claim for many years was the place where he would put his bed roll down for the night. But now the Yellow Rose Ranch had taken hold of him in a way he had never dreamed possible. A peaceful contentment came over him as he looked at the cottonwood trees that stood in disorganized ranks like a regiment at ease. They lay their shadows on the ground in long lines, and the sun cast long fingers of crimson light through them, gently touching the earth. The strong, pale light pooled between the trees, and the silence of the afternoon soothed his spirit like a balm.

The darkness came quickly, but even before it wrapped the earth in twilight, a pale streak of light scratched the heavens, and Clay looked up immediately. "Shooting star," he murmured. He turned to look at Jerusalem, who was sitting beside him, her eyes half closed. "Did you see it?"

"Yes. I've always loved seeing shooting stars since I was a little girl. I always made a wish."

Clay grinned, reached out, put his hand on the back of her neck, and squeezed it gently. "Did you make a wish this time?"

"Yes. I always do."

"What was it?"

"I can't tell you."

Clay squeezed her neck again and said, "You have to. You can't keep any secrets from your husband. It's not allowed."

Jerusalem reached back, put her hand over his, and held it. "Mama always told me it wouldn't come true if you told."

"That's if you tell anybody except your husband. Husbands have every right, you know." His hand caressed her neck, and he could smell the fragrance of her hair. She had washed it, and now he inhaled deeply. "You smell lots better than the cowhands do."

Jerusalem laughed and struck him a light blow across the chest. "I should certainly hope so!" she said. She sat there, enjoying his presence by her side. After watching the stars for a while, she said, "I'll tell you what it is, but I think it's sinful."

Clay turned his head quickly to stare at her. "I don't believe it!" he exclaimed. "You're not the kind of woman to have sinful wishes."

"I think this one is." She reached out, took his hand, and held it in her lap, squeezing it between her hands. "I know I'm ungrateful, but I was wishing that we could have a really big ranch."

"The Yellow Rose ain't big enough for you?"

"Oh, we're making a living, although times are tough. But I'd like to be able to leave something behind for all the children and then for the grandchildren. That would take a big place."

"It's early to be thinking about what we're going to leave the kids and the grandkids."

"Life passes by so quick, Clay. Ours is more than half over."

The two sat there quietly, and from far away the distant, mournful cry of a coyote pierced the night. Jerusalem waited until it died away, then turned to face him. In the darkness she traced his strong features and thought again how wonderful it was to have a husband who loved her and cared for her and was not ashamed to say so in front of others. Jake had not been demonstrative in any romantic way. Clay seemed to be totally unaware of how unusual it was for a man to hold his wife's hand wherever they went. He was the only man she knew who had no qualms about showing his affection for her no matter where they were.

Clay caught her glance and grinned. "You know I don't mind bein' a grandpa, but it sure makes me feel funny bein' married to a grandma."

Accustomed to Clay's mild teasing, Jerusalem thought about the children and those to come in the years ahead. "Maybe it was a foolish thought, but I'd like to have a really big place."

"Well, there's plenty of room in Texas."

"I don't want to be greedy. I'm so grateful for a place of our own. I guess it was just a foolish whim of mine."

Clay sat there quietly, his hand wrapped in hers. They were strong hands but feminine. He admired her beauty for a time in the falling darkness and then said, "I didn't mean to say anything to you, but Kyle Morton is selling a big chunk of land."

Instantly, Jerusalem turned to him. "You mean that big tract just to the north of our place?"

"That's it. Devoe Crutchfield was talking about it last week. He said Kyle's sellin' out and goin' to California."

"How many acres is it?" she asked excitedly.

"About fifty thousand."

"Fifty thousand! Why, that's . . . that's *enormous*!"

"It's not bad land. Not as good as some we got, but it's got water. That means a lot in this land, especially when you're raising cattle."

"Fifty thousand acres. It makes my head spin just to think about it."

"Well, there'd be one problem with it. The Comanches think it's theirs. Of course, for as long as they remember it is the land of The People. They might take exception with us pushin' north."

"It's going to come sometime, Clay. Sooner or later the Indians will be pushed back as more people come to Texas."

"It makes me a little sad to think of it. They're losin' everything they got."

Jerusalem did not answer. She was thinking of the land that lay out there. Her mind went far beyond the fifty thousand acres to the plains that stretched up northward. "One day," she whispered, "all of that land will be ranches. There'll be plenty of towns springing up."

Clay felt the pressure of her hand and said, "You really want that place, don't you, Jerusalem?"

"Oh, it's foolish. It would take more money than we could ever get together. We've got about as much chance of buying the moon as we have that land."

"Don't know about that," Clay murmured. "Maybe we ought to pray about it. The Bible says somewhere that if any two of us agree that it'll happen."

The two sat there and watched as the stars spangled themselves in fiery points across the ebony sky. Those distant spots of light seemed to be alive as they twinkled and blinked overhead. Clay was silent for a long while, and then he shook his head. "Sure is a passel of them stars. The Lord did Himself proud when He made 'em all, didn't He?"

"Yes He did," Jerusalem said. "And the Bible says He knows the name of every one of them."

Ethan raised the hammer and then brought it down on the pecan, which he had placed on the upturned flat iron. Bits of shell and tasty morsels of meat flew everywhere, and Jerusalem laughed. "Don't hit it so hard, Ethan. Here. Let me show you." Taking one of the pecans, she held it and struck it sharply with the hammer. Then she rotated it and hit it lightly until the shell fragmented. "Now. You see? You can pull the shell off and pull the nut right out. Here. Taste it."

Ethan took the pecan half that came out whole, popped it in his mouth, and chewed it. His warm, brown eyes glowed. "That's good, Grandma."

"You bet it's good. Came off our own trees too. One thing Texas is good for is good pecans. Now you try it."

Jerusalem had cracked a bucket full of the thin-shelled pecans and watched as Ethan began to break the pecans. She studied his strong features, and her heart warmed toward him. He was a sturdy seven-year-old, and the blood of his Indian father showed in the high cheekbones and the slight coppery tint of his skin. He was no darker, however, than the cowhands that rode for the ranch. In fact, there was a latent handsomeness in the boy that spoke of a fine man to come. He was smart too. She watched as he obeyed her instructions. She smiled as he concentrated on breaking the shell of the pecan and then dropped it into her bucket.

"You know what? I'm going to make a pecan pie just for you, Ethan. You can eat the whole thing if you want to. Make yourself plum sick."

"Really, Grandma?"

"Really. Of course, the other children will be jealous, so I'll have to make them something nice too."

"I'll give them some of my pie."

Jerusalem laughed, leaned forward, and gave his jet black hair a tug. "I knew you would. You're a very generous boy."

Ethan grinned at her, then turned again to the pecans and began breaking more of them. He was serious in a way that most seven-year-olds were not. Sometimes he was almost somber, but at other times his eyes would flash, and he would shout as he entered into the childish games with the other youngsters. She saw some of Moriah in his features, for her daughter's traits had gentled the strong side of Ethan's Comanche father.

"Grandma, did you ever see my father Bear Killer?"

"Once, and only from a distance."

"I wish I could see him."

It was a critical moment for Jerusalem Taliferro. She picked a pecan out of its shell before answering, giving herself time to think of what to say. "Have you ever talked to your mother about him?"

"She won't talk about it. Why is that, Grandma?"

"I think she had a hard time when she was living with the Comanches. They are a fierce people, as I've told you, Ethan. They lead hard lives, and when they capture white people or other Indians, they make life pretty hard for them." She hesitated, then said, "Do you think about your father a lot?"

"Sometimes."

A reticence hung in the boy's tone, and he did not speak until he had finished cracking the pecan. When he looked up there was a strange look on his face. "Will he come again to try and take me away?"

"No. That will never happen again."

"Grandma, is he a bad man?"

"The Comanche ways are different from ours. We do things that they think are bad, and they do things we don't like." She went on for some time, trying to explain to Ethan the difference between the two races. He studied her carefully as she talked, and there was a poignant light in his brown eyes. Jerusalem finally said, "One thing about the Comanches that I hope you get from your father is his courage."

"Are they afraid of anything?" Ethan asked.

"If they are, I guess nobody ever found out about it," Jerusalem said. "So you'll have your father's courage and your mother's gentleness. That'll be a good combination."

Suddenly, Ethan dropped the hammer on the floor and stood up. "Somebody's coming."

"I don't hear anything," Jerusalem said. She knew the boy's hearing was acute. Clay said once the boy could hear an owl hoot all the way from New Orleans. She got up, however, and went to the window. "I don't see anything."

"They're coming. It's a wagon. I hear it." Ethan ran to the door, and Jerusalem followed him. They stepped out into the warm morning sunlight, and Ethan said, "There. It's comin' around the bend through the trees."

Jerusalem saw them and heard the faint sound of the wagon wheels turning. "There are two Indians with them, Grandma."

"I see them."

The sight of Indians was not disturbing, for she knew that when they came like this there was no danger. The real danger was when they would appear suddenly without warning. These two, however, rode in front of a wagon that she recognized at once.

"It's Mr. Nightingale," she said. "You remember him?"

"No, ma'am."

"Well, of course you don't," Jerusalem said. "You've only seen him once, I think." The two stood waiting as the wagon made its way toward the ranch. This wagon was unlike any that she was likely to see in these parts. It was the same wagon that Fergus St. John Nightingale had been driving when she and the others had met him when they left Arkansas for

Texas. Clay and Brodie had saved the Englishman from a slow death by torture inflicted by a band of Kiowa Indians, and he had become a close friend. She smiled as the wagon pulled up to a stop and the tall, lanky Englishman climbed down and walked over to her. He was wearing clothing that no Texan would be found dead in. His attire would have been most acceptable at a high-society ball in London. He was very careful about his clothes, this Englishman, and he lifted his stovepipe hat, probably the only one in Texas, and swept it in front of him in a grandiose bow.

"Well, my dear Jerusalem, we have the pleasure of meeting again."

"How are you, Fergus?"

"Better than one might expect at my advanced age. I hope we are not inconveniencing you, but can you put some travelers up for the night?"

"You know we can. You're always welcome here, Fergus. Take your horses over to the corral and have one of the hands stable them and give them a good feed."

Fergus swept his arm and said something in the Comanche language, then he turned, and the two Indians slid off their horses. "I want you to meet two good friends of mine. This is Fox," he said, indicating a tall, lanky Indian. "And this is One Eye." He was a short, muscular man with one eye. Fox was staring at Ethan and seemed fascinated by the boy. He spoke in Comanche, and Ethan, who had grown up learning the Comanche language, responded instantly.

"Who is your father?" Fox asked.

Ethan glanced at his grandmother, then said, "Bear Killer."

"Ho!" Fox said, and the two exchanged a glance with One Eye. "I was in his camp for a while, but your father ran me off."

"Why did he do that?" Ethan said, fascinated by the two Indians.

"I was too good-looking. All the squaws were after me."

One Eye laughed, showing a large gap, where two teeth were missing. His one eye was half-closed and had a milky look to it. "He's lying. Bear Killer ran him off because he was lazy." He shrugged and said, "Me too."

"These are my assistants. They're teaching me the ways of the Comanche," Fergus said. "Deuced hard language to learn, I must say."

"Ethan, why don't you go down with Fox and One Eye and give their horses a feed."

"Yes, ma'am."

Ethan went at once with the two Indians, and Jerusalem listened as the two spoke to Ethan in Comanche. She looked at the wagon and said, "James, you look dusty and hungry."

James Langley was almost forty, a chubby bald man with sad, brown eyes. He was Fergus Nightingale's manservant and took care of the professor's clothing and cooked the English meals Fergus was so fond of.

"Yes, ma'am, I suppose I am, but those are occupational hazards in Texas—hunger and dust."

"You wait 'til supper, I'll fill you up with plenty of good home cooking. Go take care of the team, and I'll fix you a snake that'll hold you until suppertime. Come on in, Fergus. I want to hear what you've been doing. I'm sure you have some interesting stories to tell."

"Yes, ma'am, that I do."

Fergus was sitting at the large table talking to Clay. The kitchen was crowded, for the supper was almost ready. The smell of roasted meat and vegetables and strong coffee made an agreeable aroma in the air. Clay looked over at Fergus and said, "Well, how have you done with that book you're writing about the Comanches?"

"Oh, it goes . . . it goes. It's slow progress, and I don't know if I'll ever finish that book. I've got to go back to England. That will be an interruption to my work."

"Back to England!" Clay said, startled. "Why are you doing that?"

"I got word that my brother has died."

"Oh, I'm sorry to hear that. Were the two of you close?"

"No. We didn't get along too well over the years. Still, he was a good fella."

"I suppose you have to go back and take care of family business."

"Yes! Now I've got the title."

"The title?" Clay said.

"Oh yes. I'm now officially the Earl of Minton. It sounds important, doesn't it?"

"What do we call you? Your Lordship?"

"You will call me Fergus as you always have," he said. "Unfortunately, I have to leave here soon. I won't stay long, though. As soon as I get the family matters settled, I'll be on the first ship back."

"I have a favor to ask, Clay," Fergus said.

"You name it."

"I'd like to leave my wagon and my horses here until I come back. It'll probably be six months."

"No problem. What about those two?" Clay motioned toward Fox and One Eye, who were sitting on the floor with Ethan. "They going back to their tribe?"

"No. They're going with me. They want to go across the big water, as they call it."

"They ought to make quite a splash in England."

"I suppose so," Fergus said idly. He shook his head and then said, "I hate to go, but a man must take care of his family matters."

"I say. You two seem a little depressed." Fergus stared across the table at Clay and Jerusalem. "Not something wrong, is there?"

The three had sat up late talking about all the experiences they had shared since they first met. Now Fergus leaned forward and said, "Not like you two to be so downhearted."

"Oh, it's nothing really," Jerusalem said quickly. She picked up the coffee mug, sipped at the black coffee, and then put it down. "Nothing to trouble you about."

"Why, of course, it is. What are friends for but to share trouble?" Fergus grinned. He was rather a horse-faced individual, homely but with bright blue eyes and a courage that would put most men to shame. No other white man, except a few traders, had made themselves friends with the Comanches. Fergus Nightingale had gone blundering in as if for a stroll in a park in England. The miracle was that the Comanches had not roasted him over a slow fire.

"Come, now. What's going on with you two?"

"Oh, it's just there's a piece of land that we'd like to buy," Clay said, "but it's just a dream. It's too big for us to handle."

"How much land?"

"Fifty thousand acres. It's just north of here," Clay murmured. "Good land, too, with water. Someday when the Comanches are gone, it'll be a great ranch."

"And you two want to buy it?"

"Oh, it's just my own foolishness," Jerusalem said quickly. "I should never have mentioned it to Clay. It'll be a long time before there'll be peace with the Indians. Besides, we don't know which way things will go with this new state of ours."

Fergus Nightingale pulled out a cigar, smelled it, and bit the end off, then produced a kitchen match. He struck it on the sole of his boot and lit up. When the purple smoke was rising in the air, he said mildly, "This is a new land, friends. England is on the way down. The day of empires is long gone, I fear. The future lies here with America."

"You really think so, Fergus?" Clay asked.

"Yes, I do. Nations have their day. They rise and they fall. England is falling. America is rising. I think it will be the greatest nation the world has ever seen. If I had my way, I'd sell out everything in England and move here."

"Build you a castle on the Brazos River," Clay said, smiling.

"Something like that. Tell me more about this land. It sounds promising."

For a long time Clay and Jerusalem talked, growing more excited about the idea of enlarging the Yellow Rose Ranch. Finally, Clay laughed and slapped his thigh. "Jerusalem, you do get a fellow into wild, outlandish notions. Gettin' that land and makin' it into a ranch would be harder than puttin' socks on a rooster!"

Fergus laughed. "I never tried such a thing as that, but I think it's time for you to buy the land."

Both Clay and Jerusalem stared at him. "Why, it would cost a fortune!"

"How much?" Fergus asked abruptly. When Clay gave him the price, he said, "You must buy the land. I'll deposit a check to your account tomorrow at the bank for the price."

"Why, we can't let you do that!" Jerusalem protested, but her eyes danced with excitement, and her lips were parted with wonder. "It's too big a risk."

"I came to this place to take risks," Fergus Nightingale said. "I can't think of two other people I'd rather take a risk with. I'll be a silent partner. You'll do all the work, and I'll watch as you build the Yellow Rose into the greatest ranch in Texas!"

CHAPTER
ELEVEN

I declare, wife. This coffee's so strong it'll walk across the room and climb into your cup!"

Jerusalem looked up with surprise. She was sitting across the table from Clay, and the table was littered with papers, bills, notices, and notes of all kinds. She studied her husband for a moment, knowing that he hated bookwork worse than he hated sickness. A sharp reply jumped to her lips, but she bit it off. She knew full well what was wrong with Clay. It had been a full year since they had bought the new land with the money Fergus and loaned them. Every month at the same time he got ornery when the payment at the bank came due.

"I'll make some fresh," she said.

"Oh, it don't make no nevermind," Clay said. He looked at the papers scattered out over the table. As always, when the two of them sat down to try to wade through the bills and make the payments necessary to keep the ranch together, he grew despondent. He reached out, picked up a piece of paper, looked at it, and then shook his head. "I thought we was poor when I was growin' up," he said sadly. "We was so poor the wolf wouldn't even stop at our door, but trying to run a ranch this size with all the bills is worse."

Jerusalem got up and walked around the table. She came and stood behind Clay and, leaning forward, put her arms around him. "I know it's been hard this last year," she whispered, "but just think what we'll have one day. Please don't be discouraged. I hate to think that I've become a burden to you."

Clay turned his head and pulled her around and gave her a kiss, then laughed. "Why, don't pay no attention to me, wife. We're gonna be all right. This old Yellow Rose Ranch is gonna be safe as granny's snuff box."

Jerusalem laughed and gave him a hug. She picked up the coffee cup, went over, and poured it full, noting that the coffee was not as bad as he had said. She stopped to put three heaping spoonfuls of sugar in his coffee and then poured in some rich cream. After stirring it, she set the cup before him and smiled. "I think you just drink coffee to get the sugar and cream."

"Well, aside from you, that's the only sweet thing I got around here— except for the kids, of course."

For the next half hour, the two of them talked about how they were going to handle the bills. At one point Clay remarked, "The Mexicans took a bunch of our cows. I'm gonna take a bunch of the boys down and steal 'em back one of these days."

"With all that has to be done around here, you don't have time for that," Jerusalem said.

"You're right about that. Some days I don't know how it'll all get done, but somehow it does. The Lord has been looking out for us, Jerusalem. But I'm thinking we're gonna have to sell off some cattle to make ends meet this month. I've been thinkin' about takin' a drive to New Orleans."

"I don't want you going, Clay."

Clay looked up with surprise, and then a smile tugged at the corners of his lips. "It is downright aggravatin' to have a wife so in love with me! You don't want me to get ten feet away from you."

"That's right. I've been thinking about it, and I believe we ought to put Clinton in charge of taking the herd to market."

"He might preach 'em to death on the way down to Louisiana."

"He's been a good hand, hasn't he?"

"Real good. I think you're right. We'll try to get the herd off within a few days." He looked at the bills and shook his head. "We need the money pretty bad."

June had brought with it heat and dust and flies, but that was Texas, and neither Clinton nor Quaid seemed to pay any attention to it. They were trailing a group of longhorns that had wandered off and now appeared to be docile as they grazed on the prairie grass. It was a state that was not natural to the critters, for Texas longhorns had tempers that could flare up with the slightest provocation. Many a rider had learned a hard lesson at the end of those sweeping horns.

From time to time one of the two would spur his horse and drive one of the steers back in the general direction of the ranch. For the most part, it was an easy job, unless something spooked the herd and caused a stampede.

The two made a good team because they both loved working with cattle, and over the years, they had become quite experienced. Clinton loved to talk, and as a rule, Quaid didn't mind listening to the young man. This time Clinton was rattling on about his beliefs about the end times.

"Quaid, I've been givin' a lot of thought about this business of the antichrist."

"Who's he?"

"You don't know who the antichrist is?"

"I don't reckon so," Quaid said as he sat high in the saddle.

"Well, that just shows how ignorant you are, Quaid. If you would read your Bible, you would know more about him. The antichrist," he proclaimed, "is gonna be the one to take over the world in the end times just before Jesus returns for all His followers. He's just what his name sounds like. He's against Jesus, the church, and everything that's good."

"And you've got it all figured out who he is, I suppose," Quaid said.

"Why, of course I have! I've been studyin' on it for a long time," Clinton said loudly, "and I know who it's gonna be."

Quaid could not help smiling. He was well aware that Clinton's notions about certain parts of the Bible would change like the phases of the moon. "Well, who is it?" Quaid asked.

"It's Santa Anna! I thought everyone knowed that."

Quaid laughed aloud and shook his head in mock despair. "Santa Anna? You think he's the antichrist?"

"Why, I'm plum shore of it! No question about it. It's him, all right."

"He was finished at the Battle of San Jacinto."

"No, he wasn't. He came back, and they made him president of Mexico. First thing you know, he'll take over the world."

"He couldn't take over San Antone."

Clinton launched into a long and involved discussion of the Scripture, and Quaid let it go over his head. He had learned to simply put his mind in neutral while Clinton babbled on with one of his doctrinal morasses. Finally, without a break, as was habitual with Clinton, he changed the subject for no apparent reason.

"Why don't you marry Moriah, Quaid?"

Quaid was taken aback by this unexpected question. He turned to look at Clinton and shrugged his shoulders. "She won't have me."

"Why not?"

"Who knows why a woman does something or doesn't do anything?"

"Well, she's got to have a reason. She needs a husband. And Ethan needs a father."

"I think she's afraid of what could happen to Ethan."

"Like what?"

"She's afraid that Bear Killer's coming to get him."

Clinton suddenly pulled his horse out and drove a pair of steers back into line. When he came back, his face was solemn, and he said soberly, "Maybe we ought to get him."

"Get who?"

"Why, him—Bear Killer."

"What do you mean 'get him'?"

"I mean shoot him. That way he wouldn't come back and try to take Ethan away from us."

"I thought that was against your religion, killing folks."

"Well, I haven't got that quite figured out yet, at least as far as the

Comanches are concerned. Especially the mean ones like Bear Killer. Maybe we could just convert him."

Quaid turned and stared at Clinton. A sober thought clouded his eyes, and he shook his head. "That ain't likely, Clinton."

"Come on in the house, Clinton. We need to talk."

Clinton and Quaid had arrived after settling the cattle in with the rest of the herd. Clay had been waiting on the front porch, and when Clinton approached, he said, "Did you get a bunch of strays?"

"About thirty. Shore is dusty and hot out there."

"Come on inside. We've got business to talk about, Clint."

The two men walked into the room that had been made into a study, and Clay turned at once and said, "Clint, we're going to have to have some money soon. I want you to take three hundred head to New Orleans and sell 'em for a good price."

"Why, sure, Clay!" Clinton brightened up. "You mean I'm to be the boss?"

"You're the boss. You think you can handle it?"

"Handle it! Why, them cattle buyers won't know what hit 'em. They won't have a dime left to buy a beer after I get through dickerin' prices with them."

Clay's face assumed a mock solemnity. "You've got to do something about this lack of confidence you've got, Clinton. Now, you pick some good hands and be careful on the way home with the money."

"Why, shore, Clay. It'll be a cake walk."

"I want you to leave in the morning and get back as soon as you can. Like I say, we need the money to pay the loan at the bank."

Except for Oney Pierson's cooking, the drive to New Orleans had gone fairly well. They did not encounter any marauding Mexicans or Indians along the way. Fortunately, no threatening storms had blown up. Clay had warned Clinton not to try a river crossing if a storm came up suddenly. Flash floods could come without warning in this part of Texas. Clay had told him of a time when a part of a herd had been caught in a flash flood, and all of them had drowned. Fortunately, they had lost no stock along the way. The rivers had been low, so the crossings had been easy.

Clinton had picked a good bunch of cowhands to help him drive the herd to New Orleans. The only regret he had was asking Oney Pierson to be the cook on the trail. Oney was so anxious to go on the drive that he had made the claim to have been a cook for Andrew Jackson at one time. Oney was a small, grizzled man of fifty, and his claim that he was a good cook was now in serious doubts by all the hands.

"He ain't never cooked for Andrew Jackson," O. M. Posey declared with disgust one day. "Jackson would never have lived through the cooking Oney puts out. Why, it ain't even fit for an ornery mule to eat."

"You got a point there," Ike McClellan said as he stuck a plug of chewing tobacco in his mouth. The two were riding along just outside of New Orleans and were sick of Oney's cooking. "I'd rather eat raw food as eat any more of that man's cookin'."

"Why don't you offer to do it for him?" Posey asked.

"'Cause I can't cook, and neither can you, but I'm gonna fill up my saddlebags before we leave New Orleans. Take some grub along with me that's fit to eat. Otherwise, I'll be as skinny as a fence post by the time we get back."

Clinton had ridden up as the two men were talking and turned to point. "Well, there's New Orleans over there." The two riders looked to the outline of New Orleans.

Posey nodded with satisfaction and said, "I'm gonna eat in a hotel and go out on the town tonight."

"When do we get paid?" Ike asked.

"I'm afraid to give you fellas any money. You'll spend it foolishly and won't have any to take back with you."

"Not me," Ike said. "I'm gonna invest it wisely in wine, women, and song."

"That's what I'm afraid of," Clinton said sternly. "I want you men to behave yourselves."

Clinton rode away, and Posey shook his head. "That'd be a fine young fella if he wasn't so religious—and so loud about it."

Clinton came away from the meeting with the cattle buyers feeling quite satisfied. He had made what he considered a good deal. As soon as he finished his business, he went straight to the bank and cashed the draft for the cattle he had just sold. He put the cash in a canvas bag but took out enough to pay off the hands. They were waiting for him when he got back to where they were staying, and he distributed the money along with words of wisdom.

"Now, you fellas stay away from these bad women here in New Orleans. You know what the Scripture says, 'None that go unto her return again, neither take they hold of the paths of life.' That's what the Bible says."

All the crew tried to assume a solemn expression as Clinton continued to lecture them. They were anxious to get away from Clinton, and Posey declared firmly, "I reckon I'll go down to the library and read a book."

"I'll go with you." Ike winked. "Maybe we can find a book of John Wesley's sermons."

Clinton saw that they were making fun of him and shook his head. "You fellas better pay attention to what I tell you." He turned and walked away, ignoring the laughs from the crew. He did turn and see them head for the nearest saloon and muttered, "Keep 'em out of it."

Before Clinton could even return to his hotel for a good, hot meal, Oney found the saloon. No sooner had he entered he spotted a poker game. Going over he sat down with some rough characters and started playing. It wasn't long before he got heated and accused one of them of cheating. A fight broke out, and Oney shot a dentist in the leg, who happened to be the nephew of the mayor of New Orleans. By the end of the day, Oney found himself behind bars, facing a month in the jail.

"Why didn't you fellas look out for him?" Clinton demanded when the crew told him the next morning what had happened.

"Well, all he did was shoot a dentist," Ike grumbled. "The man looked to be cheating, and I saw him reach for his gun first," Ike said. "Would've been self-defense if Oney had killed him." His eyes were red, and his clothes looked like he had slept in them. O. M. Posey was not much better, and Johnny Bench gave evidence of a mean hangover.

"It wasn't our fault," Bench said. "You can't blame it on us."

"Well, looks like you can do without a cook on the way home."

"Good!" Ike said. "We'll do better off with cookin' our own grub. Oney never could cook for sour apples."

"I'm leavin' right now," Clinton declared. "Clay needs this money. I'm gonna make a quick ride of it back home."

None of the crew argued with him as Clinton mounted his horse. He took one look at the bedraggled crew. "The whole lot of you is a sorry sight," he said indignantly. "I warned you not to go drinking. Drinking in saloons and chasing women will only lead you away from the path of life." Shaking his head, he spurred his horse and rode off.

As he disappeared, Ike shook his head. "I feel so bad I think I'd better go get another drink."

The other two agreed, and the three punchers made their way back to the saloon.

"What are we gonna do?" Posey muttered.

Ike McClellan shook his head. "We're going to get drunk again—and do I dread it!"

CHAPTER
TWELVE

Clinton stared morbidly at the carcass of the jackrabbit he had dressed and impaled on a stick. The small mesquite fire sent up tendrils of smoke that burned his eyes and then rose higher into the air to dissipate. Taking out his pocketknife, he opened it and sliced a strip of the meat free and then put it in his mouth and began to chew vigorously. "Might as well eat saddle harness," he muttered but continued eating his meager meal. Finally, he gave up and threw the remains of the rabbit over his shoulder. "I doubt if even the coyotes will eat you."

The sun was midway down in the sky, and the July heat poured itself over the land. He leaned back against the trunk of a mesquite tree and watched idly as his horse clomped at the scrawny grass. "It'd probably take five acres of this sorry ground to raise one steer." The sound of his voice sounded loud in the silence. After a while he lay back and put his hat over his face and went to sleep. He was awakened some time later by the sound of hoofbeats. He quickly shoved his hat back and got to his feet. A man had to be careful when traveling alone, for danger lurked everywhere in Texas these days. He brushed his hand against the Colt he wore at his right side. As he looked out over the plains, he saw a single rider astride a lanky, blue-nosed mule coming toward him.

Clinton's eyes narrowed as he studied the rider. As the mule got closer, Clinton saw that it was a woman with red hair done up in pigtails that hung down her back. When she pulled the mule up and slid off of it, he noted that she was wearing a pair of man's britches and a man's shirt that seemed a little too small. Her eyes were green, and she was studying him in a calm way.

"Howdy, ma'am," Clinton said. "Surprised to see you out here."

The woman stood there holding the mule by a braided bridle, obviously handmade. Suddenly, the mule edged forward and bared his teeth, intending to bite her. Clinton yelled a warning, and the young woman turned around and hit the mule in the nose with a tremendous blow with her fist. She also called him a name that Clinton had never heard from a woman's lips before.

She turned back to face him but kept an eye on the mule, who was wild-eyed and rolling his eyes, obviously waiting for another chance. "Don't mind Judas here," she said. "He's meaner than a skillet full of rattlesnakes." Then without a pause she said, "My name's Maggie Brennan."

Clinton pulled off his hat. "Pleased to know you, Miss Brennan. I'm Clinton Hardin." She was a tall, young woman with the summer sun laying an even creamy tan over her face. Aside from her outlandish garb, she was rather attractive. She had a squarish face, a wide, generous mouth, and her eyes were well shaped and very direct. "Like I said—didn't expect to see a lady out here. Are you lost?"

A look of disdain crossed Maggie Brennan's face. "No, I ain't lost!" she said. "I ain't never been lost a day in my life!"

"Why, I ain't neither," Clinton said, "although I did get sort of confused for a couple of days once up in the north country." He was still considering the profanity that had escaped from her lips and couldn't figure out what kind of a woman she was. She didn't have the look of a saloon woman. He knew that well enough—a hard, brazen look that couldn't be mistaken. The cussing just didn't seem to go with the face.

"I'm lookin' for a doctor."

"A doctor?" Clinton said in surprise. "Well, ma'am, there ain't no doctor here closer than New Orleans or maybe San Antone—that I know of anyway. Are you sick?"

A look of disappointment swept across Maggie Brennan's face. "No. It's not me, but there's a feller in camp. I think he's about ready to die."

"Did a hoss pile him up?"

The young woman swept off her low-crowned black hat, and the sun brought out the reddish tint of her hair. "Me and my pa, we left Missouri headed for San Antone through freight wagons. That's what Pa does. He's a freighter . . . and me, too, I reckon."

"That's a mighty long trip all the way from Missouri."

"Sure is. But we would have made it, though."

"What kind of freight you haulin'?"

"General merchandise. Pa and me always been freighters. That's all we've ever done."

"And who's sick? Is it your pa?"

Maggie Brennan chewed her lower lip and looked down at the earth. For the first time she showed some hesitancy. Finally, she lifted her face, and he saw that her jaw was tense, and her eyes were cloudy with some sort of trouble.

"We're haulin' two people with us. A man and his sister. Charles Campbell. His sister's named Rose Jean Campbell. He's some kind of preacher, I think."

"And you were haulin' them to Texas?"

"They said they're goin' to preach to the Indians out there. The woman, she's a preacher, too, I reckon."

Clinton waited for her to go on, and when she didn't, he said, "Was it one of them that got sick?"

"Yes. It was the woman first. She took bad sick. Cholera, I reckon, it was. And then just when she started gettin' better, her brother and my pa both got sick."

"Well, I reckon we'd better get a doctor. I can ride back—"

"I think it'd be too late." She wiped her arm across her eyes, and her voice was thick when she said, "Pa—he died the day before yesterday."

"Why, I'm right sorry to hear that, miss."

"I buried him myself. The other man was real sick, and the woman, too, but they had a service. They said some real kind words over Pa." She blinked fiercely and said, "But the man, he's likely to die too. I don't know what to do."

"Let me saddle up and I'll go with you."

"You might take the cholera," Maggie warned.

"No, I won't. God will take care of me."

Maggie Brennan stared at him, her green eyes filled with grief. "That's what them preachers said, but it didn't seem like He cared enough to take care of Pa."

As Clinton rode into the camp beside Maggie, his eyes swept the mules that were hobbled and tied out on a line that stretched between two sturdy cottonwood trees. The two wagons with the canvas over the hoops were on either side of a fire that had been built but was now dying. A woman had stood up to greet them, and Maggie said, "That's the preacher lady."

Clinton stepped out of the saddle and took the lines of the horse, and Maggie slid off the mule. The mule tried to bite her again. She cussed him and kicked him in the belly and then struck him in the nose. "Let me hobble this ornery mule. This here's Rose Jean Campbell. This here's Clinton Hardin."

She left without another word, and Clinton held his hat in both hands, turning it by the brim. "I'm right sorry to hear about your trouble, ma'am," he said.

The woman regarded him steadfastly. She was a small woman, and her blue eyes were the same color as the azure sky above. She had a wealth of brown hair that was tied back in a bun, and she had a slightly sunburned pale complexion.

"Thank you, sir," she said. "You can call me Sister Rose. You say your name is Hardin?"

"Yes, ma'am, but everybody just calls me Clinton. How's your brother? I hear he's doin' poorly."

"He's going to be with the Lord very soon," she said matter-of-factly.

The words struck Clinton with a force that caused him to blink his eyes and robbed him of words for a moment. "Maybe not, ma'am. People get over cholera."

"God's already told Charles that He's taking him home."

Rose Jean Campbell had a calmness both in her face and in her voice. She stood facing Clinton straight as an arrow, her hands folded in front of her. She was wearing a light blue dress that matched the color of her eyes and a pair of black leather boots laced up past the ankle. She wore a small white cap such as Clinton had never seen before. Somehow she seemed out of place in this Texas plain country. It seemed to Clinton she would have fit more easily in a drawing room in a big house in St. Louis. He noticed that she had a lilting accent. "You say you come from Missouri, ma'am?"

"My brother and I were born in Scotland, but my parents left there when we were very young. I suppose I still have a little of the accent."

Clinton shifted his feet and said, "I'd better go ride for a doctor. Maybe you're wrong about your brother. He might live if he had a doctor."

"No. He's going to be with the Lord, but you were kind to come. He said he'd like to see you before he dies."

Her blunt words startled him. "See me? What does that mean? He couldn't see me ride in, could he?"

"He's been saying that God was going to send someone to him, and I think it has to be you, Mr. Hardin."

"Just Clinton, ma'am. Well, I'd be proud to talk to him if that's what he wants."

"He's on the other side of the wagon. It's so hot in there we put a tarp out so he could catch some shade."

Clinton followed the woman around one of the wagons, and there on the shady side he saw a tarp stretched out. He watched as the woman stooped and whispered, "Charles, God has sent the man He promised." She straightened up and said, "He's awake. You'd best be quick."

Clinton leaned over and saw a small man lying on a piece of canvas. When Clinton saw how pale his face was from the cholera, he remembered Rose's words about her brother going home to be with the Lord.

"Howdy. My name's Clinton Hardin. Sorry to find you in such poor shape."

Charles Campbell was a small man with a pale, thin face. He looked a great deal like his sister, with a straight nose and the same sky blue eyes. His face was emaciated, and his lips were cracked.

"Can I get you something?" Clinton asked.

Charles Campbell's voice was weak, and he said, "Come closer, please." Clinton got down on his knees. "Not much time left. God has sent you to me."

"What can I do for you, Reverend?" Clinton asked.

"I prayed for God to send someone to look out for my sister after I'm gone, and He has answered my prayers. He sent you."

"Why, sure, Reverend," Clinton said. "I'll be glad to take care of her."

"You give me your promise on that?"

"Yes, I do," Clinton said solemnly.

"Are you a Christian man?"

"I sure am, Reverend, and I give you my word. I'll do my very best for your sister just like she was my own sister."

"That's . . . that's kind of you," Charles said, laboring to breathe.

He lay still and closed his eyes, and Clinton did not know for sure if he was still breathing. But he saw that the man's chest was rising slowly and falling. Finally, his eyes opened, and the cracked lips turned up in a slight smile.

"Things don't always turn out like we plan," Charles said.

"That's right. They don't."

"My sister and I felt the call of God to go preach to the Indians. I thought that's what I'd do, but it looks like I'll be going to be with Jesus."

Clinton hardly knew what to say. He had never seen anyone actually die before, and he was impressed by how calm the man seemed to be in the face of death. "He knows best. The Scripture says no man knoweth the day nor the hour of his death."

"That's right," Charles said. "I'm glad you're a Christian man. My sister's a strong woman, but this is a hard country for a single woman."

"You want me to take her back to Missouri?"

Charles Campbell did not answer, for he was slipping away. His eyes fluttered and closed, and his breathing grew even more shallow. Clinton moved out from under the tarp, stood up, and walked quickly around the wagon. "Sister Rose! Your brother, you'd better see to him." He stood still and watched as the woman moved quickly under the tarp. He could hear her voice but could not make out the final words she was saying to her brother. He turned and walked away, putting his hat back on his head. He saw that Maggie had hobbled the mule and now was standing beside his horse.

"Your horse didn't run away," she said.

"No, ma'am. He's trained to stand where I drop the reins." He looked back at the tarp and shook his head. "That preacher's not going to make it."

"No. He ain't."

"He seemed like a right nice fella."

"For a preacher, I guess he is."

"You don't like preachers?"

"Don't know much about 'em. I reckon they're just like all other men." She turned and pointed a ways from the wagons. "I dug Pa's grave over there. See? I reckon we'll bury this fellow right beside him." She turned and looked at Clinton. She was not as tall as he, but she had to lift her head slightly to look up at him. "Be kind of peculiar, a preacher and a sinner being buried side by side."

Clinton stood there, not knowing what to say, and finally the woman said thoughtfully, "The preacher was so sick he could hardly stand up. His sister had to hold him, but he come and stood over Pa's grave to pay his respects. I thought that was right nice of him. His sister, she sung a really pretty song. A church song, I reckon, and the preacher, he read from his Book and said some good words over Pa."

"That was kind of him," Clinton said.

"I reckon he's a brave man."

"If he was going to preach to the Indians, he is. It's a shame he's not gonna get to do what he had his heart set on."

"You hungry?" she asked.

"As a matter of fact I am. All I had all day was a skinny piece of a jackrabbit. It was so tough I couldn't finish it."

"Come on. I got some stew on. It ort to be ready by now."

Clinton tied his horse to the line along the mules, then went over to the fire and sat down. Maggie filled a tin bowl with stew, gave him a spoon, and said, "I call this my varmint stew."

"Why you call it that?" Clinton grinned.

"Because I put in it all the varmints I shoot."

Clinton took the stew and said, "Well, Lord, I'm grateful for varmint stew." He tasted it and said, "Why, this is plum good, Maggie!"

"I'm a good cook," the woman said simply.

"I remember I had a fit once when I was just a kid. We was goin' through some hard times. Food was scarce, and my ma made a stew. She put some snake in it. I thought we'd all go to perdition for eatin' snakes. I was sure it was that evil snake got us all into that mess."

"How'd a snake get us into it?"

"Like the Bible says. A snake tempted Eve."

"Eve who?"

"Ain't you never read the Bible?"

"No. I've been to preachin' once or twice, but I guess it didn't take."

Clinton ate the stew hungrily and was finishing his second bowl when the woman suddenly appeared from behind the wagon. He rose to his feet and waited for her to speak. Her face was smooth and her eyes were clear. He was surprised at the peace he saw in her countenance.

"My brother just died," she said. "He's with the Lord now."

"Right sorry to hear that, ma'am."

Maggie watched the woman for a moment, then said, "I reckon as how, if you'd like, we'd bury him there beside my pa."

"Yes. That would be most kind of you."

"I'll go dig the grave."

"No," Clinton said. "Just give me a shovel. I'll dig the grave."

The offer seemed to surprise the woman. "I can do it well enough."

"I know you could, but I need a little exercise." She turned, walked to the wagon, pulled out a spade and handed it to him. As she turned and walked away, Clinton began to dig a grave beside the one where Maggie's pa was buried. As he worked, he thought about what Maggie had said earlier, that a sinner and a preacher would be side by side.

I hope Maggie's father knew the Lord, he thought and then began to make the dirt fly.

The service did not last long. They had wrapped the body of Charles Campbell in a blanket, and Clinton had filled in the grave. When he was done, Rose Jean came with her Bible in her hands. She took her stand at the foot of the grave and bowed for a moment of silence. Then she opened it and began to read in a strong, clear voice. She read from the fifteenth chapter of the first book of Corinthians. Clinton knew it almost by heart. The words were very familiar to him, but he saw that Maggie recognized none of them. He turned his eyes on the face of the young woman who read and thought of how attractive she was. He thought to himself, *I couldn't be that calm if one of my folks had just died and I was buryin' them out here on this prairie.*

The woman continued reading from the Bible she held. "But now is Christ risen from the dead, and become the first fruits of them that slept. For as in Adam all die, even so in Christ shall all be made alive." She read on for a long time, and finally she bowed her head, and immediately Clinton did the same, although he had time to glimpse at Maggie, who made no attempt to do so.

"Our Father and our God, You have taken Your servant Charles to Yourself. I thank You for the life that he led, for his salvation, and that he is now with You forever in joy and peace. I pray, O God, that You would give me comfort, for I cannot help but feel the loss of one so dear. But I know that he is happy with You, and one day I will be with You and with him and with all the saints of God forever."

The prayer was not long, but it was spoken in a strong voice until the very last. Clinton thought he heard it break a little bit when she pronounced the words, "And now may the grace of the Lord Jesus Christ be with us all. Amen."

Clinton waited until night fell before he spoke to Rose Jean. He kept waiting for her to weep, to show some sign of grief, but the only indication of her loss was in her eyes, which she kept turned down. He knew that he had to say something of comfort, so he went to her and said, "Sister Rose?"

"Yes?"

"Your brother asked me to take care of you before he died."

"I know he was worried about me, but I'll be fine."

"Well, you're way out here in the middle of the plains with no kin to look after you."

Rose looked at him steadily, as if trying to read his intentions, and then he said, "I'll take you back to Missouri if that's what you want."

"No. I have no intention of going back there."

Her words were definite, sharp, and clear. "But you don't want to go on to the Indians now, do you?"

"Yes, Mr. Hardin. That's exactly what I'm going to do." She straightened up, and although there was a slight tremor in her lips, her voice was clear. "God called me and my brother to take the gospel to the Indians. He's gone now, but I'm going to do it."

Clinton started to speak but then cut his words off. He knew the dangers of an attractive white woman trying to preach the gospel to the Comanches. His sister Moriah had been kidnapped and held hostage for a number of years by the Comanches. He said nothing about that, however, and said, "If you want to go to San Antone, you can go with me. I expect Maggie will want to take these wagons on through. You could stay with us for a while. As a matter of fact, my sister speaks the Comanche tongue. You might learn a little from her."

Instantly, Rose said, "That would be fine. Why, thank you, Clinton. That's very kind of you."

"I'll see if Maggie's going on," Clinton said. He turned and walked across to the tall young woman and said, "Miss Maggie, do you intend to take these wagons on through?"

"I sure do. That's what we set out to do, me and Pa, and I won't let him down."

"Well, I'll drive one of them for you, if you'd like. Our place isn't far from San Antone, if that'll suit you. You could spend some time there with us. My kin would be glad to have you."

"That'll suit me fine. I reckon we'll be ready to leave by sunup in the morning."

CHAPTER
THIRTEEN

The journey back to the Yellow Rose Ranch was a strange one for Clinton Hardin. There could hardly have been two more different women on the face of the planet than Rose Campbell and Maggie Brennan! As he drove the wagon during the day, Rose Jean Campbell sat beside him on the seat talking for hours.

At first Clinton had been delighted to speak with Rose Jean. The Scottish woman was alert and well read, especially in the Scriptures. He enjoyed discussing some of his ideas about the Bible with her as they rode along. To his surprise, she took more delight in speaking of the Bible and its doctrines than he himself. And as they talked, he realized she knew more about certain things in the Scriptures than him.

She had, however, a way of becoming very personal in a way that made Clinton nervous. He had been driving the mules at a steady pace for hours and was looking for a place to pull up to camp for the night when she turned to him and asked, "Are you married?"

"No. I ain't."

"Why not?" she asked directly.

It was exactly the sort of question that Clinton would have no qualms asking someone else, but he was unaccustomed to being questioned so sharply about his personal life. He always liked to have the upper hand in a discussion, and her direct questions made him nervous.

"Well, I guess I'd have to say my girl wouldn't have me." He was thinking of Aldora Stuart and how foolish he had been over her for several years. He had always planned to marry Aldora, but she had seemed to lose interest in him.

"Well, if she won't have you, then she's not the one God has planned for you," Rose Jean said.

Clinton turned and faced her. She had turned her head and was watching him carefully. Although her skin was fair, she had a few faint freckles across her nose. Her hair was neatly in place, and the rigors of the trail had not seemed to trouble her. "You believe that God puts people together, I take it?"

"Why, of course!" His question seemed to surprise her. "God is interested in every detail of our lives, Clinton, so naturally He'd be interested in seeing that the right man got married to the right woman."

Clinton lifted his eyes and studied the trail ahead. They had passed a few wagons and a few horsemen, but the road was scarcely traveled at all. He was thinking about what she had said, and then she surprised him by speaking again.

"If people will wait until God moves, they'll get the right mate. But people won't wait for God's best. They're in too big a hurry."

"Well, that's not true with me. I haven't hurried. I'm twenty-five years old now, and that's waitin' around long enough. How old are you by the way?"

"I'm twenty-three," Rose Jean said. Clinton had no time to respond, for she said at once, "Do you believe God has a mate picked out for each one of us?"

"I sure do. It's all predestinated. Wrote down in a book."

"So you're a Calvinist, then?"

"Don't know what that is, but I just believe what the Bible says." Rose Jean fell silent for so long that Clinton looked over and saw that she was in a thoughtful mood.

After a while, she said, "I have a sister who isn't a pretty woman."

"Isn't she?"

"No. She is very plain. And she loved a man named Duncan McDowell with all her heart. They were engaged for over a year, and she was so in love with him. She dreamed of marrying him and growing old together with a family."

She didn't speak for so long that Clinton said, "Well, what happened? Did they get married?"

"No. A week before the wedding Duncan broke it off."

"Why'd he do that?"

"He didn't give the real reason, but I know that a rich woman with good looks stole his heart away from my sister. He married her, and she made his life terrible." She turned, and her gaze was intent. "He missed what God had for him."

"Well, I guess your sister missed it too."

"No. She married another man. A good man, too, but she didn't love him the way she did Duncan. Duncan was the one that God had picked out."

Clinton was fascinated by the assurance she seemed to have concerning the things of God. "What about you, Rose Jean?"

"God may want me to be single. If He does, that's what I want."

"You ever had a man ask you to marry him?"

"Yes, I have. Two, as a matter of fact."

"But you didn't take 'em up on their offer?"

"No. Neither of them was the right one for me."

"How will you know when the right one comes along?"

"God will tell me. The Bible says He speaks to those who are His own. We only have to take the time to listen." She turned then and asked, "What about this woman who won't have you? What's her name?"

"Aldora Stuart."

"Do you think God has picked her out to be your wife?"

"I thought so once. Now I'm not so sure."

"Don't be in a hurry, Clinton. God isn't."

Rose Jean's questions were making Clinton feel uncomfortable, so he quickly changed the subject. When they finally pulled up for camp, Maggie slid off her mule and said, "You take care of the stock, Clint. I'll fix us a supper."

"All right," Clint agreed and went to see that the animals were watered. He took his time at it, and when he got back, he found Maggie making biscuits in a Dutch oven.

"I been taking care of this sourdough starter for five years now," Maggie said. Her face was flush from the heat of the fire, but when she pulled the biscuits out, they were tender and a golden brown. "Try one of these, Clint."

Clinton took a biscuit and juggled it around between his hands, for it was hot, then bit off half of it. "Why, this is mighty fine, Maggie!"

"Can't stand bad biscuits," she said and soon began to serve the rest of the meal. The main dish was some sort of hash that was delicious. "This here is what I call Red Flannel Hash," Maggie announced. "My own recipe."

"What all has it got in it?"

"Oh, beets, potatoes, onions, some salt pork, a little ground beef. Some eggs. A little bit of this, a little bit of that. Whatever I have to throw in it," she said.

"Why, that's plum prime!"

"If you think that's good, you ought to taste some of my Hopping John. It takes some black-eyed peas for that. Pa always said that set him free." She finished the meal off by producing a tin and pulling the lid off. "This here is molasses candy. Sweetest you ever saw."

Both Clinton and Rose Jean took some of the delicacy. Clinton popped his piece into his mouth, and his eyes closed with pleasure. "I'll tell you, Maggie, that's the best candy I ever had."

"Shoot! You ought to taste some of my caramel candy, then you'd think this tastes like dirt."

After they finished the meal, they all sat around the campfire watching the flames. Rose Jean, in her direct manner, began to ask Clinton about his family.

"Well, my pa got kilt at the Alamo," he said, "but my ma's fine. After Pa died she married a real good man named Clay Taliferro."

"What about brothers and sisters?"

"Well, I got an older brother named Brodie. He's with the Rangers now. I got a sister named Moriah. She got captured by the Comanches."

Clinton fell silent, and it was Maggie who said, "Did you get her back?"

"Brodie and a fella named Quaid Shafter, they got her back after tracking the band a long time. Took over a year to find her." He hesitated, then added, "She had a boy while she was there. Named him Ethan."

"He's half Indian?" Maggie said.

"That's right. Fine boy too."

Not wanting to give all the details about his sister's kidnapping by the Comanches, he hurriedly began to tell about the history of the Yellow Rose Ranch. Rose Jean listened with interest as he told her how they had built up the ranch. After a while she said, "I'm sleepy. I think I'll turn in now." She got up and noted that Clinton rose when she did. She came over to him and put her hand out. "It was nice of you to take care of us, Clinton. I sure appreciate it."

"Why, sure. No trouble at all. You go to bed now and rest up. We've still got some miles to go, but we'll be home in another day."

Rose Jean disappeared into the wagon, where she had made a bed for herself. Maggie kept her eyes fixed on Clinton. When he sat back down by the fire, she continued to ask him about his family. She was very interested in Texas and the Yellow Rose Ranch, which Clinton enjoyed boasting about. Finally, Maggie looked at Clinton and said, "I got to take care of myself, Clint."

"You mean stay in the freightin' business?"

"It's all I know. My ma, she died when I wasn't but five, and I had to take care of Pa."

"Guess you didn't have much of a life."

"All I've done most of my life is look at the rear end of a bunch of ugly mules. But it wasn't bad," she said defensively.

Clinton listened as she continued to ask about the possibilities of the freighting business. He finally had to admit that he didn't know much about it. He got up and said, "I reckon I'll go to bed myself."

Maggie got up and came over to stand in front of him. She looked up into his face, and he saw a quizzical look in her green eyes. The fire set off the red glints of her hair, and without warning she reached up and put her hands around his neck and pressed herself against him. He was shocked at the firm roundness of her body as she held him. As he looked at her, he saw that she was waiting for him to kiss her. She was a strange-looking woman, tall and dressed in man's clothes, but there was no doubting the expectant look in her eyes. He suddenly reached up, pulled her hands down, and cleared his throat. "Well, good night."

Maggie laughed at him. "Don't you like women, Clinton?"

"Well, sure I do," he said nervously.

"Well, what are you waiting for, then?"

Clinton tried to think of a proper answer but didn't have one. He finally said lamely, "I reckon you're in a state of shock losin' your pa and all."

"That's what you think, is it? You know what I think? I think you're afraid of women."

She was challenging him, and Clinton felt the temptation as he stood there. But he quickly said, "We got a hard day's journey tomorrow. I'll see you in the morning."

He heard Maggie laugh as he turned, and his face turned red. "Why, that hussy!" he muttered under his breath. He grabbed his bed roll and went to bed, but he had difficulty going to sleep. When he finally did, he had strange dreams.

Clinton was up early the next morning. While he hitched the horses to the wagons, Maggie made a quick breakfast for everyone. Clinton ate in a hurry and went to finish tightening the reins on the horses as Maggie put out the fire. Every time he looked her way, she smiled in a way that made him feel awkward.

"All right, let's get going. We should make it back to the ranch tomorrow if we make good time today." Before long the wagons were rolling along at a fast clip. Clinton kept the mules going to keep up with Maggie's wagon in front. "She sure is in a hurry to get to San Antone," he remarked.

"I guess we all are," Rose Jean said, touching his arm.

Startled, Clinton turned to look at her. "What is it?" he said.

"I admire you, Clinton."

"Admire me? What for?" he said, very aware of the feel of her hand as it squeezed his upper arm.

"I couldn't help seeing how you resisted temptation last night. It takes a strong man to say no when a woman tries to work her charms like that."

"Well, I try to be."

"She'll try it again," Rose Jean warned. "I think she's that kind of woman. She doesn't have any sense of right or wrong."

"It won't do her any good to try me," Clinton said firmly.

"Don't be too sure." Rose Jean's lips turned upward in a smile, revealing a dimple in her left cheek. "Let him that thinketh he standeth take heed lest he fall." She nodded and said, "That's in First Corinthians chapter ten verse twelve."

"Well, she can try, but it won't do her any good. I've given a lot of thought to women who try to bring men down. I'm on my guard."

At his confident words, Rose Jean laughed. It was a delightful sound. "What if you're tempted by a good woman?"

"Why, a good woman wouldn't tempt a man!"

"Don't be too sure about that. Even good women have their bad moments."

Clinton changed the subject, for he hated for this woman to think that he could be seriously tempted by any woman. Finally, he started talking about what it meant to pray the prayer of faith. For the rest of the afternoon, they discussed what the Bible had to say about the importance of prayer. He found himself enjoying it, even though it was humiliating to learn that she knew more Scripture than he did. She seemed to have the whole Bible memorized and could give chapter and verse to any section they discussed. Still, he held his own as well as he could.

They were interrupted late that afternoon when Maggie drew her wagon up alongside of a creek. She jumped out and said, "This would be a good place to camp tonight. We got good water here. Let's get these mules tied out. I aim to fix a good supper."

Clinton jumped down and unhitched the mules while Maggie gathered wood along the bank to start a fire. He came over and stood beside the creek, where both women were looking at it. "Probably fish in that creek," he said. "If I had a line, we'd have fish for supper."

Maggie looked at him and said, "Creeks are good for fishin', but I'm dirty as a pig. Haven't had a bath in a week at least. Let's wash some of this trail dust off."

Clinton and Rose stared at Maggie as she unbuttoned her shirt and threw it on the ground. She was wearing a thin cotton chemise and a vest, which revealed the fullness of her figure. She was preparing to pull it over her head when Clinton suddenly realized she had no intimidation of undressing in front of him. She was not bluffing! He turned quickly and walked away, saying, "I guess I'll have my bath upstream."

Maggie pulled off the vest, and she stood there, her eyes dancing. "He's bashful, ain't he, Sister Rose?"

"And right he should be," she said.

"Well, I ain't. I'm gonna have me a bath if it hairlips Texas. Come on and join me."

"I guess I'll wait until we get to the Yellow Rose Ranch tomorrow."

Maggie unlaced her boots and kicked them to one side. Next she pulled off her socks, and then shucked out of the jeans. She saw that for once she had shaken Rose Jean Campbell's confidence. It delighted her, and she said, "You ever sleep with a man, Sister?"

The woman's brash question took Rose Jean off-guard, and she stammered, "N-No."

"Didn't figure so," she said as she waded out into the creek. She sat down in it and then lay down, letting her pigtails float behind her. "Well, Clinton's a man. He'll talk religion, but sooner or later some woman will come along and he'll fall. All men are alike."

"I don't think so," Rose said firmly. Her cheeks were red. She was terribly embarrassed by the woman's absolute lack of modesty.

Maggie said, "Get me that bar of soap in the floor of the wagon, will you?"

Rose turned and went and got the soap. She tossed it to Maggie, who was splashing in the water. Maggie caught it and began to lather up. "Going to wash my hair right good, then dry it out by the fire." She continued to lather the soap and gave Rose a sly grin. "You'll fall for a fella someday," she said firmly. "Then you'll find out you're as weak as the rest of us." She held the bar of soap in one hand and looked defiantly at Rose Campbell. "All women are alike, Rosie. Just like the men!"

PART THREE

THE PRODIGAL

CHAPTER
FOURTEEN

Jerusalem reached into the bag, pulled out a handful of chicken feed, and threw it over the chicken yard. As always, the birds came clucking and flocking, surrounding her and pecking at the feed as it fell to the earth. The twins, Sam and Rachel Belle, stood inside the fence, for they had followed her. The August sun was going down in the west, and the heat of the earth was reflected upward. Both Sam and Rachel Belle were dirty, and, as usual, they were pestering their mother with questions. Rachel Belle was wearing a straw hat that looked as if it had been through the war. She had pulled it firmly down over her head but now took it off and let her hair fall free.

"Ma, don't you feel bad about feeding these chickens?"

Jerusalem turned and gave her daughter an odd look. "Why should I feel bad about that? They've got to eat."

"I know they have to eat, Ma, but you're feeding them up just so you can wring their necks. That don't seem very fair to me."

Sam turned to give his twin a look of disgust. "Don't you know nothin'? That's what chickens are for—for folks to eat. I swear, Rachel Belle, you're dumb as last year's bird's nest!"

Fast as a striking rattlesnake, Rachel Belle hit Sam in the arm, who yelled and dodged behind his mother.

"You two both hush and stop that fighting!" Jerusalem threw the last of the chicken feed out, then turned and looked down at the two. "If you've got to fight somebody, go find strangers."

"They ain't no strangers here," Sam remarked logically. He had that kind of mind that took things very literally. Rachel Belle, on the other hand, had a vivid imagination and took almost nothing literally. She also had a mind that hopped around like a grasshopper from one subject to another.

"Ma," she asked abruptly, "are we poor?"

The abrupt change of subject gave Jerusalem pause for a moment. "Well, we're not rich," she said. "What makes you ask a thing like that?"

"Yeah," Sam put in. "You're gettin' plenty to eat, ain't you? And you've got dirty, old ragged clothes to wear. That's all you need."

"You hush, Sam. I'll take care of this. Why would you ask a thing like that, Rachel Belle?"

"'Cause I heard you and Pa talkin' late last night. You were talkin' about how we didn't have enough money and how bad things were."

"Little pitchers have big ears! You shouldn't be listening to other people's conversations."

"Well, she couldn't help it," Sam said. "I heard it too. When you got ears and people talk, you can't help but listen, can you?"

"Come along. I've got work to do, but you mind what I said. Don't worry about money. Worryin' is for grown-ups, not children."

Rachel Belle reached up and took her mother's hand. She turned her face upward and said seriously, "Mama, you can have my money." Rachel Belle had been saving coins in a lard can for some time. Every night she would take it out and count it as if it would grow.

Jerusalem leaned down and gave her a hug. "Bless your sweet heart, honey, that's generous of you. I hope when you grow up you'll always be as good-hearted as you are now."

The three left the chicken yard, and Sam latched the gate. As they headed back toward the house, he said, "Mama, why does Quaid always take Ethan hunting and not me?"

"Why, he does take you hunting."

"Not as often as he takes Ethan. He took him this morning and wouldn't let me go. Why does Quaid like Ethan better than he likes me?"

Jerusalem stopped abruptly and turned to put her hands on Sam's shoulders. She said very carefully, "You have to remember, Sam, that Ethan doesn't have a pa."

"Sure he does. Bear Killer's his pa."

"But that's different from, well, from you. You've got a father to do things with. Sometimes Ethan feels bad because he doesn't have a daddy around to do things with him. Quaid feels for him, so that's why he pays special attention to him. Don't you be jealous, son."

"Okay, Ma. I won't. Can Rachel Belle and me go fishin' down at the creek?"

"I guess so after you get your chores done."

At that instant Rachel Belle said, "Look, Ma, there comes some wagons. Who can that be?"

"I don't know. They're freighting wagons, it looks like."

"Ma, that's Clinton drivin' that wagon. His horse is tied on the back."

"I guess we'd better go see who he's bringin' home."

The three went around to the front of the house and waited until the wagons drew up. Jerusalem's eyes took in the neatly dressed woman sitting beside Clinton, then she glanced at the driver of the other wagon. At first she had taken the driver to be a man, but she saw, on closer examination, it was a woman dressed in man's clothes with a hat pulled over her face.

"Well, I'm back, Ma," Clinton said, jumping down and coming over to give her a big hug.

"I was gettin' a mite worried, son. Did the drive go all right?"

"Went fine. I made a good sale. The only problem was Oney got in a fight and shot someone in the leg. He'll be spending the next month sitting in a jail."

"Oh my," Jerusalem said. "Clay will chew his ear off when he gets home, for sure."

She could tell Clinton seemed nervous, and she said, "You picked up a couple of wagons on your trip."

"Yes. I met up with some trouble on my way back." He turned and went over and helped the woman down and said, "Ma, this is Miss Rose

Jean Campbell. She and her brother was on their way from Missouri to Texas, but her brother took cholera and he died."

At once Jerusalem stepped forward and put her hand out. "I'm so sorry to hear that, Miss Campbell."

"Thank you, Mrs. Taliferro. I hate to impose on you."

"No imposition at all," Jerusalem said. Her eyes went to the driver of the second wagon, who seemed to keep her distance. "Introduce me to your other friend, Clinton."

Clinton seemed to find it difficult. "Well, this here is Miss Maggie Brennan, Ma. She's had tough luck too. She lost her pa to that cholera just like Miss Rose lost her brother."

"I'm sorry for your loss, Miss Brennan. Indeed I am. Won't you get down, Maggie?"

"I've got to take care of this stock."

"I'll do that," Clinton said. He went over to offer the woman a hand down, but Maggie jumped lightly to the ground and stood there uncertainly.

"You two come with me. I know you need to freshen up after a hard trip. Clinton, you take care of the animals."

"Sure, Ma."

Clinton moved toward the wagon but stopped to watch as his mother led the two women inside, followed by the twins. Maggie was lagging behind as if she felt out-of-place.

"Well, Clinton, I swear I wouldn't have believed it of ya!" O. M. Posey had kept his distance until the two women had disappeared into the house, but now he grinned broadly and said, "What happened, Clinton? You rode out a full day head of us, and we still beat you back. Look at this, Ike. I don't know no other fella that could go off to take a bunch of cattle to New Orleans and come back with two women, one for each arm."

Ike McClellan, tall and lanky with one eye covered by a patch, was grinning also. "Ain't one woman enough for you, Clinton? I think there's somethin' in the Bible against a man havin' more than one woman."

Clinton flushed and said sharply, "Never mind about them women! Help me get these mules unhitched and watch out for 'em. They're meaner than snakes! Better watch 'em. They'll try to bite you every chance they get."

The three men set out to unharness the mules, and the rest of the crew gathered around Clinton. They all fired questions at him, all grinning slyly, for Clinton was a favorite target of their teasing. Finally, Clinton said, "I want you all to hush. Them two women have had a terrible loss. Miss Rose lost her brother, and Miss Maggie lost her pa to cholera."

His words brought a look of contrition to all of them. Ike said, "We was just teasin', Clinton. I'm plum sorry to hear about that."

With all the help he had, the contrary mules were soon put into a corral and fed.

As Maggie entered the house feeling awkward and out-of-place, she hung back, noticing that Rose Jean Campbell had no problem at all fitting in with the Taliferros. *She's used to nice things,* she thought. *She's like Clinton's ma.*

Two women were in the large room into which Jerusalem had led them. Turning to Rose Jean and Maggie, Jerusalem said, "This is my daughter Moriah and my younger daughter Mary Aidan. Girls, this is Miss Maggie Brennan and Miss Rose Jean Campbell."

Maggie nodded but did not speak as the two younger women greeted her and Rose Jean.

"You sit down and have a cup of coffee, and then I'll take you up to your rooms."

"Was that Clinton that came in with you two?" Mary Aidan said.

Rose Jean looked at Maggie, whose lips were tightly clamped together, and said quickly, "Yes. Miss Maggie and her father were bringing my brother and me from Missouri to Texas, but the cholera struck, and I lost my brother and she lost her father. Clinton came along and brought us this far."

"Is someone meeting you?" Moriah asked. She was studying the two women carefully, noting that the tallest of them was very nervous and ill at ease. "No. Never mind. I shouldn't be asking questions. Please sit down. The coffee's on the stove."

Maggie sat down awkwardly and took the cup of coffee that Mary Aidan gave her. She saw the younger woman studying her through half-lidded eyes. *She don't like me. I can tell,* she thought.

Jerusalem made the two women comfortable and said, "You two need to rest up. You're welcome to stay with us as long as you'd like."

"That's very kind of you, Mrs. Taliferro," Rose Jean said. She sipped the coffee and then said, "My brother and I are both Mennonite ministers."

"Mennonite? I don't believe I know that denomination," Jerusalem said.

"There aren't many around here. Our group came from Europe originally. Charles and I were born in Scotland, but we came to this country when we were very young." She hesitated, then said, "We both felt the call of God to preach the gospel to the Indians."

"The Indians!" Mary Aidan exclaimed. "I don't know how you could do that. They'd scalp you before you could say a word."

"God would just have to protect us," Rose Jean said with a smile.

"Well, I think your dedication is wonderful," Jerusalem said.

Rose Jean turned and said, "Miss Moriah, Clinton said you speak the Comanche language. He suggested you might be willing to teach me."

"Yes, I do speak Comanche," Moriah said. "I'll be glad to teach you what I know."

"I'd like to know about what the Indians are like."

"Well, I can tell you that," Moriah said. "I spent several years with them."

Jerusalem turned and said, "Well, that's settled, then. We've got plenty of room here, and you two can have lessons, and you can rest up, Miss Campbell." She turned and said, "What about you, Miss Brennan?"

"Just Maggie, ma'am. I don't know nothin' but freightin'. That's all I've ever done with my pa."

"I'm so sorry about your loss. Will you keep on freightin'?"

"Well, I've got to take these two wagons on into San Antone and deliver the goods. Then I reckon I'll look around and see if I can get some freightin' jobs."

"There's no hurry. You stay with us and rest up and rest the animals. Now, then. Moriah, you and Mary Aidan finish cooking, and we'll have a good meal for our guests. You two come along. I'll show you to your room."

Maggie and Rose Jean followed Jerusalem upstairs. She walked down a hall, opened a door on the end, and said, "You two will have to share a room for a while. This is a big, old house, but we've got a large family. Now, you two freshen up. Lie down if you want to, and take a nap. Whatever. Supper will be ready in about an hour. I want you to meet my husband. He'll be glad to see you."

"Thank you, Mrs. Taliferro," Rose Jean said.

Maggie suddenly said, "This is too fine for me. I can sleep out in the wagon."

"You'll do no such thing, Maggie. I'll call you when supper's ready." Jerusalem turned and went down the stairs, her mind filled with the problems of the two young women who had suddenly appeared in her life. When she got downstairs, she heard Mary Aidan saying to Clinton, who had entered the house, ". . . and you have no business bringin' strangers home. You don't know a thing about them."

"That's enough out of you, Mary Aidan!" Jerusalem said sharply. "I'm ashamed of you! Now, you go out and milk the cow, and I'll hear no more talk like that."

Mary Aidan gave her mother an angry look, then turned and left the room.

"Mary Aidan's spoiled, Ma," Clinton said.

"She's too pretty. Men fall over themselves following after her." She shook her head and added, "At times I wish she was plain." Then she went over to Clinton and put her arms around him. "But you did the right thing, son, in helping them. You've got a good heart."

Moriah laughed and said, "I don't notice him bringing any homely women home."

Jerusalem tried to withhold a smile and then couldn't. She laughed too. "Well, that's all right, Clinton. Pretty women need to be taken care of too."

For the next two days the talk around the Yellow Rose Ranch had been about nothing but the two young women Clinton had brought home with him. Clay was amused by it and slyly made remarks to Clinton, who finally said, "You hush now. I'm tired of people makin' fun of me. I didn't have no choice but to bring them women here."

As for the two themselves, Rose Jean settled in, enjoying the hospitality, as if she had been a long-lost relative. Within two days she knew everyone's name and had thrown herself into learning the Comanche language. At the same time, she worked hard, and there was always plenty of work to do in the house and outside. The children loved her, for she told them stories and read to them books that she had brought, wonderful books with stories they had never heard before.

Maggie Brennan did not meld in as easily as the young Mennonite woman. Maggie absolutely refused to stay in the room with Rose Jean and insisted on sleeping outside in the wagon. On the second night she heard the hands complaining about the bad cooking. Finding out that the cook, such as he was, was in jail in New Orleans, she immediately volunteered to cook a meal. Her offer was accepted eagerly, and she cooked up a supper for the hands that night. When they trooped in and sat themselves down, she put before them a huge chuck roast and big bowls full of peas and onions.

"By golly, I hope that tastes as good as it smells, Maggie. It'll be a wonder," Ike McClellan said. He started to cut the roast beef and exclaimed, "Why, this here meat just pulls apart!"

"That's what meat's supposed to do. Ain't no sense in puttin' tough meat on a table," Maggie said. She took her seat with the men and helped herself.

As the cowhands ate heartily, they all exclaimed over how excellent the food was. Johnny Bench, six feet tall and husky, grinned at her and said, "Why, Maggie, if you hadn't shown up, I think we all would have died with Oney Pierson's cooking. I tell you right now, when he gets back from New Orleans, he can hang up his pots. In fact, I'll marry ya just to get to eat cookin' like this every day."

The rest of the hands all volunteered to do the same. Maggie smiled at their compliments and then rose from the table and brought in the pies she had baked, one cherry and one apple.

"They ain't no better pie in the world than this, Maggie! Where'd you learn to cook like this?" one of the hands exclaimed.

"I learned on the trail from an old fella that had cooked for all his life."

"Well, he taught you good," Johnny Bench said. "It's the best pie I ever ate."

Maggie sat back feeling relieved. She felt more comfortable around the tough men in the crew headquarters than she did in the big house. Johnny Bench insisted on helping her do the dishes, and to her surprise, she found his attention pleasant.

"This is a nice ranch, Johnny," she said.

"Sure is. Best ranch in Texas. Gonna be the biggest one of these days too." He was drying a dish and said, "What about you, Maggie?"

"I reckon I'll go on to San Antone tomorrow and deliver these goods and see if I can find some work."

"Be glad to drive your other wagon in."

"That'd be fine, Johnny."

Johnny, however, did not drive the wagon in the next day. Clay sent him and some of the other hands out to brand a new herd that had been brought in. Clinton elected himself to go with Maggie, and before they left, Clay came to Maggie and said, "You know, I think I'm gonna have to keep you here."

Startled, Maggie looked at Clay Taliferro. She had liked him instantly when Jerusalem had introduced him. He had a teasing manner about him and walked with a decided limp from a brush with the Indians Moriah had told her about. "What do you mean 'keep me here'?"

"Well, the hands have been doin' nothin' but singin' your praises on what a good cook you are. I wish you'd stay on and cook for us. Of course," he said, "we've got plenty of cooks in the house, but the hands get mighty hungry with all the hard work they do around here. You could even go on the drives and drive the chuck wagon, since you're used to freightin'."

Maggie smiled. "That's mighty good of you to offer, Mr. Clay. I'll think on it and let you know."

"You do that. We can't pay much, but we'd be glad to have you."

Clinton and Maggie drove the two wagons into San Antone, found the store that had ordered all the supplies, and left the two wagons to be unloaded. Maggie asked the owner of the store, Jeb Hawkins, about opportunities for freighting in these parts.

"Well," Hawkins said slowly, "the fella you need to see is Tim Hankins. He does most of the freightin' around here, and he can tell you how business is. Pretty tough, from what I hear."

"Where could we find him?" Maggie asked.

"Why, he was at the saloon a little bit earlier. Probably still there." Grinning, he added, "He seems to enjoy saloons more than freightin', appears to me."

"Why don't you wait here, Maggie, and I'll go find the man and bring him to you," Clinton said.

"Why, I'll just go right along with you."

"That saloon can be a pretty rough place," Clinton said.

Maggie laughed. "I've been in saloons before with Pa many a times. Most men are like ornery mules, and I've been handling them since I was a little girl."

"You might hear some bad talk not fit for a lady," Clinton said.

"You've heard some bad talk from me, Clinton."

"I been meanin' to talk to you about that, Maggie. You ought to stop cussin' them mules. As a matter of fact, you ought to stop cussin' altogether. It's unseemly for a lady to cuss."

"I ain't no lady!" Maggie said sharply.

"Well, you could be if you wanted to."

"Well, I don't want to. I want to do just what I've been doin'. Now, let's get to that saloon and find Hankins."

Clinton led her to the Golden Lady Saloon, and they found Tim Hankins without any problem. He was a short, muscular man in his mid-fifties, and Clinton had to interrupt his poker game, which irritated him.

"What is it you want?" Hankins snarled.

"This here is Miss Maggie Brennan. She wants to talk to you about getting into the freightin'."

"You got somethin' you want freightin'?" Hankins demanded.

"No. I'm thinkin' about goin' into business for myself."

Hankins got up and said, "Come on over in the corner to that table and we'll talk."

The two went to the table, and Frisco Farr came up and greeted Clinton. "You've been gone on a cattle drive, I hear."

"Took a herd to New Orleans."

"How was the prices?"

"They were pretty fair, Frisco."

"You want a soda pop?"

"No. I don't reckon so."

Farr was a medium-sized man, very neat and a fancy dresser. "Who's the woman?"

"I ran across her out on the prairie. Her pa and another fella had died of cholera, so I helped her get the wagons in. She wants to get into freightin'."

"She always dress like that?"

"I reckon so. She can cuss a blue streak too. Her pa was a mule skinner, and you know what their language is like."

Farr grinned. "Well, maybe you can convert her, Clinton."

"I hadn't had any luck with you."

Farr looked at Clinton, and the smile disappeared. "Don't give up on me," he said briefly, then turned and walked away.

Clinton stood at the bar greeting friends, for he knew most of the men in there. Finally, he saw Maggie get up, and Hankins went back to his poker game. "Did you find out anything, Maggie?"

"He's going to lease my wagons and my mules. He's got all the contacts, and I may drive some for him."

"I think that'd be—" Clinton didn't finish his sentence, for two men had approached. He turned quickly to see Dee Nolan and Lou Burdette. They both worked for the Skull Ranch, a big ranch just south of the Yellow Rose. Lou Burdette was the foreman, six feet tall, lean, and dark complected. He had little use for the Yellow Rose Ranch. He was an ornery man, and he had had words with Clay on more than one occasion. Dee Nolan was a huge man with yellow hair and hazel eyes. He was grinning broadly and looking at Maggie.

"Who's your lady friend here, Hardin?" Dee asked.

Instantly, Clinton knew the two were looking for trouble. There had been arguments over land boundaries and so-called stray cattle, and the two never lost an opportunity to cause trouble. "Come on, Maggie. Never mind these two."

Maggie was staring coolly at the two, not in the least disturbed, but when she turned to leave with Clinton, Dee Nolan reached out and grabbed her arm. "I reckon there's a real woman underneath all them men's clothes. How about you come along with me, and we'll have a drink."

Maggie turned and struck Nolan's upper arm, driving his grip loose. She called him a name that Clinton had never heard a woman use, and he saw the anger rise in Nolan's eyes.

"You two move along. We don't want any trouble," Clinton said.

"You don't want any trouble? I don't know who this woman is, but she ain't no better than she should be, going around dressed like a man," Nolan scowled.

"Shut your mouth, Nolan!" Clinton said angrily. "Come on, Maggie."

But he had no chance to say more, for without warning Nolan threw a punch. He was a huge, muscular man, and his blow caught Clinton high on the head, knocking him to the floor of the saloon. The world seemed to turn into a storm of yellow and green and purple spots. After a moment, Clinton got to his feet, addled. Nolan laughed and started toward him. He struck Clinton with a blow that knocked the young man totally unconscious this time. He moved forward to kick him, but suddenly a shot rang out. Nolan yelled in surprise and reached down and grabbed his calf. He turned to see Maggie, who had drawn a thirty-eight and was holding it trained on him.

"You shot me!" he cried.

"I should have shot you in your ugly head! Now, you pull out of here before I do!"

Lou Burdette had no particular liking for Dee Nolan, but Nolan was one of his hands. He started for Maggie, saying, "I'll take that gun and maybe give you something else."

Instantly, the gun in Maggie's hand was leveled and pointed straight between Burdette's eyes. He stopped as if he were staring eye-to-eye with a rattlesnake ready to strike. "Hey now. Watch out. That thing might go off."

"It will go off if you don't get out of here as well. Now git, the both of you!"

"I reckon you boys can leave now." Frisco Farr had made his approach, and his bouncer, Jumbo Jones, a huge man who was known to destroy an opponent with one blow of his massive fist, came and stood by him. "You fellows drift along," he said in a strangely gentle voice.

Burdette stared at the two, then snarled, "Come on, Dee. We'll have to get a doctor to look at that."

As they left the room, Farr turned to Maggie and smiled. "That was good shootin'."

Maggie smiled back at Frisco. "It was a pleasure," she said. She went over and knelt down beside Clinton. "You got some place we can put him until he wakes up?"

"Jumbo, let's get Clinton back in my office. We can put him on the couch."

When Clinton woke up, he did not know where he was. His head was throbbing, and the room seemed to be spinning in circles. He groaned and sat up, and then a voice said, "How do you feel?"

Reaching up, he felt the side of his face, which seemed numb, and saw that Maggie had drawn a chair up beside the couch and was sitting there looking at him.

"What happened?" he moaned as he rubbed his head.

"Oh, them two fellas from Skull Ranch decided to leave."

Frisco Farr came from across the room, where he had been sitting at his desk. "Maggie here helped them. She shot Dee in the leg."

"I should have shot the other one," Maggie said, then added an unprintable name to Burdette's description.

"I wish you wouldn't cuss like that," Clinton said.

"Well, I'm sorry if I hurt your feelings, but they made me mad."

"Do you feel like movin' now?"

"I guess so." Clinton was embarrassed, and he stood up and glanced over at Frisco. "I didn't make much of a show."

"They caught you off-guard." Frisco grinned and said, "Just keep Maggie handy with that thirty-eight of hers and watch out for those two. They'll try to get back at you if they can. They're always looking for trouble, those two."

"Thanks, Frisco," Maggie said. "Come on, Clinton."

The two left the office, and Clinton felt everyone looking at him as they left the saloon. When they got outside, he said, "I thought I could take better care of myself."

"He got you with that first lick, Clinton. You was addled after that and didn't have no chance. Now, what you should have done is hit him first. Never let a fella get the first lick in. Bust 'em with somethin' if you have to. That'll get 'em to understand you're serious."

As the two walked along the boardwalk, Clinton asked, "What are you gonna do, Maggie, work for Tim Hankins?"

Maggie seemed happy. She took his arm and said, "Nope. I got another plan."

"What kind of a plan?"

Maggie laughed and squeezed his arm. "I think you need a woman to take care of you."

"I don't need a woman to take care of me! What are you talkin' about?"

"I reckon you do, so I've decided to do the cookin' at your ranch. That way," she grinned and squeezed his arm, "I can keep an eye on you."

Clinton stared at her, and he grunted, "Well, the hands will be glad. They sure like your cookin'!"

CHAPTER
FIFTEEN

D ad, you've got to do something about that . . . that *woman*!"
Clay looked up from the harness he was mending and
frowned. "What woman are you talkin' about?"

Mary Aidan had hunted Clay down, and her face was flushed. "It's
that Maggie Brennan. You've got to do something about her."

"Why, she's a hard worker and a good cook. The boys are all fattenin'
up."

"It's not her cookin' I'm worried about. Why, she flirts with anything
in pants, Dad! You've got to get rid of her."

Clay had always had a special affection for Mary Aidan. She had been
a small child when he had first appeared into the life of the Hardin family,
but she had been affectionate, and he had spent many hours with her.
Now, however, she had outgrown some of her youthful qualities and was
not afraid to state her opinion.

"She's had a rough life, Mary Aidan," he said, shrugging his shoulders. "You've got to be a little more patient with her."

"Dad, there have already been two or three fights over her. She's caus-
ing trouble among the hands."

Clay laughed. "There wasn't much of a fight. Just some pushin' and shovin'. I'll keep an eye on her. The men are after her all right, but I'll bet they're not gettin' anywhere. Did you hear about Johnny Bench?"

"What about him? He's ga-ga over the woman."

"He tried to steal a kiss, and she busted him with her rollin' pin. Put a knot on his head the size of an egg that's still there, from what I hear."

Mary Aidan was accustomed to having her own way. She had been the pet of the family, and no one had ever really seriously disciplined her. A frown put two vertical marks between her eyebrows, and she exclaimed, "Why, Dad, she's been after Clinton since the day she arrived!"

Clay laughed aloud and shook his head. "Well, I doubt she'll catch him. He's pretty set in his ways."

Moriah was sitting across from Rose Jean at the kitchen table as they continued with their daily lessons to learn Comanche. Jerusalem was busy at the stove cooking some jam from some berries the children had picked.

"I can't seem to make the right sounds, Moriah," Rose Jean said.

"I know. It's hard. The Comanche language sounds like someone speaking with a rock in his mouth—or maybe a mouthful of hot mush."

"Well, I suppose our language sounds just as odd to them."

Suddenly, Moriah said, "I think you ought to change your plan, Rose Jean."

"You mean not go to the Indians?"

"No, I didn't mean that. I believe God has really given you a calling, but did He say specifically to you and your brother that you were to go to the Comanche?"

"Well, no not really. As a matter of fact, we didn't either of us know much about the Indians."

"Well, there are some other Indians down on the coast around Galveston. Some of those tribes there are not dangerous at all."

Rose Jean considered Moriah's words. She had gotten very close to the young woman over the past two weeks. "I don't want to be stubborn, but, to tell the truth, I'm not quite sure what to do. But it's a help just to learn from you about the Indians." She hesitated, then said, "I know your captivity must have been terrible."

Moriah grew still, and memories flooded her thoughts. "It was bad," she said, "but not as bad as for some. I had some good friends among the Comanches. One of the women especially. We were like sisters." She went on to tell about her life with the Indians, and Rose Jean sat there listening attentively. She had made many long lists of words that would be helpful in learning the language, and eagerly tried to throw herself into the study.

Jerusalem finally said, "I think Moriah may be right. The Comanche are the fiercest of all the tribes."

Rose was silent for a moment, then said, "I think the world of Ethan. He's such a fine boy."

"Thank you. He is a good boy," Moriah said.

"You never told me how you got away from the Comanche."

"It was my brother Brodie and Quaid. They never gave up looking for me all that time. After over a year, they came upon an Indian who knew where Bear Killer camped during the winter. I don't know how they did it, but it was a miracle."

Jerusalem said, "Quaid's in love with you, Moriah." When Moriah did not answer, Jerusalem said, "The way he looks at you and the attention he gives Ethan, why, that's the way a man watches the woman he loves."

"I can't be thinking about that, Ma."

"Why not?" Rose Jean said. "He's a good man, isn't he?"

"Yes. He is a good man."

Rose Jean exchanged glances with Jerusalem, and the two women seemed to agree. "We'll pray that you get a good husband and a good father for your son."

Right then the women heard a knock on the door.

"I didn't hear anybody drive up," Jerusalem said.

"I'll see who it is," Moriah said quickly. She went to the front door and opened it and smiled at once. Rice Morgan stood there smiling on the porch.

"Good morning, Miss Moriah."

"Why, Preacher, it's you! Come on in."

"Thank you, ma'am."

"Why didn't you bring Julie with you?"

"Oh, Esther was fussing some today. Julie didn't want to take her out."

"Well, come on back. I want you to meet our guest."

"That's why I came. I heard about her."

"She's a fine woman, Rice. You'll like her." Moriah led him to the kitchen and introduced the pastor to Rose Jean Campbell.

"I came by especially to see you, Miss Campbell."

"How kind of you, Pastor. They've been so good to me here. Moriah's teaching me the Comanche language."

"I understand you feel God's called you to preach to the Indians."

"I suppose you don't like the idea of a woman preaching."

Rice suddenly laughed. "None of my business whom God chooses to do His bidding. If we won't preach, the stones will preach. That's what the Book says. No. Just the opposite. I'm so sorry about the death of your brother," he added. "What a loss."

"You would have liked him, Pastor Morgan."

"I'm sure I would have. What I came to ask was if you would come to church Sunday and give your testimony."

"Why, that's most kind of you. I'd be most happy to."

"You understand," Rice warned, "that you won't be the most popular person there. There's strong feelings against the Indians in this part of the country."

"I know that. I've heard some of it already, but God loves them just like He loves me and you."

"Right you are. Well, I'll look for you then. Now," he said, "I have one more call to make. I understand there's another young lady here."

"You mean Maggie," Jerusalem said as she stirred the jam on the stove. "I doubt if you'll get her to put one foot in your church."

Rice smiled. He was a trim, good-looking man in his mid-forties. The sound of old Wales colored his speech, and he had a way that made people like him immediately. "I'll have a try at it. All she can do is shoot me like she did Dee Nolan."

"You heard about that, did you?" Moriah said. "I'd like to have been there to see it."

"Maggie said she should have shot him in the head," Jerusalem said. "She's very rough, Brother Morgan."

"Well, God can use rough ones and smooth ones. I'll have a try at least."

"You'll find her somewhere around the bunkhouse, probably getting a meal ready."

"I'll look for you Sunday, Miss Campbell. It's so good to meet you." He turned and left, and went at once to the bunkhouse. He had no trouble finding Maggie, for he spotted her outside hanging some clothes on the line. She was wearing men's boots and a man's hat, which was shoved back on her head. He came up and said, "I'm supposing this is Miss Margaret Brennan."

"That's me, but everybody calls me Maggie. Who are you?"

"I'm what people have to use for a preacher in this part of the world. Rice Morgan. I've come by to invite you to the services Sunday."

Maggie did not smile. "I'm not much of a one for church."

"Well, that can change. I'd like very much to have you come. Miss Rose Jean will be coming. Perhaps the two of you could come together."

At the sound of a horse approaching, Rice turned and saw Clinton step off his horse. He looked hot and dusty, but he smiled when he saw Morgan.

"Hello, Rice," Clinton said. "Good to see you."

"Hello, Clinton. I've just met Miss Maggie here and invited her to church. She tells me she's not much of one for coming to the Lord's house."

Maggie was looking at Clinton, and a light suddenly danced in her eyes. She had learned to tease him without mercy, and now she said, "Preacher, I'll come to your church if Clinton will take me."

Rice grinned. "Well, there you are, Clinton. You're always wantin' to serve the Lord, and here's a golden opportunity. You'd be glad to take Miss Maggie to church, wouldn't you?"

Clinton actually would have preferred not to, but he was trapped. He made the best of it, forcing himself to smile. "I'll be glad to, Maggie. We'll leave here about eight o'clock."

"I'll save you a place on the front row," Rice said. He lifted his hat again. "Good to meet you, Miss Maggie," he said as he turned and walked away.

Before he was out of earshot, Maggie said loudly, "He's too good-lookin' to be a preacher."

"What's that supposed to mean? No law against a preacher looking nice. He's married to my aunt, you know."

"No. I didn't know. You don't have to take me to church. I was just makin' fun of you."

"You said you'd go, and we're going and that's that!"

Maggie found it amusing that Clinton seemed upset about having to take her. "All right. I'll be ready."

Clinton had risen early on Sunday and taken a bath, shaved carefully, and put on his best suit. He had told the rest of the family he would take Maggie in the small buggy. Mary Aidan had given him a hard look at breakfast and said, "You be sure she behaves herself in church."

Jerusalem had said, "You mind your own business, Mary Aidan. It's always a good thing when someone goes to church to hear God's Word preached. Now, you help me clean up these dishes so we can get to church too."

"Yes, ma'am," Mary Aidan said, frowning at being corrected.

Jerusalem was proud of Clinton for taking the young woman and whispered to him, "Good for you, son. We'll see that young woman saved yet."

Clinton went outside and hitched up the buggy and drove it to the wagon, where Maggie slept. "Maggie, are you ready?" he called out. He stood there loosely in the seat, when suddenly she appeared.

She jumped to the ground and said, "Reckon I'm ready."

Clinton stared at her, for she was wearing the same men's clothing she did every day, which were none too clean. "Well, Maggie, you're not wearin' that to church, are you?"

"You go to church to be seen in your pretty clothes, Clinton?"

Clinton found it hard to meet Maggie's eyes. "Well, it's just that most people put on their best clothes to go to church."

"These *are* my best clothes. Do you want me to go or not?"

Clinton definitely did not, but he knew he couldn't back out now. "Well, get in and let's get goin'."

Maggie grinned at him and got into the buckboard. "That's a fine team of horses," she remarked. When he did not answer, she said, "How long does church last?"

"A couple of hours."

Maggie waited for him to speak and saw that he was tense. "You don't have to take me if you don't want to. I don't care."

"We're goin'," Clinton said grimly.

Mary Aidan was sitting close to the front over on the right. The small church was filling up in a hurry, and she turned and saw Clinton come in with Maggie. "Mama, look at that, would you?"

Jerusalem turned to look, and even she received a shock. "Well, she doesn't know any better, Mary Aidan."

"It's disgraceful. You should go tell Clinton to take her out of here."

"I'll do no such thing. This is God's house and not mine."

Maggie Brennan was actually petrified with fear as she entered the church. She had not believed that Clinton would bring her to church dressed in ragged men's clothing. Now, as they entered the building, she desperately wished she were anywhere but here. Every eye turned to stare at her, and she knew she looked terrible.

"Well, it's Miss Maggie and Clinton. Glad to see you both," Rice said as he took Clinton's hand and shook it. Turning to Maggie, Rice said, "This is my wife, Julie. Julie, this is Miss Maggie Brennan."

Julie Morgan smiled and came to greet Maggie. "I'm glad to see you. I've heard you're the best cook in Texas."

"Not really that good."

"Well, that's what I hear, and I believe it. I'm coming out to have one of your suppers with the crew this week, then I can see for myself. There are some seats right up here," she said. "You can sit with me."

Maggie wanted to turn and run, but she could not. Julie took her by the arm and led her to the front along with Clinton. As Maggie took a seat, she could feel every eye in the church fixed on her. *Whatever made me do a fool thing like this?* she asked herself fiercely. She sat there feeling more humiliated than she had ever felt in her life. *This ain't the place for me. I've made a fool out of myself!*

The song service began, and after a number of hymns, Rice Morgan came and stood at the front and said, "We have a very special guest this morning. Miss Rose Jean Campbell, originally from Scotland, but lately from Missouri, is with us. She and her brother felt the call of God to preach the gospel to the Indians of the Southwest. Her brother unfortunately died on the journey, but Miss Rose Jean is still determined to fulfill God's call on her life. I'm going to ask her to come and share her testimony with us."

Rose Jean went to the front and turned to face the small congregation. She was wearing a simple light gray dress, every hair was in place, and she looked very young. "I thank you, Brother Morgan, for allowing me to share my faith in Jesus Christ. My brother and I were both converted when we were very young, just in our mid-teens. This was in a revival meeting . . ."

As Rose Jean Campbell spoke, Jerusalem was watching the congregation. She saw what she expected. The very idea of preaching the gospel to the Indians was offensive to many of the people. Many had lost family and friends to the savage attacks of the Comanches and the Kiowas, but others looked interested, and Jerusalem thought, *She's a courageous young woman, but she doesn't know Texans and how they hate the Indians.*

Finally, Rose Jean said, "I hope you will pray for me that I will be faithful to the task that God's called me to."

Suddenly, a voice spoke up. "I ain't prayin' for no hostile Comanche! They killed my two sons and scalped them." It was Les Emery who spoke up, a man filled with grief and hatred toward the Indians.

Instantly, Rice was there standing beside Rose Jean and said, "Les, we're all sorry for the terrible loss you've had. It's a hard task that Miss Campbell has given herself to, and I ask you all to show respect for her calling."

The congregation had such respect for Rice Morgan that not another word was said. When the message was over, Morgan noticed that many left without speaking to Rose Jean. A few had taken interest and took the time to speak with her. Morgan waited until the last person had finished, then he went to her, saying, "You did fine. There will be those who will have trouble with your ministry, but God will be with you."

⋆   ⋆   ⋆

On the way home from church, Maggie had not said a single word. Clinton glanced at her from time to time and tried to start a conversation. He asked her how she liked the service, and she had replied, "It was okay," and would say no more. Finally, he stopped at a creek and pulled the horses up. "It's mighty hot today. We'll give 'em a rest and let 'em have a cool drink." He watched as the horses lowered their heads and drank thirstily, their front feet in the cool waters of the creek.

The silence grew on. The only sound was a bird singing in a cotton-wood over to his left and the horses drinking. Clinton turned and saw that Maggie had turned her head away. "Is somethin' wrong, Maggie? You haven't said hardly a word. You're not mad at me, are you?" He was shocked when she turned to face him and he saw tears in her eyes.

"I . . . I miss my pa. He was all I had, Clinton."

It was the first time she had mentioned her father since arriving at the Yellow Rose. It was not like her to show this kind of feeling. From the time he had met her, she seemed like a hard woman who could handle anything life brought her way. But then Clinton realized it had been all bottled up inside her. She had no one to talk to. She had not bonded well with the women in his family, and now he saw the deep grief in her eyes. "I'm real sorry about your pa. You and him was real close, wasn't you?"

"All we had was each other after Ma died."

Suddenly, Maggie's shoulders began to shake, and tears spilled out on her cheeks. Maggie had teased him unmercifully, but a great compassion filled Clinton Hardin at that moment. He realized suddenly, *Why, I've been put off by the rough clothes she wears and her rough ways, but she don't know nothin' else.* He put his arms around her, and as he did, she seemed to collapse against him. He turned to face her, pulled her around, and held her against his chest. "Maybe," he said quietly, "I can help."

His words seemed to loose the fountain of grief and loss in Maggie's heart. She wept inconsolably and held on to his arms, her face buried against his chest. Clinton had never heard such deep, tearing sobs, and all he could do was hold her. It went on for some time, and finally her body ceased to tremble and the sobs faded. He waited for her to move, but before she did, he suddenly heard the sound of horses. He turned and saw Clay, Jerusalem, and Rose Jean Campbell seated in the larger buggy. They passed by on their way home from church, and Clinton flamed with embarrassment. He knew what it looked like, him holding this woman. He saw Rose Jean staring at him and remembered her words, how that he could be taken in by Maggie's wiles if he wasn't careful.

And then the wagon had gone by, and Maggie pulled herself back. She saw Clinton's face filled with embarrassment. Then she turned and saw Rose Jean look back from the wagon. Suddenly, she cried out, "You see there, Sister Rose, I told you men wasn't to be trusted!"

Clinton was mortified and angry and confused. "Why'd you say that? You do all this on purpose?"

And then he knew he had said the wrong thing. Her grief had been real, and he had been the one to whom she had turned. He saw the hurt in her face, and then her features hardened. "Sure I did! What about it?"

"I was trying to comfort you, nothing else."

"You had your arm around me, didn't you? You was huggin' me."

Clinton opened his mouth to reply, but he could not think of anything to say. He slapped the lines on the horses and said, "We'd better get home." He drove the horses slowly to avoid catching up and wondered what he would say to Rose Jean and the others.

As for Maggie, she felt crushed and humiliated. She had never wept like that, and she certainly had never turned to a man for comfort. *Now he thinks I'm nothing but a hussy,* she thought. *I've got to get away from here!*

CHAPTER
SIXTEEN

I see where Cyrus McCormick is going to produce five hundred of his new reapers in time for the harvest."

Jewel Benton looked across the breakfast table at her husband and smiled. "What does that mean for us, John?" She was a sweet-faced woman who had just turned fifty. Both she and the room were furnished in the latest styles. She wore a light gray dress that complemented the deep maroon color of the dining room furniture. She picked up her coffee and sipped it daintily, studying her husband. He was looking at the paper—a bad habit at the breakfast table in her opinion—but he put it down and smiled at her. He was a big, strong man with English features and a straightforward manner.

"If we don't move ahead, it may mean we're going to have to go out of business."

"John, that can't be true!" Jewel gasped.

John Benton tapped the newspaper. "Things move on, Jewel. We hit at the right time with the factory. When we started, we were producing the latest in equipment for farmers. Now it's a whole new world. When

McCormick invented that reaper, it put a million horses out of business. That means the harness makers will hurt as well. It's just the beginning."

"Are you thinking of producing reapers yourself, Dad?" Tom Benton, a younger version of his father, had been silent during breakfast, but now he looked at his father carefully, knowing that something was on his mind.

"It's a quick-moving world, Tom," Benton said with a shrug. He picked up a piece of bacon, bit off a large bite, and chewed it, speaking with his mouth full. "Things are happening I don't understand. There's a crazy Russian Revolution, where they are killing people and saying they're going to make every man equal."

"That's quite a switch, Dad, from a czar to a democratic society."

"I doubt they'll make it happen." He tapped the paper again and said, "And here. That gold strike they made in California at Sutter's Mill. Everybody's gone crazy. Why, twenty of our workers have quit their jobs and rushed off to California."

"I know. I've tried to talk them out of it. They think that the gold's lying around on the ground ready to be picked up like ripe apples that have fallen from a tree," Tom said. "Fred Mason ran off in search of striking it rich and left his wife and three children. Money drives people crazy."

Jewel listened to the two men as they talked about the news items in the paper and finally signaled for the maid to take the dishes away. "Bring us some fresh coffee, Eileen."

"Yes, ma'am," the black maid said. "I'll be right back with it."

"I see where John Jacob Astor died," Tom remarked. "He was the richest man in America. Left over twenty million dollars."

"Well, he was a rough, old cob," John Benton said solemnly. "He was absolutely ruthless in his business dealings."

"Poor man. His money won't help him now," Jewel said.

"No. I asked a friend of mine how much he left yesterday. Know what he said? He laughed and said, 'All of it.' It struck me as pretty blunt truth, but it's the truth, all the same."

"Memphis is changing too," John Benton remarked. "The place seemed like no more than a big village when I first came here as a boy. Now it's getting to be one of the biggest cities in the South." He looked across at Tom and said, "We've got to put our heads together and come up with some new products, Tom. I'm depending on you to lead the way. We need innovation. We either ride this crest or we go down."

Tom Benton was a serious young man of thirty. He had come to work in his father's factory as soon as he got out of college. In many ways he was much like his father. "It looks like Zachary Taylor's going to be our new president."

"That's a mistake." John Benton shook his head. "Americans make that mistake thinking because a man's a good military commander he'll make a good president. They're dead wrong, though. It's one thing to storm a city and take it by force. It's another thing to guide the financial problems of this country. Taylor will be elected, but we'll have to take care of ourselves. What I think—"

Benton broke off, for James Trenton had entered the room. "What is it, James?" he said.

"There's a gentleman to see you, sir."

A frown creased John Benton's forehead. "This early in the morning?"

"He says it's urgent." The butler cleared his throat. "He's from the police, Mr. Benton."

Surprise widened Benton's eyes. He glanced at his son and his wife. "What in the world can the police—" He suddenly broke off again, and his features hardened. "I'll see him in the study."

"Yes, sir." As the butler left the room, Benton got up. "It has to be something about Mark. He's in trouble again."

"Maybe not, Dad," Tom responded. "Maybe there's been some kind of trouble at the factory."

John Benton did not answer. He left the room in a hurry and walked down the hall. Turning into the study, he found a large man with blunt features and a pair of steady gray eyes waiting for him.

"Mr. Benton, my name is Harlow. I'm with the police. Sorry to disturb you at your home, but I thought it might be best."

"What is it, Detective Harlow?"

"I'm afraid it's not good news, sir. We have your son in custody."

"On what charge?"

"Drunk, disorderly—and perhaps a more serious charge of assault and battery."

"He was in a fight?"

Harlow shrugged his beefy shoulders. "He assaulted the police officer who tried to arrest him. I'm afraid it took considerable force to restrain him. He's not hurt, but he's been beaten around a little bit."

John Benton was a fair man, and he said at once, "Detective, I appreciate your coming all the way out to my home to inform us. I know it's not usual for you to go to such trouble."

"I think it will be all right, sir, if you'll settle the damages at the bar and pay the fine. I've already spoken with the judge, and he was upset, but he agreed to at least negotiate."

"I'll either come, or I'll have my son come down at once, Detective Harlow, and again I appreciate your kind consideration."

"Not at all, sir. I hope it all turns out well." He hesitated and said, "He seems a bit disturbed for a young man of his position. If I were you, I'd have a straight talk with him."

Benton's face took a hard cast. "You may depend on that, sir."

"Good-bye, sir."

As soon as he had shown Harlow out, John Benton went back into the dining room. As he entered, Jewel said, "Was it about Mark, dear?"

"Yes. He's in jail."

"In jail!" Tom exclaimed. "On what charge?"

"The usual. Drunk, disorderly, but this time he beat up a police officer. If I didn't have influence down at City Hall, he'd be going for a public trial. As it is, I think I can speak with Judge Smith and get the charges dropped. We'll have to pay the fines, of course, and there was some damage to the bar he was in."

Jewel Benton's hand fluttered at her breast. "Will you go at once? I'm worried about him."

Tom Benton got up. "Let me go, Father."

"All right, Tom. You take care of it, but bring him straight back home. I'm going to have a man-to-man talk with him."

Tom cast a glance at his mother but said only, "I'll bring him right back here."

Tom left the room hurriedly, and John Benton went over to the large window and stared out. He was silent until Jewel came over and stood beside him. He turned around and said, "Try not to worry any more than you have to, my dear."

"How can I help it?" She clung to John, and he held her protectively. She was a small woman, and her heart had been giving her some trouble lately. Benton gazed at her face now and said, "We're going to have to be a little bit hard on him this time, Jewel. This behavior has to stop."

"Not too hard, John. You don't know how hard you are sometimes."

Surprise washed across John Benton's features. "I don't think I'm all that tough. I try to be fair."

"Oh, you are, dear, you are. But you grew up in such a hard world. You still have some of it in you."

"We've tried being gentle with him. That hasn't worked. I think it's going to be hard to make Mark face up to his responsibilities as a man," John Benton said softly. He put his arms around her and embraced her, trying to think of a way to prepare for what he had made up his mind to do. "It takes hard lessons to make a man, and we've made life too easy for Mark. He's different from Tom, so we'll have to try a firmer hand." He felt her tremble and patted her shoulder. "Don't worry, my dear. We gave both our boys to God when they were born. Tom's been on the right track all of his life, it seems, but Mark's got a different spirit. He's a good young man, but he's terribly undisciplined, and that's what we have to work on."

Tom was waiting as Mark entered the outer room of the police station. His face was scratched on one side, and he had a large purple-green bruise on his other cheek. Seeing Tom study his face, Mark grinned cheerfully. "If you think I look bad, you ought to see the copper who I got into the scrap with."

Tom didn't smile. He turned to the officer and said, "Is he free to go?"

The sergeant, a red-faced Irishman, nodded curtly. "You paid the fines. Try to keep him sober and keep him out of bars. And most of all, if he ever takes off on another policeman, his stay won't be as short in this place."

"And the top of the mornin' to you too, Sergeant," Mark said breezily. "Come along, Tom. I'm starved. I don't recommend the food in this place."

The two left, and Tom said, "Father wants to see you at once."

"Well, of course he does. I'm all prepared for lecture number two hundred and sixteen." He drew a scowl and imitated the same tone that his father would have used if he had been there. "'Now, Mark, you've got to learn to behave yourself. After all, you're a Benton, and you've got to learn to act like a Benton. You weren't put into this world to enjoy yourself. You've got to be miserable and be a success.'"

Tom did not smile as Mark mimicked their father. Mark could do it perfectly. Usually it amused Tom, but he knew that this time was different and he said so. "You'd better get yourself braced, Mark. Dad's not going to take it easy on you as he has before."

"He's really on the warpath, is he?"

"He's very upset, and so is Mother. I try not to preach at you, Mark, but you really need to consider Mother. She's not well, and she's very worried about you."

The smile left Mark's face at once. He chewed his lower lip and said, "I know, Tom. I'm a rotter. Why can't I be a straight arrow like you, upright and going to work every day and always doing the right thing?"

"You're just a little bit slower to grow up, Mark," Tom said. He put his arm around his brother's shoulder and squeezed him. He had a real fondness for the young man. "You've got something that I like. You seem to get more joy out of life. I envy that. I'm an old sober side."

Mark Benton nodded and looked up at his older brother, who was three inches taller than he. "You're the good one, and I'm the bad one. That's all there is to it."

"Stuff! You don't believe that any more than I do. But listen to Dad carefully and do what he says. We'll come out of it all right."

"Sure. I'll charm him like I always do."

Tom Benton shook his head. "Not this time you won't."

Mark held himself perfectly straight as his father continued to speak firmly. He couldn't believe what he was hearing. He had prepared himself for a rough session with his father, but he had expected nothing like this.

"You don't mean that, Dad," he said finally. "I've told you I'd try to do better."

"I've heard that before, Mark. It won't wash this time. It's time you learned that life is not always about having fun all the time. You need to learn to be responsible and think of others for a change."

The sounds of the factory drifted up, and the midday sunshine threw a slanting beam of light across the two as they stood facing each other in John Benton's office. Benton's face was stern, and his voice was even firmer. "You've wasted your life, Mark. Your mother, your brother, and I have been waiting for you to grow up for years now. When you were younger, it just seemed like youthful high spirits, but you've done absolutely nothing with your life and the talents God blessed you with. You washed out of college when you could have graduated with honors. You weren't able to take hold here at the office, although Tom and I gave you every chance. You spend your nights carousing with a worthless crowd, and there's no purpose in your life."

"Just give me one more chance, Dad."

"All right. That's what I'll do, and here's what it is. You can come to work here on a trial basis."

"Sure, Dad, I'll be—"

"You'll start out as a floor sweeper, and if you prove you can do that, we'll let you be a helper to one of the mechanics."

"Floor sweeper!" Mark stared at his father. "You can't mean that! Why, they'd laugh me out of the factory."

"They're laughing at you already, son. They call you the prodigal son. Not one man in our factory or even in our acquaintanceship has any respect for you. So that's my offer."

"I won't do it!" Mark's anger flared. "I can take care of myself, and I don't need you, and I don't need Tom!"

"If that's the way you see it, then it's your choice. You won't get any help from either one of us anymore. We've already agreed." John Benton's heart was breaking, but he did not let any emotion show in his face. "You can't take care of yourself. You never have. You're not a Benton. You're not even a man. Go and grow up if that's what you want."

"All right, I will." Mark wheeled and left the office, his face set in anger. He slammed the door behind him and stomped out of the office, aware that his father's secretary was giving him an odd look.

Leaving the factory, he went straight home and began to pack his things. With each passing moment, his anger grew more intent. "He can't treat me like this! All I want is a chance, but I'll show him! I can get along without him, and he'll find it out."

When the suitcase was packed, Mark hesitated. He knew he had to say good-bye to his mother, and he dreaded it. *There's no way to make it sound good, but I'll do the best I can*, he thought. He loved his family, even his father and certainly his brother, but his mother was different. She had always been on his side whenever he had confrontations with his father and with Tom. Now he had to go tell her he was leaving home. "She'll be proud of me when I come back," he said. He stood there looking at the room that had been his for so many years and doubted he would ever come back to it.

The restaurant was full, but the waiter found Mark a place in a corner in the back. He had ordered his food, but when the plate came, he sat there pushing it around with his fork. His thoughts were grim and gloomy, for in the two months since he had left home, he had done absolutely nothing that he had promised himself he would. He had not found a job that fancied him, nor any other kind of opportunity. By now he had gone through most of the money that he had in his bank account.

"Mark, it's you!"

Mark looked up, and his face suddenly lightened. "Dave! What in the world are you doing here?" He got up and shook hands with Dave Matthews, his old roommate in college. The two of them had enjoyed good times together. Dave had finished college. Some of Mark's best memories were of this tall, young man who had been such a good friend to him. "Sit down. Have you eaten?"

"Yes, I've eaten, but you go ahead," Dave said as he took a seat.

"I'm not really hungry. What in the world are you doing in Memphis?" Mark asked.

"Looking for you."

Mark stared at Dave Matthews with surprise. "For me! What for?"

Dave Matthews had a lean, earnest face. There was a goodness in his expression that was a reflection of the kind of young man he was. He was excited now and said, "I'm going into a venture, and I'm looking for a partner. You're the first one I thought of."

"What kind of a venture? Tell me about it."

Matthews leaned across the table, his eyes flashing with excitement. "Did I ever tell you about my uncle Oscar who lives in Chicago?"

"I don't think so."

"Well, he owns a large stockyard on the south side. I've been visiting him, and he told me all about the cattle business. The thing is, Mark, beef prices are sky high in Chicago. The cattle market is the stock market of the world, really, but my uncle is gettin' desperate. He has to pay such a high price for the cattle, so he's looking for new sources, and I think I found one."

"I didn't know you knew anything about the cattle business," Mark said.

"I don't. I don't know anything about the meat business, either, but I know a friend who went to Texas. I hear from him pretty often. Mark, you wouldn't believe how cheap cattle are down there! Sometimes you can pick up good steers, Fred says, for two dollars a head. You know what they'd sell for in Chicago? Why, we'd make a killing."

Mark sat there, leaning forward, and Dave's excitement began to creep into him. From time to time he posed questions about Dave's scheme, which was to go to Texas, buy a big herd of cattle, and drive them to Chicago.

"But, Dave, why aren't people doing that already if there's money in it?"

"Well, in the first place, it'll take a little money. In the second place, they probably never thought of it. In any case, we can do it. I know we can."

"Well, we don't know a thing about driving cattle. We'd be babes in the woods."

Dave shook his head, and his face grew intent. "I know we don't know anything, but there are men in Texas who know this work. We get the money, and we head down there and hire a good trail master. He hires good hands. You and I can learn to sit on a horse. We're young and strong. It'll be an adventure."

"How much will it cost?"

"Well, the more we take, the more money we'll make. I'd say we need at least five thousand dollars. I've got about half of that. What about you?" Dave paused and said, "But I guess you'd be crazy to do a thing like this. I mean, your father owns one of the biggest farm machinery factories in the country. You'll go right to the top there. I guess you already are."

"No. That's not going to happen. As a matter of fact, my father and I have disagreed. I've been looking for something to do, but I never thought of a venture like this."

"We can do it, Mark. You know we always did everything we set out to do when we were in college. Some of them were pretty wild ideas, but this is the biggest thing we'd ever try."

Mark sat there for a long moment. "I can't go to my family for money," he said. "But I have one asset. My grandfather left me some money. I think it's at least a couple of thousand."

"That'd be enough. Finish your meal. We've got a lot of talking to do."

The steamship *Essex* nosed into the harbor at Galveston, and the two young men at the very prow were excited. "There it is . . . Texas. Pretty big place, Mark," Dave said.

"I can't believe we've really done it," Mark replied. He gazed out at the flat country that stretched all the way to the horizon and tried to let his imagination roam to the immense distance from Texas to Chicago. "Sometimes I think we're the world's biggest fools to think we could do a thing like this."

The two of them had gathered their assets and taken a riverboat from Memphis down to New Orleans. There they had secured passage on the *Essex*. Now that they were actually within sight of Texas, both of them felt a little odd. Mark said suddenly, "This is my last chance, Dave. It's just got to work."

Dave was staring at the land, and his face was sober as well. "It'll be hard, but it's a great opportunity. We'll give it the best we've got."

The *Essex* eased up beside the wharf, and for one moment a wave of doubt swept across Mark Benton. It was a risky, daring, and even dangerous venture they were proposing, but he was remembering his father's words. *You're not a Benton. You're not even a man.* He turned and slapped Dave on the shoulder, suddenly filled with resolve. "We'll succeed, Dave. We'll get those cattle to Chicago if we have to carry 'em on our backs!"

CHAPTER
SEVENTEEN

Black Eagle fingered the scalp that he held in his hand. The thrill of being on the warpath ran thick in his Comanche blood. He looked up, and his eyes narrowed. "Lion is coming back."

Bear Killer was already looking in the direction of the approaching horseman. The war chief of the Comanches was not tall but erect and had obsidian eyes. "If you weren't toying with that scalp, you would have heard him coming much sooner. It's a habit that will kill you one day, Black Eagle."

Black Eagle laughed. "A warrior deserves his rewards."

The two Comanches waited until the rider came in. Lion was the youngest of the three brothers still alive. He was barely twenty years old, but he was already a tried and trusted warrior. He came off his horse with one smooth fluid motion, and his face shone with excitement. "They are bedding down for the night. We could take them now."

Both Lion and Black Eagle looked eagerly at Bear Killer. Neither of them dreamed of making any further suggestions, but they were both ready for more scalps. It was now the eleventh day of their war party, and they had cut a swath of death across the country looking for isolated cabins. Once they had scouted them out, making sure there were not too many men, they would ride in and rape the women and kill the children, at times even pausing to torture their victims.

Bear Killer did not speak, and his silence held his brothers still. He was a deep thinker and seemed to have some natural gift of knowing what to do. He was silent so long, however, that Lion could not keep quiet. "Why are we waiting, brother? These white eyes are fools."

"They may not be such fools as they look." Bear Killer removed his knife from the sheath, held it in his hands, and tested the edge of it with his thumb. "We have found the whites to be foolish in many ways, but these men seem to have a secret."

"What secret?" Black Eagle asked with surprise. "They never even put out a guard at night. They're like dumb cattle, brother. They act as if nothing could kill them. We've never had an opportunity like this."

Indeed, the war party of nine Comanches had been puzzled by the actions of the men herding the cattle toward the north. Ordinarily, the men who herded cattle were tough, hard men adept with guns and pistols that shot many times. Some of them were as dangerous as the Rangers, whom the Comanches had learned to respect and avoid. And they always had guards watching for danger all night.

But these men acted as if they were alone in the world. They stayed drunk most of the time. One night Black Eagle himself had crept in close enough to listen to them arguing and drinking themselves to sleep. Bear Killer had insisted on following them for three days now, watching them while staying invisible. He had been puzzled at their lack of concern for safety. Now, however, he looked up and said, "I have not believed that even white men could be such fools. Do they think The People are all dead?"

Black Eagle stared at his older brother. He knew that when Bear Killer's fury was ignited, nothing could stand before him. But now he felt his brother was showing too much caution. "They'll be drunk by the time the moon is high. It is our time to attack and take their scalps. The warriors are restless."

Suddenly, Bear Killer shoved the knife back into the sheath and turned to face south, the direction from which the large herd was coming. "I have been wrong," he said. "I thought there was a trick here, that somehow they were trying to draw us in so that they could surprise us. But we have looked behind them for many miles, and there is nothing there. No one is guarding them. We will take them at dawn," he said.

Black Eagle grinned. "There are no women there, but we will have sport with the men. I love to hear them scream. They sound almost like women when they die at our hands."

Bear Killer stared at his brother but said only, "These white men had better enjoy their drinking tonight, for it's the last drink they will have on the earth!"

As the sun edged slowly down into the west, Mark got off of his horse with effort. Every muscle in his body was sore from head to foot. He had thought he was in fair physical condition, but he had found out differently after riding so many hours in the saddle each day. He was so saddle-galled on his inner thighs that it was an agony to stay in the saddle.

"This drive has been a nightmare, Dave," he said wearily as he watched his friend dismount. He noted that Matthews seemed as worn out as he himself. "We should never have tried it."

Dave Matthews straightened up and put his hand in the center of his back. He had discovered after the first few days that he had a weak back. The jolting of the horse for hours at a time had become agony. His face, Mark saw, was gaunt, and his lips were white and parched.

"You're right, Mark, but if we stop now, we'll lose all that we've invested."

The sound of the men yelling and laughing drifted to the two. "We hired the wrong man to make this trip," Mark said grimly.

"You're right about that, but he seemed tough enough," Dave said as he rubbed his back.

Rance Mottler was the man who had agreed to head up the cattle drive. He had, indeed, seemed tough enough when they hired him. The man had hired a group of riders who claimed to be experienced cowhands, but they had looked ragged and run-down to both Dave and Mark. Not only had Mottler proved to be a drunkard, but most of the men he had hired loved to tilt the bottle at night around the campfire as well. They had been on the trail now out of Galveston for over a week, picking up cattle as they went and drifting them toward the northeast. Unfortunately, the whole ordeal was not turning out as they had expected. The men stayed drunk most of the time, and they had made the mistake of not hiring a cook. The food had been practically inedible, and both Mark and Dave had lost weight.

Mark turned to Dave, shaking his head, and said, "Dave, I think we'd better call it off."

Dave Matthews stared at him, his eyes seemingly shrunk back in his head. He did not answer for a time, and then he said, "I think you're right. We're going to lose our shirts, Mark. We paid too much for these cattle in the first place."

"More of Mottler's advice," Mark replied bitterly. "We were a couple of babes in the woods. In the morning we'll start back to the coast, sell the cattle for what we can, pay off these drunks, and call it quits."

Mark awoke long before daylight. He looked at his watch and saw that it was nearly two hours until dawn. Getting to his feet, he groaned, for every movement he made was painful. He had not undressed the night before, so he put on his hat and glanced over at Dave, who was still sleeping soundly. The rest of the men were scattered around. They looked like bodies thrown down from a height, all dead drunk. With a disgust such as he had never felt, Mark picked up his rifle and walked away from the camp. They had passed a spring a ways back, and he had the idea that a deer or an antelope might come for a drink. He could kill it, and he and Mark could skin it and cook it themselves. Roasted venison would be better than what they had been eating on the trail lately!

It took him longer than he thought to get to the spring. He found some brush for cover and sat there waiting for some game to show, but nothing did. The moon was bright overhead, and he remembered what an older man had told him in Galveston. *That there's a Comanche moon, young feller. When it's full like that, them hostiles love to ride down out of the north killin' and rapin' and torturin'. Ain't a good time to be makin' a trip.*

The moonlight was bright enough that Mark could see very clearly off into the distance. He had seen the outlines of the mountains farther to the north, but the land they were on for the last few days was flat and covered with thin grass and trees called mesquite. They were twisted and gnarled, and when you tried to burn them, they burned with a greasy smoke. Dave had especially hated the sight of them. "If there are trees in hell," he had said to Mark, "they must be mesquite trees. What I wouldn't give to see a good, tall, straight pine or an oak."

From far off came the lonesome sound of a coyote. The mournful quality of it seemed to reach down deep inside Mark Benton. It touched a nerve somehow, and he sat waiting there, wishing he had never heard of Texas or of a cattle drive. He knew now that he only had one choice, which was to go back to Memphis and tell his father that he was right. Yet the thought of admitting his failures was bitter.

He watched overhead as a small cloud drifted across the heavens. He wondered if it would hit the moon or miss, and as he watched, it slid across the moon and partially covered it.

The time went on, and after a good half hour he got wearily to his feet. "I might as well go back. Mottler's not going to like going back. They might all quit. We may lose all these cattle, but we've got to get out of here."

As Mark moved in the direction of the camp, his thoughts went back again and again to the scene where his father had told him, *You're not a Benton. You're not a man.* As the light crept along the edges of the horizon and dawn began to show itself, Mark Benton felt as sorry for himself as a man could.

His feet hurt, and he dreaded the idea of another day in the saddle. As he approached the camp, he decided he would let Dave break the news to Mottler. After all, this whole crazy venture was Dave's idea. He was merely a silent partner. *A broke silent partner now*, Mark thought bitterly.

Suddenly, a jolt ran along Mark's nerves at the sound of rifle fire. He stopped dead still. His first thought was that the men were shooting off their revolvers in a drunken spree, but then a scream split the air. It was high-pitched and full of mortal agony.

"Indians!"

Mark began to run forward, thinking of the warnings that he and

Dave had received from people about Indians. Mottler had said there was no real danger. He had told them that the Indians were farther to the west, and that they had missed them by heading east. But the horrible screams continued, and Mark ran until his breath was ragged. He came up over the small rise, and the sight he saw made his blood run cold. The camp was filled with half-naked savages. They were attacking with their tomahawks and screaming blood-thirsty cries. Mottler had come out of his blanket and was trying to get his gun free, but a tall savage struck him in the neck with a tomahawk. As he fell to the ground, blood gushing, the Indian hacked at him, killing him with one swift blow to the skull.

Mark began to tremble. He tried to put a shell into the chamber of the rifle, but his hands were trembling so much with fear that he had difficulty doing it. The screaming and yelling continued to fill the morning air. When he finally got the shell in the chamber, his hands were still trembling so much he could not hold the rifle steady enough to shoot. He saw immediately there was no hope and dropped down so that the Indians would not see him. As he did, he saw that two of the savages had pulled Dave Matthews out of his blanket. One of them struck him with a tomahawk, but it was with the flat end, and Dave cried out and fell to the ground. As Mark looked on in horror, the rest of the men were slaughtered without mercy except for Dave and two others.

Mark watched as they staked the three men out spread eagle and ripped their clothes from them. He had heard of Indian tortures, but the horror of this was more than he could bear.

I've got to help Dave, I've got to! he told himself, but as he raised the rifle, it wavered so that he could not draw a clear bead. He knew that once he shot and gave away his position, he would join the dead or those about to be tortured. He saw one of the warriors bend over with his knife, and Dave Matthews's scream went straight to the center of Mark Benton's soul. With a desperate cry that he suppressed, he turned and ran blindly away. He could not run fast enough to drown out the sound of Dave's screams and the cries of agony of the other two men. He threw the rifle down and put his hands over his ears and ran until he could run no more. He did not look back as he headed through the mesquite trees toward the north—anything to get away from the nightmare that he had just witnessed.

★   ★   ★

The sun had become a single white spot in the sky, pouring its rays down mercilessly on the dry ground. Mark had lost his hat, and his face and hands were now sunburned to a brilliant red. He had lost track of the days that he had been moving. He thought it was four, but he could not be sure anymore. Twice he had found small springs among the rocks, but he knew he could not stay there. The fear of being discovered by the Indians and suffering the same fate as the others kept him on the move. He'd had nothing to eat, and now as he staggered along, his vision was betraying him. He thought he could see mountains, but they seemed to be wavering off in the distance. He closed his eyes hard and blinked and opened them again, but the mountains were gone. He had seen not a single sign of life except for vultures soaring high above him.

For the first two days he had looked fearfully over his shoulder, expecting the Indians to be trailing him. Now, however, he had stopped expecting anything except death. He knew that unless he found food soon he wouldn't survive. His boots had been too tight, and now his feet were blistered. He had taken off his boots and washed his feet at the springs, but it had been agony to put his boots back on.

His lips were dry and cracked, and there was no moisture in his mouth. His tongue was swollen, and he could hardly swallow. Finally, with a small cry he collapsed, and consciousness began to leave him. He tried to pray, but he couldn't. His mind, his heart, and his soul were filled with the sound of Dave Matthews's dying screams.

I should have gone to help him. I should have! The guilt of leaving his friend to die overwhelmed him as he lay there.

He knew he was dying, and the last conscious thought was, *I wish I'd done things differently.*

"Well, Brodie, we missed him again." Captain Mac looked worn by the trail. His beard, which was usually trim, was ragged. He looked out into the desert and said wistfully, "It was Bear Killer all right, your old friend."

Brodie was exhausted, as was every member of the Rangers. He looked over and saw Snake Jones and Simon Gore, and farther back Sally Duo and Hack Wilson. Peach, the black tracker, was up ahead, but they all knew they had missed out again on catching the most feared war chief of the Comanche.

"We can keep goin', Captain," Brodie said. "I hate to let him get away from us again."

"He's got the best of us this time."

"But all them people he killed, Captain. I can't stand the thought of it."

They had followed the trail of Bear Killer's rage. At several cabins they found butchered carcasses, tortured men and women, and slaughtered children. The Rangers had followed the trail hard, but the trail led into the Llano Estacado, and then it disappeared.

"We can't follow him out there. He knows where the water is this time of the year, and we don't. Our horses are in poor shape. We'll be lucky to get back to Austin."

Brodie felt a wave of disgust at having to give up. "I hate to be outsmarted by an Indian."

"You're not outsmarted by an Indian. It's the country. He knows it like we don't. Come on. I've got to tell the men we're starting back," Captain Mac said.

The troop was so worn out from tracking the Indians for days that they didn't mind obeying Captain Mac's instruction to turn back toward Austin. They had lost two men already, and he wasn't ready to risk losing any more to surprise attacks from the Indians.

They traveled steadily, yet slowly, that day, and late that afternoon Peach came back from scouting ahead, his eyes troubled. "Another massacre up ahead over that rise, Captain."

"A cabin?"

"No. I think it was a bunch of drovers. There's cattle wandering everywhere, but the drovers, they're all dead."

Macklin's face hardened. "We'll have a look," he said briefly.

A look was all they needed. Brodie had no desire to do more than glance at the scattered bodies. Three of the men had been staked out and tortured to death, and the others had been slain in a surprise attack.

"We'll have to bury these folks," Macklin said. "As few as they were, they were fools to try to drive across this country."

When they had finished burying the dead, the Rangers mounted their horses to continue on. Brodie looked at the cattle and said to Pokey Reese, "A lot of cattle here. Don't belong to anybody now, I guess. I'd like to get 'em to our place."

Pokey Reese, undersized with tow-colored hair and freckles, shook his head. "There's plenty of ornery longhorns without drivin' these, I reckon. I wonder who these poor fellers were."

"Hard to recognize 'em," Brodie said tersely.

After riding hard for hours, they made camp late that afternoon. The next day Captain Mac sent Peach out again as a scout, and Brodie rode with him. Both men kept their eyes alert, but Peach shook his head.

"I ain't seen no sign of them Indians. I think we'd have to go into their country to catch 'em now."

"I guess so." Suddenly, Brodie narrowed his eyes. "Look there, Peach."

Peach shaded his eyes and looked in the direction Brodie pointed. "That looks like another body."

"Come on. It probably is, but how'd he get so far away from the camp?"

The two men spurred their mounts and rode toward the huddled body of a man. They both came off their horses, and when Peach bent over him, he said, "He's alive, Mr. Brodie, but he's in bad shape!"

"Has he been shot?" Brodie asked as he knelt beside the man.

"No, he's just starved and about to die. Let's give him just a little water." They rolled the man over, and his face was cooked from the scorching sun. "Don't look like no cowboy," Peach said. He tilted the canteen up, but the man's lips did not move. Finally, the man coughed and swallowed, and Peach said, "Maybe he'll make it."

"I don't think so. He looks more dead than alive to me," Brodie said as he held his head while Peach gave him more water.

The two waited until the rest of the Rangers got there, and Captain Macklin said, "I don't know what to do with him."

Brodie said, "Captain, our ranch is not too far from here. If we make a travois, I could take him there. My ma is good with hurt people—better than most doctors."

"All right, if we can find enough wood to make somethin' to haul him with," Mac said. "You want someone to ride with you?"

"No, Captain, I can make it fine on my own. This fellow's probably gonna die on the way, but it's the best chance he's got."

Two of the Rangers managed to find some saplings and quickly made a travois in the Indian fashion. When they had finished, they lifted the sick man onto the travois. They covered him up best they could, tied him in, and then hitched it to Brodie's horse. Brodie mounted and said, "I'll see you fellas later in Austin."

"Hang on to your scalp, Brodie," Pokey said.

"You too."

Jerusalem and Mary Aidan had seen the horse approaching. At first they did not know who it was, but Mary Aidan said, "That's Brodie! I know his horse."

"Looks like he's hauling something," Jerusalem said. The two women were standing on the porch, and now they went out into the yard and waited. When Brodie stopped in front of them, he tried to grin, but his lips were parched.

"Howdy, Ma. Howdy, Mary Aidan."

"Brodie, are you all right?" Jerusalem asked.

Brodie came off his horse stiffly. "I'm all right, but that feller there is in bad shape."

The two women went back and removed the cloth from the face of the injured man. "Why, he looks dead!" Mary Aidan said.

"He near about is," Brodie said. "He's all dried out. Hasn't been shot or nothin', but he's pretty far gone."

Mary Aidan looked at the sunburned face. It was peeling badly. "You brought him home to die, Brodie."

Jerusalem Ann shook her head. "I'd not be too quick to say that. We'll do our best for him, and the good Lord will help us. Come on. Let's get him into the house."

CHAPTER
EIGHTEEN

For a long time nothing but darkness, black and intense, surrounded him on all sides. It was as silent as the inside of a tomb. After a time he began hearing sounds, which he slowly came to identify as voices. At first, they seemed far away and faint. Though he struggled to understand the words, he could not make them out. It was merely mumbled voices, which meant nothing to him.

Slowly he was able to distinguish between the voices. Some were male, some were female. He became aware of the hands that touched him too. Some were rough and others were gentle. At times he could feel himself being lifted, and liquid was put on his lips. This was the best time, for he soaked up all of the water that touched his lips. He wanted to ask for more, but he didn't seem to have the strength yet to speak.

Finally, a moment came when he was aware of the light. His eyes had been swollen shut at first, but now a milky, translucent light was coming from somewhere. Cautiously, he opened his eyes and then had to shut them, for the light was too bright after the darkness. He slowly opened his eyes again and could barely see his body. He was lying on a bed, and the light was coming from a window over to his right. It was a pale, opaque light that illuminated the room.

His first conscious thought was, *I've been hurt.* He opened his eyes a bit farther and looked around. The room was large with a high ceiling and two windows, one at his right and the other on his left. The head of the bed he was lying on was against a wall without a window. He did not know where he was, for nothing was familiar. A blanket was hanging from one wall for decoration. A picture of some man he had never seen was on the opposite wall. A table beside him had a pitcher of water. Just the sight of the pitcher made the raging thirst make itself felt. With a grunt, he swung himself over and tried to grasp the pitcher. Instead, in his weakness, he hit the pitcher and sent it off the table. It fell with a resounding crash, and he fell back on the bed.

Almost at once the door opened, and a woman rushed in. She was young with bright red hair and green eyes, and he tried to think if he knew her, but his thoughts were jumbled.

"Well, you woke up at last and managed to break the pitcher, I see." The woman came over and stood looking down at him. "Can you understand me?"

Mark tried to speak but had to lick his lips. "Yes," he mumbled finally. "Where am I?"

"You're at Yellow Rose Ranch. My name's Mary Aidan Hardin."

She was looking at him critically, he thought, and he felt he had done something wrong. "Could I have . . . some water?"

At that moment he heard another voice, and he saw an older woman enter the room. She came and stood over him with a smile and put her hand on his forehead. "Well, you decided to live." She looked over and said, "What happened to the water pitcher?"

"He broke it, Mama."

"Well, go get some more. I'll bet you're thirsty, aren't you?"

"Yes," Mark whispered. The red-haired girl turned to leave, and he looked up and saw that the woman had the same red hair and green eyes. "What . . . what happened to me?"

"Don't you remember anything?" When Mark shook his head, the woman said, "My son found you just about dead out on the desert and brought you here. You were in pretty poor shape, but you're going to be better now. What's your name?"

For a moment Mark had to think, and then his mind seemed to clear. "Mark Benton."

"What were you doing out in the desert like that? Were you lost?"

"Yes. My friend got killed. The Indians killed him."

At that moment the girl came back carrying another pitcher of water. She poured a glass full, reached down, and hauled Mark upright rather abruptly. "Here, drink some of this," she said tersely.

She seemed harsh and bothered by him for some reason. He wondered why she was treating him like that. Slowly, his thoughts began to settle down now. He gulped the water thirstily, and some of it spilled, running over his chin and onto his chest.

"That's all you can have for now," the girl said, and quickly pulled the glass back. "You need to take it a little bit at a time," Mary Aidan said. She moved his arm, and his head plopped back on the pillow.

"Don't be so rough, Mary Aidan!" Jerusalem said sharply. "You need to eat something as quick as you can. I've got some broth. Been waiting for you to wake up for two days. I'll go get it. Mary Aidan, you stay here with him."

"All right, Mama."

Mark watched as Jerusalem left, and then he turned to look at the girl. She was watching him critically with a half-lidded attention. Her eyes were wide-spaced, and their green color seemed to have no bottom. Her lips lay together almost willfully, and a summer darkness lay over her skin. She was wearing a simple blue dress, and as weak as he was, Mark noticed that she had clean-running, physical lines.

"How'd you get out there in the desert?" she asked directly.

Mark considered the question. It was difficult to organize his thoughts. They swarmed in his head almost like bees, and he had to wait for a few moments before he said, "My friend and I were taking some cattle to Chicago."

"You're no cowboy. Look at your hands. They're soft."

Mark was too tired and weak to think clearly. "No," he finally admitted, "I'm no cowboy."

"Then what were you doing driving cattle? Seems like a dumb thing to do if you didn't know what you were doing."

Her questions became too complicated for Mark, and he whispered, "Could I have some more water?"

Once again the girl lifted him up, and he drank thirstily. "That's good," he whispered. "I never thought anything could taste so good."

"You nearly died out there in that desert. You would have if my brother Brodie hadn't found you."

"The others are all dead," he said as he lay back.

Mary Aidan stared at him. "The Indians killed them?"

"Yes. They . . . they killed my friend and all the others."

"How'd you get away, then?"

At that moment Jerusalem came back with a bowl with a spoon sticking out of it. "Prop him up, Mary Aidan, and we'll get somethin' into him. He can answer your questions later."

The girl reached down and pulled Mark up to a sitting position. Roughly, she shoved the pillow behind him, and Jerusalem gave her a disgusted look. "You treat him like he's a sack of feed. You're not much around sick people, daughter." She turned to Mark and said, "This isn't hot, but you need to eat something. You're just about starved to death."

Mark felt no hunger at first, but as she spooned the broth into his mouth, his hunger returned like a famished wolf. He ate all of it, and Jerusalem said, "Now, a little bit at a time and water too." She put the bowl down and pulled a chair up. "You feel like talking?"

"I . . . guess so."

"Your family is probably worried sick about you. We need to get word to them. Where are you from?"

"Memphis."

"In Tennessee? Well, what's your people's name?"

Suddenly, Mark was growing sleepy. The water and the broth had dulled his senses. His eyes drooped, and he suddenly went to sleep.

"Well, look at him. Weak as a newborn kitten. A man ought to be tougher than that," Mary Aidan said with dissatisfaction.

"Hush, Mary. You don't know anything about what he's been through. Here. Help me get him laid down." They pulled Mark until he was lying flat on his back, and Jerusalem put the pillow under him. She stood up, then said, "He's had a hard go of it. Did he say anything while I was gone?"

"He said his friend was killed by the Indians."

"That was Bear Killer," Jerusalem said grimly. "Brodie and the Ranger troop were on his trail. They didn't catch 'em, though." She looked down at the still face, reached down, and laid her hand on his cheek. "He'd be a good-looking fella if he'd fill out a little bit and had some of these whiskers off."

"He must be a fool of a greenhorn to try to drive cattle all the way to Chicago. Only a fool would try that."

"We're all fools at one time or another, so don't be judgmental. Now, let's get out of here and let him rest. He needs it."

"We didn't find out much about that crew that got wiped out," Brodie said. "We chased Bear Killer halfway through Texas, but we couldn't catch him. He's gone back to the Llano Estacado now." Brodie's face turned grim and moody. "No catching him there." He turned and said, "How's that fella I brought in? What's his name?"

"His name's Mark Benton," Mary Aidan said. "That's about all he said so far."

"He almost didn't make it," Jerusalem said. "Another day and he would have been dead. You did good, Brodie."

"He can't be a sensible sort of man," Mary Aidan said. "Doesn't know anything about cattle. He's a greenhorn from Memphis, Tennessee, trying to drive cattle all the way from Texas to Chicago. Sounds foolish to me."

"Men do foolish things sometimes," Clay remarked. "Why, I can recall a time or two I done some myself. Is he gonna be all right, Jerusalem?"

"Oh yes. He's sitting up now and feeding himself. He doesn't say much. There's an odd look in his eyes."

"I guess that's understandable. Anybody who survives an attack by Comanches is not likely to come out of it without some changes."

"Reckon I'll go in and have a talk with him," Clay said.

"If he's asleep, don't wake him up, Clay."

"I'll go with you," Mary Aidan said. "Time for him to have something else to eat. I think he could have something solid, couldn't he, Mama?"

"I think so. He needs all his strength."

Clay rose and limped away from the table. Mary Aidan filled a plate full of food and went in after him. When she entered the room, she found Clay sitting in a chair beside Benton's bed, and she moved to the other side. "I brought you something more solid. Some green beans and squash and some meat. I'll have to chop it up for you."

"Thanks, miss."

Mark was sitting up in bed, and his eyes went to the young woman. He already knew that she disapproved of him, and it troubled him. His eyes went back to Clay, and he said, "So that was the scheme my friend and I had. He came to me with this idea of driving cattle to his uncle, who owns a stockyard in Chicago. I didn't know any more about it than he did, but he made it sound pretty reasonable at the time."

"Here. Eat this while it's warm," Mary Aidan said. She put the plate down on Mark's lap and set the glass of milk on the table. "Try not to spill any."

"Bossy, ain't she?" Clay grinned. "She gets that from her mama. I guess if I put up with it, you can, too, Mark." He leaned back in his chair and shook his head. "I don't know as anybody's ever driven a herd all the way to Chicago. If it could be done, I'd like to try it myself, but it would be a tough job."

"We never should have tried it." Mark put a bite of squash in his mouth and said, "This is good, Miss Mary."

"Mama cooked it. Her cooking is always good." She pulled another chair up and stared at Mark.

He could almost feel her displeasure. "I guess you think I'm not much."

"Mary Aidan's hard to please," Clay remarked. "She's been spoiled, and I guess I'm to blame for spoiling her. You'll have to pardon her. Her manners ain't very good."

"Why, my manners are fine! I just can't see why a man would do something as foolish as this one."

Clay frowned. "Why don't you wait until he's on his feet before you start kickin' him around. Now, you hush. I want to hear more about this."

"Not much really to tell," Mark said. "We hired the wrong man to herd the cattle. He was a drunk, and he hired others who were no better. They didn't even put out a guard at night."

"Well, you had the bad luck to run into the worst of the Comanche war chiefs. We know him pretty well. His name is Bear Killer."

"You know him?"

"Better than I'd like. He raided our ranch and kidnapped our daughter Moriah years back. Kept her a prisoner. She had his baby while she was held captive. You'll meet him when you get up. His name is Ethan. Fine boy." He suddenly said, "Well, by jimminy, Ethan was at the table when Brodie was talkin' about Bear Killer! We got to remind each other to keep our mouths shut."

"How old is the boy?" Mark asked.

"He's eight now."

Mark did not comment, and Clay said, "I expect we'd better get word to your folks?"

Mark seemed disturbed by the question. "Well, the truth is I'm not getting along too well with my people. When I get a little better, I'll write them a letter."

"Well, that's thoughtless!" Mary Aidan could keep silent no longer. "The least you can do is write to them and tell them you're all right."

"You stay out of this, Mary Aidan. Let the man eat in peace. He's old enough to know how to take care of himself."

The two sat there, and Mark found himself thinking of Dave Matthews. He put the fork down abruptly as a memory of Dave's cheerful face came before him. He felt the two looking at him and swallowed hard. "Dave Matthews was my best friend. We went to college together, and it's my fault he's dead."

"Why, that don't sound likely," Clay said with surprise. "He's the one that got the trip up, wasn't he?"

"Yes he was, but when the Indians attacked, I wasn't there. I had gone out hoping to shoot a deer or something. I heard the screams and the guns going off, and when I got back to camp, most of the men had already been killed . . . and I saw them—" His words broke off, and he looked down at his hands, which were trembling. "I saw them stake Dave out. I had a rifle in my hand, Mr. Taliferro, and I just stood there. He began to scream, and I . . . I ran away." His head was bowed, and tears were running down his cheeks.

Clay reached out and put his hand on the man's shoulder. "There wasn't anything you could have done, Mark. You'd be dead if you'd tried to help him." He got up hurriedly and said, "Come on, Mary Aidan. Let's let Mark rest some more."

He left the room, and Mary Aidan followed him. As soon as they were outside, Mary Aidan exclaimed, "Why, he was crying! What kind of a man is he that would cry?"

Clay's eyes blazed. He reached out and took Mary Aidan by the arm, and his grip caused her to cry out. "You hush your mouth, girl! What do you know about what he just went through? Have you ever seen your best friend staked out and tortured by Comanches? I don't want to hear any more about this. Stop bein' any more of a fool than you have to." He let go of her and then turned and stomped down the hall.

Mary Aidan stared at him with astonishment. Clay had been nothing but kind to her ever since she had known him, and she loved him dearly. She felt angry but also ashamed at his rebuke. She rubbed her arm, which hurt from his iron grip, but she lifted her head and said, "I love you, Clay, but he's not much of a man that would cry like a baby. Men don't cry!" She gave a disgusted look toward the room where Mark Benton lay, then turned and walked away, filled with indignation.

CHAPTER
NINETEEN

As Maggie approached the big house, which she called the main ranch building, she found Rose Jean sitting in a chair drying her hair.

"Hello, Maggie," Rose said.

"Just washed your hair?"

"Yes. I'm going to church later, and I felt rather grimy."

Maggie paused long enough to look down at the smaller woman. "How's that sick fella doin'?" she asked.

"His name's Mark Benton. He's doing much better. Able to get around a little bit now." She ran the comb through her glowing brown hair and shook her head slightly. "He'd do better if Mary Aidan didn't make things so hard on him."

"Why is she doin' that?"

"She's very young, Maggie, and she hasn't found out yet that life hurts people."

Maggie grinned. "She'll find out sooner or later."

"Yes, she will, but the truth is she's been spoiled to death by everyone in the family. By her brothers, her mother, and Clay's the worst. One day she'll find out that we all get hurt, and we need people when times get tough. She doesn't know it yet, though." She put the brush down and began to dress her hair. "They're having a revival meeting in town at the Methodist church. I wish you'd come and go with me."

"I don't have nothin' to wear."

Rose was wise enough not to give the stock reply that it didn't matter. Instead, she said, "We need to fix your wardrobe up a little bit." This was as tactful as she could put it, but Maggie laughed.

"My wardrobe is these britches and this old shirt."

"Don't you have a dress at all?"

"Never had no place to wear one to."

"You're larger than I am, but you're about Jerusalem's size. I'll bet you could wear one of her dresses." She saw Maggie hesitate and said, "We'd love to have you go."

Maggie's eyes grew cautious. "Who all's going?"

"Just Clinton and me."

Instantly, Maggie shook her head. "Don't reckon I'm much of a one for church." She turned around and walked off without another word.

Rose Jean watched her and shook her head. "It's a shame the way that young woman was raised. I don't think she'll ever listen to anybody."

Brodie stepped off of the sweating horse he had been breaking and patted her. "You're gonna be a good girl when you learn how to behave," he said. The mare tried to bite him, and he smacked her on the nose and laughed. "You got spirit. I like that in a female. Now, you get out of here. We'll have another session when we both get rested up."

Leaving the corral, he realized he was ravenously hungry. It was still two hours before suppertime, but he turned and went to the kitchen built off of the bunkhouse where the crew stayed. As he approached, he smelled something very good. When he stepped inside, he saw Maggie standing at the table cutting steaks. "Hi, Maggie," he said. "I'm so hungry my stomach thinks my throat's been cut."

"You can wait 'til suppertime, Brodie, just like the rest of 'em."

"No, I can't. What's that I smell?" He walked over to the oven and opened the door of the old ancient stove. "Pies!"

"You stay out of those pies!"

"Oh, come on, Maggie, you got a tender heart. I'm gonna die if I don't have somethin' to eat right now."

Maggie had liked Brodie from the time she had met him. He had been free and easy with her, and he always had treated her with respect, even though he teased her from time to time.

"I'll tell you what I'll do. You give me some of that pie, and I'll let you ride my new mare I'm breaking."

"No deal."

"Well then, how about this? I'll take you into town, and you and me will have us a good time."

"Doin' what?"

"Anything you like."

"I like to play poker."

"Then we'll go to the Golden Lady and bust the bank there. Frisco Farr made too much money off of me, anyhow. Are you any good at poker?"

"Yes, I am," she said, smiling.

"Well, how about it? Is it a deal, then?"

Maggie found it hard to resist Brodie's cheerful grin. "I guess one piece wouldn't hurt."

"Okay, but I get to cut it."

Maggie laughed. "I know what you'll do." Nevertheless, she walked over and pulled the pie out and cut him a quarter of it. "That's all you get now."

"You're a hard woman, Maggie Brennan, but a fine cook." Brodie took the fork she handed him and began to eat.

"You're gonna choke yourself eatin' so fast. Eat slow and enjoy it."

"No, I like my food quick and fast. Tell you what," he said. "Tomorrow mornin' real early let's me and you go fishin'. It's coolin' off, but I know a spot on the river where there's some mighty fine catfish. Then we'll come back, and I'll clean 'em, and you can cook 'em all for me. We'll make a day of it."

Maggie smiled warmly. "Okay, Brodie. I always loved to fish."

"Be up early. I want to be there about dawn. That's when the fish bite the best. I'll dig us some worms after the sun goes down." Brodie sat there eating the rest of the piece of pie and drinking the cup of coffee she had put beside him. As she continued to cut the meat for the evening meal for the cowhands, he could tell something was bothering her.

"What's the matter, Maggie? You look down in the mouth."

"'Tis nothin'."

"Sure it is." He got up, came over, and put his arm around her shoulder. "Come on. You can tell me. We're buddies, ain't we?"

"I can't never be no lady, Brodie."

Brodie was shocked. "What do you mean you can't be a lady? You can if you want to. I thought you liked to wear pants and walk around like one of the fellas."

"It's all I ever knowed, Brodie. My pa was a mule skinner, and my ma died when I was little. From the time I was little, all I ever did was help my pa drive mules. Pa never had no other woman, so I ain't never been around genteel people. I couldn't be like your sisters." She hesitated and said, "Or like that preacher woman."

Brodie turned her around and looked into her eyes. "Why, Maggie, you're wrong about that. You just haven't had the right kind of opportunities, but it's not too late. How old are you?"

"I'm nineteen."

"Why, you're just in the prime of life. I'll bet if we would wash you down and put you in some store-bought clothes, and you quit smokin' cigars and cussin', you'd be surprised."

"That ain't no use," she insisted.

Suddenly, Brodie had an intuition. "Wait a minute. Don't tell me you like one of the fellas around here." When she didn't answer, he said, "Who is it?"

"Well, if I tell, you can't ever tell nobody else."

"Cross my heart and hope to die. Now tell me."

"Well, it's Clinton."

Brodie's eyes opened with surprise. "Well, you've got good taste. That Clinton, he's a fine-lookin' fella and a good young man too."

"But he wouldn't ever like me."

Brodie stood there thinking hard, and then he said, "Here. You sit down here and let me tell you what we're gonna do." Maggie sat down on the high chair and looked up. Brodie studied her, noting the finely shaped blue-green eyes and the hair that was done in pigtails. "Look, you've got good features and a good figure too. Oh, I seen it in spite of them forked pants you wear and them ratty old shirts. I'll tell you what. I've just decided that I'm gonna help you out. You just see if I don't," he said proudly.

"What do you mean, Brodie?"

"I mean I'm gonna make a fine up-standing lady out of you! Why, it's a chance of a lifetime. I'll teach you how to dress, and we'll keep it a secret. I'll give you lessons on how to be a lady and how to make the men like you. Why, old Clinton won't have a chance when I'm done with you!"

"You really think you can do it, Brodie?" Maggie asked.

"Well, Clinton is always going around saying there ain't nothin' he can't do, so I reckon I can do this because, Maggie, I got somethin' real good to start with. You just wait and see. You and me will be best friends."

"What about your rangering?"

"Oh, I don't have to be back for a while. We'll have plenty of time to start."

"Start right now, Brodie, while I'm finishing supper."

"Sure. Well, the first thing you got to learn is how to walk."

"How to walk!" Maggie stared at him in astonishment. "I know how to walk."

"No. You walk like a man with big strides. You watch Moriah or Mary Aidan. Watch how they walk. They kind of take smaller steps. We'll practice on that." He smiled at her and winked. "It's gonna be fun makin' a lady out of you. Clinton's a dead duck and don't even know it."

The revival meeting at the Methodist church had lasted until eight o'clock. The mourner's bench had been packed with people who had given their lives to the Lord. Clinton and Rose Jean had stayed until the very last one of them had been prayed for by someone.

"I guess we should have come home earlier, Sister Rose," Clinton remarked.

"Oh no, I wanted to stay for all of it. Wasn't it a fine service?" Rose Jean turned to him and smiled. The moonlight was bright, and the September air was cool after the heat of the day. "Can we go back again tomorrow?"

"I don't see why not," Clinton said.

The two rode along, bouncing over the ruts and laughing until they finally arrived back at the ranch. Clinton drew up in front of the house and gave it a glance. "I reckon they've all gone to bed. Don't see no lights at all except that lamp in the parlor Ma always leaves on when somebody's out late."

Clinton leaned back in the seat and then turned to face Rose Jean. The moonlight had coated her face with a silver hue, it seemed, and he said, "I never met a woman like you."

"What's so different about me?" Rose Jean smiled and turned so the two were facing each other. He had removed his hat, and she could not help noticing what a strong, kind face he had. "I'm no different from any other woman."

"Yes, you are. You know more about the Bible than any woman I ever met. More than most preachers, I expect. Of course, that's what you are."

"I don't think I know as much as you do."

"Ah, you're just bein' nice." He suddenly had a thought and said, "It seems funny sittin' here with a nice-looking woman who's a preacher at the same time." He grinned slyly and said, "It makes a fellow wonder how to behave."

"What do you mean, Clinton?"

"Well, I mean if you was a man preacher, we could talk about Scripture. But if you was just a nice-lookin' woman like you are, why it wouldn't be like that."

Rose smiled. "What would it be like, then?"

"Why, I reckon I'd do what men do with good-lookin' young women. Tell them how pretty they are . . . how nice they smell. Maybe try to put my arm around them."

Rose whispered, "Well, that wouldn't be wrong for a young man like you to like a young woman."

The moonlight cast a shadowy glow across Rose's upturned face, and Clinton was stirred by her beauty. He was captured by the tenderness and gentleness of her demeanor. Her face fascinated him, for it was like a mirror that changed as her feelings changed. She was serene, but a provocative, teasing light danced in her eyes. Clinton reached out and pulled her close. His head bent down, and he gently kissed her, hoping that she would not draw back. Her lips responded tensely at first, but she did not pull back, and a warmth swirled through him. He felt the touch of her hands resting upon his shoulders.

Suddenly, her hand was on his chest, and she was staring at him, holding his glance. He could see the hesitation in her eyes.

"You . . . you shouldn't have done that, Clinton."

"I guess," Clinton whispered huskily, "I got more carried away with the good-lookin' woman than I did with the preacher woman."

"We . . . we should go in now."

"Okay." Clinton jumped out and walked around the wagon. He took her hand and helped her down.

"Good night, Clinton," she whispered. "I had a fine time."

"We'll go again tomorrow."

"That would be nice."

Rose Jean walked into the house and went straight to her room. As she got ready for bed, she felt disturbed. It was not the first time she had been kissed. She knew that she would think of Clinton's embrace and kiss for a long time, and she wondered if it were wrong.

Quaid had walked away from the bunkhouse and lit a cigarette. He stood there watching the sun as it sank behind the low-lying hills in the west. The talk at the bunkhouse of Bear Killer's brutal raids had disturbed him. He had said little, although he knew Bear Killer better than most and had more reason to wish him dead.

He heard the cry of an owl, and he looked up into the fading colors of the sky but saw nothing.

A movement caught his eye over to his right, and he waited until he was sure it was Moriah. He threw the cigarette down and ground it with his boot, then walked resolutely toward her. She turned to greet him, startled, and he said, "Hello, Moriah."

"Hello, Quaid. Beautiful evening."

"Where's Ethan?"

"Oh, he's with the other kids. They're playing some game out behind the house."

Quaid stopped directly before her, and she started to speak but saw a determination in him.

"I've been wanting to talk to you, Moriah."

She could sense an urgency and also the manly power that she admired in him. He had the power to stir her, which she had tried to shake off, but something about his confident ruggedness had moved her ever since he had rescued her from Bear Killer's winter camp. Now she grew apprehensive, for there was no sign of a smile, which he usually had for her.

"I can't go on living like this," he said abruptly. "You don't know what it's like being around you and loving you like I do. I can't make pretty speeches, Moriah, but I love you as a man ought to love a woman, and I always will. And I can't stay here loving you and not be able to show you how I feel. I've decided it's time for me to leave."

"No, Quaid, please don't do that," Moriah said, touching his arm.

"Then marry me. We can have a good life together," he said. He reached forward and pulled her to him, and his caress was rough. He had reached the point where he didn't care. He knew she was a woman with a great degree of vitality and imagination, but her time with the Indians had caused her to put these qualities under restraint. She had a temper that could swing from extremes of laughter and softness to anger at times. He knew deep within himself that she had a tremendous capacity for love, but for some reason, she was holding back. When he looked at her, he saw a strength that drew him to her. No weak woman could have survived being a captive of the Comanches as long as she had. "I've got to know right now, Moriah. Do you care for me at all?"

Moriah was taken aback by his sudden embrace, his caress, and his words of love. Fear gripped her heart, not for herself so much as for Ethan. She also had a fear about Quaid. She had known for a long time of his love for her. Yet she still had doubts about his feelings for a woman who had been forced to be an Indian squaw. She was not sure she could make a man happy. For all of these reasons, she whispered, "I'm afraid, Quaid."

Quaid did not argue. He stood very still for a moment and then said quietly, "You can't live with your fears, Moriah. I've got to have an answer and soon."

As he turned and walked away abruptly, Moriah felt the winds of doubt sweep through her. She also knew she had a hope in her heart that had been there for a long time, a hope that was tied to Quaid. She turned and walked slowly down the road. For a long time she walked in silence. Finally, she stopped, looked up at the moon for a moment, then straightened and walked back toward the house.

CHAPTER
TWENTY

M ark paused under the large pecan tree that was part of a grove east of the ranch house. September had brought cooler breezes. The two weeks since he had been found and brought to the Yellow Rose Ranch had seemed like a long time. He took a deep breath and looked down at his body, which had been nothing but skin and bones when he first arrived.

"You're a pretty scrawny specimen," he muttered, then shook his head. "But I ought to be grateful that I'm alive at all." The sun filtered through the trees, making puddles of light on the ground. The pecans had not fallen yet, but he could see the fruits on the branches above his head. A red squirrel suddenly appeared midway up the tree. He perched on a branch, then folded his hands. It reminded Mark of a priest saying his prayers. He smiled and said, "You better get out of here, or you'll wind up being part of a squirrel and dumpling supper."

He watched until the squirrel frisked his tail wildly and then disappeared up into the upper branches of the tree. He took a deep breath and realized that he had walked a fair distance without having to stop to rest. He wandered on beneath the pecan trees, trying to compose in his mind a letter to his family. *Whatever I say sounds foolish. I'll wait until I get there, and then I can explain it all to them.*

He reached the outer edge of the pecan grove and leaned against the scaly bark of one of the trees. Zeno Bruten and Johnny Bench were digging post holes nearby, and he could hear their voices clear on the morning air. He watched idly for a while, but his mind was occupied with the horrible ordeal he had experienced. He had not slept well since regaining consciousness, for no sooner would he go to sleep than he would have nightmares about the Indian attack. The awful sound of Dave Matthews's screams filled his mind, and he shook his head now, trying to drive away the disturbing thoughts.

One thing had been coming to him more and more as he had slowly recuperated. The family had all been kind to him—except for Mary Aidan, who, for some reason, developed a contempt that she took little trouble to hide. He had picked up enough from the family to know that she liked strong men and had little respect for those who showed any kind of weakness. She saw in him none of the strength or virtues that she admired in other men on the ranch.

God's given me a second chance. I've got to do something with it. He had been thinking along these lines for a week now, and a thought had been forming within him. Now, as he stood there watching the two men dig the post holes, an idea started to take shape. *I could stay here and prove that I can do a man's work. It would be hard, but I need something hard. Dad always said that it was the hard things that made one a man. Most of my life has been pretty soft and easy up until now. If I could throw myself into this life on this ranch and become a good hand, I believe I could go back and face my family with some respect for myself and do just about anything.*

For a long time Mark Benton stood there. A resolution began to gather strength inside him, and he knew with certainty that this was what he had to do. He straightened himself and walked over to where Zeno and Johnny were digging post holes. "Can I give you fellas a hand?" he called out.

Zeno Bruten, who was a short and barrel-shaped man, grinned at Mark's offer. "Here, you can dig with these while I rest a spell. Better take these gloves, though."

Mark took the gloves and put them on. They were hot and sweaty and too large for his hands. He lifted the post hole digger and struck the earth with it, but it seemed to make little impression in the ground.

Zeno laughed at Mark's feeble attempt. "It's hard ground. Nothin' I hate worse than diggin' post holes. I should have been an undertaker like my folks wanted me to be."

Mark continued to try to use the post hole digger, but he had little success at making a hole in the ground. He was very aware that the men were watching him.

"It looks like the first time you ever had a pair of diggers in your hands," Johnny Bench said. He was a husky six-footer, a tough man in every way, and used to the hard work on the ranch.

"It is," Mark said. "I've been spoiled."

The two men exchanged grins. "Well, diggin' post holes is a good way to get unspoiled."

Mark stuck at the task for thirty minutes and then was trembling with fatigue. Zeno came over and took the post hole digger. "You better go sit down, Mark. You wasn't born for this kind of work."

"What'd you do, work in an office?" Bench asked.

"I didn't work at all. I was nothing but a parasite."

"A parasite! What's that?" Johnny asked.

"It's a fellow that lives on others without doing any work."

Zeno's grin broadened. "I wish I could get in on doin' that. Well, you rest awhile and tell us about what life's like down in the big city of Memphis for a rich young feller."

Mark looked down at his hands, which were reddened by the effort. He was panting and felt dizzy. "Well, I can tell you it was a lot more fun than digging post holes."

"Most anything is," Johnny Bench sighed. "You rest, then you can spell me after a while."

Jerusalem had been watching the scene as the men were digging the post holes. She said to Moriah, "I wish you'd look at that."

"What is it, Mama?"

"It's Mark. He's trying to help with post hole digging. He's too weak for that. I ought to go out and stop him, but it's a good sign that he's improving."

"He's a strange man, isn't he?"

"He's had an easy life, but that Indian raid shocked him. He'll never be the same again."

"Most people aren't after they've met up with Comanches."

Jerusalem suddenly turned to her daughter and said, "You'll never forget the time you spent there. It was terrible, but you and Ethan got out of it."

Moriah smiled briefly. "Yes, I did, thanks to Brodie and Quaid."

Jerusalem knew she had to speak what was on her mind again. The last time she had mentioned anything, Moriah had simply brushed it aside. "Moriah, Quaid loves you." She saw Moriah glance up at her with shock in her eyes. "And I think you love him."

Moriah's eyes suddenly filled with tears. "Mama, I don't know what to do."

"Then I'll tell you." Jerusalem stepped closer and then put her hands on Moriah's shoulders. "You've got to move on, daughter. You're robbing Quaid of a woman's love, and you're robbing Ethan of a father. And most of all, you're robbing yourself of a man who wants to love you."

"Robbing myself?"

"Yes. You're refusing to take the good life he's offering you. The thing a woman should treasure most, which is being a wife."

Moriah began to sob. "Mama, I've been so afraid. Quaid said that I couldn't live with fear, and he's right."

"He is right," Jerusalem said.

"I was afraid he couldn't forget that I . . . that I had been a squaw of a Comanche."

"Don't be foolish," Jerusalem said at once. "That wasn't your doing, and Quaid's a kind man. That's what you need, a strong man and a kind man. Marry him and give Ethan a father and give yourself a good husband."

"I'll . . . I'll think about it, Mama."

For the rest of the day, Moriah thought about nothing else. She knew her mother was concerned for her, but she still did not know what to do. When the family sat down to eat the evening meal, Moriah wondered where Quaid was.

Jerusalem noticed he wasn't there as well and said, "Where's Quaid tonight," as she carried the food to the table.

"Why, he decided to eat with the hands tonight," Brodie said. "Seems that Maggie had a new recipe to try out on them."

While Mark talked about his failed attempt to try to dig post holes that afternoon, Moriah sat quiet for most of the meal. As soon as she had finished, she excused herself and went to her room to retire early.

For a long time she lay awake, thinking about Quaid. A rainstorm came sweeping over the plains, and the raindrops hit the tin roof like bullets. Moriah got up once and stared out the window at the lightning flashing and dancing over the plains. The rain came down hard, and the lightning and thunder were frightening.

Most of the crew had gone out to bring in a new herd, and Moriah knew the dangers of a stampede was almost inevitable at a time like this. She prayed, "God, don't let any of our men get hurt."

After listening to the storm for a long time, she finally fell asleep. She rose early the next morning, dressed Ethan, and helped her mother cook breakfast for the family.

Ethan was standing at the window. He said, "Somebody's coming, Mama. He's riding hard."

"Who is it, Ethan?"

"I can't tell."

Moriah went outside and watched as a rider galloped toward the ranch. When he got closer, she saw that it was Will Perkins, a young man of seventeen who had not worked long for the ranch. His horse was covered with sweat. He swung off the horse, and Moriah cried, "What's the matter, Will?"

"It was a stampede, Miss Moriah! We got one man kilt and two more bad hurt. Mr. Clay sent me in to bring the wagon out to take the hurt men to the doctor."

Moriah suddenly felt a cold fear grip her heart. "Who was killed?"

"I heard it was Quaid, but I don't know for sure. But that's what they said. Ma'am, I've got to get back with the wagon."

"You go hitch up the team. I'll go with you. I'll get some quilts to make a bed for them. Hurry, Will."

A few minutes later, they were in the wagon, and Will Perkins drove the team at a fast pace all the way back. Moriah had hung on to the seat, worrying about the men. She had tried to question Will about who had gotten hurt, and he told her all he knew. "Monty Nolan, he got throwed and stomped by some cattle. I think his leg's broke. But the other guy, he was hurt real bad. I was with him, and I saw him go down. I tried to help him, but he got run over. Maybe slashed by a horn. When it stopped, somebody said that a feller was killed, and I asked who it was. And Posey, he said he thought it was Quaid."

A darkness gathered in Moriah then. As they approached the crew, her heart seemed to stop at the sight of a still form lying on the ground, covered with a blanket. She came out of the wagon at once, and Clinton ran toward her.

"I'm glad you came, sis. We got to get these two men to the doctor."

She started toward the form under the blanket, and Clinton caught up with her and grabbed her arm. "You ought not to look at him, sister. He's messed up pretty bad."

Moriah pulled away from him and started for the blanket, but then suddenly she saw a rider approaching. In an instant she recognized that it was Quaid. She ran forward, crying out, "Quaid—Quaid!" heedless of the stares of the crew.

Quaid came off his horse and reached for her. "What's the matter, Moriah? Something wrong with Ethan?"

"No. I thought you were dead!"

"Why, no. I loaned my horse to Shorty. They both went down, and they thought it was me."

Moriah threw her arms around him and pressed her face against his chest. She was weeping and said, "I thought you were dead and that I'd never see you again." She lifted her face and said, "I love you, Quaid, and I want to be your wife."

She said this loudly enough so that the entire crew heard it. Clinton stared at his sister with astonishment and then smiled. "That's a good thing," he said to Clay, who had come up to watch the scene.

"It sure is," Clay said. "And it's about time."

As for Quaid, he was smiling, and taking his handkerchief out of his pocket, he wiped her tears away. "Do your cryin' now because we're gonna be smilin' a lot from here on in."

PART FOUR:

ACROSS THE RIO GRANDE

CHAPTER
TWENTY-ONE

Moriah was startled, for the touch of a hand on her hair had caught her off-guard. She laughed and turned from where she was sitting in front of the dressing table and exclaimed, "Quaid, you scared me! I wish you wouldn't sneak up on me like that."

"I wasn't sneaking." Quaid stood over Moriah, looking down at her, and reached out and ran his hand down her hair again. "You've got about the prettiest hair I ever saw," he said.

"No. You've got the prettiest hair. One of these days my hair will be silver like yours."

"I doubt it. Your ma doesn't show any sign of havin' silver hair." Suddenly, Quaid reached down and pulled Moriah to her feet. He pulled her close, leaned forward, and breathed deeply. "You smell mighty good," he said. "I don't know why women smell so much better than men, but they sure do."

"Maybe you need to get some kind of perfume."

Quaid laughed. "Wouldn't that be somethin'! A tough hombre like me wearin' perfume." He leaned forward and kissed her, and as his lips lingered on hers, she seemed to melt against him. When he released her, he grinned and said, "Too bad I have to go to work. I'd like to do what the old Bible said a newly married man ought to do."

"And what's that?"

"I remember a preacher I heard down in New Orleans once. In fact, I don't know what I was doin' in church. Don't remember anything else he said, but he read out of the old Bible that when a Jewish feller got married he didn't hit a lick of work for a whole year. All he did was stay at home and please his wife."

Moriah's eyes sparkled. "I'd like that," she whispered. "Why don't we do it?"

"It would suit me, but I don't reckon as how it would put any groceries on the table." He hesitated, then said, "I got a real problem, wife."

"What's that?"

"We only got time to do one of two things. Either we can love each other, or you can fix breakfast and we'll eat it."

Moriah grinned and turned her head to one side. She made a pretty picture as she stood there. Marriage had agreed with her more than she had thought. "Which will it be?" she said.

"Oh, bacon and eggs, I reckon. After all, the Bible says a man can't live by love alone. You've got to have somethin' more solid than that. And besides, I've got plenty of hard work to do today. Some good food will help a heaping, I guess."

Moriah suddenly doubled up her fists and struck Quaid playfully on the chest. "All right. The next time you come wanting some affection, I'll tell you to go fix some ham and eggs." She gasped, for he reached out and wrapped his strong arms around her and squeezed her.

"Maybe I was wrong about that," he said huskily.

"Never mind that! Get away from me now. I know where your heart is. It's in the middle of your stomach." She laughed and said, "You go shave while I fix us some breakfast."

She left the bedroom and went to stir up the fire. As soon as it caught again with the wood she threw on it, she walked out of the kitchen, down the hall, and glanced in to where Ethan was asleep. He always slept on his stomach with his face turned to one side. She resisted the impulse to go over and smooth his hair, which was black as night. As she stood there, she thought of how good her marriage had been for Ethan. Ethan had always idolized Quaid, and now the two spent every available moment together. She had remarked once to Quaid, "I believe you married me just to get to be a dad to Ethan." She had not been altogether joking. A sense of gratitude filled her heart as she thought of how much Ethan had blossomed as Quaid had taken him with him on every possible occasion.

Turning, she went back to the kitchen, and by the time Quaid had come in, his face glowing from the shave and his hair wet as he ran his hands through it, she said, "I fixed you four eggs. Do you think that'll be enough?"

"I reckon I can scrape by on that."

Quaid sat down at the table, and she filled his plate with bacon, eggs, and biscuits and butter. "I've got some fresh blackberry jam from your mother."

"One thing I like about fall. You get some good berries. I wonder if we can have a blackberry cobbler with supper tonight."

"I'll go pick some, but I always get chiggers on me."

"Don't blame 'em for bitin' you. I've been known to do that myself, haven't I?"

"You hush such talk as that!" She sat down beside him, and the two talked some about how things were going on the ranch, but most of the conversation was about Ethan. Finally, Quaid glanced in the direction of the bedroom. "You ever think much about your time with the Comanches?"

"I try not to."

"That's probably best."

"I can't always keep it out of my mind, though. Sometimes I can't sleep." She reached forward and held on to his wrist. He covered it quickly with his free hand.

"What's wrong, Moriah?"

"I'm afraid he'll come for Ethan again one day."

Startled, Quaid's eyes widened at her words. He studied Moriah's face and saw the fear in her eyes. "Maybe not," he said.

"You know Comanches better than that. They never forget an enemy, and he sees me as the enemy."

"He'd have to be a pretty tough bird to get through all the men around here."

Moriah did not answer, for she knew how a Comanche could steal into a camp unnoticed like a phantom. The mere thought made her shudder. Despite Quaid's reassurance, her fear did not totally go away. Looking into his face, she squeezed his arm and changed the subject. "I'll go get those blackberries. I know where some fresh ones are. We'll have fresh beef and blackberry cobbler for supper tonight."

"You know what? I've been thinkin' about somethin' lately," Clay said. He was sitting at the table sipping from the big mug of coffee and watching Jerusalem as she washed the breakfast dishes. A strange thought came to him, and he said, "I saw a cardinal feedin' his mate yesterday morning."

Jerusalem smiled as she washed the dishes. In the whole time she had known Clay, she had never gotten accustomed to his remarks that seemed to come from nowhere. He'd say the most outlandish things that had absolutely nothing to do with the conversation. They had been talking about getting another herd together and driving it to New Orleans when suddenly he started talking about birds.

"What in the world do cardinals have to do with driving a herd to the market?" she asked, turning to face him.

"Oh, it's got a lot to do with it! See that cardinal? The male one was pickin' sunflower seeds apart, and the lady cardinal . . . she's the plain one, you know." He sipped his coffee and turned his head to one side, an amusement alert in the depth of his eyes. "Ain't it funny, Jerusalem, how the males are always prettier than the females? You look at them cardinals. That male's got those bright red feathers, and the poor old female is just a dowdy old brown." He shook his head sadly and said, "That's just the way it is. The male's always better lookin' than the females."

Jerusalem snorted with disgust. "I'll remember that."

"Well, I think you should. You ought to be real grateful to have a fine-lookin' husband like me. But like I was sayin', this male was crackin' the seeds, and instead of eatin' 'em himself, he was pokin' the seed down the female's throat. All she was doin' was sittin' there with her mouth open, gettin' fed while that poor husband had to be out findin' seeds, crackin' 'em, and puttin' 'em where she didn't have to do nothin' but swallow. It's kind of like us, wouldn't you say?"

Jerusalem suddenly laughed. "You're a crazy fool, Clay Taliferro! If you didn't have me to take care of you, you wouldn't know what to do with yourself."

"Well, you're probably right about that."

The two sat there, and Clay watched Jerusalem closely as she continued to finish with the dishes. He had been a bachelor for such a long time that he had grown accustomed to doing without. For years he'd eaten whatever was handy and worn whatever he could find. He had found married life to be startlingly wonderful, and although he teased Jerusalem often, he also was quick to tell her how much she meant to him. He did so now without embarrassment. "You know, wife, sometimes I love you so much it's all I can do to keep from tellin' you so."

Jerusalem smiled and came over and ruffled his hair. "Oh, you get pretty eloquent at certain times."

"That's the way with us men. We just love to go on about how pretty and sweet our womenfolk are." He put his arm around her, let his hand fall across her body, and winked. "I'll see you later," he said. "You wear that pretty pink nightgown I brought you back from San Antone the last time I went."

"I'm wearin' my flannel nightgown. These nights are gettin' colder, and I don't intend to freeze."

The two sat there talking some more about the ranch, and then Jerusalem said, "Clay, I know times are hard, but there's something I'd really like to have."

Clay was surprised, for Jerusalem very rarely asked for anything special. "What is it?" he said curiously. "You need another pink nightgown?"

"No, Clay Taliferro, I don't. What I'd like to have is a piano for the parlor."

Clay stared at her. "A piano? Can you play one of them things?"

"No, I can't, but I think our kids have musical abilities, and I want to develop them. It's just something I want for them."

Clay swallowed the last of his coffee, then said, "Don't have any idea where one of them things would be. I might have to go all the way to St. Louis to get one."

Clay said no more, but already in his mind he was beginning to wonder where he could find a piano way out there in the middle of Texas.

Rose Jean Campbell had discovered that one of the most enjoyable things about living with the Taliferros was the talks she had with Clinton. She loved to read Scripture and then discuss different passages with him and see how they applied to life. She had done this for years with her family. Now that she was all alone, there seemed to be a gap in her life, and she missed it.

Clinton, however, was always ready to discuss doctrine. As they rode along in the buggy headed for town, he had been expounding on his particular views of the Second Coming of Jesus. Rose Jean's father had been fascinated by this particular doctrine and had managed to communicate an enthusiasm for it in his daughter. Rose Jean kept her eyes scanning the horizon, but from time to time, turned to look at Clinton. He was holding the lines with his left hand and gesturing eloquently with his right, and he spoke with force and vigor.

". . . so, don't you see, most of these preachers have got the wrong idea about the Second Coming of the Lord."

Rose Jean had learned that the one quality that identified Clinton was his self-assurance in whatever he believed wholeheartedly. She had never met a young man who believed so fervently in himself as Clinton Hardin, and now she asked curiously, "But you think you've got a better answer?"

"Well, you stop and think about it. Before Jesus came the first time, Rose Jean, what were the Jews lookin' for?"

"They were lookin' for the Messiah."

"That's right," Clinton said, nodding in agreement. "And I reckon most of 'em that was serious studied it pretty deeply in their Scriptures. Remember when the wise men came to Herod, he asked them where the Messiah would be born, and they knew that right off. They had been thinkin' about it, don't you see? And the old prophets, Daniel and Isaiah, they had their ideas about what He would be like when He would come. And you know what?" Clinton waved his hand so expressively that he struck Rose Jean a light blow. "Oh, sorry about that!"

"Don't beat me, Clinton, I'm listening!"

Her eyes sparkled, and Clinton thought of what an attractive young woman she was. He had heard several of the hands remark that they'd never expected to see a pretty preacher before, but now they had.

"I guess I kind of get carried away."

"That's good. I like to see people who are excited about the Lord, but what about the Second Coming?"

"Well, they knew all about it, or thought they did, but the thing is that they were all wrong. They was expectin', you remember, a great king to come and take over the whole world and defeat the Romans down and make the Jews rulers over everything. But it didn't happen that way. They had the wrong ideas about the Second Coming."

Rose Jean sat listening as Clinton spoke about his theories of eschatology, and then finally she said, "I think God hardly ever does the same thing in exactly the same way."

"Why, that's right! So, whatever those fellows believed about the coming of the Lord, it's not going to be like they say. God's going to catch us all by surprise, I reckon."

The buggy rode along, raising a cloud of fine dust behind it, for there had hardly been any rain that month. Rose Jean listened to Clinton as he continued to enlighten her, and then he turned and looked at her in a strange way.

"What are you looking at me for?" she asked.

"Well, Rose Jean, I've been meanin' to talk to you about somethin'. Somethin' pretty serious."

"What is it?"

"Well, this business about your bein' a preacher. I just can't see that in the Scriptures. When the Bible talks about elders, it always sounds like they're men."

"Don't you think women should have a witness for Jesus?"

"Oh yes!" Clinton exclaimed quickly. "Shore they should, but it ought to be at home with their children or with other women, don't you see?"

"I know the New Testament mostly talks about men being the evangelists and preachers, but these are different times, Clinton."

"Time don't have nothin' to do with it."

"Don't you think so? Well, just think about this. In Paul's day the women couldn't come into the synagogue proper. The men were all there. The women were all shoved off into a little balcony somewhere. Would you want your mother or your sisters to have to stay in the balcony while the preaching was going on?"

Clinton fell silent, which was so unusual that Rose Jean turned to watch him. She could almost see his thought process turning in his mind from the expression on his face. Finally she said, "Well, why don't you answer me?"

Clinton laughed. "Because I don't know how to get around that, but I'll be thinkin' on it." Then he twisted his head around and asked abruptly, "You ever been in love, Rose Jean?"

The question caught Rose Jean off-guard. "Why would you ask a thing like that?"

"Well, maybe you just don't know how interesting you can be for a feller," Clinton said. "A nice-lookin' lady like you must have been in love."

"No, I haven't. Have you?"

"Oh, land yes! Several times."

"Oh, Clinton, I don't believe that."

"Well, maybe not several times, but I was in love with Aldora Stuart."

"She's a very fine young lady."

"I shore thought so. The first time I seen her I thought she was a boy. She was all dressed up in men's clothes and had her hair up under her hat." Clinton went on to speak about his meeting Aldora and then laughed at a sudden thought. "The thing is Ma knew the first time she ever saw Aldora that she was a girl, but it took me a few tries. But I was in love with her, all right. But I'm not anymore," he said quickly.

"Then I don't think you really loved her."

"I'm tellin' you I did!" Clinton insisted.

"I don't think true love is like that. I think it lasts forever. You know what the Bible says about a man and wife. They are man and wife as long as they both shall live."

Clinton thought about what she had said as they rode along. The reins hung loosely in his hands, and once he lifted his eyes to watch a herd of antelope make their graceful way across the prairie. "Them antelope sure can run, can't they?" Suddenly, a thought came to him, and he said, "You know what? You and me, we're a whole lot alike, Rose Jean."

"You think so?"

"Oh, sure. We're both smart and good-lookin' and healthy."

"Well, I guess that's better than being poor, sick, and ugly, isn't it?"

"You'd never be poor, sick, or ugly!"

"I might be. You never know. If we were married, and I lost my looks, say in a fire or something, would you stop loving me?"

"Why, no, of course not!"

"Well, I wouldn't stop loving you either." She flushed slightly. "If we were married, that is."

"Well, I never knew a woman that was as smart as you about the Bible—except Ma, of course."

"Well, that's quite a compliment. I admire your mother a great deal. She's a wise woman."

"Why, everybody does. I want the woman I marry to be just like her."

"Not many women are as strong as your mother."

"I expect you are—almost, anyway."

Rose Jean smiled. "That's the nicest thing you ever said about me, Clinton." She sat beside him and saw that he was embarrassed about the compliment he had paid her. She knew he was devoted to his mother, and it touched her to think that he would say such a thing.

David came running into the kitchen and said, "Ma, Pa's comin', and he's got somethin' in the wagon all covered up."

Jerusalem dried her hands and followed David, who was pulling at her skirt through the halls. She stepped out through the screen door just as Clay pulled the wagon up in front of the porch. He was grinning broadly, and his eyes sparkled, as they did when he was excited. "Well, there never was such a woman for gettin' her own way."

"What have you got there, Clay?"

Clay didn't answer. He rose, stepped over the seat, and reaching down, he pulled the canvas off the object in the back of the wagon.

Jerusalem cried out, "A piano! It's a piano!"

"It ain't nothin' else. It came all the way from New Orleans."

The other children came scurrying from everywhere, and Clay got two of the ranch hands to help him carry the piano inside. When it was safely placed on the living room floor, he shook his head. "I don't know anybody that can play the blamed thing. The only piano player I know is Rooney Blent."

"Who's that?"

"He plays the piano at the Golden Lady Saloon, but he plays by ear. I don't reckon he can teach anybody how to read music."

"I don't want any saloon piano player teaching my children!" Jerusalem said. She ran her hand over the fine rosewood surface and smiled. "But we'll find someone. I know we will!" Then turning to Clay, she said, "Clay Taliferro, you sure do know how to make a woman feel loved."

CHAPTER
TWENTY-TWO

A gust of acrid smoke tinged with the odor of burning hair and hide struck Mark Benton so forcefully that he had to close his eyes and turn his head to one side. Branding cattle was not something that life in the city prepared you for, and he had learned to hate the ordeal fervently. He was holding on to the sweeping horns of a large steer that longed for nothing more than to gore him. As he waited for Zeno Bruten, who was holding the branding iron, to step back, memories flashed through his mind concerning the time he had spent at the Yellow Rose Ranch.

As he struggled to keep the steer's head twisted, he thought of how hard life had been. Never had he worked so hard in all his life. He had vivid memories of the first time he had offered to help dig post holes. The task had given him such terrible blisters on his hands that he could not even clench his fists for several days. He remembered the ribald remarks he had endured from the crew, who had laughed at him constantly, as they did at all tenderfoots. He also thought of the time when he had first begun mucking out the barns, shoveling the fresh animal droppings that practically smoked. It had turned his stomach, and more than once he had lost his breakfast, which also amused the crew immensely.

"Okay, let her go, Mark!" Zeno grinned and stepped back cautiously, his eye on the brindle steer.

Mark released his grip on the horns and scrambled to his feet. When the steer came to his feet, there was a wild look in the animal's eye. Mark grabbed his hat off, slapped the animal on his nose, and hollered, "Get away from me, you ugly critter!"

"That's the way to handle him, Mark! Slap him with your hat!" hollered Johnny Bench. He and Will Perkins were doing the roping, then they dragged the fresh steers at the end of their lariats toward the branding fire.

"Here's a fresh one for you, Benton. Don't hurt him now." Will Perkins was only seventeen but an expert roper. He was a tall, raw-boned, young man, strong and burned bronze by the hot Texas sun. He laughed and said, "If you need to borrow my hat to get this one down, I'd be glad to accommodate you."

Mark managed a grin, for he had learned that nothing pleased the hands more than to hear him complain, which he had done plenty of when he first arrived. He had learned quickly, however, that the more he complained, the more they enjoyed teasing him. Now, no matter how grim the job or how dirty, he always acted as if it were a pleasure. "Just think, Will," he said. "I'm gettin' all this fresh air and sunshine for nothin'. Why, people pay hundreds of dollars to go on vacations like this."

Will grinned and shook his head. "Ain't my idea of a vacation."

"Mine neither," Zeno said as he rearranged his branding iron.

Mark watched for his chance and managed to throw the steer and hold him while Zeno slapped the brand on him. He was sore in practically every muscle, but not once did he show it. A strange thrill filled him as he realized all that he had learned since he was first hired on at the Yellow Rose. As he got to his feet and beat the wild-eyed animal with his hat until she went scurrying off, he felt a sense of pride that he was able to last all day now no matter how hard the job. *I'm going to make it,* he said to himself. *This time I'm really going to make it.*

Johnny Bench had been critical from the beginning about Mark Benton. He had no bones about telling everyone that Mark would never last. Johnny was convinced that Mark would wind up as all city slickers do—running out on the job. Now, however, Johnny drew his horse up, rolled a cigarette expertly, and struck a match on his thumbnail. When the cigarette was glowing, he inhaled deeply and turned his horse, saying, "You know, I was wrong about that feller. He's come a long way."

"Sure has," Will agreed. "For a city feller he's made a pretty good hand."

"The boss told me to give him a hoss and teach him how to ride."

"Can't he ride? I thought everybody could ride!" Will said.

"No, you ignoramus—everybody can't ride!" Bench said. "You know you're dumber than a ball of hair! You've got to *learn* how to ride. Oh, he can stay on an old plow horse, I reckon, but what good does that do you? Clay said that I was to give him some lessons." Bench grinned. "So, I'm gonna give him a good mount."

"Which one?" Will asked.

"I thought I might let him start out on Vulcan."

Will stared at Bench. "Why, he can't ride a hoss like that! I can barely stay on him my own self."

"Ain't no sense foolin' around with horses that ain't got no spirit."

"Well," Will said, grinning, "Vulcan's got that, all right. He piled Ike up so he could hardly walk for a week, and Ike's a better than average rider."

"Don't say nothin' to him—to Benton, I mean. It'll be a nice surprise for him," Bench said.

"Ain't you afraid he'll get hurt?"

"Why, no, I ain't afraid a bit. It'll be him not me," he said cheerfully.

Word had gotten around about the joke that Bench was arranging for Mark Benton, and a small crowd had gathered around the corral. Mark had been surprised when Johnny Bench had approached him and said, "Hey, Clay told me to teach you how to ride."

"I can ride."

"Why, shore you can, but I mean really ride like a cowboy. That means learnin' how to throw ropes. Don't do no good to be on a hoss unless you're able to do somethin' with the cows, does it, now?"

"I guess not, Johnny."

"Well, come on. We'll get you started."

As soon as Mark stepped into the corral, he knew something was wrong. He had grown accustomed to the jokes of the men. Now as they sat on the top rail smoking or chewing or dipping, some doing all three at the same time, his heart sank. He knew it would do no good to protest, for whatever he'd say would be wrong.

"Right over here, Benton," Johnny said. "I got your mount all saddled up and ready to go."

Mark actually knew very little about horses. He was able to stay on a horse that was well behaved, but the wild look in the roan that Johnny was holding by brute force by the bridle did not fit this description.

"This here is Vulcan. Pretty good mount," Bench said, but something in his eyes confirmed Mark's suspicion.

"I suppose he's gentle," Mark said, watching Johnny's face.

"Oh, he's downright lovely. Here. You need help to get on?"

"I guess not."

Mary Aidan had been crossing the yard when she heard the sound of laughter coming from the corral that the men used to break horses. Curiously, she swerved and went over to stand beside O. M. Posey, who was leaning his arms against the top rail and watching with interest the scene before him.

"What's going on, Posey?" she asked.

"Oh, hi, Miss Mary. Looks like a ridin' lesson."

Mary Aidan lifted herself up and stood on the lower rail, draping her arms over the top. She saw Mark slowly approaching, caution on his face, as the roan snorted and rose high in the air. She also heard the whispers of the men that lined the corral fence.

"That's Vulcan! That tenderfoot will never stay on him."

"Well, I reckon he's gonna give it a try." Posey turned and grinned. He winked broadly and said, "Johnny's givin' him ridin' lessons."

"He could get hurt. That's a bad horse," Mary Aidan said.

"Clay said to give him lessons," Posey explained, "and Johnny figured he might as well start out with a good 'un."

"I wouldn't call Vulcan 'a good 'un.' He piled Ike up, didn't he?" she said.

"Yeah, he piled me up too. I wouldn't want nothin' to do with him. You know how Johnny is. Always playin' a joke."

Mary Aidan watched closely. She had a clear view of Mark Benton's face and saw the apprehension in his eyes. She knew she should try to stop what was about to happen, for it could be very dangerous, but something inside stopped her from saying anything. She watched as Mark put one foot in the stirrup, then swung his leg over the horse. He had grabbed the reins from Johnny, and as soon as he did, Vulcan exploded with raw strength. Humping his back, he went straight up in the air and came down stiff-legged. Mark was jolted up off the saddle. He made a grab for the horn but missed. He was thrown sideways as Vulcan twisted and turned like a corkscrew. Three more jumps and Mark lost all control. He sailed up in the air, his arms flailing, and turned a complete somersault. He landed flat on his back with a distinct *Whump*, and Mary Aidan made a face. "That was a bad fall."

"Shore was," Posey said. "I hope he ain't hurt nothing serious."

Bench waved his hat at Vulcan and then turned to bend over Mark. "You okay, partner?"

Mark did not answer for the simple reason he had no air left to form words. He tried desperately to draw air in, but nothing would help him.

"Well, that was a pretty bad fall," Bench said. "It ain't no fun havin' all the air knocked out, but you'll be okay. Here, let me help you up."

Mark felt Johnny's arms pulling him up, and he stood there until finally he began drawing deep gasps of breath.

Bench stopped laughing when he saw how pale Mark's face was. "Well, we better demote you to a little bit gentler horse, I reckon."

"No. That's the one I want," Mark insisted.

Bench was surprised, and it showed in his face. "Aw, come on, Mark, I was just havin' a little bit of fun with you. You don't want that hoss. He's a mean one. You could get hurt something fierce."

"That's the one I want." There was a stubbornness in Mark's voice, and his mouth was drawn into a tight line. "Catch him up for me, will you?"

Mary Aidan said, "What in the world is he doing?"

"Looks like he's determined to ride that critter."

"Why, he can't!" she said.

The cowboys had been laughing at first, but after Mark was thrown four times, two of them dangerously hard falls, they stopped laughing. Posey shook his head and said, "You'd better break this up, Mary Aidan. He's liable to get hurt."

"None of my business," Mary said. "You break it up."

"That feller's stubborner than he looks."

Mary Aidan looked at Mark, who was getting up again. He was dusty from head to foot and had lost his hat. He moved slowly, but he doggedly walked back toward the roan, which Bench had caught. She heard Bench say, "That's enough, Mark."

"I'll ride him if it takes the rest of my life!" he said stubbornly.

Clay had heard all the noise and had come over to the corral. For a while he stood there watching Mark take a couple of hard falls. Finally, he entered the corral, went over, and said, "Come along, Mark."

"I'd like to try again."

"You can try later." He turned and faced Johnny and didn't say a word, but Bench's face grew red. He tried to think of some way to explain his behavior, but nothing came. Clay said, "Come on, Mark. Somethin' I been wantin' to talk to you about."

Mark walked over, picked up his hat, and settled it on his head. He knew he would be sore as a boil the next day, but he tried not to let it show. He followed Clay to the back of the house.

"That Vulcan's a bad hoss," Clay said. "The boys was raggin' you a little bit."

"I guess they were."

"He's thrown just about everybody, including me and Johnny Bench. He's not really a good mount for you."

"I can't quit on him," Mark shrugged. "It wouldn't look right."

Clay turned to look at the young man without breaking stride. A brief grin touched his broad lips, and he murmured, "A part of wisdom is knowing when to quit."

Mark stared at the older man. "I wouldn't think you'd know much about quitting." He had not meant to say that, but it had come out without his intention. He studied Clay Taliferro, thinking of all he had heard about the man. Taliferro had been a mountainman who had survived when weaker individuals had failed. He had been in town once with Clay and the crew when they went into the saloon. Johnny Bench had winked at him and said, "Watch how the tough ones keep their eye on Clay. They treat him like he's a stick of dynamite that'll go off any minute without warning."

Such indeed was Clay Taliferro's reputation as a tough man. He had a distinct limp as a result of a brush with the Comanches, but still his reputation was what had made the Yellow Rose Ranch secure. "I never heard of you quittin' on anything, Mr. Taliferro."

"Clay will do fine for a handle, I reckon, but I quit on lots of things." He limped along toward a stand of cottonwoods down by the river. "I remember I got bottled up by a bunch of Kiowa once. I quit right whatever I was doin' and took off. A man's a fool arguing with a bunch of Kiowas when there's a way to hightail it out of there."

"That's different from a horse. The fellas all expect me to ride him."

"No, they don't," Clay said. "They expected you to walk away from him."

"Well, I won't do it."

"Yes, you will. I'm ordering you to stay off that horse. I've got a few words to say to Johnny Bench. He knew better than to put you up on that animal."

"He just likes to hooray a greenhorn."

"That's all right, but it's gone too far this time. I intend to have a word with him." Clay said no more until they reached the river, then he turned to face Benton. "You've done better than anybody expected, Mark. I don't know what you're doing here. You was made for better things than muckin' out the barn or wrestlin' steers."

Clay waited for Benton to respond, but when the young man said nothing, he shrugged. "None of my business, but as long as you stay here, I'm gonna try to make use of you. The ranch needs every good man it can get, and you're turning out to be a good one." He suddenly reached down, took off his gun belt, and said, "Strap that on. Time for a shootin' lesson."

Startled, Mark took the weapon and stood staring at Clay. Slowly, he buckled it on and said, "I don't think I'm cut out to be a gunman. That's a little out of my line."

"May not be," Clay said. "If the Comanches come callin', you'll be a gunman just like the rest of us. You do much shootin'?"

"Just birds with my brother Tom."

"Well, shootin's shootin'," Clay shrugged. "See that saplin' over there? See if you can hit it."

Mark pulled the revolver, cocked it, leveled it at arm's length, and fired. He was pleased to see his slug shake the sapling. "Beginner's luck," he said.

"Maybe so. Try it again."

Mark emptied the revolver, hitting the sapling twice.

"Well, I hit it twice and scared it once."

"That's pretty good shootin'. You need a little practice. Some folks can shoot and some can't. Mostly, it's like pointin' your finger." He laughed and shook his head. "Most folks can't point very good. Let me reload it." He reloaded the revolver and said, "Put it back in the holster. When I say go, pull and shoot quick as you can."

Mark stood facing the sapling, and when Clay's voice broke the silence, he pulled the revolver, pulled the hammer back, and then fired.

"That's not bad, Mark."

"I missed the tree."

"If it had been a man, you wouldn't have missed. Try it again."

For the next twenty minutes, Mark received expert advice on the art of pulling a gun. It was a new skill to him, and he was pleased inordinately when Clay said, "You got a gift for it, Mark. I've got an extra gun at the house. I want you to take it and practice every day a little bit. You don't always have to fire right away. There are times," he said, "when you got plenty of time. If you do, hold that weapon out at arm's length, brace your wrist if you want to, but sometimes you don't have time for all that. You just have to pull and shoot and hope for the best."

"You expectin' trouble?"

"Sure am," Clay said. "Man is born to trouble as the sparks fly upward."

"Is that from the Bible?"

"Yep. I think it was Job or some other cheerful character that said it. Anyway, when trouble comes, I'll need you. So you keep practicin'. If those Comanches ever show up here again, we're going to need all the help we can get."

"Yes, sir, I'll do that."

As the two walked back to the house, Clay spoke of the drive that was coming up, and Mark asked with surprise, "Am I going?"

"I think so. You need a little experience, and that's a good way to get it. Hard work, though." When they reached the path that led to the house, Clay stopped and turned to face the young man. "You're doin' good, Mark. Don't let these galoots harrass you too much. If they give you any trouble, just bat 'em down."

Benton suddenly laughed. "I don't think I could do that, Clay."

"Well, maybe we can find somebody else for you to bat down. Plenty of thievin' Mexicans and no account Indians around. If we can't find any of them, we'll go down to the saloon. There's always some characters in there that need a good stompin'."

Maggie was always very careful about how she made her biscuits. She was inordinately proud of her cooking skill. In the silence of the kitchen, she broke out into the song "Old Ben Bolt" as she worked. She enjoyed making biscuits and went about it methodically. She pulled out the flour and salt from the cupboard and then the eggs and the milk. Taking a large white bowl from a shelf, she began dumping the flour into a sifter and letting it fall into the bowl. Next, she added a pinch of salt, cracked two eggs, and then added a little milk. She stirred all of the ingredients with a large wooden spoon, forming a small hole in the middle of the mixture, and then added more milk and stirred again. She repeated this process until the mixture became the consistency she required. When it was ready, she put her hands into a jar of lard and began to grease the pans. She then scooped a small amount of the mixture into her hand, formed it into a ball, and placed it on the pan, repeating this step until all the dough was gone.

As she slipped the biscuits into the stove, she heard footsteps on the porch. When the door opened and Brodie stepped in, she smiled. "If you had waited a little while, you could have had fresh biscuits."

"I got nothin' to do but wait. A man that won't wait on biscuits don't want 'em bad enough." He winked and said, "Just like lovin'."

Maggie never knew how to understand Brodie. He had been around Clay Taliferro so much he had become sort of a tease himself, but she felt comfortable around him in a way that she did not around most men. "Sit down. I got some pie left over and some coffee."

"Sounds like what a hard-working body needs right now—some nourishment."

Brodie sat down in a kitchen chair. When Maggie brought the apple pie and the large mug of scalding black coffee and put it before him, he said, "Lord, I'm shore thankful for this pie and this coffee." He winked at Maggie and said, "And for good company. Amen."

Maggie grinned. "You always say the blessing even for pie and coffee?"

"My grandpa used to say blessings over everything. Every time he took a glass of water, he would say, 'Thank you, Lord, for this good water.' If he didn't have anything else, he would say, 'Thank you for the air I'm breathin'. He was some fella. I sure miss him."

"When did he die?" Maggie asked.

"A few years back. You know, Maggie, he was with George Washington during the Revolution."

Maggie stared at Brodie. "That couldn't be. That was too long ago."

"Not as long as you might think." Brodie cut a piece of the pie with the edge of his fork, stabbed it, and put it into his mouth. "This here is right good pie. I couldn't have made a better one myself."

"Tell me about your grandpa. Did he ever see General Washington?" She took a seat across from Brodie and listened as he spoke of how his grandfather had fought in the Revolutionary War.

Finally, when Brodie finished the pie and swigged the last drop of coffee, he said, "Well, you ready to get some more lessons on how to be a lady?"

"I thought you was teasin' about that, Brodie."

"Teasin'! I reckon not! If you want old Clinton, you're gonna have to work on it."

"It's too late for me. My pa raised me to be a boy."

"Well, he didn't do a very good job about it 'cause you ain't no boy. I can see that even under them ugly, old shapeless clothes you insist on wearing. Why do you wear them old clothes, anyway?"

"They're all I got."

"Well, there's nice clothes to be had."

"I don't know what you could do to help me. You have to start bein' a girl when you're young . . . playin' with dolls and things like that. All I ever had was ornery mules and stubborn oxen to play with. I don't ever remember havin' a doll."

"You can have one now if you wanted, but my main job is to wake Clinton up and make him see you for a lady. Now, get up. I want to give you your first lesson. I'm going to show you how to walk."

"I know I can't walk like no lady."

"You can," Brodie said, "if you want to. Let me see you walk."

Maggie got up and walked across the kitchen. "I feel foolish," she said as he watched her.

"You're walkin' like an Arkansas plowboy takin' great big steps. You got to take shorter steps, and you got to kind of—I don't know. You got to *sway*."

"Sway?" Maggie said. "What do you mean *sway*?"

"Oh, you know. Women sort of *twitch* when they walk."

"Well, show me how."

Brodie laughed. "I can't do that. Did you watch Ma or Moriah or Rose Jean, like I told ya?"

"Yeah, but it just ain't natural for me."

Maggie tried to convince Brodie he was wasting his time, but he wouldn't give up. Finally, Brodie said, "I'm gonna get you some good-smelling perfume the next time I'm in town. That always helps turn a man's head."

"I never had no perfume."

"Well, I'll get some that comes all the way from France. I guess that's where they make the best perfume. Now, there's a dance comin' up, and you're gonna show Clinton what it's like."

"I can't dance."

"Well, I can. Come on and I'll teach you."

"I can't dance, Brodie. There ain't no music."

"Well, I'll hum a little bit. It doesn't matter much. You just need to learn the right steps. Watch me now. You'll catch on fast."

Brodie began to hum, and he reached out and put his arms out, but she stared at him. "Here," he directed, "you seen people dance."

"Yes, but I ain't never done it. Why, I'll just trip and fall flat out."

"No, you won't. I'll hold your hand like this, and you put your other hand up on my shoulder." He waited until she reached up. "And then I put my hand on your back. Now, that's the way we do it. Be sure you look up."

"Well, I can't look up at Clinton."

"Why not?"

"Because I'm as tall as he is," she said. "You're so much taller than Clinton."

"He takes after Ma. I take after Pa. Anyhow, we'll figure that out later. Now, let's continue with your dance lesson. I'll show you the steps now. Just follow my lead. They ain't hard to learn."

After they had moved around the kitchen floor carefully, Brodie said with surprise, "You must have danced before."

"Never did, Brodie, not once. Of course, I seen people dancin'."

"Well, you must have a natural rhythm, then. You're gonna be good at it. Now, here's the next thing. You gotta lean."

Maggie stared at him. "What do you mean *lean*?"

"Well, if you really want to catch a fella, you have to get his attention. That's a shore way to do it. Just kind of *lean* on him."

"You mean like this?"

Brodie was startled as Maggie stepped closer and leaned into him. He cleared his throat and said, "Well, yeah, like that—only you got to be careful."

"Careful of what?"

"Well, leanin's good, but it can't get a fella all stirred up."

"Stirred up how?"

Brodie could think of no way to put his answer. "Just be careful, that's all. Now, let's try it again." They waltzed around the room, and finally he said, "You got this dancin' thing down. You're just naturally good at it, Maggie, but let me remind you not to get in the buggy by yourself."

Maggie was still in Brodie's embrace, and she looked up at him. "What do you mean by that?"

"I mean let him help you in."

"What if he don't? He might just go around and get in by hisself."

"Then you just stand there, Maggie. Old Clinton's thick-headed, but sooner or later he'll get the idea." He suddenly realized that they were very close and stepped back. "This is gonna work out fine. I'll get that perfume tomorrow. I don't reckon you got a party dress."

"No, I don't."

"I'll get you a whole outfit tomorrow when I go to town."

Maggie stared at him. "But how do you know they'll fit?"

"Well . . ." Brodie stared at her and walked around her stroking his chin. "I guess maybe we both better go."

Maggie laughed. "That might be the best."

CHAPTER
TWENTY-THREE

B arton Singleton was a big man, and he was accustomed to using his bulk as a method of getting his own way. This tactic worked very well in most cases, for Singleton was not only a bruising man in a fist fight, but the son of one of the wealthiest men in Texas. He was not a handsome man. His face was florid and his features were blunt. His eyes were a dirty brown and too close together, but Singleton never depended on good looks to get what he wanted out of life. He simply saw what he wanted and took it.

He had taken dinner with the family and afterward had sat in the parlor talking with some of them. Then, by some signal, Mary Aidan made it known she wanted to be alone with him. Barton stood and thanked Jerusalem for the meal, and as soon as everyone left the parlor, he sat down close to Mary Aidan.

Now, none of the family particularly cared for Singleton, and Sam had asked once, "Mary Aidan, why do you want to have that big, ugly guy around?" Mary Aidan had scolded him, but despite her own objections about Barton Singleton, he was not a suitor to be ignored. Anyone who married him would have a comfortable life with no worries.

"Come on, now, Mary Aidan, don't be shy," Singleton said.

She put her hand on his massive chest and turned her face away as he attempted to kiss her. "Behave yourself, Barton," she protested.

Singleton merely laughed and put his arms around her. His strength was almost frightening. At that moment Mary Aidan thought of the one remark that her stepfather Clay had made about Singleton. "He can tie his shoes without bending over about like an ape." Mary Aidan had been angered by the remark, although it was true enough that Singleton did demonstrate certain simian traits.

Singleton was not to be denied his intentions, and Mary Aidan could not avoid the kiss. She tried to turn her head, but his thick lips slid across hers. Struggling was useless. Suddenly, a sound came from her right, and she felt Barton stiffen and turn. She reached up to smooth her hair, and when she turned, she saw that Mark Benton had entered the room carrying an armload of split logs for the fire.

"Don't you ever knock before entering?" Mary Aidan said. She was humiliated that she had been caught kissing a man in the parlor. It made it even worse that it was Mark Benton who had walked in on them. "Get out of here and knock the next time you come in!"

"Mind if I dump the wood first?"

"Yes! Dump it and go!" Mary snapped. She knew that her face was red, and she hated to blush. It made her feel foolish. She watched as Benton walked across the room and dumped the wood, which made a sound of miniature thunder in the wood box. Then he turned to leave the room without looking at either of them. He had to pass close by Singleton, and as he did, the big man reached out and caught him by the arm. Pulling him around, he lifted his fist, and she said, "Leave him alone, Barton."

Barton shrugged and shoved Mark away. The force of the push threw Mark off balance, and he had to struggle to keep from falling. When he straightened up, he turned and faced Barton Singleton, staring at him without saying a word.

Mary Aidan knew that any other man on the ranch would have fought back. Even if they had been smaller than Singleton, they would have done something—picked up a piece of stove wood and tried to whack him. She waited, half-hoping that Benton would at least try something, but he did not. He turned without a word and left the room.

"What kind of a softy is he? He won't even take a fight if it's offered."

Mary Aidan said stiffly, "Don't pay him any attention, Barton. He's not a real man at all. From the time he first showed up here, he's been nothing but a soft tenderfoot."

"Well, he spoiled my evening," Singleton said. "I better be going," he said as he stood. "You're going to the dance with me week from Thursday?"

"Yes. That ought to be fun." She walked to the door with him, and he tried to put his hands on her, but she shook her head and said, "Good night, Barton."

"Well, good night."

Mary Aidan watched him as he walked away from the house. He got on his horse, slapped him with the reins, and rode off at a dead run. Mary Aidan glanced toward the bunkhouse, shook her head in disgust, then went back into the house.

Lucy had been brushing her hair, but she paused suddenly and leaned forward, examining her features in the mirror. A dissatisfaction spoiled her looks for that moment. She forced herself to smile, as if speaking pleasantly to someone. The expression did not last, however, and she turned and threw the brush across the room in a violent gesture. The brush hit the wall, bounced off, and fell to the carpet just as Mable Abbot entered the room.

"What was that?" she asked, then saw the brush. She went over, picked it up, and handed it to her daughter. "What's wrong with you, Lucy?"

"Nothing."

"Of course there is. You haven't said a single pleasant thing in three days." Mable Abbot sat down on a chair and looked at her distraught daughter. She was a mild enough woman as a rule, but at times she could be very blunt. "Is this about Harry St. Clair?"

"No!" Lucy said tersely.

The answer came too quickly, and Mable said, "I think it is." She leaned forward and studied her daughter's face. "You don't have anything to be ashamed of. He's gotten himself engaged to one of the richest women in the country."

"It was all about money, then, not about me," Lucy said bitterly. Harry St. Clair had called on her several times, and Lucy had felt that he was interested in her. When the news had come that he was engaged to marry Helen Duvall, the daughter of a wealthy shovel manufacturer from Chicago, she had cried all night long, although she had not let her parents see it.

"What's wrong with me, Mother?"

"Nothing's wrong with you, my dear. The right man just hasn't come along yet."

"I thought it was Harry."

"Did you love him?"

"Oh, I don't know. He was . . . eligible."

"Meaning he was rich. Having a rich husband doesn't solve all the problems of life."

"Neither does having a poor husband."

Mable Abbot began to speak to her daughter quietly. "I've been thinking quite a bit about Clinton Hardin lately."

"About Clinton? Why?" Lucy said, turning to look at her mother.

"I always liked Clinton, and I think you did, too, at one time."

"Well, I did like him, but—"

"But he wasn't romantic enough for you."

"Mother, all he ever talked about was the mark of the beast or church things. I don't mind some of that, but Clinton's obsessed with it. Why are you talking about him?"

"If you had married Harry St. Clair, you would have gone off and lived in Chicago or New York."

"I suppose that's true enough. Would that be so bad?"

Mable smiled and leaned forward. Putting her hand on her daughter's shoulder, she said, "It wouldn't be for you, perhaps, but it would be for your father and me. You're all we have, Lucy. Seeing you marry someone who would take you far away to a big city would break my heart."

Lucy's face softened. "I know, Mother. I thought about that too. It would be nice to visit those places, but nothing is like home."

"I suppose that's why I thought of Clinton," Mable said.

"He's never going to be rich."

"I'm not so sure of that. The Yellow Rose Ranch is doing well. Your father tells me that it's nearly doubled in size in the last two years. When the beef market opens up in Chicago, he says, whoever owns the cattle will be in the driver's seat. And that will be Clinton's family."

"Well, it's a big family. They would divide it up."

"I'm not sure about that. Brodie's the oldest, but he's restless, and he's gone off with the Rangers to fight the Indians. He'll never settle down and be a rancher. Clinton will. Now that Zane's gone, Clinton's the logical one to inherit the Yellow Rose Ranch. And even if they do divide it up, it's the largest ranch in these parts. But it's not only that. Clinton's a steady man . . . dependable."

Lucy Abbot reached up and ran her hand down her hair. She was thinking of Clinton in a way that she had not for some time. Finally, she smiled and said, "Well, Clinton wouldn't be a demanding husband." She took the brush her mother handed her and began to brush her hair again.

"I've been thinking we might have him over for dinner one night this week."

Lucy smiled and nodded. "I think that would be nice."

Quaid took one final swing with the ax and looked up at the large tree as it shivered and fell. He grinned and said, "I think we were a little bit ambitious. I don't know if we can even get this tree in the house."

"Ma said to cut down a big one," Clinton said. "She'll fill the living room up with it, I reckon."

The two men had come out looking for a fir tree, for Christmas was only five days away. For the last week, the children had been begging to help decorate a tree. So with a smile, Jerusalem had ordered Quaid and Clinton to go and cut a tree for this year's festivities.

All of them wanted to come and help chop one down, but only Ethan had been allowed to come with them. The rest of the children were being punished for some mischief concerning some "missing" Christmas baking.

Ethan would have been guilty, too, but he had not been around when a dozen cookies had disappeared.

Quaid tied the end of his rope to the base of the tree, looped it around his saddle horn, and started toward the house. They talked about how the ranch was doing for a time, then Quaid turned and gave Clinton a smile. "I hear you been gettin' some free meals over at the banker's house."

"I've been there a few times," Clinton said quickly. "They've got a good cook over there."

Quaid laughed. "We've got a good cook too. Your ma can cook better than anybody else. And if she doesn't feel like it, Maggie's a better cook than most. What's going on, Clinton?"

"Nothing's going on. Can't a fella go have a meal or two without being questioned about his intentions?"

"But you don't know how interesting you are," Quaid grinned.

"Why is it," Clinton said with his lower lip stuck out, "that when a man gets married, he wants to marry everybody else off?"

Quaid winked and said, "I just hate to see you missing out on the blessings of married life. Nothing like it."

The two men rode slowly together, dragging the tree behind them. When they got to the house, all of the youngsters came roaring out. For the next hour there was all kinds of activity as Quaid and Clinton made a base for the tree. Once it was set up in the house, everybody gathered around to decorate it. As the decorations were unpacked and placed on the large fir tree, Belle was sitting at the piano trying to play. From time to time, the other children would come by and hit the keys.

"Will you children stop banging on that piano!" Jerusalem called out.

"Mama, how am I going to learn to play," Belle said, "if you won't let me practice?"

"Well, practice. But the rest of you stop banging on the keys. That piano came all the way from New Orleans, and I don't want any keys broken."

Jerusalem listened as Belle began to pick out the tune she had learned all by herself. She didn't know the words of it, but she had heard someone singing it and had managed to find the keys. It had pleased Jerusalem that Belle had proven to have at least an ear for music.

The door opened, and Mark Benton came in carrying a load of wood. December this year had been cold, and he had been kept busy cutting firewood and hauling it.

"Just put the wood over in the box, Mark. Then come and have some hot chocolate."

"Thank you, Mrs. Taliferro." Mark went over and dumped his load of wood and then took the mug that Jerusalem handed him. After taking a sip, he said, "That's mighty good. Helps to warm my cold bones."

Mary Aidan had been decorating the tree, but when she saw Mark, she came over and said, "Go bring in some more wood, Mark."

"You let Mark alone, Mary Aidan," Jerusalem said. "I don't know why you have to be so bossy."

Mary Aidan gave Mark a hard look. She had not forgotten, he well understood, how he had caught her kissing Barton Singleton in the parlor. He grinned at her and winked, which made her furious. She turned her back abruptly and went back to help decorate the tree.

Mark turned to watch Belle as she continued to pick out the tune on the piano.

"That's a good song," Mark said.

"You know it?" Jerusalem asked in surprise. "Belle heard it somewhere, but she doesn't even know the name of it."

"It's called 'Oh Susannah.' It was written by a southerner named Stephen Foster. It's a good song, but the C is flat on the piano."

Jerusalem turned her head to face Mark. "It is?"

"Yes. Can't you hear it?"

"No, but I don't have an ear for music."

Mark grinned and said, "Mind if I show you?"

"No, of course not. Please do, Mark."

Mark reached out with his left hand and played the tune of "Oh Susannah," and he sang too. "Oh, Susannah, don't you cry for me." He turned and hit the key for C. "Don't you hear that? It's flat."

"What's it supposed to sound like?" Belle said.

"Well, I'd have to do a little work on the piano."

"Can you tune a piano, Mark?"

"Well, it's not my profession, but I learned a little bit. I got interested in it when I was taking lessons."

"You play the piano?" Clay said. "You never told me that."

"I was too busy digging post holes," Mark said, grinning.

"Play something, Mark," Moriah insisted. "I love piano music."

Mark glanced at Jerusalem, who smiled at once. "Oh yes, do play that song with both hands."

Mark shrugged and sat down at the stool after Jerusalem pulled Belle up. He ran his fingers over the keys lightly. "A good piano," he said, and then he immediately began to play. Everyone in the room stopped dead still and could not take their eyes off of Mark. He lifted his voice, and the power of his rich, mellow voice filled the room. Every note he sang was true and clear. After playing all the way through the song, he gave a fast trilling noise with his right hand and turned around and said, "Your piano needs tuning, ma'am."

"Mark, why, you can make a living playing the piano!" Jerusalem exclaimed.

"I thought I might do that at one time."

"Why didn't you, then?" Mary Aidan demanded. She had been impressed as the others but refused to show it.

"Good musicians, Miss Hardin, have to have discipline. I didn't have any."

"You must have had some," Jerusalem commented, "to play like that!"

Rose Jean said, "I'll bet you know all the Christmas carols, Mark."

"Well, I know a few."

"Play some for us," she urged. Her eyes were shining. "Christmas isn't Christmas without carols."

"Which one would you like?"

"All of them," she said.

Mark laughed. "Well, that would take too much time, but how about this one." He began to play "Joy to the World," and once again his voice filled the room.

It was the most effortless singing that any of them had ever heard, and when he had finished, Belle exclaimed, "I don't see how you sing and play at the same time. Don't you have to think about what your fingers are doing?"

Mark shook his head. "Not if you practice hard, Belle. If you have any talent, you'll get so good you can study your arithmetic while you're playing."

"Play some more," Clay said. "I do admire listening to good music."

Mark played "Hark! The Herald Angels Sing" by Charles Wesley and then several more. When he played "Silent Night," his voice grew soft, and everyone joined in with him. Mark had been listening to Rose Jean sing. "You got a real voice, Miss Campbell. Why don't you and I do one together?"

"Do you know 'My Love Is Like a Red, Red Rose'?"

"Sure. From the form of Bobby Burns. You're not Scottish, are you?"

"With a name like Campbell, what else would I be?"

Mark grinned at her and played the introduction. He began to sing, and Rose Jean joined in with him. Their voices harmonized perfectly as they sang.

When the sound of their voices died away, Belle said, "That's just lovely, Mark. You've got to teach me to play."

"That's right," Jerusalem said. "Would you, Mark, give the children lessons?"

"It's your ranch, ma'am." He grinned, and his teeth looked white against his fresh tan. "Be a lot easier than digging post holes."

Later, after everyone had gone to bed, Rose Jean was talking to Mary Aidan. "Hasn't he got the most beautiful voice you ever heard? And such skill with the piano. He has a great talent."

Mary Aidan said stiffly, "He can't even ride a horse without falling off!"

Rose Jean laughed. She had a delightful laughter that seemed to tinkle. "Well, every man you see around here can ride a horse, but how many of them can play the piano and sing like that? If I had to choose, I'd rather have a husband who could sing like that to me than one who could stay up on a horse."

"He doesn't fit in this country."

Rose Jean stared at the woman, shocked. "You don't like him, do you, Mary Aidan?"

"No, I don't. He was just showing off tonight."

"I don't think so," Rose Jean said. "He was practically forced to do it." She hesitated, then said, "I hate to see you filled with that kind of feeling. It's not good."

"I don't feel any way at all about him," Mary Aidan said, turning her head and staring at Rose Jean. "I don't think about him."

Mary Aidan spun on her heel and left the room abruptly. A small smile touched the corners of Rose Jean's lips, turning them upward. "Oh, you don't? I doubt that seriously."

CHAPTER
TWENTY-FOUR

Christmas had always been a special time for the Benton family. Now, at the end of that particular day as the year of 1849 began to fade, Mark was depressed. Because it was the holiday season, he had thought a great deal of his family during the last week. It was the first year he had actually been away from them for Christmas. He remembered how his father used to say that he was not very sentimental about that day. Yet, his time away and the twists life had thrown his way made Mark miss his family as he watched the Hardins enjoy one another. He also began to think about some of the words his father had said to him. Somehow, they started to take on a different meaning for him.

The day was almost faded now. The stars had started to come out and twinkle faintly in the sky. Mark had not yet gotten over how much bigger the sky seemed in Texas than it was in Memphis. As he stared up, it looked like an enormous bowl as it stretched high above the flat country. Mark had grown to like the feel of it. Now, as he walked along the bank of the Brazos River, he thought of the months he had spent at the Yellow Rose Ranch.

A part of the moon had already taken its place in the sky. Mark stood and watched to see if the tattered remnants of clouds would hit or miss it. The clouds slowly drifted across the moon, and for a moment the brilliant sliver was blotted out. He watched until slowly, bit by bit, the clouds moved on and once again the crescent moon shone down, casting its pale, lucent light over the prairie.

The weather had turned cold for Christmas, but it had not snowed this year. Mark remembered the one Christmas he and his brother, Tom, had spent in Connecticut with a distant relative. The snow had fallen and covered the ground with a beautiful white carpet. Long icicles lined the house, hanging like crystal daggers around the eaves. He remembered all the fun they had with their cousins. They spent hours shooting down the hills on toboggans and skating on the frozen ponds. They even built a large snow fort and staged a war with plenty of snowballs flying through the air. It had been a wonderful Christmas, but most of his Christmases had been spent in Memphis, where snow was unusual. Christmas was all about family, and this year he did not have them to enjoy.

"I could go home."

Mark spoke the words aloud, and the sound vibrated on the air, seeming to hang there motionless, frozen into time and space. He had surprised himself. "I could go home," he murmured again, "but then again, what would it prove?" He had set out to prove that he could stick with something till the end. Surely he had proven that here at the Yellow Rose Ranch. All the hardships and the months that he had put in had made a change not only in his body, toughening him up, but in his attitude. He had had plenty of time to think about the more serious aspects of life at the ranch. He had spent many a long evening sitting out on the porch and listening to the rest of the men talk about horses and the things that composed their world. He had thought mostly about how he had failed his family, and he could never get away from that.

Far away in the distance, the lonesome cry of a coyote came to Mark. "I feel a little bit like you do," he said aloud.

"Well, have you started talking to yourself?"

Mark turned quickly and was surprised to see Mary Aidan Hardin bundled up in a heavy coat with a wool cap pulled down over her ears. "I guess I am," he said. "The next step is the lunatic asylum."

Mary Aidan had been standing underneath a tall pecan tree. It was stripped of leaves now, and its bare branches seemed to reach up for the heavens. He had not seen her, for she had been standing in the shadows. "I'm surprised to see you here."

"Why should you be surprised?"

Mark did not know what to say and merely shrugged his shoulders. He started to walk off, but her voice caught him. "I've been meaning to tell you something."

Mark turned and braced himself. "I bet you have," he said.

"What's that supposed to mean?"

Mary Aidan's face was framed by the darkness, and he still caught the sharpness in it. Mark shook his head, for he had learned there was little point in arguing with this woman. "What was it you wanted to tell me?"

"I . . . I wanted to tell you . . . that I appreciate your giving lessons to the children. It means a lot to Mama and to the children too."

"It's been a pleasure. They're bright youngsters, and they're learning fast."

"You think they have some talent?"

"All of them have some, but Belle is really gifted. She could be a concert pianist if she put her mind to it. She's starting a little late, but she's got a great instinctive feel for the music. Tell her something once, and she never forgets it."

Mary Aidan stared at him. "You don't really mean that . . . that she could play the piano for a living?"

"Yes, I do."

"Have you told Mama?"

"No, I haven't."

"Why not?"

"It might not be a good thing."

"It might not be a good thing to be a concert pianist? What do you mean by that?"

"Being that kind of musician takes everything you have, Miss Hardin."

"Oh, for heaven sakes, will you call me Mary Aidan like everybody else!"

Mark grinned. "If you promise not to bite my head off."

Mary Aidan started to snap back a reply, then suddenly she laughed. "You must think I'm an ogre."

"Not really."

"You must. I've done nothing but tell you what's wrong with you ever since you came here."

"Most of it was right."

Mary Aidan stared at the man silently. He was not as big as most of the men in her family, or in Texas, for that matter. Somehow it seemed that Texas produced big men. Most of them were tall and rangy. Mark was small, but he was well proportioned. She noticed that his neck had filled out, and there was a healthy glow to his face. She remembered how pitiful he had been the first time she saw him. Suddenly, she said abruptly, "Why don't you go home?"

"I was waiting for that."

"I didn't mean it that way," Mary Aidan said quickly. "But you couldn't be happy here. You've led a different kind of life."

"How do you know that?"

"Why, it's written all over you. I'll bet you went to college, didn't you?"

"Some."

"And you know about music, and you're educated. What's your family like? Wait. I'll bet they have money."

"How could you guess that?"

"I don't know. It just seems that way to me."

"Well, I wish I could go home, but I can't."

"Why can't you? What did you do that was so awful they won't let you come back?"

It was Mark's turn to grin. "It's not that they won't let me come back, Mary Aidan. I'm the one who decided to leave, and I can't go back until I—"

Mark broke off suddenly and shook his head. When Mary Aidan saw he intended to say no more, she grew curious. "What did you do that was so awful?"

"Everything."

"I don't believe that!"

"Well, I'm glad you don't, but I was a bad son and a bad brother. I wasted my talent and my family's money, and brought plenty of shame to them. Oh, I didn't kill anybody, but my dad's a proud man, and so is my brother. It hurt them when I didn't live the right kind of life they had in mind for me. It hurt my mother most of all." He stood there and dropped his head, looking at the ground. "I'd like to do something good, something worthwhile, before I go home."

Mary Aidan stepped closer so she could see his face. "What sort of thing?" she whispered.

"Oh, I don't know. I had the crazy idea that if I could stick it out here at the ranch and become an honest working man, I could show that I had some backbone."

"Well, you've certainly done that. You've even ridden that awful Vulcan."

"Somehow I don't think riding a wild horse would impress my family."

"I think it would impress them if I told them how hard you've worked and how you've taken all the ribbing the men have given you and—"

"And what you've given me, too?"

"Yes, that too!" she said defiantly.

They stood there for a moment, and Mark felt a sadness that he could not express. "Maybe I'll go home someday. Good night, Mary Aidan."

Mary Aidan did not want him to leave. She had seen more of Mark Benton during these few moments than in all of the months that he had been there. From the time he had arrived, she had taken great pleasure in ridiculing him. No matter what she had said, not once had Mark ever snapped back at her. Her words only seemed to make him try harder. During the few times when he had opened up to her, she saw a strength in Mark Benton that few men possessed. He had come into a situation totally foreign to him, and he had stuck it out despite the difficulty. She had done her best to make it hard, and he had not flinched. But now she felt ashamed for her behavior. She watched him as he disappeared into the shadows. As she made her own way home, she whispered aloud, "He's not the kind of man I thought he was."

At the same time that Mary Aidan and Mark were speaking on the bank of the Brazos, Lucy and Clinton were having a conversation in the Abbot liv-

ing room. They had celebrated Christmas, more or less, with both families. They spent the morning with Clinton's family, and in the evening they
had dinner at Lucy's house. Clinton was full of turkey and dressing, as well
as the other dishes Mable Abbot and their cook had prepared for the holiday. He leaned back on the couch and listened as Lucy spoke with excitement about the trip that she had made earlier that year to Savannah. He
finally said, "You like to travel?"

"Oh, I like Savannah. It's such a pleasant place. So beautiful. You
should see the houses, Clinton. They're magnificent."

"Maybe I will someday."

Lucy was sitting beside Clinton. She leaned over and put her hand on
his arm. "It would be good for you to travel some," Lucy said. "All you've
ever seen is Texas."

"No, I saw Arkansas, and I've seen New Orleans four times."

"I know, but you were working then, taking those old cattle down
there to market."

"Well, those old cattle paid the bills."

Lucy moved closer and reached up and put her arm on the back of
Clinton's neck. He was so startled he straightened up and turned to face
her. "This has been a wonderful day, Clinton," she whispered.

Clinton felt intoxicated by the faint perfume she wore. He had always
admired her beauty, and when she had seemed to lose interest in him
before, he had fancied himself heartbroken. Now she looked into his eyes
and leaned against him. All he could think of at that moment was the fragrance of Lucy's perfume and the softness of her body close to him. He
said huskily, "Lucy—!" Then he pulled her forward and kissed her. He felt
her arms go around his neck, pulling him closer, and her touch stirred
him. He was the first to pull his head back, saying, "Lucy, you're so
sweet!"

"Do you think so, Clinton?"

"Of course I think so. I've always thought so."

"You and I do seem to fit together so well."

"I reckon we do." Actually, Clinton could not think of any way they
fit well together, but he would have agreed with anything as she smoothed
the hair on the back of his head and did not move away. "I reckon a man
could live with you a hundred years and never get tired of you."

"Oh, Clinton, do you really mean that?"

"Mean it? Why, of course I mean it. Any man would be proud to have you."

"Would you, Clinton?" Lucy said demurely.

Clinton felt overwhelmed. His thoughts were racing, and he hardly knew what he was saying. The smoothness of her cheek and the firmness of her body against him stirred him. "Why, of course I could spend a lifetime with you and never get tired."

"Oh, Clinton, I've been waiting so long to hear you say that!"

Clinton blinked. "To say what?"

"Yes. I've always thought we'd make a wonderful couple, and now I know you feel the same way."

Clinton suddenly realized that he had backed himself into a corner that he could not easily get out of. "Well, Lucy, I'll tell you—"

"Oh, I know. We can't talk about it for a while, but now I know how you *really* feel about me. I promise I won't tell a soul. It'll be our secret."

"Our secret?" Clinton said, wondering what just happened.

Lucy kissed him quickly. "You sound like a parrot," she said. "Now, go home. I'm going to go write it all up in my diary the night you proposed to me."

Clinton felt like a man who had suddenly been plunged into cold water. Before he could think of a single thing to say, he found himself out of the house, standing there staring at the buggy. When he finally got in, he looked at the horse and said, "Molly, what have I went and did?"

Molly whinnied at him, as if to say, "You did it all right this time, Clinton."

"Clinton, you're going around in a daze," Brodie said sharply. "You're gonna run into a tree or somethin' if you don't wake up."

"Leave me alone, Brodie."

Brodie stared at his younger brother and shook his head. "Now, don't forget. You've agreed to take Maggie to that dance. You be nice to her, you hear?"

"When did I agree to that? I don't remember."

"Yes, you do. You agreed a week ago. I asked if you'd take her to the dance, and you said, 'Shore, I will.' That's all there is to it."

"Well, things are somehow complicated now."

"What's complicated about taking Maggie to a dance?" Brodie said. "Now, she'll be waitin' for you to pick her up."

"All right, but I don't know if it's gonna work."

Brodie was puzzled by Clinton's attitude. He did seem to be in a daze. Later that afternoon Brodie went to see Maggie. When he knocked on the door, she didn't say, "Come in," as she usually did. He knocked louder and said, "Maggie, are you there?"

"Yes. Come on in, Brodie."

Brodie stepped inside and then stopped dead still. "Why, Maggie, you look plum splendiferous!"

Brodie couldn't believe what he saw. The two had gone to town to pick out a dress. Maggie had insisted on something plain, but Brodie wouldn't hear of it. After looking at what was available, Maggie chose one without even trying it on. She simply declared it would fit. The dress she was wearing was made of a light blue silk with an off-the-shoulder neckline and short puff sleeves edged with a delicate white lace. The bodice was trimmed with white lace and had tiny white artificial flowers flowing from each shoulder in a V-shape. They met at the middle of her waistline and then continued outward to each side of the skirt and along the bottom. Maggie had also bought low-quartered shoes, hoping that if Clinton wore high-heeled boots, she could look up to him. Her hair was drawn back and tied, and she appeared to have put on some sort of make-up.

"I put on some rice powder," she confessed, "and some lip rouge that your sister gave me."

"Well, you're as pretty as a pair of red shoes with green laces!"

"Do you really think so, Brodie? Do you really?"

"I sure do. Now, you're all set. You remember what I told you?"

"I got on the perfume you gave me. Do you smell it?" She stepped forward, and Brodie took a deep breath.

"Oh, that's good!" he sighed. "That's real good!"

"And I'll lean on him too. I been practicin', just like you showed me."

Maggie was so close she was practically leaning on Brodie. "That's fine. When you come back, I want to hear all about it. Don't forget. Make him help you in the buggy."

Maggie had thoroughly enjoyed the dance, but she was puzzled about Clinton. When he had come to get her, he had complimented her on her new dress and on her looks, but he didn't seem to be himself. She asked him once, "Are you worried about somethin', Clinton?" and he had quickly denied it. She realized then that perhaps he was ashamed to go with her to the dance, and she said, "I know you could have found a more fittin' girl to take to the dance than me."

Clinton was a sensitive young man and realized immediately that he had hurt Maggie's feelings. "Well, leapin' lizards, don't feel that way, Maggie! We're gonna have a great time at the dance."

Maggie had been doubtful, but she had been pleased with the way she had danced with Clinton. Several times that night, she tried to talk to Clinton, but he seemed distracted. She had tried to look up at him as they danced, but his boots were only an inch taller than her, so they were practically eye to eye. She had tried leaning on him, but he had apparently not even noticed. He seemed to be in some sort of a daze. When several other young men cut in, asking for a dance, Clinton didn't seem to mind. When she finished each dance, Clinton had complimented her on her dancing.

Now, as the horses moved down the road at a fast trot, she said, "That was the first dance I ever went to."

Clinton turned. "Well, you done real good, Maggie. You're gonna have those fellas lined up wantin' to take you to all the dances."

"I don't want to go with any of them."

"You don't? Don't that make you proud to have fellas clamorin' over you?"

"No, it don't. I don't know those men, Clinton."

She remembered Brodie's insistence on leaning and moved closer to Clinton. She took his arm and pressed herself against him. "It was the best time I ever had in my whole life, Clinton."

"Well, I'm right proud of that. You shore prettied up for the occasion. You remember the first time I seen you in those old, ragged clothes?"

"I know I was a sight, but it was all I knew, Clinton."

"Well, you come out of that now."

Maggie continued trying to speak to Clinton but saw that he was thinking deeply about something. Finally, she said in desperation, "Clinton, I was afraid you wouldn't like me."

"Like you? Why would you be afraid of that?"

"Well, I ain't like other girls."

Clinton was aware of Maggie's pressing against him. "You're gonna do fine, Maggie."

"You think anyone will ever want to marry me?"

Clinton had a sudden memory of his conversation with Lucy, but he forced it out of his mind. "You bet," he said.

"I don't know how to talk to fellas much."

"Well, you're talking to me."

"You're different, Clinton. You're easy to talk to."

"I'm glad of that. You know what we need to do, me and you, is spend lots of time together."

"Oh, I'd like that. You could tell me all about the Bible."

"Why, sure I could." Clinton was always interested in the spiritual life of anyone he came in contact with. "What would you like to know?"

"Oh, just whatever you want to tell me. I'm so ignorant."

Clinton pushed Lucy Abbot out of his head and began talking to Maggie about getting saved and living a godly life. She sat close beside him, for the night air was cold. After a moment, she sighed and said, "It's so good to have a fella to talk to."

Clinton meant to say, *I hope you always have someone.* Instead, he heard himself saying, "Well, Maggie, I hope you'll always have me."

"Really, Clinton?"

Clinton had not realized yet what he had said, but Maggie hugged his arm tighter. "Do you really mean that, Clinton? You want to have me always?"

Clinton felt like he had stepped with his left foot in one bear trap, and now he was stepping with his right in another. He tried desperately to think of some way to avoid the inevitable, for he saw the direction of Maggie's thoughts. He opened his mouth, but she leaned over and put her head on his shoulder.

"That makes me feel just wonderful. No man ever wanted me before, and now you do. It's gonna be great, Clinton, when we get married."

Clinton opened his mouth to say something, but no words came out. He listened without hearing as Maggie talked until they got in front of her house. He sat there, and she finally said, "You're supposed to help me out, Clinton."

"Oh, sure!" Clinton jumped out, ran around, and helped her down from the buggy. She turned to him, put her arms around his neck, and kissed him. "Good night, Clinton. I'll never forget this night for the rest of my life."

Clinton stood there until she entered the house and shut the door, then he turned and went back to the buggy. Climbing in, he settled into the seat wearily and looked down at his feet. "Feet, I wish my mouth wouldn't work so good. Now I'm engaged to two women. There couldn't be nothin' worse than that!"

For some time Gray Deer, one of Bear Killer's best warriors, had known something was wrong with the chief. He had watched him carefully, and after pondering on it for a long time, he approached his leader. "What is wrong with you, my brother?"

Bear Killer stared at Gray Deer. "Nothing is wrong with me."

"You are not being honest with me. The light has gone out of your eyes. There is no laughter in your teepee. Can you not tell me what it is?"

Bear Killer sat silent in front of the fire that had almost died out. He had spoken to no one all day and had hardly eaten anything. Picking up a few sticks of wood, he threw them on the fire and stared at the glowing embers.

"Some burdens a man must bear alone."

"But some of his brothers can help him carry that burden. I feel bad that you do not call on me, but I know what is troubling you."

Instantly, Bear Killer lifted his head and stared at Gray Deer with his dark eyes. He trusted Gray Deer as much as he trusted any man, and he said, "I do not think you can know my heart."

"I do not know your heart, but I know your history. For many years you have thought about the son that the Silver Hair and the Tall One took from you. Is it not so, brother?"

Bear Killer was silent. Finally, he nodded reluctantly. "It is a wound in my heart."

Gray Deer leaned forward. "Then why do you not go for the boy? The longer he stays with the white eyes, the more he will be tied to them. Let me get a party together. We are many now. We can mount forty warriors. They cannot stand against us."

The crackling of the fire was the only sound, and Gray Deer waited eagerly, his eyes reflecting the light of the coals.

Finally, however, Bear Killer got to his feet. He pulled his robe around his shoulders, gave Gray Deer one implacable look, then turned and walked away. Gray Deer watched him go and shook his head. "He will never know peace until he gets his son back and the scalps of the Silver Hair and the Tall One hang before his teepee." He watched as Bear Killer walked slowly through the camp. "He will change his mind, and we will take many scalps and many slaves. I will help him to see the path he must take."

CHAPTER
TWENTY-FIVE

Brodie had remained behind after the crew had left. He had seen that Maggie had something to tell him. After they had all cleared out, he went into the kitchen where she was washing the dishes. She turned around, dried her hands, and then came and looked up at him. He saw that something was different about her, and he said quickly, "Is something wrong, Maggie?"

"Oh no," she replied quickly and smiled, but there was a tension in her face. "I figured I better tell you first, since you're the one who done it all."

"What did I do?"

"Well, you taught me how to be a lady and how to make Clinton like me."

Brodie grinned. "Well, that wasn't too hard. You had it in you all the time. I just helped you bring it out. How'd the dance go?"

"Oh, it went fine," she said. "I danced with lots of other fellas, but mostly with Clinton. It happened on the way home."

"What happened? Did Clinton get up nerve enough to kiss you?"

"He proposed to me," Maggie said, her eyes sparkling.

Brodie blinked with astonishment. "You don't mean it!" he exclaimed. "Not really!"

"Well, that's what you wanted him to do, wasn't it?"

"I thought it was what *you* wanted. I guess that ought to make you happy."

"I guess so."

The two stood there for a moment, both of them feeling uncomfortable. "Well, I guess I don't have to give you any more lessons," Brodie said. "Looks like you did *really* good."

"I guess."

"I guess I got to congratulate you too."

"But you can't tell anybody else. It's a secret. I don't want people to know just yet."

"Oh, I won't," Brodie said, "but I'm mighty glad that you got what you wanted."

Maggie looked up and parted her lips to say something, and then she clamped them together. "I guess I'll always be grateful to you, Brodie, for teachin' me how to be a lady."

"Well, we'll be, more or less, brother and sister now."

Maggie suddenly frowned. "No, we won't."

"I guess that'll be the way of it," Brodie said. He could tell she was nervous about something, but it was clear she didn't want to talk about it.

"I got to finish washing all these dishes."

Brodie watched her as she turned. "Congratulations, Maggie," he said. "I won't tell anybody, but I'm happy for you. You'll make Clinton a good wife."

"I reckon so," she said without turning around from the sink. When Brodie left, Maggie flung the dish towel across the room. "I'm happy. That's all. I have to be, don't I?"

Barton Singleton seemed to fill the parlor in the big house. He always seemed larger than life to Mary Aidan, and he certainly was too large for the chair he was sitting on.

Belle and Samuel rushed through, followed by David, all yelling like Indians. Next, Mark appeared in the doorway of the parlor, following the kids and yelling at them to come outside.

"Can't you keep them kids quiet, Benton?" Singleton snapped at Mark.

Mark turned quickly to look at him, and then his glance went to Mary Aidan, who was watching. "Apparently not. They're just kids full of life."

"Well, get 'em out of here!" Barton said.

"I'll just do that."

Mark's answer did not please Singleton, who had yearned to use his fists on him for a long time. He moved closer and said, "What does it take to get your goat, Benton?"

"I've delegated all my fighting to my dog," Mark said. Singleton was not particularly swift of mind, but he understood the illusion. He cursed and stepped forward, but Mary Aidan quickly stood up and stepped between them.

"Let's not have any trouble, Barton."

Singleton looked as if he was about to start a fight with Mark, but instead he mumbled something under his breath, grabbed his hat, and left without another word.

"I think I insulted your suitor. Sorry about that," Mark said.

Mary Aidan was displeased with the obvious tension between the two men. She had thought much about the conversation she had had with Mark Benton, but the idea that a man's courage was tied to his willingness to use a gun or his fists was deeply ingrained in her. It was part of life in Texas. Violence lay just around the corner, and a man who would not stand up for himself or his family was less than nothing.

"Don't you have any pride, Mark?"

"Not the kind you like."

"What's that supposed to mean?" she demanded instantly.

"I mean that you can only judge a man by the way he fights, with a fist or a gun or a knife. If he's willing to do that, then you think he's a real man. But there are other things that make a man, and you need to learn what they are."

Anger flared in Mary Aidan. "I didn't ask to be lessoned to by you, Mark!"

Mark had been standing sideways, ready to leave the room in pursuit of the children. Instead, he turned and came and stood before her. He also had thought of the conversation they'd had. Ever since then, he had been unable to stop thinking about her. He knew it probably seemed foolish, but she had something in her that he found desirable. She had treated him cruelly for months, and even now he saw the disdain in her eyes. He reached out suddenly, and before she could back away, he pulled her close and pinioned her in his arms. He leaned forward, but she was too late to avoid his kiss. She struggled briefly, and then when he lifted his lips, she was furious.

"Take your hands off me, you brute!"

"Your trouble, Mary Aidan, is you won't let a man get close to you no matter how hard they try."

"Get out of here!" she snapped.

"A woman," Mark said quietly, "should have gentleness, but that trait is missing in you."

The accusation touched off something deep inside Mary Aidan, which caused her to flare out at him. In one swift motion, she swung her arm and slapped him hard on his cheek. It resounded loudly, leaving the white print of her fingers. "Get out of here and leave me alone! You don't know what you're talking about!"

"Somewhere there's a woman in there, but I doubt she'll ever get out," Mark said, then turned and left the room.

Mary Aidan's hands were trembling, and her knees felt weak. She did not understand the tumult of feelings that stirred in her, for she was a young woman who was accustomed to being in charge of situations—especially where men were concerned. She clasped her hands together as if to hide their trembling and walked quickly toward the window and stared outside. She saw Mark walking toward the bunkhouse with his head high. He didn't look back, and anger flared in her again. "He's wrong! He doesn't know anything," she whispered aloud.

The moment would not go away. She carried it with her all afternoon. Even that night after she had gone to bed, she could hear his voice saying, "Somewhere there's a woman in there, but I doubt she'll ever get out." A mindless rage swept through her as she thought of his words. She gritted her teeth together and lay stiffly in the bed with her fists clenched. "Who does he think he is? He thinks he knows so much about women. What makes him an expert? He's nothing but a weak man!"

Time and again her mind relived the scene in the parlor, then finally she drifted off into a restless sleep, broken by shattered dreams.

Will Perkins was the youngest of the four men who kept circling the large herd of longhorns. At seventeen he was two years younger than Monty Nolan and Bake Teague, and he was at least twenty-five years younger than O. M. Posey, who was the oldest hand on the ranch. It was generally considered that Will had the loudest voice and the most opinionated spirit of any man in Texas. Will was not aware of how his voice carried, and once Monty said, "Just speak up, Will. They'll hear you all the way back at the ranch."

At the moment, they were discussing the subject of slavery. Will Perkins was a devoted disciple of those who believed that slavery was nothing more than the way things should be. "It's all spelled out clear as day in the Bible," he said, his voice carrying over the lowing of the steers. "I'm surprised you fellers can't see it."

"How many slaves you own?" Bake Teague asked. He was a small, thick-boned young man with guileless blue eyes and a broad face.

"Why, I don't actually own none," Will said from atop his mount.

"Well, how many does your family own?" Monty Nolan added, winking at Bake, for they both knew the answer.

"We don't own none, but we got a right to."

"You won't have it long," O. M. said.

"What you talkin' about, Posey?"

"There's a war shapin' up over slavery. The South would do well to get rid of their slaves right now. Be cheaper in the long run."

Will shook his head in disgust. "Posey, I'm surprised at smart fellows like you. You know them Yankees ain't got no right to tell us what we can or can't do."

"You'd argue with a stump, Will, and you don't know nothin' about it. I don't care—"

Suddenly a shot rang out, and Posey was rocked back in his saddle. The younger men were so shocked they couldn't speak. They looked at Posey's chest, which was blossoming like a red rose.

"I think I've been shot!" Posey said. He reached out, touched his shirt, and then without another word, he began to fall over. He fell sideways, not trying to catch himself, and his horse started off, dragging him in the stirrups.

"Rustlers!" Will yelled and pulled out his six-gun. "I'll take care of Posey. You fellas try to hold 'em."

The battle that followed was short. The three young men did their best, but the rustlers had planned their ambush well. Posey was dead, and they were forced to leave him to save their own skins. As they rode out, leaving the herd, Will turned back and yelled to the other riders, "They was Mexicans. I heard 'em talkin'."

"Well, they're takin' all those cattle we worked so hard to catch and brand," Bake said.

The three were galloping at a dead heat, and Bake had to yell to be heard. Will Perkins shouted back, "No they won't get to keep 'em, not if I know Mr. Clay. He'll get them cattle back or die trying."

Clay listened silently as the three young men described the cattle raid. He said nothing, but his eyes had a cold glint to them. Perkins said, "We tried our best to fight 'em off, but we didn't have no chance. They took us by surprise. There must have been at least a dozen of 'em."

"That's right," Bake said, "and they killed poor old Posey without no warnin'."

"They got all the cattle too," Monty Nolan said sorrowfully. "I suspect they're halfway back to the Rio Grande by now."

The room fell silent. Clinton, Quaid, and Brodie had stepped inside, and the women stayed in the background, but every eye was on Clay. "I knew it would come to this sooner or later," he said.

Jerusalem did not even have to ask. "When will you leave, Clay?"

"As soon as you can get some grub together. We'll take the best horses. Every man take three mounts."

"I'm gonna take my best horse Caesar," Clinton said quickly. "He'll outrun anything they got."

"You're not going, Clinton," Clay said flatly.

Clinton blinked with astonishment and then anger. "Why, I am so goin'!"

"Somebody's got to stay here. You'll be in charge."

"Well, I'm goin'," Brodie said. "Don't try to tell me not to, Clay."

"I won't. I want you to go, too, Quaid. We'll take four of the hands, the young fellas and Mark. Now, we'll stop by town and get plenty of ammunition before we head out after them."

Jerusalem said to Moriah, "Come on. We need to fix some food."

Mary Aidan helped get the food ready. After Clay came back in from saddling his horse, she found a chance to ask him, "Why are you taking Mark? He's no gun fighter. He'll be no good to you."

Clay's mind was on Posey. He said gently, "Posey didn't have too many years left, did he, but he never got 'em."

"Did you hear what I said?" Mary Aiden asked.

"I'm taking Mark because I'll need him."

"He's no fighter."

Suddenly, Clay's eyes turned cold. He turned to face Mary Aidan, and the words that dropped from his lips seemed to burn into her spirit. "It's good we got at least one person on this ranch who never makes any mistakes, who's always right."

Clay's anger was so shocking that Mary Aidan took a step backward. She had always been Clay's pet. He had practically raised her and had never once raised his voice to her, but now he stared at her with such a hard look that she could not speak for a moment. Finally, she whispered, "I . . . I didn't mean—"

"Stay out of this, Mary Aidan. I don't want to hear any more about Mark from you. You've judged him wrong." Then he turned and walked outside the house.

Mary Aidan simply stood there and could not say a word. She found herself trembling at the second rebuke he had given her. Ever since she was a little girl, she had adored Clay. He had been more of a father to her than Jake had ever been, and now she felt she had lost something—something very precious, and she didn't know how to get it back.

Maggie had helped gather some supplies so the men could ride out soon. It was as if they were going to war, she thought, as she watched them pack blankets, guns, food, and plenty of ammunition. Something about it frightened her. She had grown up in a rough world, but this spirit in Clay Taliferro she had not seen before. She had heard some of the tales of what a fearless fighter he was, and now she was seeing that side of him.

Brodie came over to Maggie, who was still helping pack food supplies, and said, "I reckon we might take a little more coffee if you got it, Maggie."

"I'll put some more in a bag." She sacked up the coffee in a cloth bag, tied it firmly in a knot, and gave it to him.

He stood looking down at her, but his mind was on the dangers that could lie ahead. He realized she was watching him intently. "That's a mighty serious look for a woman to have."

"I'm worried about you, Brodie."

"Why, it won't be nothin'. The whole Mexican army couldn't kill me. How could a bunch of rag-tag Mexican rustlers do it?"

"When bullets start flying, anything can happen."

Brodie laughed. He leaned forward and kissed her on the cheek. "Now, sister, you stop worrying right now. I'll be back before you know it."

Maggie flushed. "I'm . . . I'm not your sister."

"Well, I think you are, and if I didn't love Serena, I'd sure give Clinton a run for his money with you. Of course," he said quickly, "you love Clinton."

Maggie stood very still, then she reached up and put her hand on his cheek and whispered, "Oh, be careful, Brodie, be very careful!" She watched as he winked at her, then turned and walked away. He acted as if he were going to a picnic, but her heart was filled with fear. She watched as the men rode out with extra horses all heavily loaded with gear. She stood there waiting, watching until all she could see was the dust from the horse hooves, then she suddenly began to cry.

CHAPTER
TWENTY-SIX

W ell, this has been a pretty tough venture, Mark."
Mark looked up from the frying pan and saw that Clay's face was lined. He looked tough in the early morning light. Fatigue had worn away at him, as it had on the rest of the men. The men were all tired from long hours in the saddle as they continued to look for Mexicans who had stolen their cattle.

"Toughest thing I've ever done," Mark agreed.

Clay watched as Mark broke three more eggs and added them to the skillet over the fire. "We had a cook once up in the mountains. He was so bad that somebody finally shot him."

"Shot him because he couldn't cook?" Mark said, looking up at Clay in amazement.

"Well, that was one of his failin's. It was only in the leg, though," Clay said, grinning. He suddenly changed the subject and asked, "You wonderin' why I brought you along?"

"Yes. I've never been in a fight."

"You may not be this time. We may get out of it easier than you think."

"You don't believe that, do you?"

"No." Clay grinned and shook his head. "I don't. I think it'll be quick, though. I brought you along," he said, "because you're a good man, and I want you to know it."

"I wish my dad could hear you say that."

"I'd like to tell him. You two have a ruckus of some kind?"

"Lots of 'em." Mark turned the eggs over skillfully, for he knew Clay liked his over easy. When they were done, he let them slide into another pan. Then he put some bacon on and some biscuits that they had brought along. "That's the last of the biscuits," he said. He looked over at Clay, who was drinking coffee from a tin cup, and said, "Do you reckon the horses are gonna hold out?"

"They won't have to. We're almost there."

"You know where we're goin'?"

"I've had a pretty good idea all along. The biggest horse thief in Mexico is sort of a friend of mine, or used to be."

"How could he be a friend if he stole your cattle?"

Clay picked up a fork and began picking out little bits of debris out of the bacon. He was finicky about his eating. Finally, he took a big bite and chewed it thoroughly, adding a biscuit for texture. "His name is Mateo Lebonne. His dad was one of the best friends I ever had. We partnered together in the mountains a long time ago."

"Lebonne. Is that the girl I heard Brodie was sweet on?"

"That's the one. Of course, she was a beautiful girl. Still is, I guess. A woman now. She let Brodie down pretty hard. He's never gotten over it."

"Why is Mateo stealing from you?"

"I don't know. He just hates Texans. He fought with Santa Anna's army at the Alamo. Brodie saved his life at San Jacinto, but Mateo's got a screw loose about Texas. He wants to take it all back for Mexico. He never will, of course."

Mark had fixed his own meal and now filled his tin plate and sat with his back against a mesquite tree. He ate slowly and methodically, pausing to take a drink of his black coffee from time to time. "Won't it be pretty hard fightin' against an old friend?"

"It's Mateo's choice, Mark. He's been stealing all around us, and I've said nothing, but now he feels like it's a personal thing. I hate to see it come to this, but I have to stop him."

Mark stared at Clay's face and tried to understand the man. From working at the Yellow Ranch, Mark knew that life for Clay Taliferro had been hard in earlier years. It had molded Clay into something that Mark could not understand completely.

"Would you really shoot him, Clay?"

"If I had to—just like he'd shoot me."

The two sat there and finished their meal. After a while, Mark got up and stared at the horses. "They'll just about make it. You think they're up ahead of us?"

"The herd? No, they're behind us."

Mark stared at Clay. "What do you mean 'behind us'?"

"We rode around them, Mark. We'll get to Mateo's ranch before they will. He won't be expecting it so quick." He grinned without mirth. "That will give us the advantage of surprise."

"I don't know how well I'll do. I've never shot anybody."

"Well, I'm suspectin' nobody ever shot at you, but it'll be different this time. I'm hoping we can surprise 'em."

Clay's plan from the beginning had been to ride around the herd that the Mexicans were stealing. He was fairly certain that Mateo had sent them to raid the cattle. While he could not understand Mateo's reasoning, he knew that it could not go on. They could not afford to lose any more cattle. The Yellow Rose Ranch meant everything to him and Jerusalem, and he intended to do everything within his power to protect it.

He drove the men hard that day. That night he called them all together when they had eaten almost the last of their provisions. "Mateo's ranch is just five miles over in that direction."

"Are we going to ride in tonight?" Brodie asked.

"No. We'll be there in the morning. We'll take 'em when they get up."

"You think they'll put up a big fight, boss?" Perkins asked eagerly.

Clay did not answer immediately, but when he did, his voice was low and soft. "I hope not," he said. "We'll meet whatever they got."

The next morning, Clay had everyone up well before the sun's rays crested over the hills in the distance. He led them within sight of the ranch house, which was barely discernible at dawn.

"We'll leave our horses here," he said. "Hobble 'em and tie 'em good. We won't be ridin' 'em back to the ranch, though. We'll take fresh stock."

"I'm takin' my horse back," Brodie said. "He's too good to leave with these Mexicans."

"Do as you please," Clay said. "Now, nobody shoots until I say so. I'm hopin' we can get out of this without anybody gettin' hurt."

"Posey got killed," Brodie said, "so somebody's goin' down for that."

"Maybe so. It's up to them." Clay outlined his plan, which was to surround the ranch house and move in as close as they could. "If we're lucky, nobody will see us, and we can take them without a fight. If they do see us and start to fire, do what you have to do."

Mark stayed close to Clay at his command. As they approached the house, he felt himself gripped by a strange feeling. It was not fear exactly but uncertainty. He battled with the fear that he would not be able to handle the trouble. He had always run away from trouble before, but there would be no running away from this fight.

They were only a hundred feet from the house when suddenly a man stepped out from the house. He took one look at the circle closing in, yelled something in Spanish, pulled his gun, and got off three shots. He fell at once, riddled by at least a half-dozen bullets. The gunfire awakened other men, and suddenly, for the first time, Mark Benton heard the whistling of bullets flying past them. He recalled from a book he had read that George Washington had found that sound pleasant. He himself disliked it intently, but he kept moving forward and dodging the gunfire that cracked in the early dawn.

When they were within twenty feet of the house, Mark saw a man who suddenly had come around the corner of the house. Clay was forging straight ahead, unaware of the man pointing a rifle at him. Mark yelled, lifted his pistol, and got off one shot. It beat the rifle shot by a split second. Clay's hat was plucked off his head, and the Mexican was driven backward and lay still.

Clay turned and flashed a grin. "I owe you one for that, Mark. Now, follow me."

"They rushed into the house, and a young man was reaching to pull a rifle from the wall. Before he could get it down, Clay had his gun on the back of the man's head. "Let it stay there, Mateo," he said, and the man stopped dead still. He turned around, and although the sound of gunfire continued outside, it was fading away.

"So it's you, Clay."

"You were expectin' me, weren't you?"

"I guess I was." Mateo Lebonne was a fine-looking young man. He had one silver streak in his coal black hair. He stood there staring at Clay, and there was no fear in his eyes. "I'm sorry it's come to this."

"It was your choice, Mateo."

"Go ahead and hang me. Do it quick, Clay. Don't do me any favors."

Clay reached out and pulled the rifle off the wall, then holstered his own gun. He stood there holding the long weapon in his hand. "No need for that, Mateo. You and I are goin' to have a little talk."

"It won't do any good."

"It might," Clay said. He turned and said, "Mark, go see what's going on outside. We've got to get ready to beat those fellows comin' with our cattle. Have everybody tied up and out of sight somewhere."

"All right, Clay."

When Mark stepped outside, he saw three bodies lying on the ground. They were all Mexican. "Anybody hurt?" he called out.

"I got nicked in the butt," Bake said. "Ain't that disgraceful?"

"We're supposed to tie all these fellas up and put 'em in the barn or somewhere until Clay decides what to do with 'em."

Brodie came over and said, "Is Mateo inside?" The look on his face was cold and hard, for he was determined to make these Mexicans pay for Posey's death, especially Mateo Lebonne.

"Yes."

"I guess I'll get in on that talk." Brodie turned and stepped inside the house. He saw Mateo sitting at a table. When Mateo looked up and their eyes met, a silence hung in the room for a while. Then Brodie said, "I didn't think you'd do a thing like this to a friend, Mateo."

"Anglos are not my friends."

"You were ready to take us for a friend at San Jacinto."

"And I saved your life before that, if you remember, so we were even. I figured it was a debt you owed me."

Clay came and stood in front of Mateo. "Mateo, this is foolishness.

Give me your word there will be no more raiding of our ranch, and we'll take the cattle and leave."

Mateo shook his head and would not answer.

"You always were a stubborn fellow," Clay said, "but it could kill you this time."

"What difference does it make?" Mateo said bitterly.

"Where's Serena?" Clay asked.

"In town, but don't waste your time," Mateo said.

"You better go talk to her, Brodie. Maybe she can talk some sense into Mateo."

"Yes, go on and talk to her," Mateo snapped. "You'll find her in the cantina. You'll be surprised at what you find."

Brodie stared at Mateo, then said, "How do you get to town?" He listened to Mateo's instructions, then went out and got on his horse.

The town was only seven or eight miles from Mateo's ranch. After riding for over an hour, Brodie finally reached the outskirts of the town. When he rode down the main street, he asked the first man he saw, "Where can I find Serena Lebonne?"

"Serena Lebonne? She works at that cantina over there," the man said. He laughed and said, "It's early for her. You'll have to get her out of bed."

"Go away!"

The voice was muffled, but as Brodie stood outside the door, he recognized Serena's voice. "Open the door, Serena. I've got to talk to you."

He heard someone stirring in the room. After a few minutes, the door slowly opened. He had asked downstairs in the bar and was told that Serena had a room on the second floor. Now he stared at her and could not think of what to say for a moment. He was thinking of how sweet and how beautiful she had been when he had first met her. He had only been a boy and knew practically nothing about women. She was a beautiful young Mexican girl with a creamy complexion, black hair, and eyes like deep pools.

The woman that stood before him now had aged. It was not so much that her hair had streaks of gray or that her face was wrinkled, but there was hardness in her. She was wearing only a thin wrapper around her sheer gown and seemed careless and immodest. The life in the cantina had left its scars on her body as well as her soul.

"Well, Brodie, what are you doing here?" she asked, her voice coarse and shrill.

"I think you'd better get dressed. You need to come with me," Brodie said.

"Why should I come with you?"

"Mateo's in trouble. I think maybe you can help him."

"Come in." She stepped aside, and Brodie walked in. The room was cluttered with dirty clothing. Cigar butts lay scattered on the sparse furniture and the floor. The room had an acrid odor about it that he did not recognize. He turned to face her and tried to find the features of the girl that he had been dreaming of for so many years.

I've been a fool. This isn't the girl I knew. The thought burned into his mind as he stood there in silence for a moment.

"Look, Serena. Your brother is stealing cattle from our ranch. We came to get our cattle back. Three of his men are dead already. If Mateo doesn't promise to leave our ranch alone, Clay's liable to hang him."

"Mateo's a fool!"

"Yes, he is. He'd die before he'd admit he was wrong, but I think he might listen to you."

"He hasn't for years, but I'll try," Serena said. She slipped out of the robe and would have pulled the gown off, but she saw the distaste in Brodie's eyes. "What did you think I was—the same little girl you used to know?" She laughed harshly and said, "Go downstairs and wait while I dress."

Mateo stared at Serena, who had entered and without preamble said, "Don't be any more of a fool than you already are, Mateo. You don't need Clay's cattle. You can steal from somebody else. There are plenty of Anglos for you to steal from until one of them shoots you."

Mateo's face reddened with anger. "You don't tell me what to do, Serena."

Serena stared at Mateo. "You remember the first time we saw Clay?"

"Yes, I remember."

"We didn't have anything. Our father was dying, and we didn't have a peso. Clay took us all in, built us a house, and looked out for us. This is the man you want to steal from?" she said as she held his gaze.

Mateo suddenly dropped his head. The anger that was there seemed to fade, and he did not speak for a long time. Serena went over, and placing her hand on his shoulder, she said, "I know you hate the idea of Anglos in our country, but that's the way it is, Mateo. But Clay and Jerusalem have never done anything to us but good. Your foolishness and hatred have cost us the best friends anyone could ever have had. You think we have good friends like that now?" she said bitterly.

Mateo looked up. "No, we don't." He turned to Clay and whispered, "I don't know what got into me, Clay. I'm just crazy. You ought to shoot me."

"Can't afford the ammunition, Mateo. I've got your word, then?"

"You have my word. None of my people will ever touch the Yellow Rose Ranch again. Do you believe me?"

"Why, sure. You always were a truthful sort of fella." He turned and looked at Brodie, who had said nothing. The young man's eyes were fixed on Serena, his face filled with disbelief and doubt and disgust. Clay said quickly, "We'll be leaving with the cattle tomorrow. We'll need some supplies and fresh horses."

"Of course, Clay." Mateo seemed almost eager now to do what he could to help them. "Serena, will you help me get them ready?"

Serena turned and looked at Brodie. She said nothing for a moment, then nodded. "Yes. I will help."

By the time everything was packed up and the horses saddled, it was midday before Clay and his hands left with the herd of cattle. Serena had stayed to help her brother and the cook get supplies together. Mateo even gave Clay fresh mounts to take back with him.

She did not speak to Brodie until he mounted his horse, ready to ride out. She walked over to him, and when he looked down, he saw a faint trace of the sweetness and the purity that he remembered. She put her hand out and he took it.

"Try to think of me as I was then. Not as I am now, Brodie."

"I will, and God be with you, Serena."

She did not answer, but tears came to her eyes. She turned and walked away and did not look again until the Texans were a mere speck in the distance.

That night after supper the hands sat around the fire talking about how easy the raid had been, boasting about how they had taken the Mexicans without much of a fight. Clay and Brodie sat off to one side. Clay had stuck close to Brodie all day long. Brodie had said hardly a word since early that morning when they left Mateo's place. Now he turned, and when he looked at Clay, his face was filled with misery.

"You know, Clay. Sometimes a fellow bends over to pick up something, and when he straightens up, the whole world has changed."

Clay sat there looking at Brodie. For years he had loved this young man as if he were his own son. Now he saw the pain and grief and disillusionment in his eyes. "Sometimes, son," he said, "the whole world needs to be changed."

Brodie kept his eyes on the older man. Finally, he nodded and summoned a smile. "I reckon you're right about that." He leaned back, lay down, and looked up at the stars and said no more. The sky was brilliant with stars, and the moon was a pale, ghostly circle. As Brodie Hardin thought about a lost love, somehow he knew that despite the grief he felt, it would not always be that way.

PART FIVE:

CLINTON'S CHOICE

CHAPTER
TWENTY-SEVEN

The day was fading, and Jerusalem was sitting on the porch, looking out across the plains. The trees nearest the house stood in disorganized ranks, laying their shadows on the ground in long lines. The large pecan trees that surrounded the house helped keep most of the sun out of the way. A peace filled her as the fading sunbeams stretched their long fingers of light through the trees and touched the earth with gentleness. The quiet was almost palpable, and Jerusalem was startled when Rose Jean suddenly appeared and broke the silence.

"I wonder if the man who married Mary Magdalene had trouble with her past," Rose Jean said.

Jerusalem laughed softly as she rocked back and forth in the chair. "That sounds exactly like something Clay would say." She turned to trace the features of the young woman who sat beside her. "He's always coming out with some outlandish statement that has nothing in the world to do with the conversation. What made you think of a thing like that?"

Rose Jean stared at the trees that lined the riverbank before she answered. This young woman had a quietness about her that Jerusalem liked very much. She had told Clay that a woman needed a silent side, and Rose Jean Campbell possessed that to a large degree.

Finally, she shrugged and said, "I was just reading about her in the Scriptures early this morning. Apparently, she was not a good woman before she met Jesus."

"I don't think she was," Jerusalem said. "She was full of demons."

"The Bible doesn't say so, but I expect she was a very immoral woman too. So, as I read it, I was just wondering if she ever married, and if she did, did her husband ever hold it against her—what she had been in her past, I mean."

"Not if he was a good man," Jerusalem said, noticing that her comment caused Rose's eyebrows to lift in question.

Rose turned, and one last sunbeam outlined her form. At that instant Jerusalem realized again what an attractive woman Rose Jean was. Everything about her seemed neat. Her wealth of light brown hair was always washed, combed, and brushed. She was small but very well-formed, indeed, with a tiny waist and hips. Her oval face was dominated by well-shaped eyes of an odd, dark blue color.

"Do you think so?" Rose said. "Some people find it very hard to forget other people's pasts."

"When a man and a woman come together, they start where they are. If they don't, there's bound to be trouble." Jerusalem made a little gesture with her shoulders, and then a smile turned the corners of her lips upward. "Every married person ought to have a good forgettery."

"Forgettery?" Rose Jean smiled. "I never heard that, but it sounds like a good idea."

The two women sat there enjoying the quiet evening, each occupied with their own thoughts, until Jerusalem said quietly, "I'm worried about the men. It's always dangerous to cross over the border. A lot of Mexicans have never forgiven us for taking this land away from them."

"They'll be all right, I'm sure. God's going to put His protection on them. We've agreed on that, Jerusalem, and you know the Bible says that where two or three are agreed on anything, it will be done."

The soothing silence flowed around them, and from far away came the sound of one of the hands singing a song. He sang very badly, and the guitar that accompanied him was terribly out of tune.

"He can't sing much, can he?" Jerusalem said. Then abruptly her voice changed. "It would be terrible for me if Clay died."

"He'll be all right." Rose Jean reached over and put her hand on Jerusalem's arm. Her eyes were warm and confident. "And the Lord has given me peace about it. They'll come back safe. You'll see."

Jerusalem reached over and covered Rose Jean's hand. It felt strong but soft, compared to her own, which was worn with years of hard work. "What do you want, Rose Jean, besides taking the gospel to the Indians?"

"Why, I suppose I want what all women want. I want a husband and children, a place to call home someday."

"You and Clinton would make a good marriage."

Surprised by Jerusalem's comment, Rose Jean said, "I don't think that will ever happen."

"Why not? He's a good young man. I don't know of one better."

"He's in love with Lucy Abbot, Jerusalem."

"No, he's not." Jerusalem pronounced the words almost harshly. "He's dazzled by her the way any man would be. But I will have to say that Clinton is not the world's greatest authority where women are concerned. He thought he was in love with Aldora Stuart. He was practically walking into things he was so taken by her." She waited for Rose Jean to speak, and when she didn't, Jerusalem continued. "You two have so much in common. You both love the Bible more than any young people I've ever seen. You'd never run out of things to talk about."

Rose Jean did not speak for a moment. She had straightened up in her chair and then said, "Listen. Someone's coming."

"You have the sharpest ears, Rose Jean." Jerusalem waited and listened intently, and then she said, "You're right. Someone is coming." Both women rose and stood and watched as a single horseman came at a fast gallop out of the falling darkness. "It's Clay," Jerusalem said. "I'd know that horse anywhere."

Rose Jean said, "Go out and greet him like a good wife should."

"All right. I wonder where the rest of the crew is."

Jerusalem stepped off the porch and walked a ways in front of the house and then waited until Clay came in. He swung off his horse and limped toward her, then caught her in a strong hug and kissed her, saying huskily, "You're about the prettiest thing I've seen lately, woman."

"Clay, are you all right?"

"Finer than frog hair."

"Where is the rest of the crew?"

"Oh, they'll be riding in sooner or later, but I had to come on ahead. I've been lonesome for a good hug, so how about it?"

Jerusalem held him tightly, reveling in the strength of his arms, as relief at his safe return flowed through her. She was not a woman given to worry or agitation, but she knew what it was to be anxious for her man. "How did it go?"

"It went fine. None of our men got hurt, but a few Mexicans died in the fight. You got coffee on the stove?"

"Yes, and plenty of food too," she said as she waited for him to take care of his horse. Then she linked her arm in his and walked to the house. When they entered the kitchen, Rose Jean greeted him.

"Is everyone all right?"

"Sure. It was easy. Brodie and the rest of the boys will be back pretty soon."

Ten minutes later Clay was eating a heaping plate of hot food that Jerusalem had set before him. Between bites he was telling her how the raid had turned out at Mateo's place.

"It was easier than I thought, and we won't be havin' any more trouble with Mateo."

Jerusalem listened closely as Clay told her how they had managed to capture Mateo and how it was Serena who had convinced her brother to stop raiding the Yellow Rose.

Jerusalem got up, refilled Clay's cup with coffee, then replaced the pot and sat down again. "What about Serena and Brodie?" she asked.

Clay picked up the coffee cup, sipped it, and when he put it down, he had a quizzical look in his eyes. "It didn't go well for Brodie when he finally met up with her. It's all over between him and Serena."

"Has she changed that much?" she asked.

"It's real sad, Jerusalem. She was a fine young woman when she left here, but she's—" Clay sought for the words and said, "She's not what she once was."

Clay's words told Jerusalem all she needed to know. "I'm sure that must have been hard on Brodie. He's had her in his heart for a long time.

Winning her heart has been his dream from the day she and her family left."

Clay leaned forward and took her hand. They were silent for a moment, and then he murmured, "Well, when a dream goes up in smoke, some men can't handle it. But I reckon Brodie will have to."

Although Maggie had said nothing about it, she had been very worried about the cowhands the whole time they were gone. She had grown up in a violent world, and she knew how quickly things could turn dangerous. When they finally rode in, she breathed a sigh of relief.

She spent the rest of the afternoon preparing them a good supper. When they all came in and sat down in the evening, she waited on them, filling their plates over and over again until they were full. She smiled at their generous compliments on her cooking. She saw, however, that something was bothering Brodie. He was quiet and seemed distant. He hardly said a word during the entire meal. She said nothing until the hands, all weary with their journey, went off to bed. Brodie did not join them but left to go outside. She was undecided about saying anything, but finally she went outside. She found him leaning against one of the poles that held up the roof of the porch.

"I'm glad you got back safe, Brodie."

"It wasn't much of a chore. It went a lot easier than we figured."

"From what I hear, it sounds like there won't be any more raiding."

"Not from Mateo's bunch, but he ain't the only Mexican bandit who's raiding Texan ranches."

"Did you see—?" Maggie broke off the question that she had been wanting to ask. She had heard from Moriah and Jerusalem and others about Brodie's hopeless love for Serena, Mateo's sister. But she knew that it was not her place to speak. She was surprised when Brodie began to speak of what had happened.

"It was a bad trip for me, Maggie. None of our guys got hurt, but some of the Mexicans were killed. Maybe you heard about Mateo's sister, Serena."

"I've heard people speak of her."

"Well, she's one of the prettiest women I ever saw. I guess I was pretty much gone on her when she and her family lived here for a while. Her father, Gordan Lebonne, was a good friend of Clay's from years ago. Clay helped them out when Serena's father died. Serena was a little older than I was and didn't care for me."

"But you cared for her?"

Brodie didn't answer for a moment, and then he turned to her. The moonlight was silvery on his face, and she could see that he was hurting.

"I sure did," he said. He looked down at his hands and then lifted his eyes. He began to speak of Serena and how much he cared for her back when he was just coming into manhood.

As she listened to Brodie, Maggie could not identify her feelings. She had become very fond of Brodie Hardin. He had always been kind to her. When he fell silent, she said, "Brodie, I'm real sorry. I know how much you loved her. I can tell from the way you talk about her."

Brodie shook his head, and his voice was unsteady. "Well, it's a strange thing, Maggie. I was in love with a woman who didn't exist. That girl that I first knew. She's gone."

A great compassion filled Maggie's heart at seeing Brodie brokenhearted over Serena Lebonne. Even though Maggie had led a hard life, she had a sweetness and a goodness in her. It bothered her to see Brodie this way. Reaching out, she put her hand on his arm. When he turned to face her, she whispered, "I don't like to see you hurting."

"Why, Maggie, you're crying!"

Maggie turned and ran away, leaving Brodie to stare after her. He was shocked by the emotion he had seen in Maggie's face. From the time he had first met her, she was an untamed young woman who was more at home with a bunch of ornery mules than feminine graces. He was surprised to see the tenderness that had leaped out of her eyes. And now as he stood there in the silence of the night, he wondered what kind of a woman was beneath that rough exterior.

All four of the youngsters that livened up the atmosphere of the Yellow Rose Ranch were gathered in the parlor for the music lesson that Mark

Benton was there to give. Sam and Rachel Belle, their red hair gleaming and their green eyes alert, were arguing, as they often did, about who would perform first for their teacher. David, though younger, was the loudest, and Ethan, by far the quietest of the three, said little but watched all that went on with his dark eyes.

"I'm gonna play first," Rachel Belle announced.

"No, I am!" Sam argued.

Mark had listened to the argument with a smile. He had sort of expected that the twins might argue and fight with each other. Yet he knew they would unite instantly against a common enemy. "Ladies first, Sam."

"Well, I don't see why ladies have to be first!"

"Because it's the polite thing to do. Okay, Belle, let me hear the piece you've learned this week."

Belle stood up with a triumphant smirk at Sam, plopped herself on the piano stool, and began to play the piece that Mark had given them at their last lesson. "That was good, wasn't it, Mr. Mark?"

"Very good."

"Now me. I can do it better," Sam said.

All four of the children took their turn at the piano. Mark noticed that Mary Aidan had come in and taken a seat. She said nothing, and the children hardly noticed her. Mark ignored her as he listened to each child play their piece. After he had heard all of them, he said, "Now we'll see about your sight reading."

"I don't see why we have to fool with them old notes," Sam said with disgust. "We can play without 'em."

"My pupils all have to know how to read music. I know it's dull, but just think what it'd be like, Sam, if you could pick up a piece of paper with notes and the words to a song and be able to play what that sheet says without anybody there to tell you."

"I like to read the notes," Ethan said. "It's almost like magic."

"Good for you, Ethan." Mark winked at the boy. "So far you're the best sight reader. I'm real proud of you."

"Well, I'm the loudest!" David said. "I can play the piano louder than anybody else!"

"You sure can, David, and sometimes that's good."

The music lesson had become a bright spot for everyone involved. The children, of course, loved it. Of the four, Belle was the most talented, but all of them looked forward to the time with Mark in the parlor each week.

As for Mark himself, he had grown very fond of the youngsters. Giving them music lessons had become a matter of pride, and he worked hard to help them improve their skills. He had never done anything along these lines before, and he was surprised at how much he enjoyed it.

Finally, after Mark had worked with each one of them, he looked at the clock on the mantel and said, "Okay, that's enough for today. You work on that piece for our next lesson."

As the youngsters ran out, they made miniature thunder over the pine flooring. As soon as they were gone, Mark gathered up the music sheets and put them in a folder. He glanced at Mary Aidan, who had not moved.

"They're doing very well," she said.

"Yes, they are. When I was their age, my parents practically had to tie me to a piano stool to make me practice. I hated it."

"I don't guess it hurt you."

"No. It didn't hurt me." A sheet fell out of his folder, and she came over and retrieved it.

"You dropped this." She held it for a moment and said, "Is it another piece for the children?"

"No," Mark said. He took the sheet and stared at it. There were no words on it, just notes. "It's just something I've been working on."

"I'd like to hear it."

He did not take the sheet but turned and began to play. It was a soft song with a beautiful melody. Mary Aidan was captivated by the intriguing melody and harmony. "That's beautiful! Who wrote it?"

"I did."

"You wrote that?" Mary Aidan was accustomed to his excellent playing, but the idea that he could write a song like this caused her to stare at him with amazement. "Why, who did you write it for?"

"My wife."

Mary Aidan suddenly blinked with shock. "Your wife! You . . . you have a wife?"

"Not yet." He laughed and said, "I suppose I'll get one someday." He turned around and started to play the piano again, and as he did, he murmured a few words. "I haven't got the words yet, but it'll be about a special woman. She'll be sweet and gentle and tender and lovely. She'll never fail her man, and she will know how to encourage him when he's down."

"You're not likely to find a woman who does all that," Mary Aidan said.

Mark turned and grinned at her. "I don't expect to. We never find exactly what we want in people."

Mary Aidan stared at Mark, wondering what his words meant. "I guess we don't," she said.

"My family never found it in me."

"What's your family like?"

"They're good people. Not like me. I'm the one who's always been out of step. It seems I never could be what they wanted me to be, especially my father. That's why I left and came out here."

Mark studied Mary Aidan. He had always found her attractive, and now the sweet fragrance she wore stirred him powerfully. It slid through the armor of his self-sufficiency. She had a long, composed mouth and a temper that could charm a man or chill him to the bone, as he well knew. She was breathing quickly, and a blushing ran freshly across her cheeks. For some reason she was moved as well. In order to change the direction of his thoughts, he asked, "When are you getting married to Singleton?"

"Why, I'm not engaged to him!" Mary Aidan said abruptly.

"What are you waiting for? He's got everything you want in a man."

"You don't know that."

"Well, you've made it pretty plain what you want. You want a two-gun man who can whip anybody in the county."

"That's not all I want in a man." She was confused by his blunt questions. Yet she had not forgotten when he had kissed her how it had stirred her more than she had cared to admit. She quickly changed the subject to avert more of his questions. "What are you going to do with your life?"

"I'm going to prove to my family that I can stick with something even if it's only digging post holes on a cattle ranch way out here in Texas."

"Do you write to them often?"

"Don't have anything to write. Not yet."

"You ought to write to them. They'll be worried about you by now."

Mark got to his feet and gathered his folder of music and put it under his arm. "They've been worried about me for a long time. A little longer won't matter."

"I think you should write, Mark, and let them know where you are. That you're not sick or in trouble."

Mark Benton was surprised at her concern. He had seen the harsh side of Mary Aidan, and now he was surprised by the genuine interest that she seemed to have in him. He looked at her for a moment and then nodded. "I think you're right. I'll write tonight. Thanks for the advice."

Mary Aidan smiled. "Tell them I said we're all proud of the way you stick at post hole digging."

Mark laughed. "I'll tell them that. They'll be proud of your good report."

CHAPTER
TWENTY-EIGHT

L ucy Abbot drew the brush through her hair listlessly, then paused and looked at her image in the mirror. She had been sitting at her dressing table now for over twenty minutes brushing her hair, and her thoughts had brought a frown to her face. Yellow bars of sunlight streamed through the window, and already the heat of summer was beginning to envelope the house.

"I wish I could live in Chicago or New York, somewhere without these blistering Texas summers."

The sound of her own voice startled her, and she put the brush down, rose, and walked over to the window. Staring outside, she felt a sense of depression settle on her as she watched a familiar scene she had watched every morning of her life. Old Mrs. Hampton from across the way was up puttering in her flower garden, as usual. Next door to her, Josh Wilhite, a veteran of the Mexican War, hobbled along on his crutches. He had left a leg in Mexico. That part of his life had been so much more vibrant than anything else that he bored everyone who would listen with the story of the battle.

The sound of footsteps and then a light tapping on the door drew Lucy around. "Come in," she said. When her mother came in, she nodded and said, "It's already getting hot."

"It's only June," Mabel Abbot said. She was wearing a lightweight cotton dress and took a handkerchief out of the pocket and mopped her brow. "I declare, I don't know what it'll be like when July and August get here!"

"It'll be unbearable as it always is!" Lucy said.

"Oh, it's not that bad."

Lucy shrugged and said, "I wish I could go shopping in New Orleans."

"We could go together downtown."

"Downtown! There's nothing decent to buy around here! There *is* no downtown to this forsaken place!" she said bitterly.

Jordan City was, indeed, a small frontier settlement. It had been raided by Comanches, and part of it had been burned by the armies of Santa Anna on their last sweep to drive the Texans out.

"I think I know every item at the general store down to the last butter churn. They don't need to take an inventory," Lucy said sarcastically. "They can just ask me."

Mrs. Abbot gave her daughter an odd look. "You're in a bad humor this morning."

"I guess I am," she snapped.

"What's the matter? You've been unhappy for some time now."

"Oh, it's nothing, Mother. I just don't like this hot weather."

Lucy Abbot could not tell her mother the true source of her discontent. She was tired of Jordan City and longed to move away to a city that suited her tastes more. She had known only one man who would have taken her away, and he had never proposed to her. For a moment she was tempted to tell her mother the truth. She could not stand her home or Jordan City or Texas, for that matter. But she quickly rejected this idea, knowing neither her mother nor her father would ever understand. They themselves were perfectly happy to live out their lives in the middle of the flat plains of Texas. Lucy longed for something more.

Her mother patted her on the shoulder and said, "When you're finished here, come downstairs and I'll get you something to drink." Turning, her mother went to the door and left Lucy to her thoughts.

For a time she moved around the room restlessly, and then finally a resolution formed within her. She spoke it aloud as if giving voice to the words would make it come true.

"I'll marry Clinton, and I'll convince him to take me to St. Louis or Chicago. He's never really been anywhere. I can do it. He just needs to broaden his horizons." The thought pleased her. A smile tugged the corners of her lips upward. She began to hum a tune, went back to the mirror, and leaned forward, examining her features.

"Clinton, I want to ask a favor of you."

Clinton had been brushing his horse down in the stable and had looked up with surprise when Rose Jean had appeared. As always, her appearance pleased him. She was wearing a light green dress that stressed her well-formed figure. She came to stand beside him, reached out, and brushed her hand across the horse's back.

"Why sure enough, Rose Jean. Anything you'd like."

"That's a pretty broad door you've left open there. You'd better be careful. Some woman might take advantage of you."

"Why, you wouldn't do a thing like that!" Clinton said. He had learned to trust this young woman implicitly. Her Christian character was stronger than his own, which had taken some force of will for him to admit. For years he had seen himself as the spiritual head of the Hardin family, but Rose Jean Campell had not only a broad grasp of biblical doctrine but also a determination to serve God, which pleased him greatly. "What can I do for you?"

"I've been trying to think of some way that I could help the Indian people, Clinton. What I'd like to do is start a school for some of the children."

"For Comanches? I doubt they'd take to it. The only thing they'd study about is killin' white folks."

"Well, not just for Comanches. There are other tribes around here. Some of them aren't as vicious as the Comanches, I hear."

Clinton nodded and said instantly, "Why, I'd be glad to help you do it. First thing you'll have to have will be a schoolhouse, and I know how you can get one."

"I thought I'd try to find an empty building and use it."

"No," Clinton said. "You need your own building, and I know where we can get the material to build one. I know a fellow that tore down an old house to build a new one, and I figure that we can get him to donate some lumber."

"I don't have much money," Rose Jean said quickly.

"Well, you just go over and smile at him, and he might give you the whole thing for free. I'll go with you to encourage him. His name's Ike Scranton. While we're there you might do some preachin' at him. He's kind of a scamp. A little bit of religion would go a long way for him."

Rose Jean reached out and put her hand on Clinton's arm. "It's so sweet of you to help me."

Clinton grinned and winked at her. "Us hyper-Calvinists have to stick together. The way I figure it is God's got this thing worked out already. Why, we'll have that building throwed up, and you'll be teachin' them Indian young'uns to name all the kings of Judah and Israel before a spotted dog can wink his eye!"

The sun had gone down now, and Rose Jean admired the sunset as she sat beside Clinton in the buggy. "That's a beautiful sunset."

"Shore is."

The two were tired, for they had spent the whole day at the site of the new school. Clinton had begged some time off from Clay to help with the project. For the past three weeks he and Rose Jean had thrown themselves into building the new school. They had encountered difficulty from some Texans who hated Indians of any sort. To Rose Jean's surprise a number of families had thrown in donations and their time to help her. Rose Jean had even charmed the crew of the ranch into lending a hand with the building.

"I'm so tired I could scrape it off with a stick," Clinton said. "I reckon we'll be all set to start the school next week."

"I'm so excited, Clinton!" Rose Jean exclaimed and began to speak of all the plans she had for teaching the Indian children.

Clinton was pleased at the expression on her face. He listened until they pulled up in front of the house, then drawing the horses to a halt, he said, "I'm right excited about this school myself. Never have seen an Indian baptized. Maybe you'll let me come and preach at 'em someday."

"Of course you can, Clinton, and I want to tell you again how much I appreciate all the work you've done. I know the Lord's going to bless you for it."

"Well, I've really enjoyed it. It shore beats brandin' cattle. You know, you're not like any woman I ever saw."

Startled, Rose Jean turned to face him. She was struck at his rugged, masculine features, and for one instant thought, *Clinton doesn't know how good-looking he is,* but she only said, "Why, I'm just like other women, I guess."

"No, you ain't. You know more Bible than anybody—except maybe me." He grinned and winked at her. "When I get your doctrine on the Second Coming all straightened out, you'll be sharp as a graduate straight out of the seminary."

Rose Jean laughed. "I doubt that." Changing the subject, she said, "You haven't had much time for courting. You're spending all your time on the school."

Suddenly, Clinton grew restless. The truth was that Lucy had been pressuring him lately to set a date for their wedding, when he himself was not even sure that he was ready for marriage. "Well, servin' the Lord has to come first."

"Does Lucy see it that way?" she said, teasing him a little.

"We haven't exactly talked about it."

"You know, Clinton, I thought a time or two that Maggie has a heart for you."

"Maggie?" Clinton was startled. "What makes you think that?"

"Oh, just the way she looks at you."

"Why, there ain't nothin' to that."

Clinton seemed embarrassed, and this amused Rose Jean. "Women just seem to take to you, Clinton. I think there's just something about you that naturally draws them."

Clinton felt awkward at her words and pulled off his hat and looked at it as if he had never seen it before. "Sometimes I get confused about women."

"That's the first time I ever heard you admit you were confused about anything."

"Well, women puzzle me."

"You're not confused about me, are you?"

"Oh no, not you, Rose!" He reached out and took her hand. "If I ever get a wife, I want her to be like you. Why, you're just the kind of woman I'd like to have."

Rose Jean wanted to laugh, but she could not resist teasing Clinton.

"Why, I never expected a proposal, Clinton!"

Clinton's jaw dropped, and he was startled. He closed his mouth and swallowed hard. "Why, I . . . I didn't mean—" he stammered.

"I'll have to know you a little better first, but you're going to make a fine husband. By the way, I don't expect a big wedding." She reached out, pulled his head down, and kissed him on the cheek. "Yes, I think you'd make about the best husband of any man I ever met. Good night, Clinton."

Stunned beyond belief, Clinton sat there and watched Rose Jean as she walked into the house. "Well, if . . . if that don't beat hens a pacin'!" he stammered. He picked up his hat, jammed it down over his ears, and then shook his head. "How'd I get in a mess like this? Dangerous enough to have one woman aimin' for a marriage, but now I got *three* of 'em. It looks to me like I done squatted down on my own spurs." He was a resolute young man, but the idea of three young women expecting him to marry them was something he had never faced before. "Well, every feller's got to clean his own catfish," he muttered. He looked up and said, "Lord, I got myself into this mess. Now it's up to You to get me out!"

"What's the matter with you, Brodie?" Jerusalem asked. "You act like you lost your best friend."

"Oh, Ma, nothin's wrong. I just—" Brodie broke off, for in all truth, he didn't know what was wrong. He had been unhappy for some time and couldn't put his finger on the reason.

Lately he had taken to moping around the house when he wasn't working with the cattle. Jerusalem had come on him sitting out on the front porch staring off into the distance. Taking her seat beside him, Jerusalem looked over at this tall son of hers and felt a sudden warmth that she always had for him.

"You need to get yourself a young woman and go party in town."

"I don't know no young women."

"Why, that's not so. You know Maggie. Why don't you take her to that dance they're having the day after tomorrow?"

"Why, she'd rather go with somebody else," he said, shrugging his shoulders.

"No, she wouldn't." Jerusalem reached over and grabbed Brodie's hand and held it between both of hers. "You're the best-looking thing on the place. Now, go find you a gal or go hunting or fishing. Do something to get out of this slump you're in."

A thought came to Brodie, and he said, "You know, that might not be a bad idea. I've been givin' Maggie lessons, and it might be time for her to sort of bust out a little."

"Lessons? What kind of lessons?" Jerusalem asked.

"Lessons on how to be a lady."

Jerusalem stared at Brodie with surprise. "How did all that come about?"

"Oh, she's pretty rough, Ma. I felt sorry for her from the first time I saw her with those ornery mules. I sort of had the idea back then that maybe I could show her a thing or two about being a proper lady. So lately, I started to teach her how to walk and stuff like that."

"What do you mean 'how to walk'? She could walk when she got here!"

"Why, she walks like a lumberjack."

Jerusalem laughed. "I can just imagine what your lessons must be like."

"Don't laugh at me, Ma. It's serious!" Brodie protested. "When I offered, she asked me to do it. She hasn't had much of a chance to learn what being a lady is all about, you know. Her pa raised her to be a mule skinner. She's had a pretty hard life. Her language is terrible, but it's gettin' better," he added defensively.

"You've been giving her talking lessons too?"

"Well, a little bit."

Jerusalem squeezed Brodie's hand. It was a big hand, strong and corded. It reminded her of her first husband, Jake. Brodie was much taller than Jake had been, but he had the same lean strength. "Oh, I don't know if you're doin' the right thing, tryin' to make her somethin' she's not, but it is real sweet of you. I think it would be good if you'd take her to the dance."

"All right, Ma. I'll do that."

"I'm sure I can help her with her clothes and with her hair."

"Oh, Ma, that'd be real good! I think she likes some fellow, but I don't know exactly who it is." Brodie tried not to appear sheepish. He had, after all, promised not to tell anyone about Maggie's secret engagement to Clinton.

"Well, with you for her teacher, she'll be able to catch his attention for sure," Jerusalem said.

CHAPTER
TWENTY-NINE

Loves The Night looked at the four puppies that were playing close to the campfire and hesitated for a moment. She evaluated the frolicking pups, then reached down and picked up the fattest one. He barked with surprise and whined, but before he had time to do more than that, she killed him with a swift blow to the back of his head.

For an instant she stood there holding the limp body of the puppy, and memories came back of the time when Moriah, her sister in all but blood, had been a captive in Bear Killer's camp. Loves The Night had a keen memory, and the face of the white woman came before her so sharply that it was almost as if Moriah had appeared. While Moriah was at the camp, they had become very close. Moriah taught her about her Jesus God, and Loves The Night taught her the Comanche language. From the time she watched Moriah ride off the day she was rescued, Loves The Night often thought of her white sister.

Quickly, Loves The Night began preparing the puppy for the stew pot. She could not help but remember the many times that Moriah had protested killing puppies for food. Her protest had caught Loves The

Night by surprise, for puppies were a staple food for The People. She smiled, suddenly remembering the first time that Moriah was shocked, and she had said, "Why, puppies were made to be eaten."

The statement had disgusted Moriah, who, for all her misery of being a captive in a Comanche camp, could never acclimate herself to the habit. She had a gentle heart and had been called the Quiet One when she was brought to the camp after a raid. Loves The Night murmured the words aloud as she continued to fix the stew and remember those times. Although she was the favorite wife of Bear Killer, she herself had borne him no children. When Moriah had given birth to Ethan, Loves The Night had become a second mother for him. Even now a poignant feeling rose in her as she thought of the boy and the woman that had been such a friend to her. Moriah and Ethan had been the gentle side of life that she had not known existed, and not a day passed that she didn't think of the two.

"Where is your husband?"

Loves The Night turned quickly to find Gray Deer standing and watching her with disdain. He was a tall, hatchet-faced man with cruel eyes and a merciless heart. He had despised her now for a long time, for in his mind, Loves The Night had been part of the scheme to allow Moriah and Ethan to escape from the camp. He never spoke his view in the presence of Bear Killer, who had a great affection for the woman, but when they were alone, he let his anger be seen.

"He's not here," said Loves The Night.

"I can see that, woman! Where is he?"

Reluctantly, Loves The Night motioned with her head. "He went to the river."

"Why did he go there?"

"Why don't you ask him, Gray Deer?" Loves The Night said defiantly. She turned and faced him fearlessly. In her mind Gray Deer was the most dangerous enemy that Bear Killer had. He was a bloodthirsty individual who always urged the war chief of the Comanches to lead them on raids so captives could be taken and scalped. Loves The Night had gently tried to warn Bear Killer that Gray Deer's desire for revenge could get them killed, but her husband would not listen.

"He is a good fighter," Bear Killer had replied once when she talked to him. "There are not many left among The People like that."

"Why don't you leave him alone, Gray Deer?" Loves The Night said.

Caught by the woman's bold words, Gray Deer whirled and stared at her, his obsidian eyes hard and flickering with anger. "Women do not tell Comanche warriors what to do!" He half-turned to go, but then the anger that always lay just beneath the surface of the man seemed to erupt. He took two steps before he turned back around, as if he would attack her. Staring at her, he said, "Bear Killer must have his honor back."

"He has not lost it."

Ignoring her words Gray Deer's voice rose. "He will not have his honor back until he kills Silver Hair and the Tall One. These and the White Ghost shamed him. They are all together in one place. We could kill them at the same time."

Although she knew it was useless, Loves The Night began to try to reason with Gray Deer. "I have heard the talk about the place where they are. It's in the middle of the white man's country. They are strong fighters, all of them, and many more surround them."

"We would kill them as if they were children!" Gray Deer began to spit out his words as if they were weapons. "They stole his son! He would be the next chief of The People. We should go kill all of the white eyes there and take the boy back. The woman, she should be killed too. She was never a Comanche woman."

"Gray Deer, have you looked around at our tribe?"

"What do you mean?"

"Have you noticed how few we are? And where have they gone? It is not sickness but your raids that have killed our young men. We need peace if we are to grow strong again."

"Peace?" Gray Deer spit out. "The Jesus God has made you weak! You are no longer a woman of The People." He whirled and made for the river without looking back. His back was stiff, and anger marked every step he took as he went to find Bear Killer.

Loves The Night watched him go with a heavy heart. Though she knew to challenge a Comanche warrior could bring serious consequences, she did not fear Gray Deer. She felt a strength inside, and she whispered aloud, "Yes, I serve the Jesus God, but He has not made me weak." She thought of how she had prayed to Jesus ever since Moriah had taught her to do so. The old gods had meant nothing but fear to her, but now that she was a believer in Jesus, she had learned that He was more powerful than any of the gods of The People. At night she would pray, and His presence would come into the teepee and fill her with a peace and a joy that softened the hard circumstances of her life. Day by day, as she went about her work, she would lift up her heart, and always the Jesus God would come in.

Gray Deer found Bear Killer standing beside the stream and looking out over the water. It was the same stream where the Tall One and Silver Hair had ridden off with Moriah and Bear Killer's son. He wondered if his chief was thinking the same thoughts. For a moment Gray Deer hesitated, for one never knew how the war chief of the Comanches would react if disturbed. Still, he himself was a war chief, and though they were not equals, Gray Deer felt it his duty to speak of his concerns to Bear Killer.

"My brother," he said, "may I speak with you?"

Bear Killer did not turn. He had heard the footsteps and identified them. "Speak," he said, his voice low and without intonation. He kept his eyes fixed on the stream, where farther down a buck and two does were crossing. He marked the spot but said no more.

"I know my place, I hope," Gray Deer said respectfully, "but when a man sees his brother headed down a wrong path, he must speak."

"And the wrong path for me is what?"

Bear Killer's blunt words gave Gray Deer pause. He hesitated and considered his next words carefully, but he could not turn back now.

"You are the greatest war chief of The People. You have proven yourself over and over again in many battles. You have taken many scalps in victory, but a dark cloud has covered you. It must be blown away with another victory that shows what a great warrior you are. You must become the great war chief that you were in your youth." Hurriedly, he said, "You must lead a raid to kill the two men who stole your son—Silver Hair and the Tall One. Until you have killed them and the White Ghost, your honor is gone."

Gray Deer took a deep breath and waited nervously, ready to flee. No one that he knew of had ever spoken such daring words to Bear Killer. It would be in Bear Killer's right to strike him dead for questioning his honor.

When Bear Killer did not answer, Gray Deer continued, "The three men are on a ranch. I have scouted out the spot already." His blood ran hot with revenge as he spoke. He hated all three, for they had shamed The People with their deeds. As if to head off the anger of Bear Killer, he quickly added, "You can even get the woman back if you want her—the mother of your son."

Still Bear Killer did not speak. The silence flowed over the two men so that only the sibilant murmur of the stream could be heard. Finally, Bear Killer said, "I've had a dream."

Instantly, Gray Deer grew still. Dreams were an important part of the life of The People. Comanche men could not be true warriors unless they had had dreams and visions. Sometimes it was necessary for a man to fast for many days until he was so weak he could hardly move in order to obtain a dream. At other times they would hang at a pole, held suspended by rawhide thongs tied through holes in their chests until a dream would come. No Comanche warrior would ignore a dream.

"May I know the dream?" Gray Deer asked respectfully.

"The white buffalo appeared in my dream. It was three nights ago."

"The white buffalo. That was a dream, indeed, my brother!"

Bear Killer turned and said, "He told me how to regain my honor."

"That is good!" Gray Deer exclaimed. "I knew that you would find your way. When do we go on a raid to get your honor back and kill the white eyes?"

Bear Killer did not answer for a long time, and when he did, his eyes were cold. "You go too fast, Gray Deer. A man does not lay a dream of the white buffalo out for anyone. Go from me now," he said and turned his back.

Gray Deer stared at him. He dared not remain, so he turned and headed back toward the camp without another word.

Loves The Night looked up and saw Gray Deer return to the camp. She knew immediately that something had happened between him and Bear

Killer. He was not a man who was particularly good at hiding his feelings. His face was stiff with anger as he walked by her. She held her tongue and did not speak but stood there stirring the stew she was preparing. As it bubbled, its pleasant aroma filled the air. Finally, Bear Killer appeared also. To her he was the most handsome chief of all The People, and she loved him dearly. He had had another wife who had died, but Loves The Night had always known she was his favorite. As he came up to the teepee, she said, "Here. Sit, my husband. You must eat."

Bear Killer looked at her with his black eyes, nodded, then sat down. He waited until she had filled a bowl with the stew and ate slowly. When he finished, he turned to her and said, "I have had a dream. I dreamed of the white buffalo."

Loves The Night drew in her breath, for among The People this was the most powerful dream of all! The white buffalo was woven deep into the legends and myths and religion of the Comanches. Such an animal was as close to a god as they had, at least a visible one. Any dream concerning a white buffalo was extremely important indeed!

Bear Killer watched Loves The Night, waiting for her to ask. When she did not question him, he said, "I will be leaving soon."

Loves The Night stood perfectly still. The first thing that came into her mind was that Gray Deer had won the battle and had persuaded Bear Killer to lead a devastating and bloody raid on the white people to recover his son and perhaps even Moriah.

Loves The Night moved over and sat down at Bear Killer's feet. She put her hand on his knee, and her voice was as soft as the summer breeze itself as she said, "You will find no peace, my husband, in killing these men."

Bear Killer did not move but studied her carefully. "Why do you say that? You know the way of The People."

"Moriah never became a Comanche woman. This you well know. As for Ethan, you taught him the ways of the Comanche, but at the same time Moriah was teaching him the way of the white men and the way of the Jesus God."

Bear Killer listened until she had finished, then he said, "You loved Moriah and the boy."

"Yes. I still do."

"You have not been the same since you began to follow the Jesus God."

"I have not loved you less because of my love for the Jesus God."

Somehow Bear Killer knew her words were true. She had always been his favorite, and he had feared that her heart would turn away from him when she had decided to follow the white man's God. But it had not been so. He had watched her carefully. She had not become a worse wife but a better one. Always a gentle woman, she showed her love for him in many new ways. As a violent war chief of the Comanches, Bear Killer knew little of gentleness, but the gentleness of Loves The Night was something that he had needed.

Loves The Night looked up into his face. "Let us adopt a son. There are several baby boys in our camp. Any of our people would be glad to have you adopt him. He will be our son, yours and mine. He will take the place of Ethan."

For one moment Loves The Night thought that she had changed his mind. She saw the struggle in Bear Killer's face, and her heart leaped up in hope. She had been praying that his yearning for a son could be answered without the bloodshed that was sure to happen if he tried to take back Ethan. But then a dark cloud seemed to pass over the face of the war chief of the Comanches.

Bear Killer sat there staring into the fire, struggling with the old ways of the Comanche that flowed through his veins. He heard his wife's words of wisdom, but he found himself too weak to go against the ways of The People.

"I cannot forget the old ways," he said sadly. He rose to his feet and looked at her with an expression she would never forget. "I must go and regain my honor."

CHAPTER
THIRTY

The celebration for the completion of Rose Jean Campbell's school for Indian youngsters had finally arrived. She had decided to invite everyone who was interested to a fine meal she had planned. Clay and Jerusalem had provided a yearling, and Maggie had agreed to barbecue it and to cook a number of her special dishes for the guests.

Brodie had also thrown himself into helping build the school, which surprised Maggie considerably. After his return from rescuing the cattle from Mateo Lebonne's place, he had become downcast and had kept to himself a great deal. Maggie had asked Jerusalem about this, and Jerusalem had spoken quite bluntly.

"He's still mooning over that Serena Lebonne," Jerusalem had said. "He fancied himself in love with her for a long time. Even when she left, I know he still hoped that something would work out."

"What's she like?" Maggie asked curiously.

"She was a beautiful young Spanish girl, but she had a streak of wildness in her. I tried to warn Brodie about it, but you know young people don't take kindly to advice when it comes to the affections of their hearts."

"I'm surprised he didn't bring her back with him," Maggie said.

"I think he had that on his mind," Jerusalem said, "but she wasn't the same person. He found her working in a cantina. That life hardened her. He's lost the young girl he thought he had fallen in live with. Some dreams are good and some aren't. This one was a bad one for Brodie. He's taking it pretty hard."

"I wish I could help him."

"So do I," Jerusalem said, "but time's a great healer. He'll just have to fight his way out of it."

Jerusalem's words had remained with Maggie, and she had gone out of her way to ask Brodie to help her get the food ready for the celebration. He had agreed, but Maggie could tell he lacked the same enthusiasm she had for the occasion, even though he had spent hours working on the building. She kept talking to him about what a good thing Rose Jean was doing, and gradually his interest seemed to improve.

"You know, Maggie, this here school-raisin' business may be a good time for you."

Maggie stared at him. The two were standing in front of a huge spit, watching the carcass of a yearling that was roasting over an enormous hole filled with burning hot coals. The smell of cooking meat was strong and enticing. From time to time she had tested the meat with a sharp knife.

"How could it be good for me? It's good for Rose Jean."

"Well, what I mean is this is gonna be a big party, isn't it? Well, it's a good time for you to try some more of your wiles on Clinton."

"I'm just the cook. 'Sides, he done proposed. The work's done, ain't it?"

"Well, you don't have to be just a cook," Brodie said as he put his hand on her shoulder. He smiled down at her and winked. "You've been practicin' up on how to get a man. But you also have to work on keepin' him."

"Oh, that was just foolishness, Brodie! I never should have tried to let you teach me to be a lady."

"No, it wasn't either."

"Yes, it was. I'm just what I am. A person can't make herself over just to catch a man."

"Well, it worked, didn't it?"

"That's what you wanted."

"No. It's what *you* wanted. Don't you remember? You told me how you liked Clinton, and now he's gonna marry you. All you have to do is spring the trap."

Maggie turned and looked up at Brodie. "You're one of the tallest men I know. It sure is nice to look up at a man instead of down on him."

"Well, you can't measure a man by how tall he is. You know that, I hope. One of the meanest fellers I ever knew was three inches taller than I am, but he was mean as a snake. Why, he would fight at the drop of the hat, and he'd drop the hat his own self just to start one. His name was Doff Peterson."

"I don't want to hear about him."

"Why, he'd steal flowers off his grandma's grave. You can't go fall in love with men just because they're tall."

"I didn't say I was fallin' in love with you."

"Why, I didn't mean *me*! It's Clinton we're talkin' about. I think you're gettin' shaky because you're a mite taller than he is. But that don't matter."

"It's not that. I just think he cares for somebody else."

Brodie stared at her. "Who would he be carin' for? He's engaged to you, ain't he?"

"Why, it could be that lady preacher Rose Jean, or it could be Lucy Abbot. I heard hints that he had proposed to her too."

"Oh, that's just gossip. Look, we'll get you all prettified up for him again. Put on some of that perfume we bought for you. Lean on him a little bit and smile at him. Just sweet-talk him."

"I don't know how to do none of that, and I don't want to either!"

"Well, you've got to. I've got too much invested in you." He put his arm around her shoulders and hugged her close. "After all, a fella's got to look out for his sister, don't he?"

Maggie suddenly flared up. "I am not your sister, Brodie Hardin!"

"Well, I know you ain't actually my sister, but kinda you are."

"No, I'm not kinda your sister!" She turned and walked away from him, leaving Brodie to stare after her.

"Well, ain't that a pretty come off!" he muttered. "What in cat hair's wrong with her? I'll go talk to Ma."

★　★　★

The celebration meal for the opening of the school had been a great success. Several good fiddle players and guitar pickers flavored the air with the sound of music as people gathered at the schoolhouse. Brodie searched for Maggie but didn't find her, so he had taken care of cutting up the barbecued meat. Finally, he asked his mother, "Where's Maggie? She's supposed to be here."

"Moriah's helping her with her clothes." Jerusalem hesitated, then said, "I think you're a fool, son."

Brodie looked at his mother with shocked astonishment. "Why, Ma, why would you say a thing like that?"

"Because of this fool experiment of yours, trying to make Maggie into a lady."

"It's what she said she wanted."

"She didn't know what she was saying. There's nothing wrong with Maggie the way she is. You ought to be able to see that, Brodie. Except for Clay, you're the dumbest man about women I ever saw."

"I expect you're right about that," Brodie said ruefully. "I proved that with Serena."

"You got to stop whipping yourself over that woman. She was never the one for you," Jerusalem said firmly.

"Well, I thought she was. I was pretty wrong, wasn't I, Ma?"

"A man's got a right to be wrong when he's young like you, but now this thing you're doing with Maggie . . . it'd be bad."

Brodie looked down at his feet. "I was just tryin' to be helpful."

"I know you were, son," Jerusalem said. She loved this tall son of hers fiercely, and her heart had ached for him. She knew that losing his dream of marrying Serena had cut deep. "You're hurting right now, but just stop trying to make something out of Maggie that she's not."

"All right, Ma, if you say so."

Jerusalem went to help with serving the food, but her eyes went often to Brodie's tall figure as she worked. "Lord, open his eyes," she said. "He's blind as a bat!"

Clinton stood on the outskirts of the platform that had been built where people were dancing. Lanterns had been hung all over the trees that surrounded the schoolhouse, and the sound of lively music and singing and laughter filled the air. Clinton leaned back against one of the pecan trees that they had left in order to shade the school and wished he was a thousand miles away, maybe two thousand!

"How in the world could I get myself engaged to three women at the same time? I reckon if brains was dynamite, I couldn't even blow my nose." He pulled his hat down over his eyes and watched the dancers as they moved under the yellow lights of the lanterns. He had been miserable for the last week, for he knew that sooner or later the whole thing was going to unravel. He was jarred suddenly when a voice broke into his thoughts.

"What's wrong with you? Come on. Maggie's here."

Clinton shoved his hat back and straightened up. "I don't see her, Brodie."

"Well, there she is! Have you gone blind?"

Clinton looked across the dancers and shook his head. "I don't see nobody but that woman in the red dress."

"Why, that's her!"

Clinton squinted and gasped. "That's *Maggie!*"

"Sure is. Ma bought her a new dress, and Moriah's been showin' her how to primp up. You better get over there because she's gonna be hard to get a dance with as soon as the fellas spot her."

"I can't do it, Brodie."

Brodie turned to Clinton. "Why can't you do it?" he demanded. "Ain't she good enough for you?"

Clinton looked up at Brodie with shock. "Good enough for me? Why, of course she is. Maggie's good enough for anybody."

"Well, I'm glad you got a little sense left in that brain of yours. For a while I thought you was as dumb as a mule."

"But I can't dance with her. I can't even talk to her—and I can't tell you why, Brodie."

Brodie stared at Clinton for a long moment. "What's goin' on in your head? You ain't been yourself lately."

"I can't tell you, but I just can't dance with her."

Brodie shook his head. "Well, *I* will! Go on off and drown yourself in the river. If you want somebody to shove you in, call on me."

Brodie turned and made his way through the crowd. When he reached Maggie, he smiled broadly. "Well, look at you! I claim the first five dances before these other hooligans get started."

"Do you, Brodie?" Maggie's face seemed to lighten up. She had been apprehensive about all of the fuss Brodie had made over her. It was only Jerusalem's urging that had finally convinced her to come to the dance. "I wish I was somewheres else."

"Well, I don't. I'm glad you're right here. I always dance with the prettiest girl at the dance, and you're her, so come on. Let's get at it."

Maggie smiled up at Brodie. "If you say so, Brodie," she said. When he put his arm around her and she took his hand, she whispered, "I'm glad you're here. I was real scared. I feel silly dressed like this."

Brodie suddenly tightened his grip. "Listen to me, Maggie Brennan. I don't want you ever to put yourself down again. You don't have to be scared of nothin'. You're a fine lady, and you're just as fine wearing forked pants and an old shirt as you are wearin' that pretty dress. It's what you are on the inside that makes you a fine lady. Now, you just keep that in mind."

Maggie smiled up at him brilliantly. "All right, Brodie, if you say so."

For some reason Mary Aidan had not enjoyed the dance. She had a new dress made especially for the occasion. It was a light green cotton with white lace around the neck and elbow-length sleeves. The bodice hugged her form tightly to the waist, where the full skirt fell to just above her ankles. Delicate embroidered flowers in pale yellow, green, blue, and pink adorned the front of the bodice and around the hem of the skirt. She was pleased with the dress, but something was bothering her.

Barton Singleton lay at the cause of her discomfort. He had claimed her for the first dance and demanded that she dance with him alone for the whole night.

"Why, I can't do that, Barton. That's not the way to behave at a dance."

"You're my girl," Singleton said adamantly, "and I'll stomp a mud hole in any man that tries to steal my girl."

"You think you own a woman, Barton?"

"Why, I don't think I would like that," he had said with surprise, "but when a man's got a woman, he don't want other fellas cutting in on him."

His domineering ways did something to Mary Aidan Hardin. If she had had any doubts at all about Barton Singleton as a husband, they were blasted by his pompous attitude. *I wouldn't marry him if he were the last man on earth!* she thought. She decided not to make a scene but simply to endure the dance.

The dance went on for some time, but she enjoyed none of it. She was keenly aware of Clinton's absence, and she asked Brodie once about it.

"I don't know where he is," Brodie said shortly. "I told him to go drown himself in the river."

"Why'd you tell him that?"

"Because he's an idiot. I went to all the trouble to help Maggie catch his interest. He was the man she wanted, and then he acts like she's nothin'. It's a good thing he left. I was ready to punch his head."

"Something's wrong with Clinton, Brodie," Mary Aidan said. "I've never seen him this way before. It's not the time to punch his head. Oh, there were times I wanted to when he wouldn't stop preaching at everyone, but something's wrong. We have to find out and help him."

Brodie stared at her, then said, "He just made me mad after all the trouble I went through to get Maggie here."

"Well, Maggie looks beautiful. The young fellas seem to like her well enough."

Brodie looked over and said, "Look at that. Devoe Crutchfield is holdin' her too tight. I'd better go straighten him out."

"Well, don't get into a fight with him. He'd knock you out with one punch if you got him angry."

Devoe Crutchfield was a powerful, young blacksmith, but Brodie seemed oblivious to that fact. "He's holdin' her too tight. I'm gonna stop him."

Mary Aidan laughed. "You're mighty possessive. She's not your girl, is she?"

Brodie gave her an odd look. "That don't matter. I've got to let Devoe know how to treat a lady properly."

Mary Aidan watched him go and waited to see what would happen.

She saw Devoe's face flush with surprise as Brodie gave him a stern lecture about the proper way to hold a lady and dance. Devoe was a good young man, however, and turned Maggie over to Brodie without making a scene.

"I think this is our dance, isn't it?"

Mary Aidan turned to see Mark standing there smiling at her. He was wearing a dark suit she had not seen before, and there was a touch of elegance about him that was lacking in the other men.

"You look beautiful," he said.

"So do you," Mary Aidan smiled. "If you drop dead, we won't have to do anything to you."

Mark laughed, his white teeth flashing against his tan. "How about that dance?"

"You ain't dancin' with Mary Aidan. She's my girl," a voice said behind them.

Both Mark and Mary Aidan turned quickly to stare at Barton Singleton, who had suddenly appeared. "Get out of here, Benton, before I put the run on you!"

"Wait a minute," Mary Aidan said, her face flaming. "You're not my keeper, Barton! I'll dance with anyone I please."

"No, you won't. You ain't dancin' with him! I told you the way it's gonna be, Mary Aidan."

"Well, I'm telling you that you're not my husband, and you never will be, so who I dance with is my choice!"

Singleton's temper was a fearsome thing, and he blurted out before he thought, "Well, you ain't no better than a saloon girl and a tease!"

His words carried, and the music instantly fell silent, and everyone stared at Singleton. Clay Taliferro and Brodie Hardin were suddenly there, and their eyes were cold with anger.

"What was that you called my sister?" Brodie said.

"Yes, I think you called my daughter a name," Clay murmured. "I hope I heard you wrong, Singleton."

Instantly, Barton Singleton knew he was in trouble. Clay's reputation as a fighting man was second to none in this part of Texas. He had won a knife fight against Jim Bowie in his younger years, had served in the army of Sam Houston with distinction, and as a mountainman had fought and won battles with some of the toughest men in the West.

"We ain't got no quarrel, Clay," Singleton said, his eyes darting back and forth at the two men who stepped nearer.

"Well, I've got a quarrel," Brodie said. He was the tallest man in the crowd. He had served with the Rangers, and the dangerous glint in his eyes warned Singleton that he had gone too far.

"I ain't got no fight with you fellas. It's this here piano player that's caused all the trouble." He turned suddenly and reached out and shoved Mark, who staggered backward. "Get out of my way, piano player!"

Mark recovered his balance, and his eyes met those of Mary Aidan Hardin. He knew what she thought of him, but he knew he had come to a crossroads. He knew how to behave properly in Memphis, Tennessee, a civilized place, but this was Texas. Right then he remembered Jerusalem Ann once saying that the eyes of Texas were on the ranchers. They would have to be men and women of a different breed, for they were going to have to settle this wild land. And it wouldn't be settled with law books or with debates. To live here with all the dangers took courage and strength. At that moment her sobering words came back. *The eyes of Texas are upon us.* He thought, *The eyes of my folks are probably on me. I've backed away from every hard thing that ever came my way, but this is the end of running.*

"I won't take that from you, Singleton," he said evenly.

Singleton laughed. "What are you going to do? Sing me to death?"

"No. I intend to fight you."

Mary Aidan's face grew pale. "Don't do it, Mark!" she cried out. She knew the fighting prowess of Barton Singleton, and she feared what would happen to Mark if Singleton fought him. "That's what he wants. He's nothing but a bully."

"I expect you're right, Mary Aidan." But then he turned and said, "What do you want—pistols, knives, or fists?"

Barton's lip snarled, and he said, "You couldn't stand up to me with fists. It'll be pistols. You might have half a chance that way, piano player."

Mark turned to Clay and said, "Can I borrow your pistol, Clay?"

Clay was silent. He wanted to urge Mark to back away, but he knew that if he did, the young man would never be the same. "I guess so." He pulled the pistol out of the holster and handed it to Mark.

Jerusalem wanted to cry out, but this was men's business, and she knew as well as Clay that Mark could not live in this country unless he stood up like a man.

"I guess it'll be a duel, then," Barton Singleton said. "Choose your seconds."

"I don't think we need any seconds," Mark said. He looked over at Brodie. Can I borrow that pretty red neckerchief you've got on?"

"What?"

"Your bandanna, let me borrow it, will you?"

Puzzled, Brodie removed the large red bandanna and handed it over. "What do you want with it?"

Mark did not answer, but he took one end of the bandanna and extended it. Barton had a pistol in the holster on his side. "Pull your pistol, Singleton."

"What's all this bandanna business?" Barton said slowly. He knew he was in the wrong for what he said to Mary Aidan, but he would not back down.

"I'm not much on dueling, so we'll even the odds. Here, you take the other end of this handkerchief. Pull your gun." He pointed his own gun right at Singleton's chest. "You put it on me. We'll have Clay count to three, and on three we blast away. Whoever is left hangin' on to this handkerchief is the victor."

A murmur went over the crowd, and Mary Aidan gasped. She felt suddenly weak, for she knew that part of this, at least, was her doing. She whispered again, "It's suicide!"

Mark did not answer. He stared at Singleton, and his voice suddenly cracked out. "Take the neckerchief, Singleton!"

"Are you crazy?" Singleton said.

"I reckon both of us are. Take the neckerchief now. Clay, you can do the countin'."

Sweat suddenly popped out on Singleton's face. He had been in fights before, both with his fists and with guns, but not anything like this.

"Why, I ain't a fool!" he said.

"Are you a coward, then? You've got the same chance as I have."

Barton Singleton was aware that the eye of every man and woman and young person at the gathering was on him. His face was pale, and he nervously wiped his forehead with his shirt sleeve. The pressure was so intense that it seemed to close his throat.

"I ain't fightin' no crazy man!" he said.

Mark Benton stood there holding the gun in his right hand, the hand-kerchief in his left. His voice was hard as a diamond as he said, "You been boasting about what a fighting man you are. Well, here's your chance to show everyone how tough you really are."

Barton Singleton looked around and saw no sympathy in any face. He took a step backward, then suddenly shook his head hard and said loudly, "He's crazy! I ain't fightin' a crazy man!" He turned and walked away.

A single voice called out, "Better start carryin' a handkerchief, Single-ton. Everybody here knows how to whip you now."

Everything around her seemed to sway, and Mary Aidan suddenly felt light-headed. The pressure had been so intense she could not move. She made a slight sound in her throat and then tried to speak, but the last thing she remembered was the lanterns seeming to dim and someone's arms catching her as she slid to the ground.

Mary Aidan sat beside Mark in the buggy. She had thought with humilia-tion of how she had awakened, sitting flat on the ground, with Mark's arm around her. Others were staring at her, but Mark had said roughly to them, "Why don't you get back to your dancing? Can you stand, Mary?"

She had gotten to her feet, and Mark had put her in the buggy. They had not said a word all the way home. Mary Aidan had never been so humiliated in her life. Finally, she said, "I've never fainted in my life."

"I nearly fainted myself," Mark said.

Mary Aidan turned to face him. "Would you have done it, Mark, shot it out with Singleton?"

"Well, you know I think I would. It was crazy, but I've run away from things all my life." He turned to her, and wonder filled his eyes. "I'm all through running, Mary Aidan."

"I'm . . . I'm glad for you, Mark." She wanted to reach out and touch him but dared not. "I've treated you as bad as I ever treated anybody. I don't guess you can ever forget it."

"I think I can. It was part of my growing up. Don't fret yourself about it."

Mary Aidan felt a rush of relief, for she saw his smile and knew that he was an honest man. She sat back in the seat and glanced up at the stars that spangled the sky. She could not help but think of the scene and the look of determination on Mark Benton's face as he faced Singleton and certain death.

"How can anybody be as wrong as I've been about you?"

"You weren't wrong."

"Why, of course I was," she insisted.

"No, you weren't. I was nothing but a spoiled tenderfoot when I got here. You know the Bible says that it takes a furnace sometimes to bring out the best in a man . . . I guess I needed that." He did not speak for a time, and then he said, "I'll be leaving here soon."

Mary Aidan suddenly turned. "Leaving!" Her eyes widened as she looked at him. "Where are you going?"

"I've got to go home and make things right with my family."

"I . . . I think that would be a good thing for you to do. I'd like to meet your family. They must be fine people."

"Would you really?"

"Why, certainly."

"Well, come with me, and I'll introduce you to them."

Mary Aidan could not believe she had heard Mark Benton correctly. "Come with you? Where?"

"To Memphis to meet my family."

Mary Aidan shook her head. "I remember that song that you wrote about the woman you want to marry. I'm not the woman in that song."

Mark pulled the horses to a halt. He tied the lines and then turned to face her. "I think you're the woman in the song, all right. Maybe you're not all of it, but I can help you to be the rest."

"You're mighty uppity!" she said, feigning anger.

"I guess I am. I'm feeling like the world's off my shoulders now." He edged over on the seat and put his arms around Mary Aidan and drew her toward him. "You know, Mary Aidan, you're the kind of woman a man would want to share life with. Sometimes you're reckless, and sometimes you're steady, but you're like a music that makes a man feel strong enough to whip the world."

"Me? You feel that about me, Mark?" His words had captured her, and she leaned over against him. "I think I'm about to faint again," she whispered.

Mark Benton laughed. "I'll take you to see my family, but Clinton will probably insist on going along to be sure my intentions are honorable."

"No. He's got problems of his own." She put her hand on his cheek and said, "I'm anxious to meet your family."

"I'll tell you what," he said. "As soon as we get home and I make my peace with my family, I'll start doing some serious courting like lovers are supposed to do."

"Yes. I demand lots of courting. Now, let's try to think of some way to break this to my folks without giving them all heart attacks."

Mark unwound the lines and spoke to the team, and as they jolted along, the sound of their voices filled the summer air. From time to time their laughter broke the still night, and Mary Aidan knew that she had found her man!

CHAPTER
THIRTY-ONE

Mary Aidan carefully folded the last dress and laid it in the trunk. After closing it firmly, she turned to face her mother. Jerusalem had been helping her pack her things, but now she had backed up against the wall and was regarding Mary Aidan with a steadfast gaze.

"I wish you wouldn't look at me that way, Mama," Mary Aidan said quietly. "It makes me feel like you don't trust me."

Ever since Mary Aidan had told her mother of her intention to go to Tennessee with Mark and meet his parents, Jerusalem had been greatly disturbed. She and Clay had talked at great length about the trip, and both of them had been mystified at Mary Aidan's sudden interest in Mark. Clay had finally thrown up his hands and said, "Well, you always said I never understood women, and I guess now this is proof of it. But she's got her mind made up, and that's all there is to it."

Jerusalem gazed out the window at the buggy that was drawn up. Brodie was waiting to take Mark and Mary Aidan to San Antone. There they would be able to get a coach to the coast, where they would embark by steamship to New Orleans and then up the Mississippi to Memphis.

Jerusalem shook her head in disbelief. "I can't believe this is happening, Mary Aidan. Are you sure you want to go with this man?"

"Yes, Mama."

"But I don't understand it at all. You didn't like him at all when he came here. Every chance you got, you criticized him. Why this sudden interest now?"

Mary Aidan came over and put her arms around her mother. "I know. I was proud and vain and thought I knew everything, but I've changed, and so has he." She stepped back and said, "I'm not sure what will come of it. I need some time with him. I don't know if I can live in his world or not."

"We'd hate to lose you, daughter."

"You wouldn't be losing me, Mama. I'd just be living in another place if I decided to stay in Memphis. But I need time in his world."

Jerusalem knew that Mary Aidan needed encouragement from her family. She found a smile and said, "Well, you're a good girl, Mary Aidan. You had good raising. You go with Mark. I trust him. He's a good man."

"I don't think Clinton does. He threw a fit when I told him what we were going to do."

"Clinton's so confused himself these days that he can't go sticking his nose into other people's business. But you go on with Mark, and you find out if he's the one for you. If you love him and he loves you, and if God is in it, you two will be all right." She stepped forward, embraced her daughter for a long moment, then kissed her on the cheek. "It's time to go."

They went outside and found Mark talking to Clay on the porch. Both men got up, and Mark said at once, "I'll bring her back safe, Jerusalem. You have my word on that."

"I guess I know that, Mark, or I wouldn't let you go." She put out her hand, and Mark took it and held it for a moment.

"My folks will want to come out and meet you."

"We'll look forward to that, won't we, Clay?"

"Shore will," Clay said. He shook hands with Mark, then embraced Mary Aidan. "You be sweet now—like me," he said, grinning.

"I will, Daddy," Mary Aidan said. She had called him this for a long time, which always gave Clay pleasure.

"I'm ready, Mark," Mary Aidan said. He flashed a smile at her and led her down the steps and handed her into the buggy, which was loaded with all they would need for the journey. Brodie was sitting there, holding the lines loosely, and said nothing until the two were in. "I'll write as soon as I get there," Mary Aidan called, and then Brodie spoke to the horses and they moved out.

Clay and Jerusalem stood watching the wagon disappear in the distance down the road. "I don't want you to worry about this, Jerusalem," Clay said. "Mark's a good man, and apparently Mary Aidan's done some growing up these last few months right under our noses. If they found each other, I just hope they'll be as happy as we are."

Jerusalem leaned over, and Clay put his arm around her. The two stood watching until the buggy was a mere dot in the distance, and then they turned and went back into the house.

Clinton had said his good-byes earlier, but he was watching as the buggy pulled out. He was in the cook shack with Maggie, and now he turned to her and said, "I can't believe Ma let Mary Aidan go off with a man, and I can't believe she'd want to go."

"I reckon she loves him, Clinton," Maggie said, "and a woman has to go with the man she loves."

Clinton turned to face Maggie. He yearned with all his heart to clear up the situation, for he knew that she was still expecting him to marry her. But when he tried to speak, his throat seemed to close up, and he could only say, "Well, I guess I'll be goin'." Leaving the cook shack, he wandered over to the corral and cornered his horse and put a saddle on it. "I don't know where I'm goin'," he said, "but wherever it is, I hope there ain't no more women lurkin' around waitin' for a wedding ring!"

Clay had been troubled about Jerusalem ever since Mary Aidan had left with Mark to travel to Memphis, Tennessee. Their absence on the ranch had left a vacuum of sorts, and Jerusalem was not her normal self, for she missed them terribly. Clay had decided to throw a big birthday party for Jerusalem to try to cheer her up. He had asked Maggie to cook a magnificent supper, which included a huge cake. When Jerusalem found out what

he was up to, she had protested, but Clay's mind was already set and he
would not be overridden.

"We're gonna celebrate this birthday, and that's all there is to it," he
had announced, and Jerusalem finally had to yield.

On the morning of her birthday, Jerusalem awoke slowly and then
realized Clay wasn't in the bed. She was about to get up when the door
opened and Clay came in carrying a tray with a white cloth over it.

"Breakfast in bed for your birthday."

"Oh, Clay, that's so foolish!"

"You just scooch up there with your back against the headboard and
eat this here breakfast. That's all you get all day. We're savin' up to com-
mit gluttony tonight."

Actually, Jerusalem was pleased at the attention. She had never gotten
anything like this from her first husband, and now as she sat there eating
breakfast, she listened to Clay as he spoke cheerfully of what he had
planned for her day. She realized how God had blessed her with a good
family and especially a good husband.

"After today, I may expect breakfast in bed every day," she said, smiling as she sipped the hot coffee. "A woman could get spoiled being treated
like this."

"Well, I plum hope so." Clay grinned. "But I doubt if you'll get it
every day. Now, you ain't doin' a lick of work today. You're just gonna sit
back, and I'm gonna entertain you."

Jerusalem laughed. "What are you going to do . . . card tricks?"

"No. We're goin' into town and buy you a whole new outfit. I'm
gonna pick it out myself." He leaned back and said, "I've got a certain
kind of dress in mind. I'd like for it to be pink with big green polka dots
on it and maybe some red flowers." He continued to describe the outlandish outfit he wanted to buy her, but in truth that was part of his
scheme. He had planned to make her birthday one that Jerusalem would
never forget.

"All right," she said. "A polka dot dress it'll be. Won't I be a sight
when we go to dances?"

Clay leaned over and kissed her on the lips. "You taste like eggs," he
said. "But then everything, more or less, tastes like eggs, don't it? Now,

get out of that bed. We're gonna hit town and do 'er up right, then we're comin' back here and have a bodacious birthday party."

The party was bodacious, but the dress that Clay bought for Jerusalem was not as garish as he had described that morning. It was a beautiful dress, one that Jerusalem had admired for a long time whenever she had gone to town to shop. The dress was light yellow with small dark yellow dots. It had a close-fitting bodice with three-quarter-length sleeves that ended in a large white ruffle. The skirt gathered around the waist, then fell to the ground with a border encircling the dress in dark yellow and brown accents. Now she was sitting at the head of the table, and cries went up as the door opened and Clinton escorted Maggie in, who was carrying a huge white cake with candles burning on the top.

"Don't stand too close to that cake," Clay said. "You're liable to get heat exhaustion."

Maggie set the cake on the table, and Clinton handed the knife to his mother. "Here, Ma. You blow the candles out first, then you cut the cake. And then we got some presents for you."

"Blow them candles out, wife. Make a wish," Clay commanded. He waited until she had done so and then said, "What'd you wish for?"

"I'm not telling. It wouldn't come true."

"Well, I'm telling you the wish that I made," Clay said. "Everybody rear yourself back and get ready for a speech because I'm about ready to turn my wolf loose."

Clay waited for a moment, and everybody looked at him. He looked around the table and said, "It wasn't too long ago I was a-rollin' stone up in the mountains with a bunch of wild, impolite, rude fellows without no social graces at all. I was eatin' my food half-cooked, expecting my hair to be lifted any day by some Indian on the warpath." He went on describing the hardships of the mountain life, and then he suddenly smiled. "And look at me now. Here I am at the Yellow Rose Ranch—one of the prettiest pieces of land in the whole United States. And I got me a beautiful wife and beautiful kids and a pretty good-lookin' grandkid, I have to admit. So,

I reckon I'd have to say that the Lord has smiled with favor on me, and I'm givin' Him thanks right now for this family and for all that they've meant to me. End of speech." He waited until the applause died down and said, "Now, wife, your turn."

Jerusalem shook her head. "I can't make a speech. I just agree with all that Clay said. God has been good to me to give me a family, a good husband, good children, and a good grandchild. We're all alive and well, and—"

Suddenly, Jerusalem broke off, and everyone at the table saw her eyes fly open wide. She made a slight incomprehensible cry, and everyone turned instantly to follow her gaze.

A Comanche warrior in full war paint and holding a repeating rifle in his hand stood framed in the doorway. He had come as silently as a ghost, and now he stood there, his dark eyes taking them all in.

Clay slowly rose to his feet. "Bear Killer," he said, his eyes narrowing. "You have come."

"I have come," Bear Killer said. He stood holding the rifle lightly, swinging it from side to side so that anyone who moved would meet a quick death. He stared at Clay, and the two men's eyes locked. "I think you expected me, White Ghost."

"I thought you might come someday," Clay said. He looked out the window and then added, "But not like this."

"I've come alone as Silver Hair and the Tall One came into camp and took this woman and my son. I have never forgotten that. What you did shamed all The People. I have had a dream of a white buffalo. The buffalo said the only way to erase my shame was to come and take the woman and child back to The People. I have come for my son and for the woman if she will go."

"You can't have them." Quaid had stood to his feet. He was not wearing a gun, and his hands were closed into fists.

"Silver Hair and the Tall One, you are all here." Bear Killer's eyes went around, and he saw that none of the men were wearing their guns. "I watched for some time. The white buffalo said I would find you here without your guns."

"You can't have her, Bear Killer," Quaid said again. "You will die if you try."

"Yes, but your woman will die first and then you next. You are a brave man, Silver Hair, but this is not your time."

A silence fell over the room. Every eye was fixed on the wild form of the Comanche. Clay and every other man in the room were bemoaning the fact that they were not carrying their guns. But all of them knew that they had little chance if they tried to reach for them. Even if they all rushed him, the seven-shot repeater Bear Killer held would take their lives.

Bear Killer turned and looked at Moriah. She had put her arm around Ethan and was staring at him defiantly. Bear Killer looked at her and then at the boy, and finally he said, "I only want my son. You can stay if you choose." He turned then to Clay and said, "Which will it be, White Ghost? Shall there be life or death?"

Clay could not speak. He felt helpless, and it was not his life that he feared for. He looked at Moriah, expecting her to speak, but she merely shook her head and remained silent.

Ethan, who had taken all this in, stood there looking at Bear Killer. He was nine years old now, tall for his age and lean, but very strong. His skin was not as dark as the father he stood watching. He looked like a sun-burned young son of the plains, but his father's strength was obvious in him. For years Ethan had been expecting his Comanche father to come and take him away. He had memories of being brought up as a child in the Comanche camp, but these had faded now, and he had become a part of the life at the Yellow Rose Ranch. He had learned to love and admire Quaid Shafter more than any other man, and it was this that prompted him to speak up. "I respect you, Father, but I will stay with my family."

Bear Killer was caught off-guard. He had fully expected a battle. That was why he had brought not only the rifle but also a pistol with six shots tucked in his belt. Ethan's words, however, came as a shock. It did not fit in with his dream. "I am your father!" he said, his voice harsh. "You will return with me to The People."

But Ethan shook his head. "These are my people. You are at war with them. If I went with you, I would have to fight them, and I can't do that."

A silence fell across the room, and Clay longed for a pistol. Just one shot would settle it all, but he had no weapon. He studied Bear Killer, knowing the merciless quality of the man. It was not past him to open up with a rifle and massacre everyone in the room. He was capable of such a thing.

Moriah held on to Ethan. She could feel his shallow breathing, but she leaned over and whispered, "I am proud of you, son. That took great courage."

Bear Killer stood still as a statue. The silence grew thicker, and then something changed in him. A flicker came into his dark eyes, and he lowered the rifle slightly. "The blood of the white eyes is strong. They have stolen you from me, my son, and from The People." A great sadness filled his face, then he straightened up and pointed the rifle straight at Clay's heart for a moment. "You have won again, White Ghost." He looked at Ethan and said almost in a whisper, "I have no son." Then with one swift catlike motion he turned and leaped out the door.

Brodie and Clinton started to go after him, but Moriah called out, "No! Let him go!" When the two stopped, she held on to Ethan and turned him around and looked in his eyes. For years the shadow of this day had lain across her, but now the shadow was gone. "He won't come again, son." She turned to Quaid, and he came and put his arms around her, then reached down and let his hand rest on Ethan's shoulder. Ethan turned to look up at the tall man with the startling blue eyes and the even more startling silver hair.

"You are my father now," he said. "I have no other."

CHAPTER
THIRTY-TWO

I've been reading about this California gold rush," John Benton said. He looked over the table at his son Tom, who was seated to his left. "It may be a bad thing."

Tom Benton was helping himself to the steak that the maid had brought in from the kitchen and put before him. He tried to cut it with his knife and said, "This steak is tough as a boot heel." He handed it to the small maid and said, "I can't eat it, Alice. Bring me something else."

"What else, sir?"

"Anything else. An egg, I guess."

"It's getting harder to get meat," Jewel Benton said. "I'm sorry, Tom."

Tom shrugged. "I'm getting fat, anyway." He looked at his father and said, "What's wrong about a gold rush?"

"Gold drives people crazy. They'll do anything for it."

"Money will do that." Tom grinned. "I haven't noticed you throwing any away."

The older man grinned. "I guess you're right about that, son. I guess we all can lose our perspective."

The three were sitting in the formal dining room. The table was covered with an immaculate white cloth and set with fine china. The silverware cast soft glows under the gas light that illuminated the room. The formal dining room was too big for three people, but John Benton liked to eat in it rather than in the smaller one.

The two men were still talking about the gold rush when the doorbell rang. Alice, the maid, was pouring coffee, and she said, "Shall I get it, sir?"

"I guess so, Alice." John frowned, not liking to be disturbed during their meals. When Alice left to answer the door, he looked at Jewel. "Are you expecting anyone?"

"No, of course not."

"Neither am I," Tom said. "Rather late in the day for callers."

"Maybe I ought to meet them and take them to the study, whoever it is."

John Benton rose from his chair and dropped his napkin, and then he stood stock still. Jewel and Tom turned to follow his gaze, and when they did, Jewel let out a small cry. "Mark!" she cried out and rose to her feet.

Tom had risen also, and he stood there staring at his brother. "Well, welcome home, brother!"

Mark stood for a moment, looking from one to the other of his family. Then he turned and said, "I'd like for you to meet Miss Mary Aidan Hardin. Mary Aidan, this is my father John, my mother Jewel, and my brother Tom."

Mary Aidan was wearing a light gray traveling dress that was nipped in tightly at the waist and fitted neatly at the bosom. She was wearing two small jade earrings that went well with her dress. "I'm so happy to meet you all," she said.

"Well, come in," Tom said quickly. "We're glad to meet you, Miss Hardin. Mark, have you two eaten?"

"We ate a little earlier, thank you."

"Well, sit down and join us," John said quickly. He was flustered as he glanced helplessly over at Jewel.

"Yes. Please sit down at once." Jewel turned to Alice, who had come in, and said, "Bring something to drink."

"What shall it be, ma'am?"

"Anything, Alice," Mark said. "Tea, water, coffee. Whatever you have is fine."

"Here," Tom said, "sit down here, Miss Hardin." He held the chair out, and Mary Aidan sat down. Mark was still standing and staring at his father, but then he turned and went over to his mother and kissed her cheek.

"I'm sorry I didn't write more often," he said. "I should have, but I wanted to have something to write about. A lot has happened since I left," he said.

Jewel reached up and kissed him. "I'm so glad you're back," she whispered. Her eyes were glowing. "You look better than I've ever seen you. My goodness, you've lost weight, but you're so sunburned."

"A fellow gets that way in Texas. That's where I've been." He looked up at his father and said, "You're looking well, Father."

"As your mother says, you look better than I've ever seen you. Sit down, Mark."

Mark moved around the table and sat down beside Mary Aidan. "You're probably wondering," he said, "about Mary Aidan and why she's here."

"Well, I think we'd be likely to, wouldn't we?" Tom grinned. "The prodigal son shows up with a beautiful young woman out of nowhere. You wouldn't expect us not to be curious."

"No, I wouldn't, Tom. Well, here's the story. I've been working for Mary Aidan's family at their ranch in Texas. It's the Yellow Rose Ranch. It's going to be the biggest ranch in Texas." He went on to describe his work, and finally he said, "I wanted to prove myself, and I didn't know how. So I thought I'd take on a hard job and give my try at punching cattle in Texas. It's about as hard as anything I could think of." He turned to face his father and said, "I haven't had a drink since I went to work for them, and I think I learned a few things about sticking to a job."

"He has," Mary Aidan said. "Mr. Benton, you wouldn't believe what he's done." She launched into the story, telling how he had arrived soft and flabby, and how the hands on the ranch had determined to give him the worst time they could. "And I was the worst. I treated him shamefully. I don't know why he didn't shoot me." She suddenly laughed. "I think he wanted to a few times, didn't you, Mark?"

"Well, maybe not quite that drastic." He turned and said, "Let me get right to it. Mary Aidan has come to stay for a visit for a while if you'll have her."

"Of course we will," Jewel said at once. "We'd be so happy to have you, my dear."

"You'd better wait until I tell you why she's here," Mark said. "She's here to try to decide whether I'm the man she wants to marry."

"Mark, what an awful thing to say!" Mary Aidan protested.

"Well, it's true, isn't it?"

"You could have said it differently. Perhaps broken the news a little bit more nicely."

John Benton suddenly laughed. "Well, Mark, I will say this. You know how to liven up an evening!"

Mark looked around at his family fondly. "I say this now. Maybe I won't ever have to say it again. I was a rotten son and a rotten brother to you, Tom. I did everything wrong. But since I've been in Texas, I think I've learned a few things, and I hope you'll give me a chance to prove it to you, Father. You, too, Mother, and you, Tom. I ask your forgiveness for all the pain and grief I caused all of you."

"And he won't give you any more," Mary Aidan spoke up. "He's going to be a fine son and a fine brother."

John Benton was not a man given to emotion, but he found tears forming in his eyes. He cleared his throat and had to look away. "Something in my eye," he said.

Mark laughed. "Something in mine, too, I guess."

"I guess it's an epidemic," Tom said. "I've got something in my eye as well." He took out his handkerchief and wiped his eyes.

"Oh, you men!" Jewel cried out. She got up and went around the table, and Mark rose to greet her. He put his arms around her. He kissed her and she said, "Welcome home, son."

And then Tom came, and last of all his father to embrace the prodigal son who had come home.

Tom stepped back and put his arm around Mary Aidan. "Welcome to the family, Mary Aidan—if you choose to have us."

Mary Aidan had been tremendously moved by the scene. Her eyes were damp also, and she whispered, "I think I just might do that, Tom."

CHAPTER
THIRTY-THREE

The family was gathered around the breakfast table, when halfway through the meal Jerusalem said, "I have a surprise. A letter came from Mary Aidan." Immediately, she had everyone's attention. It had been over a month since Mary Aidan had left with Mark. During that time they had received only one letter right after she and Mark had arrived in Memphis. The letter did not contain too many details, except that Mark's family had made her feel welcomed. Now they all waited anxiously as Jerusalem removed the letter from the envelope and opened it up.

> Dear Mama and Daddy and all,
> This is to let you know that Mark has asked me to
> marry him and I have agreed.

"Well, how about that!" Clay said loudly. "A Memphis hayseed for a son-in-law."

"He may be a hayseed," Clinton said, "but he's sound in his doctrine."

"Will you be quiet and let her finish the letter?" Brodie said. "Is she gonna get married there, Ma?"

Jerusalem went on reading the letter:

> The Bentons want to meet you all, so we'll all be
> coming to Texas for a visit soon. The three of them
> and the two of us, so make room for us.

Jerusalem read the rest of the letter, telling all she had seen and done since arriving in Memphis. Then it ended by saying:

> Oh, I love him so much, and we're going to have a
> wonderful life. We'll see you soon.
> Love, Mary Aidan

Jerusalem folded the letter up and smiled. "Look's like there's a wedding coming soon." She glanced over at Clinton and Brodie said, "If I could just get you boys married off, I could breathe easy."

Clinton could not remember being more miserable in his whole life. All he could think about were the three women who were expecting him to announce their engagement to him. He managed to avoid his family by staying out on the range for a week, making a gathering of longhorns. Finally, he came back at the end of the week at night, and Jerusalem caught him before he could go to bed.

"You're going to church with me tomorrow, so you may as well go take your bath tonight or go wash up in the creek in the morning."

"I'll go in the creek in the morning," Clinton said gloomily. "Maybe I'll die and I won't have to take one."

Jerusalem laughed and reached out and ruffled his hair. "You're filthy as a pig," she said. "It'll do you good to go to church. It always does. Rice's sermons always seem to perk you up."

Clinton shook his head. "I don't know, Ma. I think I'm backslid."

"You haven't been drinking down at the Golden Lady Saloon, have you, or chasing after any wild women?"

"Why, no, Ma. You know I wouldn't do those things."

"Well, whatever it is, you can confess it to the Lord, and He'll forgive you. Now, you're going to church tomorrow."

"Yes, Ma, I reckon I am."

Clinton slept little that night. Before the sun cast its first rays of dawn, Clinton got up. He went down to the river for his bath. When he was finished, he came home and shaved, and was ready by the time breakfast was served. He said little during the meal, but the table was noisy with talk about Mary Aidan's coming wedding. As soon as everyone was finished, the women cleaned up the table and then they left for church.

Clinton got into the wagon beside his mother and Clay. He looked over and saw that Maggie had gotten into the buggy beside Brodie. She gave him a warm smile, and he waved his hand almost listlessly. *Brodie's going to shoot me when he finds out what I've done,* he thought. *He's mighty partial to Maggie, and it's gonna hurt her when she finds out I got two more fiancées on the line.*

The trip to the church seemed very short, and more than once Clinton thought about getting out and walking back home, but he knew that his mother would never let him do that.

When they pulled up in front of the church, he got out and walked into the small building with the rest of the family. He saw Lucy Abbot sitting with her family up close to the front. He pretended not to see her, and he sat as far away from Rose Jean as he could.

All through the service Clinton Hardin tried to pray about his predicament, but nothing seemed to help the turmoil he felt. He had an image in his mind of God frowning down on him. *What do you mean,* God seemed to be saying, *misleading three fine young women? You deserve to be horse-whipped!*

Clinton endured the song service, but he did not hear one word of the sermon that Rice Morgan preached. He sat there staring at Rice so that he would not have to look at the three women who had brought nightmares into his life. Once he did meet Lucy's eyes, and she smiled and winked demurely at him. He tried to smile, but it was as though his face were frozen.

Finally the service ended, and Clinton heaved a sigh of relief. Rice pronounced the benediction and said, "God bless you all. We'll see you here next Sunday."

"Just a minute, Brother Morgan!"

Clinton seemed to freeze. Everyone in the church had risen for the benediction, but he saw Lucy Abbot leave her seat and go down toward the front. "May I make an announcement, Brother Morgan?"

"Why certainly, Miss Abbot."

Lucy turned and smiled at all those in the small congregation. "I have a happy announcement to make. That is, Clinton and I have an announcement to make. We're engaged to be married."

There was an instant response of people murmuring and a few even applauding, but Clinton waited for God to strike him dead. He wished desperately that a hole would open up and swallow him. Lucy was standing there in front smiling at him. His mother and Clay and the rest of the family were all staring at him in shock.

Suddenly, Brodie turned and faced Clinton. "Clinton, what's wrong with you? Tell that woman she's wrong. Tell her you're engaged to marry Maggie."

The earlier babble of voices was nothing to what came on now. Clinton turned and saw his mother staring at him with horror in her eyes. Then he turned around and saw Maggie watching him carefully but saying nothing.

"Isn't that right, Maggie?" Brodie said.

Maggie nodded slowly but said nothing.

Everyone seemed to be talking at once, and then Rose Jean Campbell spoke up loudly and said, "I think there's a mistake somewhere. Clinton had spoken to me about being his wife, haven't you, Clinton?"

Jerusalem could not believe what she was hearing. She grabbed Clinton by the arm and turned him around and said, "Clinton Hardin, what in the world have you done?"

The room fell silent, everyone waiting breathlessly for Clinton's answer. Clinton's eyes went from Lucy, who had turned absolutely pale, to Maggie, who was watching him clinically, and then to Rose Jean, who seemed amused by the whole thing.

"Well . . ." Clinton cleared his throat and said, "I reckon I've made the biggest mess that a man ever made in his whole life." He could get no further. He looked around desperately, and then with a short cry, he suddenly shoved his way out of the pew and ran down the aisle and out of the church, his boots echoing on the wooden floor. The door slammed behind him, and the babble increased to an uproar.

Clay, standing beside Jerusalem, began to grin and suddenly laughed aloud. "First mistake Clinton Hardin ever made, at least according to his reckoning, but it sure is a large one!"

Donald Abbot's face was livid, and so was the face of his wife and his daughter. "I'll take a horse whip to that whelp for insulting my daughter this way!"

Rice Morgan had watched all this with shocked astonishment, and he seemed to be struggling for something to say. "I take it that we can scratch one fiancée, isn't that right, Brother Abbot?"

"I wouldn't let my daughter marry that whelp if he was the last man in the world!"

Brodie went over to Maggie and stood there talking to her earnestly. Maggie didn't seem too upset, Jerusalem noticed, and then she shook her head and turned to Clay. "I think when I catch up with him, I'll whip him like he was a ten-year-old."

"Well, now, wife, he didn't actually marry all three of them fillies."

"Poor Rose Jean. How humiliated she must be," Jerusalem mourned. "I've got to go and talk to her."

Not a soul had left the church, and they all watched as Jerusalem went to Rose Jean. "I'm so sorry, Rose Jean. I don't know what to think of that boy of mine."

Rose Jean suddenly laughed. "He never actually asked me to marry him. He just talked about getting married in general, and I let him think he was asking me."

"Well, why didn't you speak up, then?"

"I knew he didn't love either one of those women, and I felt sorry for him," Rose Jean said. "You know two fiancées could have been bad, but who could take a man seriously who got engaged to three women all at the same time?"

She reached out and hugged Jerusalem. "Don't worry about him, Jerusalem. I'll talk to him. He'll be all right."

"I'm glad you think so. If you want to, we'll have Clay and Brodie hold him, and you can whip him with a belt."

"No. Right now I think the worst punishment we could give him is to talk to him. You know he's so sensitive, Jerusalem."

"He's that, all right. Especially when he gets caught in something as foolish as this. Maybe this will be good for him. He always thinks he never made a mistake. Well, he made some bad ones this time."

"Let me talk to him." Rose Jean smiled. "And don't fuss at him. He's miserable enough as it is."

Brodie had not been able to put his anger away. He helped Maggie into the buggy and drove off, whipping the horses until they were galloping at full speed. Maggie held on as best she could, and finally she said, "Brodie, there's no sense taking your mad out on the horses."

Brodie looked at her and saw something in her face that made him lose part of his anger.

"Whoa, then, horses!" he said as he pulled on the reins. Once he got the horses stopped, he turned to Maggie. "I aim to stomp a mud hole into Clinton. He's gone too far this time. It's one thing to preach at people, but toying with three women's emotions is serious."

"No, you can't do that," Maggie said.

"Why not? Why, it's awful how he's embarrassed and humiliated you and Rose Jean, and I guess Lucy feels bad too."

Maggie shook her head. "It was really all my doing, Brodie. You can't get mad at Clinton for that."

"What do you mean it was your doing? He asked you to marry him, didn't he? When a man does that, he'd better be serious about his intentions."

"Well, he never really came out and asked me."

"He didn't! But you said—"

"And I wouldn't have married him if he had asked me."

Brodie was shocked. "Why not?"

"Because I don't feel for him like—"

Brodie had calmed down now, but he was puzzled. "You don't feel like what?"

"Like I feel for you, Brodie."

Brodie sat perfectly still.

"I . . . I always liked you," Maggie said, "but I knew you was in love with that Mexican girl, so I gave up. You was so sweet trying to make a lady out of me that I just started lovin' you. I couldn't help myself, Brodie."

Brodie took a deep breath. "You are some woman, Maggie." He reached over and took her hand and studied it. "Well, I guess I'll let Clinton off the hook. He would have made a terrible husband, anyway. He'd be spoutin' Scripture all the time on your honeymoon."

"And you wouldn't, would you?"

"Not likely." Brodie grinned. "Maybe you'll let me come courtin' you my own self."

"Yes!" Maggie said. She reached out suddenly and pulled his head down and kissed him. "There. Our courtin' has done started."

"That Clinton!" Brodie said. He put his arm around her, spoke to the horses, and held her close as they moved along. "I hope this makes him realize he's not perfect. I don't reckon it will, though."

Clinton ran out of the church, grabbed the first horse he came to, and galloped off. He had ridden all day long, not knowing what to do with himself. All he could think of was the mess he had gotten himself into. Finally, he had gone back to the river, and now he sat there on a log trying to think of some way he could face his family and his fellow church members again. As he sat by the river, all his imperfections were spinning around in his head like a maelstrom. After a time he looked down and saw a rangy timber wolf with a frog in his mouth. He stared at the wolf, and the wolf stared back, then turned and trotted away.

"I wish I was an old timber wolf or even a frog gettin' eaten by one. It'd be better than this." He sat there letting humiliation bow him down, and suddenly he heard his name called. He looked back and saw Rose Jean. He did not even get up but sat there crouched over. "You found me, I guess."

"Yes." Rose Jean walked around and sat down on the log and said nothing for a while.

Clinton kept waiting for her to rebuke him sternly for what he had done. When she said nothing, Clinton cleared his throat. "I'm surprised to see you here, Rose Jean."

"Why is that?"

"Why's that? Why, after what I've done, I didn't think you'd ever speak to me again."

"Oh, Clinton, you didn't do anything to me."

"Well, I asked you to marry me at the same time as two other women were expectin' me to marry them."

"You never asked me to marry you, Clinton. You just talked about what kind of wife I'd make. That's all you did." Clinton sat so still that Rose Jean leaned forward to look into his face. "I expect that's what you did with Lucy and Maggie. You never really asked them outright to marry you, did you?"

Clinton shook his head. "I didn't think so. I'm all mixed up. I never intended to hurt anyone."

"I know that, and Maggie knows that too. We talked about it. She's not really in love with you. I wouldn't be surprised if she and your brother made a match out of it."

"Now, that would be a good pair. They're a lot alike, those two."

"Yes, they are," Rose Jean said.

Clinton sighed. "Well, that's two out of three."

"You do need to be more careful about what you say to young women, Clinton."

"Well, I know that . . . now."

The two sat there, and finally Clinton said, "I hate to go any place."

"Why?"

"I feel so . . . so *dumb*. How did I ever get in such a mess?"

"You're not very smart about women, Clinton. You have a tender heart, and you want to encourage people. That's what you did with me and with Maggie, too, I expect."

"How'd you know that?" Clinton said, turning to face her. "You know, Rose Jean, sometimes I get to thinking you're as smart as I am."

Rose Jean could not manage to restrain her smile. "Oh no, I'm not really. After all, you're a man and I'm only a woman."

"Well," Clinton said, "in some ways women are better than men, I reckon."

"Oh, really!"

"Why, sure, Rose Jean. They smell better, for example." He leaned forward and inhaled. "You smell good—just like a rose."

Rose Jean Campbell smiled at Clinton, and he took her hand and held it. "And women are softer than men except for my aunt Bea back in Arkansas. She was tough as any man. Not like you. You're nice and soft." He slowly leaned forward and looked into her eyes. "You're not mad at me, not really?"

"No. Not in the least."

"Are we friends?"

"Oh yes. Good friends."

Clinton's grip tightened on her hand. "Don't you think that friends ought to—well, show how they feel about each other?"

"Like holding hands?" Rose Jean smiled.

"Well, that's fine, but I was thinking more than that. The Bible says greet one another with a holy kiss." He leaned forward and kissed her lightly, and when she did not move, his grip tightened. Her lips were warm and soft under his, and he noticed she was clinging to him.

Finally, he drew back and said, "You're the sweetest girl in Texas, Rose Jean. Why, someday you and me might get to be—"

When Clinton paused, Rose Jean asked, "Get to be what?"

"Why, we might get serious. Now, don't go expectin' things."

Rose Jean smiled and reached up and touched his cheek. "I can't help it, Clinton. Somehow I feel we're predestined to be together."

It was a new thought for Clinton. "You mean that you think maybe God made us for each other?"

"I think so," Rose Jean whispered. "What would you think about that?"

Clinton sat very still, his brow wrinkled with thought. "Well, if that's what God wants, I reckon it will be all right with me." He drew her to her feet, put both arms around her, and said, "I'm sure glad God put us together. I'm powerful glad I figured all that out."

"I'm glad, too, Clinton."

"Well, we've got to get married now. There ain't no way out of it."

"Isn't there?"

"Well, no. It's predestined!"

"Then I expect we'll have to tell your folks."

"Why sure." Clinton nodded. He took a deep breath, looked around, and seemed to stand much taller. "You know, Rose Jean, I'm sure glad I thought of all this."

Rose Jean Campbell smiled and whispered, "So am I, Clinton Hardin. So am I."

The two made their way along the path that led to the house. Clinton went into a long explanation of the doctrine of sovereignty and predestination and election. He held her with one arm, gesturing eloquently with the other, as he talked enthusiastically. From time to time Rose Jean whispered, "Oh, Clinton, I never thought of that."

A large hunting owl floated over their heads, attracted, perhaps, by the sound of Clinton's voice. He noted the two, then arched, turned in a steep turn, and sailed off silently in search of more interesting prey.